THE RATHBONES

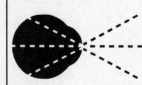

THE RATHBONES

JANICE CLARK

THORNDIKE PRESS
A part of Gale, Cengage Learning

GALE
CENGAGE Learning·

Detroit • New York • San Francisco • New Haven, Conn • Waterville, Maine • London

GALE
CENGAGE Learning

Thorndike Press® Large Print Peer Picks.
The text of this Large Print edition is unabridged.
Other aspects of the book may vary from the original edition.
Set in 16 pt. Plantin.

LIBRARY OF CONGRESS CATALOGING-IN-PUBLICATION DATA

Clark, Janice, 1954–
    The Rathbones / by Janice Clark. — Large print edition.
      pages ; cm. — (Thorndike Press large print peer picks)
    ISBN-13: 978-1-4104-6520-7 (hardcover)
    ISBN-10: 1-4104-6520-9 (hardcover)
    1. Young women—Fiction. 2. Family life—Fiction. 3. Whaling—New England—Fiction. 4. Domestic fiction. 5. Large type books. I. Title.
PS3603.L36427R38 2013b
813'.6—dc23   2013037519

Published in 2014 by arrangement with Doubleday, an imprint of Knopf Doubleday Publishing Group, a division of Random House, Inc.

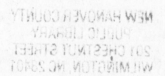

Printed in the United States of America
1 2 3 4 5 6 7 18 17 16 15 14

For my father, who sailed,
and my mother, who waited
And for Eric LeMay

CONTENTS

PROLOGUE

Moses knows what will happen. Not just how the trials will go today, or what the fathers will do when their golden sons fail and how the boys' mothers will bear it. The green of his eyes has long since been burned away by the sun on the sea, and there is no window in the little room. But he sees it all anyway, from his high blue bed. He sees the whole sweep of it.

The great herds of sperm whales that once streamed along the coast have already thinned and will soon disappear. Fleets of ships are being built with holds deep enough to provision the long voyages required to find fresh pods, to the Pacific, to the Azores and the Indian Ocean. Boys no longer climb the watchtowers that line the shore to look for whales; instead they climb to crow's nests at the tops of masts. The towers on shore will soon be torn down, their timbers used to frame the houses of captains and merchants, which will rise in the hills above the harbors as the whale gold continues to flow. Captains' wives will conduct their own searches of the sea from the widow's walks at the tops of the houses. Other towers will rise. Moses closes his eyes and sees them, the derricks, first of wood, then of steel, sprouting up across the sea of prairie. He feels the rumble as dark fountains surge up and spray across the sky; he sees black oil replace the white spermaceti. In a few years the captains will stop sailing. Some will move away and take up other occupations; some will linger, taking their wives' places on the widow's walks, staring out to sea. The houses will fall into disrepair. They will pass to city people who will use the walks for sun parlors or to store old clothes.

Moses does not choose to see such things. He longs to look back instead, to the first morning that the *Misistuck* sailed. He wishes it were that day. He strains to lift his silver head and there it all is again: the watchtower at the end of the point that curls into the sea; his son high on the tower, pointing, crying out, his voice carrying clear and strong across the bay to his brothers, already swarming up the masts and over the rigging. Moses sees the white sails billow as

the ship moves toward the bright water
where the whales are sounding.

CHAPTER ONE:
WIDOW'S WALK

{in which we meet the last of the Rathbones}

Naiwayonk, Connecticut, 1859

If I had not heard the singing voice that night, none of the rest might have happened.

Mama might yet be carving her bones; Mordecai lingering in his attic, leading me through the same old lessons on the sperm; both of my crows would still accompany me everywhere. I could have drifted through my life, forgetful of the time passing, and stayed always undersized. Maybe Papa would have finally come home.

But it's not for me to say. Though I have the keen eyes that were once the gift of all the Rathbones — standing now on shore, looking out to the horizon, I see what I know you would not if you were standing beside me: a flock of terns, a league away, diving as one upon a school of bream that darkens the clear blue sea to cobalt — I cannot see into the future, as my forebears sometimes could.

I do know that if we hadn't fled the house that night I would never have met the worn wives, or visited my grim in-laws on the Stark Archipelago, or seen the sinking island where Papa was born. The fate of my lost brother would have remained a mystery, as would what truly happened between Mama and Papa.

But I did hear the voice that night, and what I found when I followed it compelled me to flee the house with cousin Mordecai and to shed the fog in which we had both so long lived.

Though we were seeking Papa, we found our own history as we went, and that of all the Rathbones. It was a sometimes patchy tale, woven from such thread as I found: oral histories passed down and with each step altered, unfinished ship logs, journals washed and bloated by the sea until little could be read. Cousin Mordecai gathered much of it, while he could. Later I took it up from him. What wasn't provided, I had to surmise. You may think it would be difficult to assemble a story in such a way. I was used to such piecework, growing up as I did in a house populated only by remnants.

It was as easy for me to see the golden wives arrive at Rathbone House four generations ago as it was for Moses to see a school of sperm streaming through the deep.

The night I heard the singing voice began like any other that summer. I had gone to my mother's room, as usual, to help her undress. Mama's room, at the front of the house, had the best view of the sea. Its line of tall windows were kept always open, the white curtains swaying in every weather.

Each day Mama wore a dress of deep-dyed indigo with a wide collar of white linen, boiled and bleached, starched and pressed, that lifted off her shoulders and unmoored her face when the wind rose. Her underclothes were sewn from soft muslin and smelled of the cedar chest in which she kept them. Her corset was of whalebone, fine strands borrowed from a fin that had once turned in the lightless deep.

When she lifted her gown and leaned to let me unlace her, I saw again how she was double-ribbed, bone on bone. When I lifted the corset off, her body kept the corset's form, as though she always held her breath, but when I pressed my face against her for a moment, I felt the shallow rise and fall of her ribs. She placed the corset on the chair by the window. It stood sentinel there, a spare torso. For each year that Papa was at sea, she'd slid a slender bone from its channel and made me lace it tighter. The end of the ninth year was approaching. Soon Mama would be reduced. The next morning she would go down to the shore to find new sand for the hourglass she kept by her window. Her eyes turned to it whenever she walked by.

Suitors had begun showing up at the house in recent months — a retired captain, two lieutenants on leave — drawn by Mama's beauty and by the stories of Rathbone wealth. After ten years, cousin Mordecai had told me, Papa would be considered by the law to be dead. But Mama never appeared for visitors. Each suitor was ushered into a golden parlor on the second floor by Uncle Larboard and Uncle Starboard, served a plate of dry ship's biscuit and a pot of tea brewed from nettles and saw grass, and then ushered out again, hat in hand.

Mama uncoiled her braids and let them down and waited for me to unwind them. In truth, she had only to shake her head and the braids unfurled, but she knew I loved to feel the tight plaits go soft and free in my hands. When she wasn't too tired, she let me sit next to her on her bed and

16

practice my seaman's knots on her hair: sheet bend and monkey fist, timber hitch and lineman's loop. Her hair hung in a long pale wave that she sometimes allowed me to brush. I counted the strokes slowly to make them last, her hair popping and crackling as the dark bristles moved through it. When I finished, she let me step inside the curtain of hair, into her warm breath that smelled of cloves, close to the shine of her green eyes. They focused for a moment on me, and she smiled a little, then returned to her watch for Papa, her eyes trained on the sea. Long after sunset they held the horizon in each iris, split dark and pale.

I knew the tide was in when Mama smiled. I waited, hoping this would be a night for Arcady. She leaned back against her pillow, gazing out the window until the last light faded, then turned her face to me. I lay back with my head on her breast and closed my eyes as she began. It was the only story she ever told, and one I had heard since I was very young. I was, it's true, too old by then for bedtime stories, but I took what was offered. She spoke slowly, her eyes still on the sea, her fingers fondling the fine silver chain she always wore around her neck, tucked under the collar of her gown. The story always started the same way.

"A race of giants once lived on a faraway island. It was a tall island, a high atoll of pink granite, thickly sown with pine and oak and blessed with soft winds."

Here she always paused and waited to be prompted. Her hand, which had been stroking my arm, stopped. Her body went still.

"Tell me about the giants, Mama."

She breathed out and began again to stroke me, her arm so soft, the palm of her hand rough from her work.

"They lived in caves high in the pink cliffs, side by side with the swallows in their nests. They wore garments woven of rockweed and slept on beds of gull down. For breakfast they milked the manatee. At dinnertime they leaned back on the sun-warmed rock, eyes closed, while perch and mackerel leapt from the sea into their mouths."

Mama paused. I held my breath, hoping she would follow one of the pleasant paths down which her tale sometimes led: the giants diving down a waterfall that plunged from the high rocks into the sea, sporting on the sandy beach, or singing each evening to the deer who came close at twilight. I lifted my head and turned to look out the window, down to the dock, and marked by starlight where the water stood: an inch or two lower on the pilings of the pier. Mama's hair went a shade paler, her eyes a duller green. The tide was on the wane. Mama's tale took a turn.

"The giants had enough to eat and more but still they were hungry. They scoured the sand with the nails of their hands for turtle eggs until the rock was bare. They lay in the surf and sieved the sea with their teeth for spawn until the fish swam no more. They sang to the stag at evening and when he reared up to dance they speared him. They grew so fat that they lay gasping on their backs on the rocks, arms waving, while the gulls pecked out their livers. The next day their livers grew back, and the gulls pecked them out again."

The sea moved back and forth in Mama's blood. Her moods could not be depended upon.

I had felt such ebbing and flowing before. One evening, a season earlier, she had let me stay longer than usual in her room. Warm spring had arrived, and she was shifting her summer gowns into her wardrobe, first taking them from her chest to air. They hung from hooks above the open window, swaying in a salt breeze. The slanting rays of the setting sun lit the gowns to a brilliant blue, though in daylight they were a deep indigo, all the same near-black hue. Like

Mama's, my frocks were all alike, except that mine were a dun color and still had the childish shape of a jumper, while Mama's conformed to her figure. I had, at fifteen, the first outlines of a figure of my own, of which I felt vaguely ashamed but also curious. I would have preferred less shapeless frocks, but Mama made me wear them, as though I were still a little girl.

Mama seemed in good humor; at least she had not yet sent me away. I took off my loose frock and pulled one of her sea-freshened gowns over my head. I fastened its long row of mother-of-pearl buttons up the front and stood before the tall mirror that leaned against one wall. The gown, though far too long in skirt and sleeves, fit well in the bodice, and I turned from side to side, pleased with what I saw in the mirror. My crows, who had been napping atop the wardrobe, dropped down to my shoulders and began to preen. They had come with the last crate from Papa a year ago and had followed me about ever since.

Mama turned from the trunk where she was rearranging clothes and stared at me. I hoped she would offer me a gown or two; it would have been easy enough to shorten them to fit. Her eye brightened, and she seemed about to pay me some small compliment. Then her eye dulled, and she gave my figure a hard gaze.

"It will do you no good," she said. "It will bring you no joy."

She took up an awl from among her tools and in three strides crossed the room to me. She grasped a handful of my skirt to hold me firm and sliced up the front of the gown. The buttons popped and my crows scattered, squawking. The gown gaped on my breast; I felt a stinging and looked down. The sharp point of the awl had cut through the gown and grazed a fine pink line from my belly to my throat. Mama looked stricken and seemed about to embrace me. Then she drew back, composed herself, and returned to folding her clothing.

We are all descended from the fishes, Mordecai had once told me, and are still subject to the ocean's tides. So I was not surprised, these three months later, when Mama's mood changed, and her story ended not with the giants romping on the beach but gasping on the rocks, their livers coming and going.

Her story finished, she rose from her bed and returned to her work. She sat at the long black table that stood at the center of her room. The table had once been as pale and salt-scoured as the floor and the walls, but Mama had it painted black, fresh every year, so that each detail in the white bones would shine clear against the dark surface as she worked.

Each day she carved the whalebone that Papa shipped home. The crates began to arrive a year after he disappeared. Once or twice a year, a freshly docked seaman, legs still unsteady on dry land, would show up at our door, shouldering a crate trussed with chains and stamped with runes. Sometimes the crates were filled with whalebone, a single great jawbone snapped in half and packed in seaweed, or a dozen smooth sperm teeth, each as long as my forearm, nestled in a bed of kelp. Sometimes the crates held other gifts, souvenirs of Papa's travels: China Trade bowls from the Orient, cobalt blue and creamy white, big enough for me to bathe in; silk pajamas woven thick with dragons; nesting dishes for a doll, the innermost so small a cricket could drink from it; a tiny Peking dog, wrapped in a length of paisley cloth, that died of the cold soon after it arrived, having known only the warm South Seas.

Mama would question the sailors when they knocked on our door. Where did you sail from? Have you seen my husband? Do you know Benadam Gale? But the sailor never knew. His ship would have only stopped by Naiwayonk, on the way home to Nantucket or New Bedford, to deliver the crate. It had been passed from some other ship, a brig in the South Atlantic, which had it from a clipper in the Java Sea, or was it the Indian Ocean? But the crates began to come less often, and it had been more than a year since the last arrived, with my crows.

Mama kept a bouquet of bones in a willow basket on the hearth, the long curved sections of a mammoth rib, their ends sawed clean. She was working on her boat that evening. She had for some years been shaping a boat of bone, as long as her, which grew slowly in the center of the table, resting on a frame of wood. The ribs and strakes were complete, lashed together with line made from baleen, so that the form of the boat was clearly limned against the black table, though it still lacked planking. Tonight she was grinding along the edge of the keel with a rasp, smoothing its shape. She looked up at me for a moment, then back at her work.

I sat down next to her and put my hand on hers. She stopped, her hands quiet on her tool. Her fingers were raw, bleeding on the tips and crisscrossed with scars. I took the white rasp from her and felt its rough surface with a finger.

"Mama, wouldn't it be easier to use tools made from metal?"

She took the knife back from me and ran the rasp across her palm.

"Like finds like," she said. "Bone finds the true shape."

She carved no common items such as sailors made, no jagging wheels or ditty boxes, though most everything in her room but her bed and wardrobe was fashioned of bone. Her chair was bone with a caned seat, its seat posts capped with teeth. The mirror over her dressing table was framed in sperm ribs trained into an oval. Tucked into the frame was a page torn from a book with a picture of the floor of the ocean with all the sea sucked out; at the bottom stood a barren range of mountains. Scattered on the table around the boat were other objects on which she was working, among them a lantern, square-sided, its walls honed to a fine thinness.

Mama set her tools aside and walked to the hearth. She drew a soft piece of blue paper from her sleeve and held it up to the firelight to read. Light shone through the cracked seams where it had been folded and folded again. She finished reading and refolded the paper, tucking it into the sleeve of her gown. A moment later she took it out and again began to read, her eyes moving along the same lines.

I was sure the blue paper was a letter from Papa. I had often looked for other pieces of that blue paper around the house. Once, when Mama was on the widow's walk, I had searched every inch of her room, every pocket and seam of her clothing, but found nothing. I wondered if there was only one letter, the one she kept tucked into her sleeve.

"Good night, Mama."

She looked up at me, and her eyes seemed to connect with mine for a moment, then slid away. She returned to her work, her rasp scraping along the edge of the boat's keel, stopping, scraping again.

Uncle Larboard and Uncle Starboard shuffled slowly around the room, dusting the furniture. I did not then know their given names; I called them Larboard and Starboard because wherever Mama went, so they went, one to either side of her. Their bedrooms were to either side of Mama's, too. They were about her age, as tall as her, and neat in all their ways. One looked much like the other. They might have been twins. Their hair hung in tidy white queues down their backs. They wore sailor smocks washed until they were as thin as tissue, so that through the faded blue linen their old bones showed. Each had one eye slightly higher than the other, in heads that were overlarge, wobbling a little when they walked. They were mutes and never spoke, but I could usually tell what they wanted to say. Now they gently patted my head and led me to the door, pressing me away with long dry fingers. I headed for my room.

My bedroom, down the hall from Mama's, was one of the small white rooms that ran around the perimeter of the third floor. Mama's room had been made from three or four such bedrooms as mine strung together. Some of the little rooms had unfinished walls, partially plastered or ribbed with raw joists. Others were missing their outer walls altogether, except for the tall white columns between which the blue sky burned. In winter the snow would fly in and drift on the floors. Larboard and Starboard swept it away each day.

When I reached my room I stretched, yawning, and leaned to pour water into a basin from the pitcher on the floor next to my bed. After washing, I undressed and took a clean shift from a hook on the wall and pulled it on. My room had no space for any furniture except the bed, whose posts were four fluted white columns, smaller versions of the tall columns that stood in each corner. My coverlet was loomed of plain wool with a border of crabs linked claw to claw, woven in a watery green. The walls were bare plaster, the floor scoured pale. The lintel was low, the window small; if anyone but me entered, he would need to bend to see the harbor through glass panes that rippled, remembering their former life as sand on the bottom of the sea.

The room matched my size. I was small, a guppy at birth, said Mama, and at fifteen still no longer than a codling. I stood as high as Mama's breast, well-formed but of a scale like the funerary figures from a Chinese tomb.

I settled into bed, waiting for the footsteps to begin above me. Mama walked the widow's walk each night, watching for Papa's ship. The wide pine boards creaked beneath her, salt-ground and silvery. There was always the soft shuffle of sand underfoot, even up there, blown in from the shore, sloughing the wood away. Mama liked to walk above the trees, where she could look down through the leaves to see the harbor. Some nights I heard the tap of her boots above my head until dawn. She had taken to lacing them with a strand of line from an old harpoon. One day I watched her uncoil a rope, bleached white where it lay on the dock, and uncurl a strand from the center, still soft and saltless, fine enough to pass through the eyelets. Some nights she stayed up there until the fishing boats headed out from the docks and she saw them cast their nets against the first light. The boats moved to and fro, but no larger vessel appeared, many-masted and deep with sail; no fore-topmast staysail, no moonraker or mizzenmast fly. I watched from my window. I had no walk.

I had almost dozed off when my crows flew in. They often brought me treasures, gathered on their nightly patrol of the house: spoons from the dining hall, old bits of metal, any gleaming thing that caught their eye. This night one crow dropped a brass button on my bed, the other something that didn't shine, something that seemed so familiar, though I had no clear memory of it. A bracelet, woven from mariner's cord of white cotton.

I slipped the bracelet onto my wrist and turned it slowly. Its pattern alternated between simple square knots and Turk's heads. I put my nose to it: It smelled musty, not like the sea. I wondered if it was my brother's.

"Where is my brother?" I would ask Mama when I was younger, unable to shake the image of a boy, roughly my size, sturdy and dark-haired, always near the sea.

"He was smaller even than you, so we threw him back," she once replied, with a frozen smile.

Most often Mama would simply not answer my question. When I asked where my brother was, she would slowly shake her head and walk away, or stare at me silently until, uneasy, I changed the subject. Our conversations were few in any case, and brief. She would ask how my lessons were progressing and, however short my answer — "Today we began the Platonic solids" or "Mordecai is relating the woes of the queens of Iceland" — Mama's eyes and attention had already drifted back to her carving before I had finished.

I had from time to time asked Mordecai about my missing brother, when Mama refused to answer. He, too, had always insisted that no such brother existed. He always said I must be remembering a boy from the village, some fisherman's son I had seen on the dock.

Eventually I learned not to ask. But I knew better.

I didn't remember very much, only a few

flashes. A familiar form kneeling in the surf, his fat hands filled with shells, wet hair shadowing his face. A small boy diving off the end of the dock in a cold wind, bare-chested, whooping as he hit the water. But those memories always wavered and broke apart, and then I would wonder if I had imagined him, or if he was only part of some story Mama used to tell and which I had forgotten.

Not that I remembered much about Papa, either. He was always away when I was a child, Mama said, always whaling. When he did come home, it was never for long, only to load provisions and a fresh crew and sail away again.

One memory shone strong and clear, the only one that included Papa.

A ship rocks alongside the dock on a bright morning, ropes creaking, sea slap-ping against the hull. My legs dangle over the edge of the dock, swing back and forth over the water; a second pair of legs dangles next to mine, brown and bare, skin warm against my thigh.

"Push the monkey through the hole, into the cave, thrice around, pull tight."

A scratchy rope moves through my fingers. A hand guides mine, a hand the size of mine.

"No, three times, tighter!"

The loose loops of rope in my hands suddenly snap into a tight sphere.

"That's right. That's a monkey fist. Now for a timber hitch." The boy leans over the rope, intent, his dark hair thick and damp, smelling of salt.

Men move along the dock behind us, carrying provisions to the ship. I glance up to see baskets pass, full of fresh greens. Chickens' heads bob up and down from open crates. A pair of goats taps by, crying with the voices of babies. Farther down the dock someone is playing a pipe and I hear the rhythmic thud of feet on wood, men singing, and chants from the rigging of the ship. Gulls wheel and cry overhead. Through the other sounds the clanging of a bell cuts sharply. The boy — my brother — jumps up and runs down the dock. As he runs the gulls scatter and swoop; between their beating wings I catch glimpses of a man high up on the deck of the ship, leaning out over the side, raising his arm to the boy who hurries to reach him. The anchor rises from the ship's stern, streaming weed and water. A sail swells huge above me; the ship begins to glide away. I don't know how long I sit there, but it's for some time, until the ship has disappeared and the gulls have gone and there's just an empty dock, and the sea, and the bright sky. I look up toward the house. Something moves on the roof. Mama stands up there on the top of the house, a dark, slender shape against the sky. Her gown ripples and snaps in the wind. She stands with one hand clutching a lightning rod, the other raised to her brow, staring out to sea.

That must have been the day Papa sailed away for the last time, nearly ten years before, when I was five years old. That day was the start of Mama spending her nights on the walk, drifting away from me, as though when Papa's ship cast off and sailed away, he'd taken her with him, in mind if not body. And he'd taken my brother with him, too.

How I wished my brother were home. Then there would be no more lessons in the attic with Mordecai. My brother and I would wake up with the fishermen at dawn and catch our dinner off the wharf, and on warm evenings row together in the sound. We would sail up and down the coast in our little blue skiff, stopping at each town, and visit the islands I could see from my window. If my brother were home, Mama wouldn't walk the walk or carve her bones. Papa would be home, too.

But I knew Papa would leave again, and

with him my brother. Sometimes I let myself imagine that I sailed with them. Papa would not let me go; I would have to stow away. I would curl myself tight inside a great coil of rope or crouch quietly behind an anchor, or hide in a barrel deep in the hold, showing myself only when we had gone too far to turn back. I would sail away from Rathbone House, away from Mama, to the other side of the world, my brother beside me.

I lay in bed, turning the rope bracelet round and round my wrist, staring into the dark night. Gulls called over the water, and the curtains breathed softly in and out. I reached around to touch my back; among the scattered freckles floated a birthmark shaped like a ship. As I stared up at the black dome of the sky, Mama's boat of bone sailed slowly across. Its sails billowed in great sighing curves. My brother, standing in the prow, turned to look at me. His hair was thick and dark, moving like the sails; his eyes as green as mine. Against a lead sky he held up Mama's carved lantern. The flame inside beat red against the white bone like a heart.

I buried my face in my pillow, my heart pounding. He was alive. I knew he was.

Some nights I heard the sound of a boy's voice singing. It sounded in my own body, as though it was I who had sung. The song made me feel like it had always been there, waiting for me to learn how to hear it. It was the high, sweet voice of a boy before it breaks to manhood. The melody was clear, the rhythm strong, but only shreds of words came through, like a voice torn by the wind at sea.

As I lay there that night, halfway between sleep and waking, I heard it again. At the first faint note the crows left their perches on my bedposts and pulled the coverlet down. I drew a frock on over my shift and rose to walk through the dark house, the crows on my shoulders. They nipped at each other, restlessly cleaning their feathers and whistling snippets of the song.

Our house was built like a seaworthy ship. No space was wasted, each odd angle fitted with drawers, shelves, small spaces locked against light and vermin. A lingering fear of running out of stores far from land showed in its design. Each nook and cranny held stubs of ropes or ends of candles, small hoards of the hardtack that will keep a man alive at sea when the last salted beef and moldering oranges have gone.

I moved along the hall on the third floor, flanked by cupboards containing outmoded forms of illumination: candlesticks of every size and sort, tin lamps half full of old oils of vegetable origin. I was allowed to use only whale oil in my lamp, and that sparingly. The widow's walk, though, glowed at the top of the house like a great lantern, drenched in spermaceti. Mama burned as much oil as she liked. The light sprayed between the boards above us as I walked, the crows jittering and flapping on my shoulders.

The voice led us on, toward the back of the house. We passed the main stair, along which the portraits of my ancestors hung. The profiles were modeled in shallow relief of white wax and set within austere frames of ebony. The earliest, toward the bottom of the stair, were all small like me, but the profiles stretched as they mounted higher up the stair. Foreheads expanded, hairlines rose, clumped features drew apart. I sometimes sat on the staircase, staring at my forebears, wondering what they were like. I would from time to time ask Mama about them, but, as with all questions about our family, I received a reply that taught me nothing.

"A question unasked is an answer unregretted," she said.

Along the bottom edge of each image was a paler patch and two small holes, evidence of a nameplate removed. Besides the pronounced stretching from generation to generation, I observed other details such as could be seen in white wax: The hair of the lowermost was bountiful and wild, his forehead low, his features brutish. The second wore an elegant top hat distinctly at odds with features much like those of his predecessor. The third was just a boy, with a profile of balanced proportions and great beauty. The last, slender and attenuated, a little like Mordecai in profile, wore a high collar and a pomaded wave of hair leapt from his forehead. Though the nameplates were gone, the artist had incised in the wood of each frame the date: 1779, 1802, 1811, 1841. No Rathbone had been enshrined in wax for nearly twenty years. I thought the earliest portrait, the brutish one, might be my great-great-grandfather Moses; Mordecai had told me he was the first of the Rathbones.

Most of the Rathbones had long since died, though a few still lived who had moved away from the sea; a tall uncle or two sometimes visited from far inland, with a gift of maple syrup drawn from trees in the Great North Woods or a corn-husk doll from the Great Plains. My uncles tended to forget that, though small, I was now grown.

The few Rathbones besides me who remained in the house — Mama, Mordecai, Larboard, and Starboard — were all tall. They teetered around me mast-like, tilting on the stair treads, craning their necks at the sea. I was, I thought, a throwback. Small and dark.

As I passed the stair I glanced down to the first floor. A chain of seven bedrooms stretched along a narrow hallway from the front of the house to the back. Each bedroom had a door that opened onto the hallway, and doors that opened directly into the adjacent rooms. From the center of any bedroom you could look through the doorways, one behind the next, and see all along the chain: to the north, the shadowy back of the house; to the south, the bright sea. Though spare of furnishings, each room was fitted with built-in beds, one in every corner, curtained to keep the cold away. The family had once been large, Mordecai said. But no one slept behind the curtains anymore.

Now the voice seemed to be coming from the front of the house. I sent the crows ahead to scout each room, certain that if I came close enough the faint strains would strengthen and separate, that words would emerge and grow clear. The crows flew low and silent down the rooms, stopping now and then to perch above a door, to turn a head to catch some scrap of sound: the wind at a crack in a window, the creak of a floor long untrodden. The song stayed always just ahead as we made our way seaward. It was stronger that night than it had ever been, and I found my breath coming quick. Now that it seemed possible, I wasn't sure I wanted to find the source of the song. I nearly turned back.

Mama's room was by itself, on the left, near the end of the hall. Another door, directly at the end of the hall, led to the widow's walk. Coarser than the doors of other rooms, their panels planed smooth and painted in warm dark hues, this door was hinged in heavy brass, the planks broad and bare, never leveled. I was forbidden to pass through.

But the song was strong now and coming from behind the door. The crows glided back from their scouting and touched down on my shoulders, muttering to each other, leaning out to peck softly at the door. There was nothing to quiet my step in that passage. Mama kept the floor clear of carpets there. She told me it was to save them from the harsh light near the top of the house. But I suspected she wanted the floor clear so that she would hear my steps if I approached the walk. I had never been up to the walk in all my fifteen years. I had sometimes wondered what Mama was hiding, but before that day, when the singing voice had come so clear and strong, had never dared to try to find out. As it was, I hesitated at the doorway.

The crows clutched my shoulders and hunched their heads low. We entered a narrow well, cool and dank, and almost dark. At its center a rope ladder dangled. I stood just inside the door and leaned to peer up. The well brightened as it rose. Near the top was an opening, a doorway at one side.

I reached for the lowest rung but it was too high for me. I beckoned to the crows. They twined my hair around their beaks and lifted off, wings beating black in the gloom, until I could reach the bottom rung and pull myself up. The crows dropped to my shoulders, gasping. The gaps between the rungs were wide, but I was nimble and my frock was light. Mama must have had to hike up her heavy skirts and hold them in her teeth to keep from tripping. The corset bones must have bitten into her thighs as she lifted them.

I reached the top and stepped off the ladder, through the opening into the widow's walk. There was no banister or railing, just the narrow opening, a hole in the floor to one side of the walk. I pulled my arm across my eyes to block the glare. Though I had seen the walk often, looking up from the lawn, the space was larger than I'd imagined. The walls were leaded panes of glass tinged green, like sea spread thin, rough and bubbled. The panes rose and merged in a curved dome, thinning at the top until nearly clear, a bell glass.

The crows launched off my shoulders and circled high, knocking against the glass, startled by their reflections. A lantern hung from a hook in the seam of the dome. Its flame lurched and shuddered as the crows circled, their shadows careening around the glass walls and across the floor. I looked around me: Near the ladder, a ship's wheel leaned against the glass, its spokes dark and glossy where gripped by many mates. Across the walk from the ladder stood a sea chest, strapped in leather and brass-nailed, its sides mottled green, its bottom thick with barnacles.

A sudden shrill sound from the crows, a sound I knew. I closed my eyes and saw the harbor, a flash of gold braid, a line of men. The crows copied the bosun's whistle, blown whenever a captain boarded his ship, his crew at attention and ready for review. The crows knew the notes well; how often they must have heard such a whistle, in how many ports on their way from Papa to me. They flapped to the wheel and lit there, then squared their shoulders, side by side, wings closed crisply, breasts out, beaks high. I hurried to the well and peeked over the side. No captain climbed the rope ladder. It was Mama, mounting from the dark below. There was the crown of her head, pale braids coiled tight, flashes of her feet, her gloved hands opening to catch each rung. She had dressed again; the wide white collar of her gown floated above her dark shoulders. The rope creaked and swayed under her. I felt the urge to salute. My hand snapped smartly to my brow and my heart beat hard.

Where could I hide? The sea chest looked too small, but it might be deep enough and there was no other choice. Mama mustn't see me; she would be so angry. I motioned to the crows, opened the lid, and jumped inside, curling myself tight. I barely fit, slight though I was. The crows swooped down. I clutched one in each hand, stuffed them inside, and pulled the lid closed.

At first I heard only my breath, my heart pounding so loudly I was afraid she would hear it too. I kept as still as I could. Mama's boots began to click on the floor of the walk, back and forth, back and forth. As my eyes adjusted to the dark I could just make out the crows, tucked tight behind my knees. Each turned a beady eye to me and cocked its head, listening. The ladder began to creak again, the rope groaning and squeaking. Mama's boots stopped. The clump of a heavy step; loud breathing. Something bumped and rustled on the floor. Someone gasped. The sound I'd heard many times in my sleep began again, but stronger this time. Not a soft shuffle of sand but a harsh scraping, like a sailor swabbing the deck, down on his knees.

I opened the lid a sliver. A huge man rode Mama, his wide back arched over her body. A blue jacket stretched across his shoulders, but he soon tugged it off and threw it aside. His bare back was slashed with rows of pale scars that swelled with his ribs as he moved. Mama's body yawed beneath him, corset cracked open, breasts rolling on each rise. Faint crunches came from beneath her; on her lifted thighs shells had pressed their shapes: the spiral of a whelk, a cowrie's teeth. Through skin scraping against sand, I heard a faint click-click: At her neck bobbed a little trio of jointed bones on a thin chain, the chain she kept always hidden under her collar. With each new wave the bones moved in and out of the hollow of her throat, now sliding straight, now bent, beckoning.

The crows hopped up to my thigh, heads hunched low in the tight space, and leaned to dip their beaks into a deep bed of kelp under me, its bladders popping softly as the crows rummaged. They pushed something into my hands, a shape my fingers recognized: a long, smooth shaft, knobbed at both ends — a bone. I gasped and flinched. Something shifted beneath me, a soft crunch like a bird's nest compressing. My hand closed on a small warm body. A crow, crushed.

I heard the singing voice again. Not just a scrap of the song, this time, but all of it.

"Father, Father, sail a ship,
Sail it straight and strong.
Mother, Mother, make a bed,
Make it soft and long.
Sister, Sister, listen close,
Listen to my song.
For it was Father sailed the sea,
For it was Mother murdered me,
Sister, Sister, come and see,
Come see and sing with me."

I held my breath, heart hammering. The scraping sound outside the trunk had stopped.

A heavy step moved toward me, then halted. Along the seam between lid and trunk two slices of leather appeared. Knees creaked; I caught a flash of white breeches, gold buttons glaring on blue, then the shine of two eyes. The lid lifted. A broad hand reached in with the light, clutched a handful of frock, plucked me out, and held me up by my hem. My head dropped and I spun, squinting in the glare. My mother's lover inspected me, dangling upside down at the end of his thick arm. Pale eyes flared in his wide brown face. In my hand I clutched the crushed crow tighter, feather and bone squeezed between my fingers. Below me, Mama's skirts still frothed on the sand, her skin still flushed with blood. She lifted her face from the floor and held her arms out, but not to me, to him. Her legs spread wider. Her neck swelled. Her mouth opened in a croak.

When he turned away from me, to her, I reached up and smeared his face with crow. Twin stripes shone across his eyes and down each cheek. He blinked and roared, then pulled me close to his breath, to his nose black with blood. When I kicked out he

44

couldn't hold me. I dropped and found my feet, then lurched across the walk toward the well. I reached down for the ladder, first stuffing the crushed crow into the front of my frock, and called out for the other. I saw it circling above, beating against the dome. When its eye found mine, it swooped down and buried its claws in my hair. I started to sink, the rope burning my hands, and before I dropped below the rim, looked back up to see Mama; her skirts settled, hissing as she slid away. The rope jerked above me. I jumped for the floor, ran to the door, and heard the man fall heavily behind me.

I started running along the hall, toward my room, but my crow, tugging hard on my hair, pulled me down the main stair, to the bottom and into the hall of beds, my boots skittering along the boards as we turned. I heard someone behind me and looked back as I ran, but the dark swallowed everything. I kept running through the doorways, the rooms rushing by me, all the same, bed after bed, I felt my lungs would burst, until I finally reached the end of the hallway, the room farthest from the sea. I fell, gasping, onto the last bed. Legs shaking, pulse pounding in my ears, I turned and pulled the curtains closed.

My crow, just visible in the faint starlight

that washed through the curtains, dropped down from my head to lumber along the bed. He first peered into each shadowed corner, then turned to me and pushed his beak at my breast. The stain there spread, a dark, wet patch on the cloth. The crushed crow's warm body turned cold against my skin. I pressed my face further into the pillow. Still I heard no footsteps, only the beat of the sea, weaker now.

I raised my head at the sound of cloth tearing. I heard a few footsteps, then again the ripping sound, closer. My crow tugged at my gown, squawking, nipping at my hands. The man in blue was there. I felt more than saw him, a great bulk in the gloom. He walked to the bed across from mine and stripped the curtains down in one motion. Dust billowed up, and the smell of salt and mildew.

I was shaking now, hard. The bed quaked under me, its legs chattering on the floor. The curtains ripped down. The man groped in the bedclothes and his hands found me. He reached behind my neck and lifted me, this time by the collar of my gown. His body seemed to fill the room. When I tried to push him away, my hands slipped on sweaty skin and I felt his stiff hair, matted with my crow's blood. My frock started to slide up

46

my neck and over my mouth. The dead crow rustled at my breast, squeezed under the cloth as it slid by. The buttons popped, and the crow and I slipped through the frock and dropped to the bed. The man's hot hands came again, this time around my waist.

Then my crow was there, screeching, his wings beating in my face. His claws dug deep into my shoulder and I felt him strike out with his beak, once, twice. The man bellowed and his hands let go.

I scrambled off the bed, tripped over the curtains that lay in a heap on the floor, and fell. Fingers scrabbled along my thigh and tried to grasp my ankle, but I was too quick, I pulled away, struggled up off the floor, and lurched into the hall. Then I was running again, back down the long chain of rooms.

Only when I was almost to the main hall did I dare to turn around. In the faint light I could just see the man, far down the hall, his arms thrown over his face, see my crow swoop at him, squawking and hissing, beak flashing to peck his face again and again. The man groaned and clutched at his eyes, hunching away from the blows, trying to look up at me from under his raised arms. He dropped to his knees and called out in a deep, cracked voice.

"Wait, wait!"

Something in that voice thrummed through me, like a voice I had heard in dreams. I turned back around and kept running. As I reached the stairs and started up, my legs began to shake and I struggled, panting, slowing to catch my breath, hurrying again. At the second-floor landing I stopped, trying to hear over my thudding heart: nothing, only a thin whistle of wind from some window. Then my crow was flying up the stairs to me, wings beating black in the gloom. He landed on my shoulder and dropped something warm and wet there: a slice of nose, or a bite of tongue, I couldn't tell.

When I had caught my breath a little, I pushed on, up to the third floor. At the top, I hesitated. I almost turned right, toward Mama's room. For just a moment I let myself believe that I would find her there, warm, smiling, that she would take me in her arms and comfort me. But when had she ever comforted me? I pictured her on the floor of the walk, her arms held out to the man in blue. I headed for the attic.

I turned left, toward the narrow switchback at the north end of the house that led up to the attic, stopping to rummage in a cabinet for a stub of candle, striking a flame and hurrying on. My crow's shadow flared and faded on the walls in the guttering light as we made our way. Between the rows of white columns that flanked the halls, dreary seascapes gleamed from the wainscoted walls. I had lost the way to Mordecai's attic before, with all of its turns and twists; when I finally reached the base of the square tower that housed the last stair, I felt a wave of relief. The door stood open, and a silvery light drifted down.

When my crow realized where I was going, he hopped off my shoulder, croaking, onto the newel post at the bottom of the stairs. I half ran, half stumbled to the top.

I didn't see Mordecai right away. Under those beams it was always dark, except for the worn knots in the wood here and there, where sunlight or moonlight entered in slender shafts. One such beam lit up a shock of white hair. There was Mordecai, standing at his blackboard with his back to me. My cousin always moved slowly, stiffly, his long thin limbs reluctant to bend, but that night he moved feverishly, his hand dashing out with its chalk in swift little jerks. He was drawing something, a diagram of some kind, ruling off lines with a yardstick, intently focused on what he drew, but he must have heard me come in.

"Mercy, what are you doing here? It's long past your bedtime."

He turned around. His cross expression softened and his eyes widened. He was so pale that it would have been hard to say whether he went whiter.

"What has happened?"

I wanted to tell him about the man in blue. But Mordecai's face began to slowly spin, and then the room was spinning too.

CHAPTER TWO:
ROUTE OF THE SPERMACETI

{in which Mercy and Mordecai flee}

When I woke, it took me a moment to realize where I was, and why. My skin prickled and I gripped the blanket at my throat. The man in blue. Had Mordecai heard him? Had he come this far looking for me? But the way to the attic was not easy to find. A stranger would have had trouble finding it in bright daylight, unpecked by crows. The man had dropped to his knees, clutching his eyes. Maybe my crow had wounded him gravely enough that he couldn't go on; maybe my crow had blinded him. Mordecai was still standing at his worktable, as he had been when I arrived — how long ago I wasn't sure. He was hunting through a stack of books, rapidly scanning the pages of first one, then another, snapping the pages to and fro, talking to himself all the while in an excited whisper. I realized he was behaving oddly, but I didn't care; I was only relieved that everything seemed otherwise normal. I fell back against the pillow.

My face was hot, my body stiff. The cool cotton sheet soothed my skin. Mordecai had tucked me in with nautical precision, the sheet neatly turned down at my throat, over a worn woolen blanket stamped with an anchor. My hair had been brushed back, my face scrubbed clean. A steaming bowl of broth stood on a table by the cot. I glanced up at Mordecai's worktable. A beaker bubbled over a low flame, surrounded by shells from shellfish and vegetables from the root cellar.

The room was still dark, though faint gray light slanted down from the knotholes in the rafters. Then the bell clanged five times, and I knew it was near dawn. Larboard and Starboard never shirked their duty, rising each day before dawn to strike the bell that stood at the top of the stairs, as they did at the turn of each hour throughout the day.

Mordecai had not changed my frock; the stain was still there on the bodice, the cloth dark and stiff. I felt for the gobbet of flesh that my crow had dropped on my shoulder, but Mordecai had cleaned it away. I put my hand to my breast; my crow wasn't there. I sat up straight.

"Where is he?"

I started to get out of bed.

"Lie down."

Mordecai pressed me down and pointed to a corner cabinet once used for storing linens, now an infirmary for weary specimens. My dead crow lay next to a tray of crustaceans, wrapped in a napkin and guarded by cutlery, a tea towel neatly folded beneath its head. A low caw came from outside the attic. I turned my head to see my other crow clutching the outside of the doorframe, only his head protruding into the room. One eye was fixed on the tray where his companion lay.

I waited for Mordecai to question me, but he was back at his blackboard, intently working on the drawing I had noticed when I came in, referring repeatedly to the books and papers spread out around him. He had finished chalking his lines and was now plotting points on the grid.

I pulled my blanket tighter and stared up at the ceiling. Mordecai appeared to be ignoring me, but I could feel him look at me now and then. Once when I glanced up at him our eyes met and he looked away, back to his blackboard, but not before I saw a feverish spark in his pale-green eye. I was glad that he wasn't questioning me. I wasn't yet ready to talk about what I'd seen on the widow's walk. I wished it had been a dream, but the rope burns on my hands were stinging proof that it had been real. I burrowed deeper under the blanket, grateful to be warm and safe. The attic was, after all, where I spent most of my time.

Cousin Mordecai had lived in the attic as long as I could remember, under the hull of the *Sassacus.* One of our ancestors had installed her there, the bottom half of a square-rigged brig of fifty-odd feet, her upper decks stripped off and her hull turned and bolted down over the top of the house in place of a roof. Perhaps our ancestor couldn't bear to abandon her to rot in the sea after her long years of fruitful service had ended. Where the hull's halves joined, at the top of the attic, the wood was ringed from the slow seepage of the ocean, stained where barrels of beef and rum once rested. Mordecai knew the details of each voyage of the ship, gleaned from his trove of old logbooks and journals. The side of her hull had been stove in by a sperm a few generations earlier. Paler planks showed along one curve where the wood had been patched. A whisper carried easily from one end to the other. Dried strands of seaweed dangled from the rafters. As a child, I'd believed that a sleeping mermaid was trapped in the timbers.

Mordecai passed his days among his treasures, curiosities acquired by generations of Rathbone mariners. Eagerly bargained for in foreign waters, the souvenirs had soon been forgotten, their charms diluted by distance. Mordecai found them around the house, abandoned in unlocked sea lockers or fading on windowsills where curtains were no longer drawn at dusk. His collection was installed in the tall glass-fronted mahogany cabinets that lined the sides of the hull. In one, a cluster of casts of mutant hands seemed to wave gently to me as I passed, plaster fingers bloated or shriveled, some like sea slugs, others anemones. On a shelf above the hands, stuffed birds of several species perched, moldering, on branches of coral. The eye of a giant squid shone from one cabinet. In another, the heart of a sainted prelate who'd perished among the Maori endured in a coconut shell.

Each morning Mordecai tutored me, supervised by a row of salvaged plaster busts. Two heads of Socrates, large and small, flanked a startled Lord Nelson in full uniform; the chipped head of a horse who had lost a nostril observed us with a cold white eye. Other, more retiring busts hung back in the shadowy recesses of the rafters. All gazed down at us from perches that my crows would have envied if they could have forgotten their fear of the attic. They didn't care for the overturned hull. They believed, I thought, that the ship had been turned only for bailing, or had capsized in a storm, and would soon be righted. Or they were afraid that Mordecai would add them to his collection.

I had mastered most of what Mordecai knew of the arts and sciences, drawn from our scanty collection of books. An incomplete encyclopedia provided us with a thorough grounding in those subjects starting with *G, H–I,* and *U.* I was fully familiar with Unconformity, Ungulates, and the Underwing Moth. A few French volumes on natural history shared a shelf with Catesby's *The Purple Grosbeak with Poison Wood* and *Hooping Crane.* There were as well a few-score books of interest to the seaman: flag books, almanacs, *The Oriental Navigator,* books of charts, and narratives of voyages to distant lands.

I first practiced writing at five, in a salvaged logbook, copying out entries: lists of men and provisions (60 barrels of s-o-r-g-h-u-m, 30 of s-o-w-b-e-l-l-y), the name and number of whales taken on this voyage and that. We dissected creatures that washed up on the beach, or burrowed in the sand, thinking themselves safe, though these were rare; few fish swam in the waters off Naiwayonk, and I seldom saw crabs and other shore life. When I couldn't find fresh examples on the shoreline, we applied our knives to the pickled specimens that bobbed in jars of formaldehyde, whose organs, though shriveled, retained enough of shape and position to teach me the basics of anatomy. The mounted skeleton of a spider monkey surveyed our dissections from a corner of the worktable, eyeing us reproachfully from under a little sailor cap.

Mordecai had erased our lesson from earlier that day, but it was still just visible on the blackboard under his newly drawn grid, the legend still there in the bottom right corner: *"The Anatomy of the Sperm Whale."* The details of its massive body — its carefully labeled bones and organs, rendered in white chalk — had all been rubbed into one large and ghostly smear. Next to the blackboard, nailed to the neck of a headless figurehead, an aquatint showed a whale rolled on its back, impaled on all sides by men in whaleboats with lances and harpoons. With a flourish of his pointer

Mordecai had indicated the whale's blow-hole on the aquatint and asked me about its angle (*sharp, leftward, identifiable at a great distance*). He had often drilled me on the sperm's diet, nodding at my answer (*squid and skate are preferred, though he will, if pressed, eat commoner fish*), had often informed me that a lucky few evaded the whaling ships and lived to be as old as eighty, then drifted down to the ocean's bed, where smaller creatures ate them away.

I could see that Mordecai was ready for our next lesson. Lined up on his worktable was a row of jars filled with murky liquid. Pale tentacles curled in some jars; in others rows of suckers pressed against the glass. We would be reviewing the cephalopods, he had said, with particular attention to anomalies in the chambered nautilus.

How could I go back to my lessons after what had just happened?

I sipped my broth and stared up into the rafters, where the busts all dozed, trying to ready myself to tell Mordecai. Clearly he knew something had happened to send me, bloodied and fainting, to his attic in the middle of the night, my dead crow tucked into my dress. And clearly he was no more anxious to talk than I was.

Though I spent all of my time in the attic,

we never discussed anything other than our lessons. Mordecai was just my tutor, who happened to be my cousin too. Besides tutoring me, he had in recent months also instructed me in those graces a mother should teach her daughter, consulting the encyclopedia entry on "Gentility" for details. Each day I improved my posture by walking the attic with a large volume balanced on my head: *An Epitome of Navigation* or *The Eventful History of the Mutiny at Spithead and the Nore.* On days when I drifted, tired of some lesson I had long since memorized, Mordecai would mutely hand me a stack of small red missals and watch me struggle along the attic, the little tower of books teetering, my walk as stiff as his. Or he would disappear under a beam into his galley and presently I would hear spoons clinking against china. Mordecai would emerge with a tea tray. "And now, show me how you can pour with decorum," he would say, while the crows squawked outside the attic door, longing for a taste of the biscuits Mordecai had arranged on a plate.

When I was younger I would ask him to come to Mama's room with me, to choose bones from her stores, odd pieces for which she had no use; I knew he coveted them. "Your mama is busy with her own bones," he always said, with a dry little cough, and never came with me.

Staring up at the busts, something red caught my eye. At the end of the row, past the larger Socrates, stood the head and shoulders of a woman, her narrow, delicate face framed by lush marble curls. That day, her hair, until then unadorned, sported the cocked red hat of a ship's captain.

With Mordecai still busy at his board, I moved my chair under the bust, stepped up onto the seat, and lifted off the hat. The stiff red felt was trimmed in blue ribbon and boasted cockades. I held it to my nose: salt, tobacco, and another scent — more feminine, one plaster didn't produce. Mordecai looked up and, seeing what I held, snatched it away and returned it to the bust's curls. He turned back to his blackboard.

"Cousin. Where did this come from?"

He didn't turn around.

"I found it in a drawer," he said.

"A drawer?"

I frowned down at Mordecai from my chair, for once taller than him. He perched on the edge of a stool, turning a piece of chalk in his hands, not meeting my eye. One knee jittered up and down; the heel of his boot tapped on the floor. He seemed to be

60

considering some other, more acceptable answer to my question. Then he looked sharply up at me.

"Where did those burns on your hands come from? What happened to your crow?"

Now I looked away. Mordecai said nothing else. When I looked back he was running his hands through his hair, trying to smooth it down; it drifted up again in a white haze. His hair looked bleached by sun and sea, though he never went outside. His skin, too, was always pale; it looked lightly powdered, as though it wore a thin brine crust. He turned on his stool to face the blackboard and added a point to his grid. He took a deep breath and said, "He was looking for you in the night. I heard him."

My legs buckled. I dropped down onto the chair and gripped the edges of the seat.

"Calm yourself, he is gone. I heard him out there, after you came in, searching up and down the halls, but there has been no sound for hours. He must have given up."

I pulled my knees up, locked my arms around them, and hid my face. A coppery smell rose from the bodice of my frock, where my crow had been.

Mordecai's stool scraped on the floor and I heard him tiptoe over to my chair. He attempted to pat my hand, tapping it lightly a few times with three long white fingers. A few moments later I heard him begin to pace back and forth.

"Mercy . . ."

I lifted my head slightly and peered up from between my knees at Mordecai. He was standing with his hands clasped behind him, rocking on his heels, the hectic glint in his eye even brighter.

"I had planned to tell you later, but now . . ."

Mordecai flashed out a book from behind his back and thrust it in the air — a logbook, bound in frayed green linen, salt-stained.

"I have found it! The missing link!"

I looked at him, waiting.

He laid the book down and turned to his board. I saw that he had drawn more points on the grid since I last looked, a scattering of white circles, and that he had labeled the lines of his grid with numbers. With a series of quick twitches, he now connected the white points with his chalk. He stood aside and swept a trembling hand across the surface of the blackboard, glancing eagerly at me.

I looked more closely and saw that the numbers on the grid were latitudes and longitudes. The connected points now described a rough shape.

Mordecai picked up his pointer and tapped it here and there on the map as he spoke, his voice coming faster and faster.

"Certainly there were some troubling incongruities; allowances must of course always be made for slight deviations in the lunar tables, not to mention the" — here Mordecai snorted — "predictable inaccuracies of the seaman's less than keen observations . . . nevertheless, I have long suspected that the aberration in the southern loop was not a singular deviation but a periodic recurrence, mirrored in the northern portion . . . and we must certainly not neglect the effect of the currents at forty-one degrees and thirty-four minutes north, seventy-one degrees and ninety-five minutes west, owing to the Doldrums Trench —"

"Mordecai . . ."

He peered closely at the board, scratching his forehead, leaving a long white streak of chalk.

"I am in fact nearly tempted to shift my route half a point north-northeast —"

"Mordecai!" I shouted. I stood up from my chair, my hands clenched at my sides, my face hot. "What does this have to do with anything?"

He started and slowly straightened up

from the map. I had seldom seen him smile before; his eyes shone and his mouth stretched in a grin that looked painful. He opened his arms wide.

"The path of Leviathan!" He stabbed at the bottom right corner of the blackboard. The legend now read: *"Route of the Spermaceti from Summer to Winter Waters."* "They traverse the waters of the globe from pole to pole in their migration. I plotted, from the logs, the rhythms of the sperm, when and where the ships harvested the greatest numbers. They do not move at random, as sailors have so long thought. The mighty sperm departed their summer grounds off Antarctica three months ago, in late July. Based on my calculations, they are on their way north, now approaching the forty-second parallel. They may, in fact, have already begun to arrive. They will stream through for days and days." His pointer tapped at a circle near the center of the map. "Just beyond the Stark Archipelago." He picked up the green journal again and shook it at me. "I finally found the missing segment, I needed only these last coordinates to confirm it."

I tried to take it all in. "The Stark Archipelago?"

"Scarcely ten leagues away!"

I stared at Mordecai's map. I thought of whales, live sperm whales, of what it might be like to see one, its great blunt head thrusting through the waves. I had never seen any whale nor any spout, though I had often scanned the sea. I thought of being out on open water, away from this house, away from Mama and that man and what had happened on the walk. But what I saw when I looked at Mordecai's blackboard was not the map or the whales or Mama but the face of my lost brother, his features mapped in chalk like stars in a black sky.

It had been nearly ten years. Why should this not be the year that Papa finally returned, in the wake of the whales? Why else would I have heard the singing voice that night, as living as mine, calling out to me across the water, from a ship not on the other side of the world but just a few leagues away?

Mordecai picked up his chalk and drew an *X* on the Stark Archipelago. "And perhaps, just perhaps, when we find the whales we will find your papa!"

He had read my mind.

We would go to find the whales, and Papa too. And with him my brother. I felt a flood of joy.

Mordecai's grin faded.

"We must leave now, before it's too light."

He did not say before the intruder might come back, but he didn't need to.

"I'm ready," I heard myself say. "I . . . what will I need? I don't . . ."

Mordecai cleared his throat.

"I have anticipated somewhat and have taken the liberty . . ." He nodded toward a shadowy corner. A row of mismatched suitcases and sailors' ditty bags huddled there. "I have packed your clothing and gloves and boots and" — he flushed, on his white skin a faint pink — "various necessities. I need only collect a few more items."

Mordecai picked up two large leather satchels and began bustling around the attic, opening and closing cabinets, rummaging through bins. Into one bag he slid a stack of books, bundles of papers, a box full of writing instruments. He set the bags down to dash a few notes into a small journal, copying off the blackboard, tossed it into one of the bags, and picked them up again. Continuing quickly around the room, he picked up his favorite treasures, adding some to the bags, setting others back down.

There was a rap at the door. I jumped and put a hand over my mouth; Mordecai dropped an armillary sphere, shattering the outer planets. My crow's head appeared around the edge of the door and he croaked loudly, flapping his wings.

I hunched a valise under one arm, picked up two more bags, and headed for the door. I stood looking back at Mordecai, waiting.

He tossed a sextant and a roll of charts into one satchel, hung the ditty bags around his neck, and picked up both satchels again, looking longingly at three suitcases that remained with no one to carry them. He hurried toward the door and, before reaching it, stopped abruptly, then took a step backward. His gaze traveled slowly around the attic. His eyes lost their manic gleam.

I wondered how long it had been since he had walked out of Rathbone House. Maybe he never had.

Mordecai took a deep breath. He set the satchels down, picked up a broken telescope from his table and with it shattered the glass case over the eye of the giant squid. He popped the eye in his breast pocket, picked up the satchels again, and together we hurried out the attic door.

We moved as quickly as we could along the twists and turns, trying to be quiet, our cases bumping on the corners in the narrow halls. As we neared the hallway where I had last seen the man in blue, I slowed down, afraid to turn the corner and find him lying there in the middle of the hall, gigantic, blood crusting on his face where my crow had gouged it. I imagined trying to squeeze past, my skin tingling, not sure if the man were dead or alive. Hearing his giant's breath. Seeing his great chest heave, his eyes snap open —

"Mercy!" cried Mordecai.

I blinked. The hallway was open and bright. The first rays of the sun were washing in from the white rooms.

Mordecai took my hand and pulled me along — my crow flew out from the last room and clutched my shoulder, cawing — around the last corner, down all the stairs, and out the front door, into the light and the fresh salt air and toward the harbor.

And that is how our odyssey began.

CHAPTER THREE: MOUSE ISLAND

*{in which the wives of
Moses make Mercy over}*

Mordecai groaned, dropping a suitcase to throw an arm across his face as we ran down the lawn toward the sea. I glanced back but saw only the open door, the house rearing up behind us. Crow, scouting ahead, circled back and flew just above us, his wings casting a shadow over our faces as we ran. He shrieked and banked sharply to the right, toward the cliff where the lawn dropped away to the surf. I followed, pulling at the tail of Mordecai's coat.

"No, this way, we must go to the harbor." Mordecai took his arm away from his eyes to pull me the other way, then put it back, moaning.

I spotted an opening in the green, the stair of tumbled boulders that led to the beach. I tossed my bags down and leapt from rock to rock to the sand.

Mordecai sat huddled on the grass at the top of the boulders, wincing. The sunlight must hurt his eyes, I realized. I'd never seen him outside before. I untied my cloak and threw it up to him. He wrapped it around his face and hugged his knees, rocking.

The blue skiff lay on the beach, overturned in dune grass. The paint was wind-scoured, the oarlocks rusty, and it had never been tested in open sea. But it seemed sound, and there was no other choice. I squatted, reached both hands under the side of the hull, and heaved it over. The oars tumbled out. A crowd of pink crabs scuttled from the seaweed that had drifted underneath. I tossed my bags and the oars into the skiff and hurried to the stern. Digging the toes of my boots into the sand, I started pushing the boat toward the water.

Mordecai groped his way down the rocks, my cloak still draped over his face, and helped me push through the surf. When the skiff started to float I hopped in. He pushed us farther out, then climbed in and lowered himself onto the seat in the stern, wedging his suitcases between the benches, and doubling his long legs up like a crane to fit. The boat was far too small for him. I sat in the bow, set the oars in the shafts, and began to row. Mordecai leaned over and tucked his head between his knees, breathing hard.

My heart began to slow as the oars steadied. Crow hunched on my shoulder, canting his head at the gulls overhead, hopping with a squawk each time I finished pulling a stroke and leaned forward again. My skiff moved well against scant wind, through a low chop of waves. The dawn fog lifted from the surface as I rowed, a layer of warm light taking its place, as though it rose from the sea.

"Let me row." Mordecai tried to hoist himself up and fell back again, panting. His breathing was so labored from so brief an effort that I wondered if he had ever run before this day. He raised one arm again, across his eyes. When had he last seen the sun?

At first when I looked up over the water between us and the shore, only the top of the house showed above the cliff face. As I rowed, the lower floors slowly tilted into view. The widow's walk, still in shadow, crowned the roof, pricked with lightning rods and topped with weathervanes of maritime form: a merman, a manatee, a compass rose. Under the walk, the white columns of the unfinished third floor stood against a pale wash of sky. To the west, between two pediments, Mordecai's attic sloped; then the red brick of the second floor, its multipaned windows topped with keystones. Below the second story were the heavy timbers of the bottom floor, squat and dark, with small grated windows low to the ground. Now and then I glanced up at the house as I rowed. Though the hill on which it stood grew indistinct as the distance increased, the house itself seemed to me no smaller. A few other houses, none as large as ours, were hidden among the trees west of the high ground on which Rathbone House stood; once inhabited by competitors to my family in the whaling trade, they had long stood empty.

By now we were about half a mile from the house. To the east lay the harbor I had not seen in many years, and never from so far away. My only voyages had been short excursions in the cove, searching with the crows for specimens for my lessons, or hugging the shore west of the house. Mama didn't approve of my lingering near the docks where the whalers passed their time between trips, though no whaleman had docked there in nearly ten years. A few fishermen remained in the town of Naiway-onk, a cluster of cottages along the shore.

Dories and smacks bobbed against the docks, masts tilting. The shapes of men moved through fog. Beyond the docks, on the far side of the harbor, the trying sheds where the whales were once boiled still commanded the western point, their high double doors locked for generations. According to Mordecai, in Great-Great-Grandfather's time you could see the mammoth cauldrons through the open doors, the trying fires burning bright.

The air this far from shore had no trace of tidal rot, of old fish and weed turned again and again in the surf, only keen clear gusts from the open sea. A sharp breeze blew the fog into tatters; the watery blue of the sky began to strengthen. The surface of the sea was a vivid green, brisk with whitecaps. I began to feel as though my mind were clearing as well, though I wasn't yet ready to regard straight-on what I'd seen the night before: piercing glimpses of the broad back of the man in blue, of my mother turning away from me.

I reapplied myself to my oars until the house was distant and the harbor too far for even the faint cries of fishermen to carry. Though my arms began to ache it felt good to stretch them, and I took comfort in the steady rhythm of my rowing. I heard only the splash of the oars, the water humming along my hull. Crow, lulled by the motion of the boat, tucked his head beneath his wing and dozed. My other shoulder felt bare; I tried not to think of my lost companion. My gaze drifted over the side to find a school of flounder swimming nearby, all their eyes looking up at me. The water was so clear; I could see far under the surface. I let go the oars and stared for a while. The flat, silvery fish swam tight together to form the shape of one large flounder. They drifted apart, then reformed, keeping always just alongside my skiff. Beneath them groves of kelp spiraled from far below and jellyfish pulsed and swayed. Some larger fish slid below the silver school, its dark scales shimmering in the clear green. I lay my head on my knees, wondering what Mama was doing now, how long it would be before she noticed I was gone.

Mordecai finally stirred. The fleet of fish veered off and disappeared. One arm still over his eyes, he moved his free hand over the satchel in front of him until he found the open top and felt the rolls of papers protruding at one end. Before he noticed that I had stopped rowing I had found and tugged on my gloves, taken up the oars again, and returned to my rhythm. I already felt blisters forming on my palms. I glanced up at the sun; perhaps an hour had passed since we started.

"Thankfully I didn't drop the one with the charts. Though my fistulae are forever gone, and the Hand of Glory." Mordecai sighed. He pulled out an old blue bandanna, faded but clean, and tied it over his eyes with the point hanging down over his nose. Spreading his knees, he unrolled a stiff chart that cracked as he opened it across the seat between his legs. He lifted the point of the bandanna to peer down at the chart, leaning close to the faded blue ink. I bent to look at his eyes. They were red and watering; through the squeezed slits his irises were vaporous, his pupils pin dots.

I wondered if Mordecai would bring up the man in blue, now that we were safely away.

He lifted the point of his bandanna a little higher to squint at the horizon. "That chain of islands straight out, to the south?"

I turned and raised my hand to my brow and found a stuttering stretch of green.

"The Stark Archipelago."

A cold gust of wind blew hair into my eyes. Turning my face to the wind, I gulped in the clean air, so pleasant on my hot skin after rowing. I let go of the oars and half stood to look out toward the islands. I couldn't help but scan the horizon beyond for that telltale spout: *sharp, leftward, identifiable at a great distance.* I could in fact see the horizon in sharp focus, see the white crest of every distant wave as though it were close, but nowhere did I see any spout or any spray but that of the ocean itself.

As I began to row again, I noticed a sprinkling of islands far to the west of Naiwayonk, just visible, and wondered if they were among the local islands whose names I had heard Mordecai mention: Whaleback Rock, Birch Island, North Dumpling, Scraggy Island. My eye fell on another island, much closer, a few miles southwest of us. I had often watched this island from my window, a low mounded shape with a wavering, pale line of surf. The island had always been a shifting presence, seemingly changing shape and position. I longed to get closer.

"Mordecai, what about that island?" I said, pointing.

Mordecai tilted his head back to sight along his nose. Light glared off a wave and he winced. He dug again in the bag.

"Ah." From a leather case he drew a pair of dark-tinted purser's spectacles and balanced them on his nose.

"Can't we row past? It's not that far out of our way."

He saw what I pointed at and shook his head. "Not there. Too dangerous." He gazed at the island for a moment, then glanced back toward shore.

I eased up on the oars and drifted for the space of a few strokes to look to the west, toward the low gray island still deep in the fog that had already begun to burn off closer to shore. Among Mordecai's earliest lessons was one in botany in which he diagrammed the poisonous oak with its three-leaf stem of deep waxy green and told me how Mouse Island was completely covered with such plants. A brood of young ancestors had rowed out to the island one night long ago. One of the boys, on a dare, had swallowed a leaf and choked, his throat swollen closed with the poison, the scrimshaw maiden that was his prize still clutched in his hand.

"Dangerous? I wouldn't be so stupid as to swallow it."

"Not that. The rocks. The breakers."

From so close, the thin line of surf I had seen from my window was a churn of white below the island, sending high flares of spray against the green sea.

Mordecai clutched the rim of the skiff,

looked over one side, blanching, I would have said, if he weren't already so white, then fixed his eyes on me, watching me pull. My arms had begun to slow, my strokes shorten.

"Let me take the oars for a while."

I thought it was impolite to ask if he had ever rowed before. I was equally doubtful of his navigational abilities, but I was tired enough to accept the offer. I rose carefully, as did Mordecai. There was no room to pass side by side. I ducked instead between his legs and settled on the seat in the stern.

The bandanna now tied pirate-fashion over his long pale hair, Mordecai began to row, at first most unsteadily, then settling into a kind of rhythm, though one which needed frequent course corrections, veering now to starboard, now to port. With this inefficient tacking we headed south at a lubberly pace, toward the distant archipelago. Mouse Island was about a mile to the west when we passed. I could see that its low mound appeared to be gray stone. I had sometimes wondered why, if covered in poisonous oak, it didn't look green in spring or summer, instead of just a cool gray.

I closed my eyes and let my mind drift for a while. It was difficult not to, with the lapping water, the warming light.

A loud splintering sound made me sit up straight. I turned to see a jagged tear in the side of the boat. Water poured into the bottom of the skiff. With a too-vigorous downstroke of his oar, Mordecai had driven it through the brittle wood.

My first thought was to bail. I felt around under the bench and pulled a bucket from a tangle of old rope and began to bail the bottom of the skiff. I had just begun when, through the water bubbling into the boat, I heard another sound behind us. I stopped mid-bail and peered out toward the sound. Where the fog had not yet burned off, sunlight suffused it. A thick cloud of light blinded me. I heard a muffled splash and then a pause — it was hard to tell how distant; sound traveled easily on the water. Another splash. Mordecai listened too. We sat motionless.

"A pair of dolphins," Mordecai declared.

I held my tongue and listened.

"An errant buoy," Mordecai ventured.

A splash, and then another. Closer.

Mordecai plied the oars. A few inches of water now soaked my feet, seeping through the seams of my boots. Crow hopped down and splashed his wings in the water; I spoke to him sharply. He nipped my boot and lifted off, toward the sound, disappearing in the fog. Wind shivered along the face of the water. To the west the island dissolved in spray from the oars and reappeared.

"The plaster, get the plaster. The jar . . ."

I reached into Mordecai's bag and began to pull things out: a pair of Turkish slippers, a torn signal flag, a dried lungfish that crumbled in my fingers.

"At the bottom, under the eel skins."

I pulled out a jar half full of white powder.

"Take the oars."

I dove between Mordecai's legs and started to row.

He pried off the cap.

"I had hoped to cast the other . . ." He began to lift a wrapped shape from his bag, then eased it back. He glanced up toward Crow, who hovered above the boat, flapping, staring toward the splashes. "It makes no matter." He dipped the open top of the jar into the water in the hull, stirred with a long finger, and smeared the white paste along the crack. The plaster soon hardened, and the leak stopped. We switched places, Mordecai again taking the oars.

The splashing was louder now. Through the thick light I saw the curved hull of a skiff, the line of an oar. A blue back, straining. Mama's man.

Mordecai saw him, too, and leaned hard

on his starboard oar. The bow swung around and pointed to Mouse Island.

"But the rocks . . ."

He didn't reply, only bent deeper into his oars. We were not far now; patches of gray rock showed through the fog and the breakers boomed. The light chop of open water shifted to long swells as we neared the island. The skiff rose on a swell and started to dip toward the rocks, toward the roaring surf. A sudden jolt: I held on tight and leaned over the side. We had struck a rock under the surface — more rocks, dark and jagged, loomed in the water under us, all around us now.

A loud crack, behind us, cut through the noise of the surf. I looked back to see a boat shoot straight up from the water, twist in the air, and smack down with a vast jet of spray, landing hull up. An oar spun out and struck a rock, shattering. A blue shape arced down into the water.

I shouted at Mordecai, but he didn't look up, intent on avoiding the rocks, trying to crane around to see our path. I shouted again, but he couldn't hear me through the breakers. I reached out and grabbed his knee so that he would look up and began pointing, trying to direct him through the rocks.

Twice I twisted around and thought I saw the man moving toward us, gliding through the churning water, slipping around the rocks. Even if the man had survived his boat smashing on those rocks, surely he wouldn't have the strength to swim after us. But there it was again: a face lifting to one side, mouth spouting water. A blue arm driving down, lifting, driving down again.

It seemed to last forever, struggling through. We missed striking one huge rock by a hairsbreadth and glanced off another, its sharp peak jittering along the bottom of the skiff as we passed over. Then the rocks began to thin and I leaned out to try to see how close we were to the island. We were starting to round the point at the near end of the island, we were almost past the rocks, and I glimpsed what looked like calm water on the other side.

A hand shot up from the spray and seized the blade of Mordecai's oar. He lurched and grasped the oar with both hands, bracing his feet against the side of the skiff, struggling to hold on. With a single great jerk the hand pulled Mordecai and his oar half over the side.

"Mercy! Mercy!" Mordecai screamed, doubled over, clinging to the oar, his bottom half now starting to slide over the side as the hand pulled hard.

I leapt onto Mordecai and wrapped myself tight around his knees, trying to make myself heavy, to pull him back. The man's head surged up out of the water. His face was gouged all over. His eyes blazed red with salt. He reached for me. The skiff jerked and pitched and Mordecai suddenly let go of the oar and fell back. Wood cracked against bone and I saw blood gush from a black gash on the man's forehead. He threw back his head and his mouth opened in a huge howl. Blood poured down from the gash and filled his mouth with red, then the sea closed over him.

I held on to the rim, looking back through torn spray as the skiff jolted through the waves. I thought I saw the man's head bob up, but then we slapped down into a trough, the rocks now directly in front of us, and I lost sight of him. Through the noise of waves and wind I heard a deep bawl. It sounded like my name. That voice again, like something I had dreamed. Mordecai leaned out with his long arms, pushing, struggling to stave off the rocks, and then one last bump and bounce and we were finally around the point, the sea suddenly smooth and quiet.

My heart still slammed against my chest.

I felt Crow's claws settle on my shoulder and reached up with a shivering hand to smooth his wet wings.

"Mordecai?"

He was draped over the side of the boat, arms and hair trailing in the water, breath in long rasps. "I am quite well."

A thin stream of red ran into the sea from his dangling wrist. I crouched beside him and scooped water onto the wound, a long pink tear in his white flesh. I looked at it closely; the wound was shallow, but an alarming amount of blood continued to flow, and he was clearly in pain. I pulled the bandanna off Mordecai's hair and used it to tightly bind the wound.

When I had stopped shivering, I twisted the water from my hair. I knew we were not far from where we'd struggled with the man in blue. I turned nervously on my seat to look all around the skiff for the dark gliding form among the whitecaps. It wouldn't have surprised me if he had recovered to track us, breathing as easily beneath the waves as above, so strong and fishlike a creature he seemed.

We had rounded the point to the south side of Mouse Island, the seaward side. No jagged rocks, no breaking surf, only a long, low slope of gray rock curved before us, some twenty yards across. I stood to see more clearly and felt a surge of cold sea on my legs. The plaster plug was gone, forced out in the rushing water. Mordecai's boots soon sloshed ankle deep; the water gurgled around my knees. My scalp suddenly smarted. Crow was pulling a hank of my hair straight skyward, screeching. The skiff was sinking.

Crow let go of my hair and lifted off as something passed over my head and around my waist, a thick loop, not rope but something softer. It tightened and jerked me backward out of the skiff, bent over, legs and arms trawling in front of me through the water. I looked up through my own wake, spluttering and choking, to see another such loop, a lasso, pass over Mordecai's head and around his waist. He reached for his suitcases before he, too, was pulled from the skiff and towed backward through the waves. I wondered if it was the man in blue, if he had after all reached the island and was hauling us to land. I tried to turn my head and through the spray could just see three figures on the island behind me, see the taut ropes stretching back to them.

A moment later my underside struck something hard and I found myself sitting, gasping, on a ledge of rock that sloped up from the sea. Then Mordecai was beside me, coughing and unwrapping the sea wrack that had wound about his neck. Offshore the skiff, now only a tilted rim of blue in the water, sank. The bailing bucket popped to the surface and drifted slowly away.

Small hands lifted my arms, loosened and lifted away the rope, and wrapped warm cloth around my shoulders. Soft hands came under my elbow, urging me up. I was facing the sea and so couldn't see who helped me, besides which my hair, loosely braided when we left Rathbone House, now fell in wet and heavy hanks before my eyes. I pushed my hair aside. Three aged women, all strikingly similar, each closely wrapped in gull-gray cloth, and small, though not so small as me, peered into my face. Two of the women leaned and gathered up the long green ropes, coiling them in neat loops and hanging them over their shoulders. Holding me close between them, they stood straight and moved steadily through the gusting wind, leading us up the slope toward a house that backed against a sheer rock face, the same gray granite as the rest of the island. The house was clad in thick clapboard, hip-roofed, two stories with small shuttered windows, all its wood surfaces scoured clean by the wind until it was smooth and pale as driftwood. To the east were two smaller islands, shallow mounds of rock a few steps offshore, and on each a smaller house with a single large window. Behind the panes something moved — a small black face and then another. A little crowd of sheep milled in each house; I heard faint bleats. As we neared the house against the rock I looked at the uniform gray of all that surrounded me and realized that the island had not a scrap of vegetation, let alone the poisonous oak; no barnacles, none of the weed that clung to rocks on other shores.

The three women led us into the first house. As we passed through the door I looked back for Crow and saw him skim by with an egg in his beak, pursued by a tern.

We entered into warmth and firelight, the soft hands pushing us forward, patting us into chairs, pressing cups of something hot and fragrant, smelling of beach roses, into our hands. I was grateful for its heat and clasped my hands tightly around the small cup; pink-tinged tea shone through the thin white porcelain. I looked up into a face of great age, as smooth as a stone rolled in the surf year on year. The woman, one of the three, had unwrapped her shawl and wore beneath it a simple gown of soft gray wool. Her silver hair was drawn back into a neat swirl.

Our chairs were set close by the fire; the resinous scent of pine spread through the room. Stacked neatly on the stone hearth, a pile of broken planks, scarlet red, bore parts of large black letters: the stem of an *A,* a curve of *S* or *O.* Remnants of rigging sizzled in the flames, barnacles popping in the heat. I turned to face the fire, spreading my hair to dry, and rubbed my hands as I watched the steam rise from my wet frock. On the rough stone mantel above me stood a green glass bottle full of white shapes; I looked more closely and saw that they were small teeth. Behind the bottle leaned a tall mirror in which nothing reflected, its silver gone black.

Other than the small seating area around the hearth, the room held no furniture but a loom that filled the space from edge to edge, built of heavy timbers thickly tarred at all the joints. Around the loom's perimeter, the backs of their chairs pressed to the walls, sat silvery old women. Our other rescuers were among them, though I couldn't tell one from the next.

The first woman rejoined her companions, sitting on a high stool at the far end, and began to work the great lever of the warp. The others, eight altogether, worked in pairs, sitting across from each other. One pushed her spindle to the middle, passing it smoothly to her mate, who took it up and returned it, row by row. The clack of the pedal and the softer sound of the shuttles echoed in the high open space above the dames. From the rafters, across the breadth and width of the roof, hung a woven netting, a ceiling-size hammock in which I thought the women must swing to sleep at night, so that they could look down and see beneath them their weaving, like a soft sea.

I leaned close to the loom, to touch the cloth. The pattern grew no clearer no matter how close I brought my eyes.

Mordecai stood, wincing, rubbing at his elbows and shoulders. He turned and bowed to the first woman.

"Mrs. . . . Rathbone?"

I gawked up at Mordecai, amazed.

Smiling, the first woman stood and curtseyed.

"Yes, Mrs. Euphemia Rathbone."

Around the loom the others rose and curtseyed. "How do you do?" each said in succession.

The first left her place at the loom and came close to me, touching a finger to my cheek. She was, I saw then, soundly built beneath the soft gown, plumb-weighted.

"You have come from Rathbone House, dear."

I nodded and curtseyed, smoothing down my damp hair. How had she known? There was something in her that drew me. She seemed familiar, though she couldn't have been more unlike the tall and spectral Rathbones with which my world had been until then thinly populated. When she turned her head to pour more tea, I caught my breath at how closely she mirrored the profiles hanging toward the bottom of the stair in Rathbone House.

"And your boatman?" She turned to Mordecai.

"My cousin Mordecai."

Mordecai bowed again. The woman nodded and gestured for him to sit down. She stood by Mordecai, one small hand petting his head through its woolen covering, smiling into his face. Seated, his face was at the same level as hers. She conferred for a few moments with her nearest companions, all of whom nodded, then turned back to me.

"We knew your great" — she raised her eyes to the ceiling, counting back along the generations, and turned to the other women, one of whom prompted her — "yes, your great-great-grandmother Hepzibah. I'm sorry, my dear, we aren't used to visitors, or we would have welcomed you with more than our poor tea. We've seen no one from the house for many years." She took my hand and stroked it, smiling. "When you were a baby you came here often. With your mother."

"But I never came here."

The women looked at one another, smiling. They chuckled.

I turned to Mordecai for help, but his head was bent over his tea, his hand clutching a shawl under his chin that covered his head and shoulders. The pattern of the wool seemed familiar, a winding border of kelp and mollusks intertwined. Mama had taken me on visits to Mouse Island? Mama, who, like Mordecai, I had never known to leave the house?

The first woman returned to her spot at the head of the loom and placed one hand on the great lever, like a steersman at the oar of his boat. She began to speak, her voice strong and rhythmic, the others standing silently at their places around her.

"I am Euphemia Rathbone. I was Mrs. Rathbone for four years, the Thousand-Barrel Years. I bore six sons. All went to the whale." Her loom mates all bowed their heads. Euphemia moved slowly around the loom, laying a hand on each woman's shoulder and looking into her eyes as she spoke. "And Mrs. Beulah Rathbone bore three. Mrs. Patience Rathbone, five. Mrs. Eunice Rathbone, three. Mrs. Amaziah Rathbone, four. Mrs. . . . ." I lost track of names, trying to add up the numbers, wondering why she mentioned only sons.

Mordecai coughed. I looked up to see him glaring at me from under his shawl with an anxious expression; my puzzlement must have shown on my face. He looked back toward the women.

"Moses Rathbone was your husband?" asked Mordecai.

"Yes," they replied in unison.

I opened my mouth and found my chair suddenly pulled tight against Mordecai's, his hand pressing down on mine.

But my question was already in the air. "You had no daughters?"

This time they didn't reply in unison, nor so loudly.

"Stillborn."

"Sent to the country."

"Influenza."

Mordecai's hand was hurting mine. I kept quiet.

Euphemia returned to the hearth, sat next

to me, and ran a hand over my hair, over the fabric of my damp frock.

"My dear, what a beauty you are. Eunice, doesn't she bring Hepzibah to mind?"

Me, a beauty? I met Euphemia's frank and open gaze, blushing. Her size and bearing were so like mine; I saw myself some sixty years on, if I should live as long as my great-great-aunts had.

The other women left their chairs and gathered around me. They plucked at my skirts, lifted my hair to examine my collar. I tried to brush the soft hands away, embarrassed, but back they came. Since that time Mama had sliced the gown, I hadn't thought of how I dressed. Now, as my great-great-aunts fussed over me, I felt a flush of pleasure.

The women spoke quietly among themselves, then a pair moved to the baskets that lined one wall and together they sorted through hanks of spun wool stacked within them. They pulled out a skein of pearly gray, trying it against my face, draping it across my breast. Mordecai turned modestly away while they peeled off my damp clothes, patted me dry, and slid my arms into a soft nightshift, then started to push me up the stair that clung to one wall.

I hesitated, then stopped and looked back

at my great-great-aunts; a question had been nagging me since our rescue. "Excuse me, aunts, but did you . . . pull anyone else from the water? Did you see a man out there?"

My aunts looked at one another, shaking their heads slowly. One stepped close to Euphemia and whispered into her ear. Euphemia smiled and said, "No, but Amaziah says she saw a great blue swordfish plowing up the waves." My aunts, tittering softly, returned to their work.

At the top of the stair I stepped off, onto the swaying net that stretched across the space, picking my way carefully on the knots to keep my feet from falling through. I curled up on one of the soft pallets around the edges on which my aunts slept, the net creaking and swaying beneath me, and looked down, to where the women had returned to their work at the loom.

I watched the gleam of the thread as it passed across and through, again and again, but however long I watched the weft grew no wider. The color of the cloth shifted through shades like the changing sea. As I drifted off, I imagined that a darker shape appeared among the threads and spread and spread, a blob slowly sprouting limbs, a head of waving hair: There was my brother,

his arms reaching up, his mouth a great blue
O. Then the pattern shifted, his mouth
drifted away, his limbs split off, and he was
gone.

When I woke, Mordecai was lying nearby
on his back, looking up at something that
he turned in his fingers: the squid eye,
which looked intact, though less spherical
than it had once been. Beneath us the
shuttle still whispered across and back,
across and back. The slight swaying of the
net felt pleasant. Crow dozed on my shoulder. Outside it was nearly dusk and under
those rafters close to dark; Mordecai seemed
to find the dimness comforting. His eyes
were circled in white from the tinted spectacles, his face otherwise the tender pink of
a conch from the sun. His arm was now
swathed in soft cloth. His wound had not
stopped bleeding until my aunts, murmuring over the long tear, had rubbed in a green
ointment that smelled of algae.

Mama, skilled though she was, had once
cut herself while carving, a more serious
wound than Mordecai had been dealt by
the man in blue. The point of a blade she
had been using to work the surface of a
bone had slipped and driven deep into her
thumb. I had been sitting across from her,
practicing my script, when I heard her sharp

hiss and looked up to see a fount of blood flow over her hand. I had jumped up and rushed to her, clutching her about the waist and burying my face in her skirt. I was frightened of the bright blood. She pried my fingers from her waist and pushed me back to my chair, not roughly but slowly and with a cool eye. She held me there with one hand and turned her attention back to her thumb, which she brought closer to her eye to observe its small spurt for a moment longer before letting go of me to reach for a rag from the table, which she wound tightly around the thumb. I stayed in my chair and forced myself to keep my hands in my lap, though I would rather have hid my face in my hands.

There had been other times when I had felt afraid as a child. When a pack of horseshoe crabs had clattered over my boots on the beach, I had swallowed a scream. When a thunderstorm had pelted the roof with hail and drawn down lightning to its many rods so that the whole of the house crackled, I had set my mouth in a line and kept silent. Mama had watched, nodding approvingly.

I turned toward Mordecai. Crow grumbled and shuffled from my shoulder up to the top of my head.

"They've lived here all these years, just a

few miles away, and I've never known them," I whispered. "You knew. Is that why you lied about Mouse Island, about the poison oak, so that I wouldn't come find them? Why?"

Mordecai squirmed, trying to pull his nightshift down to cover his legs better.

"Well, yes, I knew of them. But I did not think their history suitable for a young lady's ears." He hesitated. "However, I did not know that some of them were still alive. Or that Mouse Island was where they lived. And it was old Bemus who told me the story about the poisonous oak. I believed it, too."

I was surprised to hear Mordecai admit to not having known about Mouse Island. I assumed he knew everything. He took such pride in his carefully hoarded collection of journals and logbooks, in knowing so much about the family. And I wondered why Bemus had lied about the island. Old Bemus had died when I was a baby. I didn't remember him at all. Mordecai had said he was the last of the old Rathbones, the ones who whaled.

Mordecai continued to turn the eye. Within its shrunken jelly the dark pupil gleamed. His vision was poor, but he liked to say that he could see more sharply than me when he held the eye, that he borrowed from the squid the great eye's power.

"Tell me more," I whispered. Crow stirred and began to preen his wings.

Mordecai sighed and hugged his knees to his chest.

"Those bedrooms on the first floor?"

I nodded. The chain of rooms. I had always loved the curtains on the beds. Their patterns were all different; one set had a border of twining kelp and mollusks. I realized that the same pattern decorated the shawl that Mordecai still wore about his shoulders. He saw me looking at the shawl and nodded.

"Your great-great-aunts wove all of those curtains, long ago, when Moses's sons slept in those beds."

I thought of other patterns in the hall of beds: starfish and sea urchins capered on a reef; gulls flew in a tight phalanx across the sky; on my favorite set, twin octopi stretched their tentacles toward the selvages.

"In your great-great-grandfather's time his sons alone were enough to crew the whalers, captain to cabin boy. When one wife was worn out with . . . breeding, another assumed her place, already with child. No time was lost, no favorable wind unmet, no bins unreadied for fresh blubber. The worn wives were exiled to an island —

this island, which, I must confess, I didn't know until today. They lived together, welcoming each new castoff."

Mordecai carefully wrapped the squid eye in his bandanna and tucked it deep into his ditty bag. He lay back with his arms behind his head, closed his eyes, and was soon asleep.

Euphemia began to speak quietly from her place at the loom below, taking up Mordecai's tale, the soft click and clack of the shuttle marking the rhythm of her voice. She told about Moses, my great-great-grandfather, and the beginning of the Rathbones. She told about the wives, and of the day when my great-great-grandmother Hepzibah came to Rathbone House. It was a story that would be taken up by others before my journey with Mordecai was done.

As Euphemia spoke, the worn wives were weaving something on the loom, new threads wound above the old on the same spindles, pearly gray. They were weaving a gown for me. Now when the thread gleamed I saw a new shape take form, my own.

Crow trundled along the net, claws catching on the threads, hopped to the window ledge, and flew off into the darkness.

CHAPTER FOUR:
MOSES RATHBONE

{in which we meet the first of the Rathbones}

1761

Before first light, the boy began to climb the tower at the edge of the dunes. It was roughly built and full of splinters, but his feet and hands were tough from hauling rope, from clambering over rocks after crabs and chasing game. The freshly felled trunks of pine, lashed together with rawhide strips, had been driven deep through the sandy soil of the dunes to bedrock, far enough from the tide line so that the tower would stand firm. Scrub pine and beach roses grew at the tower's base. Around the boy's neck hung a skin of water and a string of smoked perch to hold him until dusk.

The wood creaked under his feet and his hands grew sticky with sap as he climbed. A crow flew past him, scrawking, a fat fish in its claws, banking off toward the pines on the bluff. When the boy reached the top, he stood straight and scanned the beach from end to end. A thin line of light spread along the horizon. To the east, in low hills that rose from the harbor, the roofs of a few houses showed among the trees. To the west the beach curved out to the point, a long pale curl in the dark sea.

The boy looked across the sound to the fishing fleet at rest in the harbor, saw the gleam and sway of shuttered lanterns among the dark hulls. A few men had begun to move about on the docks and in the boats. In one bumboat near the end of the dock, a man coiled rope into a tub, while his companion sat at a wheel, sharpening lances; the screech of metal on stone cut across the water. Other men loaded their crafts with floats and fluke spades, lantern kegs, piggins, and water to wet the whale line. A sharp March wind roughened the green water to white and sent cold spray over the men as they moved to and fro, hunched into their coats, blowing on their fists to try to keep warm.

Schools of sperm and humpback had been seen out in the sound each spring for as long as anyone had lived there, but only last winter did the fishermen learn from a passing ship that a few dozen barrels of sperm oil were worth more than a long hard season's haul of cod or flounder. This spring some of the boats — dories and wherries, some larger smacks — had stowed their nets and mounted oars and racks for harpoons and lances, bought from a town farther up the coast that had begun whaling a season earlier.

Several sperm, on their way north to summer in colder waters, had been sighted a few weeks ago. Most of the whales had been too distant to pursue. Only one, an old bull of forty feet, swam slowly enough so that a few boats were able to give chase. Though all were seasoned netmen and could spear a big tunny or halibut cleanly, none of the men had ever been so close to a sperm. All pulled hard, their backs to the whale toward which they moved, glancing over their shoulders nervously, glimpsing the long shining body, scarred and puckered. For half a minute they stroked alongside the whale, their own breath and the creaking oars louder in their ears than the whale as it glided through the water. Before the harpooners could ready their weapons, the whale blew, shooting spray thirty feet into the sky, then rolled and dove down in a smooth curve, its great flukes surging up, then curling into the sea. The men rowed back to the dock in silence. None wanted to admit that he was grateful not to have had the chance to try his arm, to find out if his blade would have been the one to hold fast and make the line spin out. They had all been told, by men in the town up the coast, how the whale thrashed when it was struck, its tail slapping boats, smashing them with a single blow, how it dove deep, taking the harpoon and its smoking line with it and sometimes the boat too and all its men.

One whale had been taken by the villagers, but not through any prowess. The boy on the tower had been watching a few days earlier when a sperm drifted in on the evening tide. It was twilight, and the fishermen had long since gone home. If they had been on the docks they wouldn't have noticed the whale that the boy could see clearly on the darkening water. They would have heard the cries of birds, a horde of seabirds: white gulls and terns, black skuas and gray-tipped gannets thronged on the carcass, so thick that they made of the dead whale a living shape. The birds lifted off in a body, hovering for a moment just above the whale so that it seemed to expand, then flying suddenly off and away, the whale first becoming enormous, then dispersing and vanishing. Its body, now a diminished hulk of patched black and rotted gray, drifted to shore and came to rest on the sand.

The next morning the men towed the carcass to the dock and moored it there, head and tail, waiting for one of the larger craft to return from netting in the sound so that the whale could be towed to Mystic. Though its blubber was rotted, the reservoir of oil in its head was intact, and more valuable than the oil from the blubber. Some of the younger men sat on the edge of the dock with lances, ready to stab any sharks that followed the blood in on the tide. A gaggle of children danced along the dock above the whale, reaching down to poke at the body with oars from their fathers' boats, laughing.

On the bumboat, the older man looked up from coiling his rope, peering across the cove to where the boy stood on the tower.

"Isn't that Denison's son?"

The younger man stopped pedaling his wheel and squinted, shading his eyes with one hand. The sun had edged up, dull red behind banked clouds.

"No. No, I don't think so. Denison's son is over in Westerly today. Anyway, it's Ephraim's watch, he should be up there. That looks like the Rathbone boy."

The older man stood up to stretch, frowning.

"He has no business up there. Running wild since Amos died."

The younger man held up a spear against the light and turned it, eyeing the edge and feeling it with his thumb. "He was wild enough before. Out swimming at all hours, for no reason, sometimes out past the breakers."

"Well, now. Maybe the boy misses sailing the seas in a barrel." The older man's face twisted in a grin.

"Right, right, wrapped in a sealskin. Heard it a hundred times." The younger man turned his head and spit into the sea. "I never believed Amos found him like he said. Always full of stories. Tell you what I think. Old Amos got that boy on some heathen woman and lied about it."

"Heathen woman. You mean an Indian? Hasn't been one around here for fifty years and more. All cleared out long ago." The older man rubbed his chin. "Besides, if Amos had laid with a native woman the boy would have brown eyes and that boy's got green eyes, greenest eyes I ever saw." He pushed his cap back off his forehead and sat up straighter, hands on his knees. "Could've happened like Amos said.

Could've been set adrift from some ship that was foundering, stove by a whale. That was . . . let's see, four winters back, wasn't it, the boy showed up? Rough weather that winter, I remember. It wouldn't have been the only ship wrecked. It might've been a ship carrying skins from up north. What was that brig that passed through last fall? The *Nuuka? Nuucha?* Carrying all kinds of hides — bear, fox, some seal, I think." He pulled his cap down tight and returned to coiling his rope. "Like baby Moses floating in a basket. That's where Amos got the name, you know."

"But how would he have survived? He was just a little starved-looking thing. Amos said he lived on raw fish. Said the barrel was half full of fish bones. How would a little thing like that have caught fish, and with what? Anyway. Probably that's what stunted him, starving like that. Though he's strong enough now. Have you seen him handle one of these?" The younger man held up the spear he had just sharpened.

The older man kept staring across at the tower where the boy stood, a black shape edged in red by the low sun.

"Here's Ephraim. High time."

A tall young man stepped out of the thick pines that ran down to the shoreline and

106

stood for a moment on the beach, stretching his arms and yawning. He started, and looked up at the tower, which stood a dozen feet tall. He began to climb, quickly. Near the top he stopped and began to yell, waving his arm at the boy standing there. His angry voice wafted across to the two men in the bumboat, but they couldn't make out his words. As they watched, Moses leaned over and pushed him, hard. The man's arms windmilled backward and he fell, landing in a mound of sand.

The older man stood up from his wheel. "What in hell. Hey!"

The younger man stood staring, his mouth open.

Ephraim sat up slowly in the mound of sand, shaking his head, looking up in disbelief at Moses. Moses didn't look down. He looked straight out to sea and cried out, raised his arm, pointing.

The two men on the boat turned to look. The men on the dock and in the other boats had heard it too. All stood staring at the stretch of open water toward which the boy pointed. The surface of the sea was smooth gray, unbroken. A minute passed as the men stood there, frozen in place, their hands up to shield against the sun that now flooded, golden, across the water. Most had dropped their hands and turned away when, far out in the sound, a dark shape bobbed up, then another, the water soon as thick as chowder with them. The spouts started, bright fountains. Sperm spouts, Moses knew. He knew all the whales by their spouts: the right whale blew two vertical plumes, the sperm whale's spray angled to the left, the humpback blew one wide arc straight up. Today there were thirty, no, more than forty. Forty-two sperm.

The men on dock ran to their boats. Those already afloat bent their oars and leaned deep, urging one another on.

Moses stood on the tower, watching. He knew more about the whales. He could tell the length of a sperm within a foot or two by the curve of its back as it sounded; he knew after a minute of watching how fast each whale in a school could swim; he knew the place behind the whale's flipper where his great heart beat. But he kept such things to himself. He used to tell Amos what he felt and saw, but Amos said he shouldn't speak about such things to the other men, that they would fear or envy such gifts.

Moses knew the beat of the sea, its quick pulse along the shore and the slow swing of the tides. He felt the deep stream of warm that surged under the cold, hugging the coast, then turning in a long curve out to sea to circle back again. He was never out of sight of the water, even when he hunted in the woods on the bluff. If he walked too far away his breath went short and his limbs stiffened, and the sea pulled him back.

In the water he was more at ease than on land. With a single long draft of air he could dive down and stay under not one or two minutes, like the village men, but ten. He stroked through the light-webbed water near the surface or wriggled along the sea bottom through thickets of anemone and coral. He could see through the water as though it were air and felt everything that moved around him. Schools of small fish sparked and glimmered in his fingertips; passing sharks twitched his skin. When the whales swam near they thrummed along his spine and tolled his body like a bell. He knew the clicking sounds they made and clicked back at them, and in their answering sounds read their shapes. With eyes shut, swimming alongside a sperm, he felt the throb and jostle of its organs. He saw the white lake of oil gleaming in its head, smooth and still under the dark dome of its skull.

Where he came from, all the men knew such things. They had known the whale because their lives depended upon knowing. The village lived all the winter on a single sperm. The heart and brain were boiled in blood, the tongue and flukes and flippers dried into jerky to chew through the long dark months when the bay was frozen solid and the wind shrieked across the white sea. The blubber was eaten raw to cushion the villagers' lean bodies against the cold. His oil fed their fires and lit their lamps, and his skin clothed them. On the day each spring when the ice finally broke, when the last of the whale was almost gone, the next whale came, and the men went out in the boat to meet him. Only one whale came each year. All the village knew when it was coming. Each man, woman, and child felt it loom, their bodies attuned to what they could not live without.

But they had not taken their whale the last time. Though the ice in the bay had broken, the sea farther out, where the whale was coming, was rough that day and full of drifting ice, the wind blowing strong from the north. The men would not have willingly chosen such a day for the hunt, but they had no choice.

There were so few men by then. The village wives had produced only a few sons in the last generation, and one or two men were killed each year in the struggle with the whale. Four men remained. Only enough to crew one boat, and barely that. They needed six: four at the oars, a steersman at the tiller, a spearman in the bow. Moses, at eight the oldest of the handful of children in the village, was still too young. Boys were not usually allowed on the boat until they reached ten years. But he could handle an oar, he was strong and quick for his age, and he had begged until his father reluctantly agreed to take him. His father would be both spearman and first oar, and Moses would take fourth oar, in the stern. They would make do without a man at the tiller.

They rowed out soon after dawn. Moses matched the men stroke for stroke, his heart high. The water was rough enough in the bay; when the boat cleared the point and reached open sea the wind hit their faces like a wall of ice. If only there had been enough men on the boat when the whale breached, Moses's father would have stood ready with his spear held high, as he had stood so many times before. Instead he was still at his oar, fighting along with the other men to keep the boat from sinking. If only there had been enough men, the whale would not have crashed down and Moses would not have seen its jaws close around his father before a great wave surged over the stern and swept Moses over the side. When he came up, choking, the boat was gone, and with it all the men. Nothing remained but a swirl of splinters and an empty barrel, into which he climbed. He was alone on the icy sea, drifting for days until the man Amos spied him. Amos was heading home in his fishing smack when he noticed a crowd of gulls circling over a patch of open sea. Curious, he sailed closer and saw the barrel floating, a pair of small hands clutching its rim. He pulled Moses out of the sea and took him home.

Now Moses stood watching these new whaleboat crews begin to stroke across the sound toward the whales. They were capable enough sailors and strong oarsmen. But they would never know the sea or the whale as he did, as his father had. With their spears of metal and their ropes, they would never give the whale his due. And they were too few to man a whaleboat.

He would need to make his own crew.

The fishermen's wives and daughters were on the dock that day, seeing their men off. A dozen or so stood, hands raised against the sun, talking quietly, watching the boats as they rowed out. Moses watched the wives. A few were dry and past their time.

In one young woman a minnow-size infant curled, its mother as yet unaware. Moses felt it turn and bobble in its watery chamber: a boy. He eyed the girls who stood by their mothers in cotton dresses and laced boots, one carrying her doll. Moses felt their quivering masses of eggs and knew they would be ready to spawn in a year or two. He marked one girl and then another.

He looked out at the whales, so thick in the sea. He would need a ship, a sturdy brig with a fine suit of sails, manned by many sons. A ship full of sons.

The sperm's blubber would warm the village all winter. His flukes and flippers and tongue would be boiled and eaten to sustain them. His skin would feed the fire that consumed him to make oil for their lamps, as it always had in Moses's village. No part of his great body would be wasted. And when the whale was gone they would go out to take another from the bounty of sperm in the sound. With its warmer winter, this village would not need to wait through the long cold for the ice to thaw before they could seek out their next whale. They would go out to meet him.

In a few more minutes the first boats would be within range of the nearest whales: three young sperm swimming smoothly together, the water bubbling along their flanks. The men called out, encouraging one another, feeling strong and ready to try their harpoons.

Moses saw what would happen.

When they were within a boat length of the nearest whale, the harpooners in the first boats would stand in the bows and throw, but no blade would reach its target. One might strike the whale's side and glance off, others would miss altogether and plunge into the sea. Most of the boats would fall back, their rowers exhausted. One dory would keep on, its crew the best young fishermen of the town, the craft they rowed the fastest. Two of the whales would swim on and away; the third and slowest would soon be within reach. The headsman would shout at the rowers, urging them on. The harpooner would brace his leg against the thigh board, his arm well back, and when the headsman cried "Give it to him!" would throw his blade and strike, not well or deep, but enough to hold the line.

The whale would swim on, the shaft of the harpoon jutting from its side, the line trailing, first slack then twanging taut. The coiled line would race from its tub, smoking as the whale swam faster. The men would crouch low and hold on to the rim as the boat jerked forward and began to speed across the water toward open sea. The whale would sound, diving deep, and surface twice, three times, the line still holding, the boat bouncing behind, until the whale, exhausted, rose once more and the men closed in, plunging their lances again and again into its back, into its lungs. The boat would back off as the whale began to flurry, swimming in ever-tighter circles, striking the water with its flukes, spouting blood with each breath. At last the whale would slow, turn on its side, and go still.

Moses wouldn't let the whale die that way. He knew what he would do.

He would swim out now, before the boats were within range of the whales; with his swift, powerful strokes, he would reach the boats in no time. He would step up into the first dory and the fishermen would fall back before him. He would stand straddle-legged on the edges of the bow, at the point of the boat, balancing easily, in his hand the spear he had made and that he now drew from his belt, a sharpened mussel shell lashed to a shaft carved from white driftwood.

He would leap from the bow onto the whale's back, clutch its fin, and for a few moments cling there, green sea foaming over him, the whale swimming on. The whale would know him. The whale would turn its eye to meet his. His arm would dart out and strike deep. The whale wouldn't die at the end of a line, plunging and thrashing. It wouldn't die from a dozen jagged wounds, leaking its life slowly into the water, but in one thrust, one bright moment.

Moses would reach down and pull the shaft straight out. Blood would gush into the sea, then a watery pink stream. With his face close against the whale's shining black skin he would sing its song, and the whale would hear.

The sun was fully up, the sound a blinding blue. A stiff wind churned the water.

Moses jumped from the tower, dove into the sea, and came up spouting. He stood in the low surf and reached down to scoop up sand and shells from the bottom, rubbing them over his chest and arms until the blood came. He dove again, surged up, and shot water high from his mouth. He began to swim toward the shining water where the whales were sounding.

CHAPTER FIVE:
THE WORN WIVES

*{in which Hepzibah brims
with her own small ocean}*

1778

In the high blue bed a small bronze man floated. So high did the bed rise in the little pine room, so deep did the man drift in sleep, that in the glow of the lantern Hepzibah could see only his feet at the end of the bed, wet and smelling of the sea.

Hepzibah hesitated. She wanted to turn back but didn't know the way. The hall behind her was dark, and the boy who had brought her here was already gone. She had come directly from the dock to Rathbone House, cold and tired after the long ride across the sound on a choppy sea, hurried through the door and along the hall by the cabin boy, no offer of tea nor rest nor even a basin in which to wash before being brought to Moses Rathbone.

Hepzibah stood just inside the door, at the foot of the bed, listening. Faint moans and clicks came from above her, along with low, deep breaths. Lantern held high in one hand, she stepped up onto the frame, then knelt on the end of the bed that filled the little room. Her knees sank and wobbled. She struggled to keep her balance on the soft mattress, the light from her lantern swinging across the bed, around the walls. When she felt steady, she again raised her lantern and hung it on a peg on the wall, one of a row of pegs on which other things hung that caught the light: a string of shells, a curved tooth on a necklace of braided hair. Through the mattress she felt the stiff shafts of the gull feathers with which it was stuffed. In the close space, the air reeked with guano and pine so sharp it burned her eyes. There were no windows. On all sides of the bed rose walls of split logs, lashed together with rawhide and shining with sap. Behind her she heard a soft click. Someone had closed and latched the door.

Now that her eyes had adjusted to the dark, Hepzibah could see all of Moses, floating on his back in the middle of the bed. The circle of light from the lantern wavered over his skin, bronze-dark, scored with paler scars, over a darker knot at his center. She

118

looked away. Though he was ashore, Moses's body continued to roll as if still at sea, his arms twitching now in the motion of a half hitch, now as though he turned the wheel at the helm, his legs churning the blue blankets to whitecaps. Sun-bleached strands of his hair rode above the dark tangle that spread from his head. Hepzibah reached to touch his arm and his eyes sprang open. She started, lost her balance, and rolled to the center of the bed.

Moses checked the fresh wife over. He gripped her arms and sat her up straight. He turned her face toward the lantern to observe the sheen of her eyes, the pearl of her teeth. He lifted her hair and sniffed along her neck, then peeled her damp and heavy gown up to her waist and sniffed between her legs. He pulled a length of rope from a peg and wound it swiftly around Hepzibah's hand and his own, murmured a few words and nodded in the direction of the sea, and returned the rope to its peg. When he pulled her face close, Hepzibah smelled his sea-fresh odor of brine and cool air. Wind-borne seeds and twigs, caught in his hair, scraped her skin. He pulled her body tight against his. She was just his size. They matched end to end. From his hard flesh she felt something stiffer searching between her legs. She closed her eyes. But Moses slowed and stopped. Soon the stiffness went, and his breath came long and low again.

Hepzibah tried not to move. She shivered under Moses as he grew heavy in sleep, tugging her clammy gown down to cover her legs. Slowly she slipped from under him. She was afraid to see those bright-green eyes again, the green circles ringed in white, burned by the sun. She backed toward the top of the bed and slid her legs under the edge of a thick stack of blankets, among which were furs of bear and otter that added their own funk to the air.

Under the warm covers she began to drift. She thought of her own bed and wondered if her sisters had fallen asleep or were still sobbing, if her father was searching for her, if he would think to look so far from home. She felt a warm grip on her ankle and struggled from sleep to lift her head. Moses still slept beside her. Someone else's hand grasped her ankle from below, far under the covers. Someone drew her down into the deep.

Hepzibah surfaced and gasped for breath, the air cold around her. She was moving, slung over someone's shoulder, her face bouncing against a back, an arm tight around her knees. She struggled to right herself but her arms began to shake when she pushed against the back and the blood rushing to her head made her dizzy. From either side she heard faint snores and stirrings as they moved for what seemed many minutes, a straight path along a creaking wood floor. Then whoever carried her stopped at last and spilled her onto something soft. She landed on her back, her arms flung above her head. He leaned over her, edged in silver starlight. She couldn't make out his features clearly: a thick hank of pale hair, a smooth cheek. His mouth was open. His breath smelled sweet. She felt cold air on her thighs, a sudden weight, then sharp pain between her legs, inside her. She heard a grunt above her, a cracked voice, then the stranger dropped down beside her. Hepzibah struggled to sit up, wanting to cry out, but found that she couldn't. No sound would come from her throat. A strong, sinewy arm wrapped around her; a downy leg, with hair as soft as that of a child, pinned hers to the bed.

The darkness of the room shifted at the far end. First faint gleams of yellow, then a sudden strong glow: a shuttered ship's lantern. Behind it she could just make out a raised arm, and then a face flamed up. A boy sleepwalked the night watch, moving through the rooms as he would walk on deck, eyes open and unseeing, though his step was sure. He wore a sailor's middy with no tie and nothing below. In the light of his lantern Hepzibah saw the narrow bed in which she lay. Her fingers felt rough timber on the side. She turned her head and saw next to her the face of a sleeping boy, perhaps fourteen. She lifted her head; three other boys slept in three other beds, one to each corner of the room. Accustomed to the slender hammocks in which they lay at sea, the boys slept with arms straight at their sides, legs together, their bodies tucked close to the half-timber walls. On the wall above each bed a harpoon rested in a rack.

The space between beds formed the narrow gangway down which the watchman continued his watch, passing through a chain of such rooms, one after the other, each bearing four beds, four boys. Through windows on the east and west walls could be heard the sound of waves slapping the pilings far below and the creak of rigging from the ship just outside to the east.

The watchman's lantern faded in the distance, disappeared, then grew bright again as he turned for his next pass. *Eight bells,* he called out as he would have called out on a ship at sea, *eight bells.* No bell sounded but their bodies knew the time. Heads rose and sank back down into snores. The boy next to Hepzibah loosened his hold on her and turned to his other side. She felt herself lifted by new arms and dropped onto a new bed.

All the older Rathbone sons slept here, those aged twelve to twenty, all the crews just in from sea that morning, a ship's worth. Six men crewed each whaleboat, three whaleboats served each ship. While one sailed with Hepzibah, the others slept. She was passed from boy to boy, tossed from bed to bed like a bale, turned on each capstan, hauled and harvested until she brimmed with her own small ocean. By the time she left the hall at three bells in the last watch on seasick legs, whatever fish swam in her might have been spawned as much from the swirling plankton of the sea as from any particular son.

When Hepzibah next opened her eyes a sleepy child of five or six in a nightshirt and watch cap stood by the side of the bed in which she lay. Over his arm Hepzibah's gown was neatly draped; someone had cleaned and dried it during her travails, along with her shift and stockings. From the child's other hand her boots dangled, newly polished, laces tied together in a reef knot. Once she had dressed — she didn't at first feel steady enough to rise, but the boy waited patiently — he put his soft hand on her arm and led her out of the hall of beds, toward the back of the house. She was grateful for the warmth of her wool gown as they walked through chill air down a narrow passage on one side of the house. Wind gusted along the hall. Hepzibah's hand found a taut rope railing along the wall with which to steady her steps. The pounding of waves against the pilings below didn't fade as they moved; even the back of the house was not far from shore. But over the waves Hepzibah now heard weeping. Through a door to one side a candlelit room came into view. She stopped in the doorway and looked in.

The room was, like the chain of bedrooms, unplastered, raw joists jutting from rough wood planks. A half-dozen canvas cots stood side by side along the walls, in each cot a boy, all neatly tucked up in nightshirts under cotton sheets and woolen blankets. These, too, were Moses's sons — those not yet old enough to wield a lance or harpoon. A few were younger than her guide, boys of three and four. It was these whom Hepzibah had heard weeping. The little boys seemed to Hepzibah more distressed than ill. As far as she could tell in low light, they were sturdy little creatures with thick dark hair and healthy color in their cheeks. On a stool next to each sat an older brother, dressed in a white guernsey frock and wide-legged trousers. One of the older boys wrung water from a cloth into a basin, folded the cloth neatly, and laid it on his brother's forehead, patted away his tears, tucked him tighter into his cot. Another plied a curved needle on a piece of heavy canvas, hemming the edge of a sail, humming, his younger brother's eye listlessly following the flashing needle. The little one's face turned toward the door where Hepzibah stood and he sat up with a cry, then saw her unfamiliar face more clearly and fell back. His brother pressed him into the pillows, holding out to him a fat dolphin of whittled wood. The little one's face brightened and he snatched the dolphin with both hands. Hepzibah's guide pulled her away as the little boy's brother stood up to close the door. She longed to stop at the sick bay herself and have a cool cloth pressed to her hot head, but the boy who'd come to fetch her pulled her onward.

They arrived at a dark room at the end of

the hallway. The cabin boy tilted the wick of a candle into the flame of his lantern, set the candlestick on a table, and hurried off down the hall. A soft ring of candlelight replaced the lantern's stronger flame. In its glow a small pitcher of clear water could be seen, and a plate on which something was draped. Hepzibah pulled it toward her. She had eaten nothing since dawn. A smoked cod eyed her. She pushed the plate back and sat on the edge of a narrow bed covered in patchwork. By the bottom of the bed stood a wooden bucket with a cloth folded across its rim. Hepzibah dipped her hand and smelled it: cool seawater. She lifted her shift, squatted over the bucket, and washed herself, wincing at the sting. There was no towel with which to dry, so she used instead her shift. She crawled under the covers, curled up, and started to sob. After a while she reached for the plate and began to eat the fish. She heard something from the back of the room and stopped chewing.

This room, too, she realized, was full of breathing, high-pitched and light. Besides the breathing, a soft creak-creak came from one corner. She had heard it when she first came in and thought it was the sound of wind in the ship's rigging from outside. Hepzibah burrowed deeper and clutched the blankets around her but no one came near, only the creak and the soft breathing. She crept from under the blankets, lifted her candle, and moved toward the sound.

From hooks in the rafters hung a row of small hammocks, pale canvas flaring under her candle. The hammocks were empty but for the two nearest to the corner from which the creaking came. Hepzibah moved closer: a sturdy baby boy, wrapped in soft muslin, breathed gently in one hammock. Next to him was another boy, older, though not by much. Thick hair sprang from their heads. Their skin shone like polished copper. The hammocks swayed, one gently bumping the other. Hepzibah lifted her candle higher.

In the corner a boy rocked back and forth in a rocking chair, twin infants stacked in his only arm. His other sleeve was empty; Hepzibah wondered if he had lost it to a whale. The infants' little faces slept one above the other, in each mouth the teat of a bottle on which his lips had gone slack. Their big brother, too, had fallen asleep, though his body continued to rock. All three faces shared the same dark and bright look — the look of Moses, the look of all the faces she had seen since she arrived — like teeth in the same mouth. The boy's arm dropped lower on his chest. The infants twitched, the bottles slipped, and two thin streams of white wet his shirt. Startled, he gripped the infants tighter and looked up with his green eyes to see Hepzibah standing there. His face lightened. He rocked to his feet and tilted the twins into Hepzibah's arms, knocking her candle to the floor, and disappeared down the hall. The candle spluttered but stayed upright and soon glowed steadily again.

The boys, a few weeks old, blinked up at Hepzibah. Their foreheads began to crumple, their mouths gaped wide to wail. She bounced and shushed them and began to pace the floor. She stroked their heads to calm them. They, too, had full heads of dark hair, soft and springy in places, in others short and choppy as though it had been roughly sheared.

Enough light entered from the night sky for her to see that she was in a corner room and that the ship was docked just outside, its web of ropes and rigging darker against the dark sky. Between the ropes the sea shone, lapping softly on the piers, though it had been rough when she arrived. The tide must be turning. Behind the ship, a dull red flooded the black sky. Through the window on the other side stood stacks of crates; farther away, at the head of the pier, tall pines rustled and swayed. Hepzibah paced until the infants grew heavy with sleep, then lowered them gently into their hammocks, next to their two sleeping brothers. She gave the hammock on the end a gentle push; they bumped each other in a slow wave. On the other end of the row the empty hammocks swung.

Hepzibah tucked herself in but couldn't sleep. She was sore and still leaked between her legs. She let herself remember the moment when she'd first seen the whaleboat from the dock that morning. She had not meant to linger. The women and girls had been warned to stay clear of the docks in recent days, though the men wouldn't say why. The Rathbone method of wooing women must have already been known along the coast. But Hepzibah needed medicine for her sister's leg, a poultice of steeped seaweed that only the old lobsterman, who lived in a shack on the pier, could make. She had put on her shawl and left the house before first light, to be sure to catch the old man before he went out to check his pots. When she came out of his shack there it was against the dawn sky: a long slim hull full of fresh boys in blue middies, bright ties flying, oars flashing in perfect unison, and she couldn't take her eyes away. She couldn't stop herself from reaching for one of the hands held up to her as the boat slid alongside the dock, couldn't stop herself from stepping down into the moving prow and gliding away.

Her life had so far been spent in caring for six younger brothers and sisters. Her mother took in washing from a local merchant. In the summer she earned a few dollars on what little could be spared from the kitchen garden after feeding her family. Hepzibah's father had died in a fishing accident when she was eleven, along with the rest of the crew of his boat, the largest and finest vessel in the small village fleet. Few men remained in the town, tucked in one of the many coves along that winding coast: well north of the open Atlantic, distant enough from the Rathbones, and from the route of the whales, to have taken no part in the whaling that was burgeoning farther south.

Hepzibah was already weary of the long, hard days of cooking and cleaning. At sixteen, she saw among the men of her village few candidates for a husband, only a few depleted old clammers and indifferent netmen with leaky craft.

So when she had first glimpsed the crew

130

of young Rathbones at a distance, her mind jumped to the pragmatic: She didn't want to live out her youth taking care of her brothers and sisters. They were getting older and soon would be able to take her place as helpmeets to her mother. She wanted a life, a husband of her own.

When the whaleboat drew closer, such matter-of-fact considerations faded. The Rathbone charm took hold of Hepzibah and drew her away. It may be difficult for those not born to the sea to grasp such fishy allure. It was a charm drawn from the whale the Rathbones hunted, as though they had, like the sperm, great reservoirs of shining oil that lent a springing grace to their movements, a brightness to skin and hair, a suppleness of form that spoke of power held in check. Hepzibah had left without a further thought.

She had first spied the house from the boat, halfway across the sound: a glint of window, then a flash of golden wood that seemed to float above the sea in the fresh light of morning. By the time the whaleboat drew near at dusk, the crew's smooth strokes never flagging, hour after hour, only the long, low shape of the house showed, a darker violet on an inky sky. The house stood on pilings on a long pier, high above the surf. From its center a pale column of thick smoke surged. Three tall spikes rose from its roof, the masts of a ship docked alongside the house on the other side of the pier, its web of rigging visible between spumes of smoke.

Now Hepzibah felt like it had been days since she arrived at Rathbone House. Turning her head into her pillow, she tried again to sleep. She flipped the tear-dampened pillow over and felt raised stitching on the cotton under her face. She sat up and lit the candle. Her finger traced a name embroidered in careful loops of chain stitch on the pillowcase: "Amaziah Rathbone 1772." It had been stitched with white thread on undyed muslin so that it barely showed. She felt the same kind of stitching on the underside of the patchwork cloth that covered her bed. Turning the edge down, she saw other names on the plain muslin behind each patch: Thankful 1761, Patience 1765, Constance 1773. She turned the edge back and ran her hand over the front of the cloth, over patterned squares of calico and muslin, the cotton stiff and smelling of salt.

Hepzibah thought of the boat she had passed that morning on the way across the sound, a boat just like her own, rowed by its own crack crew. A woman had sat slumped in the stern, staring back over the sea toward Rathbone House, a woman not much older than herself, judging by her face, though by her tired breasts and slack belly Hepzibah would have said she was past forty. A woman, she now realized, who must have been Hopestill Rathbone, the name stitched on the most recent square on the quilt, dated 1775. The woman had worn a gown of the same sprigged muslin used in the quilt. Hepzibah remembered the soft rose hue, the pattern of buds and stems. She thought of the little boys of three and four, crying in their cots, and of the two infants. The woman had been tossing something from her lap into the wake of the boat — small dark blurs that curved into the water. Hepzibah had seen that they were curls of dark hair. She thought now of the roughly sheared heads of the babies. Each time the woman had tossed a curl a fish had risen, snatching at the surface and carrying it below.

Hepzibah heard a sharp cry from outside. She stood at the window that faced the sea, just above the stern of the ship that was docked tight alongside the house. Across from her, almost close enough for her to touch, ropes swayed and snapped in a low wind. Through the ropes she could see the faint line of surf that curved out to the point, on the point a wooden tower, silhouetted against the night sky. A figure at the top waved its arms in the air, then pointed straight out to sea, shouting. Hepzibah leaned out, her eyes following the pointing finger to the horizon: Nothing was visible on the mute black surface of the water. From all around the house voices were answering the cry from the beach. Feet pounded along halls, doors slammed. Below Hepzibah, to her left, loomed the dark hull of the ship. From every window of the house, all along the dock, boys were pouring down ladders, dropping onto the deck. Pulleys creaked, and barrels and crates crossed in front of Hepzibah, swung from the stacks on the pier behind the house. A bundle of piglets squealed by in a net; a crow rode on top, flapping its wings to balance, one bright eye on Hepzibah.

A roar went up from the bow. Moses swung into the rigging from a window, breeches half laced, chest and feet bare, shouting orders. Boys and men ranged over the ropes, the cheeks of some still striped with shaving soap, coffee cups in hands, losing no time. Their compact bodies moved with economy and grace, swarming nimbly up the masts, forming lines in no time atop the yardarms. In one motion they let go all along the line. The thick white rolls dropped down, the rigging drew tight, and the sails swelled in three great arcs, straining against the anchor toward open sea.

On the foredeck a circle of boys squatted around a low fire that flared up blue, sparkling each time one of them dropped something into the flames. Hepzibah couldn't see what it was from her window. They rocked on their heels in unison, chanting low, then stood as one body and stretched their arms up and sent a whoop into the sky. From the thick pine woods along the shore Hepzibah heard an answering whoop, and another, then spotted small fires flashing here and there among the trees. She heard the hoot of an owl and felt the pines exhaling warmth into the cool dark air.

Fish leapt around the ship. The sky was full of birds. On the horizon, far out at sea, spouts arced, gleaming, in the dark water.

The anchor streamed up over the stern, trailing long gouts of sea wrack. The ship drew away. Across the open water Hepzibah could now see, halfway down the shore, what the ship had hidden, what made the glow she had mistaken for dawn: a great dark shed hunkered over the water, its mouth gaped open. The dull red glow came from inside. Two new ships were drawing near it in the dark, towing behind them two great black shapes.

Moses *m.* Thankful *m.* Patience *m.* Charity *m.* Amaziah *m.* Constance *m.* Hopestill *m.* Hepzibah *m.* Euphemia *m.*

m.1761   m.1765   m.1768   m.1772   m.1773   m.1775   m.1781   m.1784

Benadam Gale   *m.*   Verity

Mercy   Brother   Mordecai

EUNICE *m.* FELICITY *m.* BEULAH *m.* EXPERIENCE *m.* DESIRE *m.* TRIAL *m.* HUMILITY *m.* SILENCE *m.* KATURAH
m.1785   m.1788?   m.1792   m.1793   m.1794   m.1798   m.1801   m.1806   m.1809

THE RATHBONES

Chapter Six:
Mordecai's Lesson

{in which Mordecai spills his story}

The worn wives all waved goodbye, their faces a line of small moons against the gray rocks. Soon fog had covered them all, hiding Mouse Island, though I still heard the bleating of sheep.

We sailed this time on a sturdier craft, a merchant brig out of Pawcatuck, a two-master called the *Able.* Her captain, a bluff, cheerful seaman of middle years named Samuel Avery, traded up and down the coast, he told us, touching at Mouse Island once each season. We were fortunate that he had arrived so soon after we were marooned there.

Though only Euphemia and Thankful really talked, the others plying their shuttles mutely, I had been happy just to sit among my aunts with a lamb in my lap while they wove, which they did from first light until dusk every day. Mordecai had slept through much of our time on Mouse Island, exhausted by our escape from the man in blue, and I kept Euphemia's stories of Moses and Hepzibah to myself. I relished having my own secrets to brood over, as Mordecai always had, though I knew I wouldn't be able to resist telling him sooner or later.

Over the two weeks we spent on Mouse Island, I had carved out a happy little niche for myself. I'd learned to card the heavy, oily wool that stood in baskets at one end of the loom, combing out lodged strands of weed and sea moss. Some days, when my aunts left their loom for a few hours to do necessary chores, I wound the wool for Amaziah as she spun on the wheel that sat by the hearth. Her small, nimble fingers coaxed glossy filaments from the unruly wool, which, like my aunts, had a silvery sheen. Other days, I fed the sheep in their little houses, pouring grain into long wooden bins into which they dipped their dark heads, and lingered to listen to them munch in the warm, close air of the houses. I shared breakfasts of tea and ship's biscuits, and modest dinners of poached fish, which left my stomach still rumbling. I wondered where my aunts' energy came from, with so meager a diet, but they rose (or, I should say, descended) every morning with the same steady vigor with which they completed each day's work, the shuttles passing back and forth as quickly at dawn as at dusk.

I would have liked to stay longer on Mouse Island. But my cousin didn't want to linger. Mordecai spent little time in the worn wives' house, preferring instead to wander the shores of the little island, observing the birds that passed overhead. He developed a brief enthusiasm for the sheep, extracting a measuring tape from one of his bags and taking note of cranial diameters and abdominal girths, noting each measurement in a little book. Mordecai grimaced each time he scribbled; his wounded arm healed slowly and was still painful, the elbow swollen, the joint a purplish-black.

Now Mordecai and I sat high atop the forecastle, in the point of the bow, which afforded us a full view of the waters through which we sailed. A keen wind sprang up and blew the fog away, leaving a washed blue sky. Mouse Island was a few miles astern. Straight ahead, some ten miles south, lay our destination: the chain of islands that formed the Stark Archipelago. Mordecai had taken the captain aside before the *Able* unmoored and asked him to alter his route slightly. The *Able* would normally have stopped at Fisher's Island first, he said, but this small change was no inconvenience at all. Mordecai had yet to explain why we were heading for the archipelago, but I was happy to be sailing farther from Naiwayonk each moment. Behind us, due north, at the deepest point of the curved shoreline, I could just make out the shape of Rathbone House and the docks and masts of the harbor.

The air had a wintry edge, though it was still early autumn. Sharp gusts of wind blew Crow from perch to perch. He first hunched on the aft rail, then clung to the fore shrouds or the mizzenmast, making short sorties at my head to worry my hair. He didn't care for my coiffure. My great-great-aunts had plaited my hair into a hundred braids, stiffened with sea salt, each end caught up in a shell. They had woven me gowns the green of sea bladder and sponge weed, one of algae-brown, one the blood-dark red of a sea urchin, and a pearly gray close to that of their own gowns. Considering that my normal dress had been a pin-tucked frock of no particular shape and a mouselike hue, I was more than pleased with gowns whose bodices were fitted to my own form and whose skirts spread wide. They'd also given me new boots of sheepskin with soft black tongues. Before we said goodbye, my great-great-aunts had taken me to a tide pool and shown me my reflection in the still water, my face strewn with starfish, my braids speckled with the small mollusks that clung to the rocks at the bottom of the pool. I felt myself color when Euphemia and Thankful spoke teasingly of suitors for me. My aunts' smiling faces formed a ring around mine. Now, when I raised my arm to wave once more, I saw that the sky was the same shale blue as my sleeve; a storm was brewing in the north.

"Just last month the *Sabine* broke up here," said our captain. "But do you see aught of it on those rocks?" On the eastern tip of Mouse Island the sharp rocks on which we had nearly smashed in the skiff disrupted the smooth curves of the island. My eye searched not for the flotsam and jetsam of a wreck but for a broken body in a blue coat. Nothing moved among the rocks except a few gulls poking between stones for stray smelt.

Captain Avery traded supplies for the wives' fine wool (much in demand, he said, among the ladies of Boston), such necessities as their austere ways required that the sea didn't amply meet: fodder for the sheep, a few tools, fresh water. Their only extravagance was the satisfying of a craving for little seed cakes like those they'd eaten in girlhood. Someone in Avery's village still remembered how to bake them. Apparently Rathbone House had once supplied the worn wives with what they needed. Euphemia told me that Mama used to bring treats for the wives — eggs, fruit from the mainland, and other small comforts — and sit with them, before I was born. I wondered at the idea of Mama visiting the wives. The picture it suggested was so unlike the Mama I knew. I imagined her pressing her gifts into my aunts' little hands, chatting about the weather or the spring lambing. The gifts Mama had given me could be numbered on one hand: barrettes for my braid; a set of knucklebones; and a ring scribed with a simple pattern of waves, the last a gift on my twelfth birthday.

I had, not long after I turned twelve, begun my monthly courses. Mama had not told me what to expect. I had woken one night, the bed wet beneath me, and when I had seen that I was bleeding I ran to Mama's room. I had long since learned not to bother her when I needed anything, but I was frightened enough that night to forget.

I stood in front of her bed, twisting my nightgown around to show her the dark stain.

"Take it off."

She took my nightgown in her hands and, sitting up straight in her bed, tore the gown into long strips from hem to neck and handed the rags back to me.

"Put those between your legs," she said, and returned to sleep.

"Shake a leg, there. Bear off, bear off."

I realized Captain Avery was speaking. He was giving orders to the mate, a small round man in faded ducks and a striped jersey, who hurried aloft. The captain peered toward the rocky point receding behind us, shaking his head.

"No, not a stick left of the *Sabine*. Your aunties have salvaged every scrap. They pick each ship's carcass clean as crabs."

I thought of the scarlet boards burning in the fireplace, warming my frock and my feet when we first arrived on Mouse Island. I remembered the partial letters on the painted wood: an *A* and part of an *S,* letters that must have once stood in the name *Sabine.*

"Have you . . . has anyone been recovered more recently from these waters?" I asked. I glanced toward Mordecai, but he sat with

146

his head bent over some book, paying me no mind.

The captain considered his answer, running a hand over his whiskery face. Though the *Able* was as neat as it could well be, the captain was not particular about his own appearance. He shook his head.

"No, but ships have broken their backs on these rocks once or twice each year for as long as I can remember. The entire crew of the *Sabine* showed up in the village next day, down at Lord's Point. Said they lost their bearings in the fog. That they were pulled out of the water by a passing sloop from Gloucester — what business, I ask, has a sloop from Gloucester this far south? — and set down again on their own dock. Don't know how they all survived. None dead — not even cut up on those rocks. And not a mark on them. I asked them myself, not two days later, down at the alehouse. They only went red and shook their heads, the lot of them."

I know better, I wanted to say, but held my tongue. During our stay on Mouse Island I'd watched the wives practice their tosses on the ewes, to keep their eyes true and their limbs from stiffening. I never saw them miss. I suppose no man with any salt would admit to such a rescue.

"I don't know how any man who calls himself a pilot could make such a mistake, even one who doesn't know this coast. Channels are clearly marked enough. Some claimed they heard singing. Others mentioned a strong light, swore it was the lighthouse at Stonington. Foolish. Everyone knows the point lies a good three miles farther west."

Captain Avery turned back to his wheel, though he continued to speak of other ships wrecked over the years. I tired of his prattle. Through it I began to hear a soft melody. I closed my eyes and listened. It sounded a little like my brother's song, and I felt myself go cold. I moved closer to Mordecai. The melody shifted and I breathed easier, realizing it was only some old chantey, which Mordecai sang in a low, keening voice.

"My clothes are all in pawn,
Go down you blood-red roses, go down,
And it's mighty drafty around Cape Horn,
Go down you blood-red roses, go down,
It's 'round Cape Horn we've got to go,
Chasing whales through ice and snow,
Oh my old mother she wrote to me,
My darling son come home from sea."

Mordecai sat cross-legged, pulling books and tools from his case and arranging them on the deck. The aunts had fashioned new clothes for him, too — trousers and waist-coats and smallclothes in dark hues — though he found them too soft. He wore only a short, tight jacket of a virile terrapin green that was not from the aunts' loom. It looked like a sailor's monkey jacket, with two rows of brass buttons down the front and heavy gold braid along the seams — salvage from some ship. And he still wore his old nankeen breeches, buff-colored, stained from our dissections.

A couple of weeks with the worn wives, soothed by their teas and coddling, had done Mordecai good. He looked almost healthful and much glossier than usual. The aunts had smeared a salve extracted from bivalves over his skin to guard it against the sun, and he had reapplied it liberally. His skin was otherwise white with a faint green tinge like the roe of a young lobster; only a few minutes in the sun caused any unpro-tected patch to become crisped. My own skin fared just fine in the sunlight. I'd inherited my forebears' coppery sheen.

Mordecai's hair hung in a single thick pigtail, which I plaited myself. At first he wouldn't let me touch his hair, though it blew in his eyes. Even in a dead calm it tended to unaccountably float before his face to form a private fog. But I persuaded him to let me braid the white mass into a neat queue. He didn't know that I had woven a strand of ribbon kelp into its center; my aunts had said it would bring him luck. That day he wore a billed and braided sailor's cap over his pigtail, which shaded his still-sensitive eyes, his spectacles having sunk with the skiff. I didn't like the cap on him. It suggested skills unearned by its wearer. Captain Avery must have let Mordecai into the afterhold, where he also found the ink and quill that lay among the books and tools he was now busily arranging on the deck.

When his song ended, Mordecai hummed on as he unrolled a clean sheet of paper that he had brought in one of his bags and spread it out, weighting its edges with a length of chain. He sharpened a pencil on a whetstone, holding the point up close to his eyes, frowning, then grinding it again.

Among Mordecai's instruments on the deck was a short spyglass I'd played with before in the attic. I held it up to scan the horizon. The view was fractured by a spiderweb crack in the lens, which split a dozen islands into a hundred. I took the glass away from my eye and looked again at the islands. I could see them more clearly with my naked eye. Earlier a single stretch of vivid green, the islands now began to separate and take shape. Reflected light from the lens flashed into Mordecai's eyes, but he took no notice. His head and shoulders were damp from occasional bursts of spray off the bow. He had ruled a grid on his foolscap and was now plotting points, referring repeatedly to the little journal he had brought from the attic — re-creating, I realized, the map of the sperm's route from his blackboard. I held up the glass again and turned it slowly, all around the rim of the sea; still no sign of sperm.

Among the books Mordecai had lined up was one in which I had seen him writing in more than once back at the house: a tall, narrow logbook with marbled covers and a leather spine. I missed my own ledger. I had thought of it as we ran from the house, but there wasn't time to run back for it. I wished I had it now. I longed to draw my brother.

I had often drawn him in the attic during lessons, tilting the cover of my ledger over my hand so that Mordecai wouldn't notice. It was an old volume bound in blue linen that held no histories, only columns of figures in a faint graphite hand, without any legend. I wondered what the numbers recorded: barrels of oil or profit gained; distances traveled.

I assembled my brother from parts of my favorite images, especially those in a set of books about the ancient Greeks, the finest books in our meager library. Each volume was bound in red morocco and stamped in silver with the head of an Olympian. Colored plates, clustered in the center of each volume, depicted the heroes of old: Achilles leaping from a parapet of Troy, Odysseus strapped to the mast of his ship while the Sirens sang. Prometheus was there, his liver being devoured by an eagle, only to grow back again. I loved to sit on the floor and turn the glossy pages, the plates vivid in the faded room: landscapes of glowing green or ochre, scarlet and crimson cloaks, breastplates and helmets stroked with sparkling silver. The volumes had suffered from the sea — the plates had melded together, and someone had tried to separate the sodden pages and torn them, so that the heroes were marred or the color stripped entirely away to rough white paper.

The day before, I had copied a figure in the aquatint nailed to the figurehead in the attic, a sturdy youth poised in the prow of a whaleboat. His head, though, was unsatisfactory, too narrow and with a weak chin; I replaced it with a profile of the young Alexander. The angle wasn't quite right; he appeared to be gazing out across some as yet unconquered country, rather than at the whale that in my drawing loomed just in front of him, but his profile was bold, his jaw firm with resolve. An earlier drawing of my brother boasted the crested plume of Patroclus, although his garment, copied from a painting of saints that hung on the hull, was impractical for whaling, draping as it did around his ankles. Every drawing of my brother included a whale, either about to be impaled or already overcome and floating lifeless in the sea.

Sighing over my missing ledger, I quietly slid Mordecai's logbook from the stack and, turning my back to him, opened the book on my lap and began to flip through it. The book sprang open at the center, at two doubled pages; I unfolded them so that together they spread as wide as my outstretched arms.

The long stretch of paper held a chart, entitled "The Rathbones" in Mordecai's narrow hand. At the top left was Moses, then came a row of names, among them three of the great-great-aunts we had just left: Euphemia was there, and Beulah, and

Amaziah. I recognized most of them from the quilt Euphemia had shown me — the quilt Hepzibah had found on her bed at Rathbone House. Moses's last wife, Katurah, who had died only a year before Mordecai and I arrived at Mouse Island, had brought the quilt to the island fifty years ago. By now the patchworked patterns had all faded to pale tones, but the stitched names, yellowed with age, remained tight and true.

I had memorized all of the wives' names, dead and living. I took up a pen from among Mordecai's tools and, first dipping it in a bottle of ink, began to add to the chart, squeezing names between those already there, so that they spread from edge to edge: Thankful, Patience, Charity, Amaziah, Constance, Hopestill, Hepzibah, Euphemia, Eunice, Felicity, Beulah, Experience, Desire, Trial, Humility, Silence, and Katurah. Seventeen wives in all.

I was adding the dates from the quilt below each name when Mordecai finally looked up from his work. Preoccupied with his grid, he only slowly realized what I was holding and reached to snatch the logbook.

"What do you think you're doing?" he spluttered.

"I'm adding the others. I know all of their

154

names now."

He stared at me, the chart dangling from his hand and fluttering in the wind.

I took the logbook back from him, folded up the chart, and made him sit down again. I told him Euphemia's stories, of Moses's first whale and of Hepzibah's arrival at Rathbone House. Crow settled on my shoulder, hunched in the chill air. By the time I had finished, the bright afternoon light had begun to fade, and the wind had dropped.

Mordecai sat for a while, quiet. He looked down at his grid, frowning, and erased a smudge.

"Some of your great-great-aunts were mentioned in their sons' journals. Though not often by name. And mostly as memories. The wives were always gone by the time their sons went to sea. I knew I didn't have all of them listed, but this . . ." He ran his finger across the long row of names, not touching the page. He hesitated. "I did wonder whether the sons of Moses were all really his."

"Four bells," the mate of the *Able* called. The bell clanged from the foremast. I closed my eyes and there was Hepzibah, being passed from one bed to the next by a son of Moses. In my mind she never left the hall of beds, was never led away by the cabin boy to rest, but was passed, at each turn of the glass and strike of the bell, from the first bed to the last and back up the hall again, in an endless circle.

I rubbed my eyes and stared down at the chart.

"Mordecai."

"What is it now?" He didn't look up, engrossed once again in his map.

"Is it true that the male uses his palp during the reproductive act?"

He froze with pencil poised and his eyes lifted slowly up to mine.

"I beg your pardon?"

Among Mordecai's stacks I had noticed a volume that I had often studied in the attic. I slid out a mottled brown book entitled *Episodes of Insect Life* and opened it, turning the book so Mordecai could see. On a tipped-in engraving a pair of spiders were interlocked. Their black-and-white bodies, at the point where they joined, glowed a brilliant yellow.

Mordecai visibly relaxed and leaned over the book, peering closely at the image.

"Indeed, yes, yes. The male jumping spider boasts light-reflective scales that attract his mate. He then transfers his . . . reproductive fluid onto small webs and hence to tubelike structures on the tips of his front appendages, or palps. Vibrating his palps, he moves stealthily toward the female." He demonstrated, his hands trembling vigorously as they approached the book. "The male then . . . his palp is . . . torn off by his mate and remains attached to her epigyny for several hours. The female may store fluid from different males inside her body and then choose which male will fertilize her eggs. Now, the Brazilian wandering spider —"

"Do men lose their palps too?"

The stream of words stopped.

"Do men . . ." His voice trailed off.

He stared at me, raising a hand to clutch at his cloud of hair, squeezing his fist tight. He looked blankly all around, then ran his eyes along the spines of his books and gingerly selected a small, thick dictionary. When he lay it on the deck the book fell open at the letter *V.* I moved closer. Tucked between the entries for "veneration" and "venereal" was a thin booklet. Its cover was a deep blue; emblazoned on it in gold were a pair of mermaids holding a scroll proclaiming *Diseases of the Seaman.* Mordecai glanced at me and began flipping through the pages of the booklet. I caught glimpses of nude male figures, but their bodies were largely hidden by captions. He lingered at one page, whose caption read *"A Night in the Arms of Venus Leads to a Lifetime on Mercury"* and accompanied an image of a man lying in a closed box under which a fire burned. Only his head, covered with blisters, emerged from the box, along with spumes of smoke, presumably vapors of mercury.

"Perhaps unsuitable . . ." Mordecai muttered, carefully pushing the booklet back into the dictionary. As he began to flip through the pages — looking, I assumed, for some other entry — a loose page slid out and floated to the deck, unnoticed by Mordecai. I looked down at a crude drawing in black ink of a sailor and his beloved clasped in what I took to be a lovers' embrace, but before I could make out any significant detail Mordecai snatched up the drawing, restored it to its place, and snapped the dictionary shut. Shaking his head, he continued work on his map.

I shrugged and looked back at the chart.

"I wonder what happened to the other wives." Some of the wives still alive were among the first on Mordecai's chart. But this meant they were among the eldest. What had become of the younger wives? I stared at the chart and tried to guess from the dates and lists of sons under each name what had happened.

"Beulah arrived at Rathbone House to find newborn triplets. But she passed no wife on her way." I checked the names. "The wife before her, Felicity, must have died in childbirth."

I ran my finger along the long line of names. No sons were listed under one wife.

"Silence. I think Silence was discovered to be barren and was made to walk the gangplank."

Mordecai looked up, his eye bright. He hesitated, then said, "The grates in the windows, on the bottom floor? Those date from just after Desire's time. Perhaps she deliberately plunged into the sea."

I opened the chart again and looked at the second row, the next generation of Rathbones. The word "Son" appeared several times below each wife's name. I counted, wondering if some of the wives had overlapped to produce so many. Though there were gaps here and there where no name appeared, the wives had borne more than fifty sons. Next to some "Son"s was an initial or number: H, B, 1, 2, 3, or 4.

Seeing my puzzled look, Mordecai leaned over.

"Harpooner. Boatheader. First-Oar, Second-Oar, and so forth."

"What about their names?"

"Those were their names."

In some lists half the sons were crossed out; in a few all were gone. I saw no mention of daughters.

"For each child born one perished at sea." Mordecai sat up straight, staring out over the water. His pencil, forgotten, dropped on the half-finished graph. "The sons returned but once in a year, later even less, their voyages stretching to three and four years as the ships ventured farther in search of fresh herds of sperm. Some died quickly during chases, thrown overboard and drowned, or consumed whole by their prey. Others were reduced by degrees, leaving their limbs behind in increments on successive voyages." He opened one of the logbooks and flipped through the pages. "One boy lost only the tip of an ear to the snap of a colossal jaw. Some were so ruined that their brothers were thankful when they sank in the sea, their entrails spiraling behind them."

I flipped back through the pages to the start of the journal and saw entries in a different hand. Not Mordecai's spidery script but the careful block letters of someone unaccustomed to writing. A boy or man whose voyage was cut short; the entries spanned only a few weeks. I wondered whose son had written these, and if his mother or grandmother was one of those still alive on Mouse Island.

Mordecai got up and began to stalk back and forth, grasping the lapels of his jacket and gazing out to sea.

"Moses reigned for three decades, the undisputed monarch of his maritime realm. Many other fishing families from Naiway-onk and neighboring towns sent their own sons to sea. All yearned to direct the flow of whale gold into their own coffers, but none had the preternatural abilities of Moses's clan. He and his sons knew before anyone else when the whales were coming, long before spouts showed on the horizon. When the whales near the coast thinned, and the ships went in search of herds, Moses and his sons always knew where to find them. They lived on land as they did at sea, their native skills honed by ceaseless practice, working as one organism.

"Other families couldn't match such prowess. They sank hope and fortune into ships that were lost at sea, ships that crawled back into port with their holds nearly empty or their meager harvest gone rancid from lingering too long in distant waters, hoping for one more whale that Moses and his sons may have missed. The Rathbone ships returned so laden with sperm oil that they threatened to sink. In the early years, whales were towed home to burn on shore, in the cauldrons of the great shed that hung over the water. Later, tryworks were built on the ships themselves, enabling each ship to harvest many whales before returning. In the great years each Rathbone ship brought back two thousand barrels, the oil of forty whales, from each voyage."

Suddenly conscious of how long he had been speaking, Mordecai stopped pacing, folded his legs under him, and went back to his graph, taking up the pen and beginning to ink in his lines.

I lay on my stomach on the warm deck and spread the pages flat, looking at the long second row crowded with sons. Below that was a third row with only a few names sketched tentatively in pencil, too pale for me to read. The fourth row was blank except for my parents: Verity Rathbone Gale and Benadam Gale. Below my parents was my own name, in the fifth row, if row it could be called, having only my name in it and, to one side and at some distance, Mordecai's name, floating, unconnected. I wondered briefly why his parents' names, Abiah and Hosea, didn't appear above him.

Mama's brother and his wife had died in a storm at sea, Mama told me, when Mordecai was just a baby, on their way to visit Hosea's family; she came from Gloucester, Mama said, far up the coast. I had always remembered Mama telling me this because she had never mentioned any other outsider woman marrying into the Rathbones. Or any other marriages, for that matter, not in her time. She had no sisters that I knew of, and the uncles who had moved away had never married. From a broad expanse at the top, the chart of the Rathbones dwindled to a trickle.

I thought of the framed silhouettes that mapped the migration of the family profile down the years and up the stairs at Rathbone House. I pictured Moses's wax profile, with its blunt features and bountiful hair. I asked Mordecai if he could identify the subjects of the other portraits. He looked up from his inking.

"The next portrait, the one in the elegant hat, was, I believe, Hepzibah's son Bow-Oar. That would make Bow-Oar your great-grandfather. Of the later portraits I am unsure."

I drew a faint line on the chart from Moses to Hepzibah with a pencil.

"I wonder what he saw when he looked at

Hepzibah? It's almost as if he could see the cluster of eggs in her stomach. The way you can see through a blenny that's not yet grown, or a squid." I looked at the lists of sons under each wife. "Maybe he wished the wives could give birth to a brood of babies in one spurt, like a splitfin. A whole whaleboat crew in one burst."

Mordecai stared at me. He tugged at his collar and cleared his throat.

"I beg your pardon, but neither Moses Rathbone nor any man could view the subcutaneous contents of his wife. Besides which, a warm-blooded mammal's eggs do not reside in its stomach, they are located . . ." He lifted a finger to point somewhere on my body, faltered, and seized a ruler. I waited for Mordecai to become engrossed in his map again, then took up the pen and drew small portraits above the names on the chart that I now knew: first Moses, looking like his wax portrait, then Hepzibah and the other aunts as I thought they would have looked as new wives, with small, neat faces and thick dark hair. In the row below, the row of sons, under each crossed-out name, I drew an oar, snapped in half. I closed the book and lay it next to Mordecai.

I picked up the telescope and wiped the

spray-spotted lens on my shawl, admiring my braids in the glass.

"Mordecai. Do you think I'm like Hepzibah?"

Mordecai looked at me warily. "How do you mean?"

"I mean, like my great-great-aunts. I look so much like them and not at all like you and Mama. How is it we're so different?"

He looked up at the mainsail above us, its long curve taut with wind.

"You did not just spring from the forehead of Zeus, you know." One side of his mouth twisted up briefly.

Mordecai turned back to his work. I lay on my side and directed my lens back toward Mouse Island.

"Mordecai."

His pen skipped on the page and he swore under his breath.

"What is it now?"

"What about the daughters? Surely Moses's wives had daughters too? And why did Mama stop visiting them?"

"Why didn't you ask Euphemia your questions?"

"I did. She just smiled and said, 'We have told our story in the cloth.' "

I had since considered the curtains at Rathbone House, and the weavings I had seen on Mouse Island, and tried to order them in my mind. The early curtains showed fishing scenes or teeming sea life; then came patterns in which I could make out sperm and harpoon, until the patterns overtook their subjects so that all I could recall were rigid geometries of square and rectangle. Then the patterns fell away until the last weavings depicted nothing I could name nor any fixed color; they looked like thin layers of the sea.

"I know my aunts were not telling the truth about the daughters. They couldn't all have been stillborn or sick . . . Maybe they were exposed on the rocks, like the Spartans did with female infants, though Moses probably would have chosen something more efficient. Then there were those fires the men made before they sailed. I wonder if those offerings they made were all four-legged or finned?"

Mordecai had stopped listening. I had been trying to speak lightly, but I shuddered, thinking of Mama's response when I asked about my brother. *He was smaller even than you, so we threw him back.* I wondered that I had not been thrown back instead.

The air grew cooler. My new shawl, adorned by my aunts with iridescent fish scales, tinkled in the freshening breeze.

"Mordecai, you should wear your new cape."

"Yes, yes, certainly. Practical. Seaworthy." He didn't look up.

I sighed. I stood and stretched, feeling the smooth roll of the deck under my feet. Avery's mate climbed in the rigging above me, adjusting the trim as the wind rose and veered south-southeast. I wrapped my shawl closer and descended a ladder into the afterhold, which was pleasantly dark and still after the bright deck. The space was filled with covered barrels and crates stacked to the ceiling. The walls were lined with shelves and drawers, packed with trade goods: bolts of cloth, casks of aromatic spices and tobacco. On a high shelf was a row of ladies' hatboxes, some striped or patterned with flowers, and next to them neat stacks of men's hats of varying styles. I chose several and returned to the deck.

Mordecai suffered me trying on each hat while he scratched at his papers. A beaver stovepipe, tall and glossy; a round-brimmed coke hat; a cocked bicorne; a sugarloaf with a high crown and stiff brim. None of them were practical at sea. I noticed a crimson brim poking out from Mordecai's suitcase, a familiar tricorne shape that had recently adorned an ivory head in the attic. First glancing at Mordecai to make sure he was not watching, I pulled the hat slowly out. Though the stiff red felt was creased and flattened, I was able to prod and pull it to something of its proper shape. Its ribbon cockades retained their former glory.

"Why not wear this one?" I held it up in the air.

Crow dropped down from the rigging and plucked the hat from my hand — Mordecai lunged for it unsuccessfully — and skimmed away over the water. Crow circled back, dropped the hat in the sea on the windward side of the brig, out of reach but in plain view, and landed on its crown. He settled to eat a sardine that he clutched in one claw. The sardine didn't look fresh; he must have stolen it from some barrel in the hold. Mordecai and Crow eyed each other. When he had stripped the fish, Crow lifted off, hovered above us, and dropped the skeleton on the foolscap. Mordecai flung the bones over the side. He bent over his paper, blotting water with the tail of his jacket, muttering.

I moved closer and leaned over to look into his face.

"Whose hat is that?"

He silently deployed a protractor, trying

to ignore me. Crow returned to his perch on the hat, bobbing beside us on the water, preening his feathers and running his beak along the brim to clean it.

"I told you. I found it in a drawer." Mordecai fanned his drawing with the billed cap to dry it.

In the attic, when I had turned the hat in my hands, it had smelled of fresh sea air, and tobacco, and something more elusive, warm and faintly sweet.

"Mordecai, I want to know."

Waiting for him to respond, I suddenly remembered a storm that had come through a few weeks earlier. The wind had been unusually powerful and had blown for days; for a fortnight afterward each tide washed a few dead creatures onto our beach, creatures I had never seen before: eyeless fish of inky black; transparent, shapeless polyps torn from deep reefs; nameless seabirds tangled in long twists of weed, all long in the water and smelling high.

Mordecai sprinkled sand on his map and lifted it carefully from the deck, then pursed his lips to blow off the sand.

"I'm not certain you're ready to hear the true story."

I stood up and crossed my arms over my chest.

"Mordecai. I may not have benefit of your years, of your wisdom, but I'm ready. I'm strong enough."

He looked startled. He lay his map aside and removed the new blue spectacles he had acquired from the captain's stores. He cleaned the lenses on a corner of his coat and returned them to his nose.

"How old do you believe me to be?"

I appraised his white hair, his pale skin and faded green eyes.

"Thirty? Five and thirty?"

He gave a little laugh, and smiled at me.

"I am twenty years old."

My eyes widened. I looked closely at his face. Mordecai was twenty? That couldn't be. The aunts' shiny salve didn't disguise the dried appearance of his skin. He looked long-salted, his flesh not wrinkled but sucked close to the bone, the water drawn away. Not that I was a keen judge of age, having lived so confined a life myself. I had first guessed my aunts' ages at perhaps seventy, though they had all passed ninety, and a few one hundred, years.

"But how could that be?"

Mordecai rolled his map and tucked it away in his case, then stood up, knees creaking. The beaver stovepipe, last among the hats I had been trying on him, fell from his head; he picked it up, looked at it absently, and put it back on. He leaned to snatch the spyglass from the deck and, holding it behind his back, began to pace, glancing my way now and again.

"But we were not talking about my age, were we? We were talking about the hat. I found it on the widow's walk." He looked directly at me, sharply, the faded eyes now bright. "It belongs to the man in the blue coat. The man with your mama."

My face went hot. I looked over the rail at the red hat, on which Crow still bobbed on the waves. I remembered now that the hat had appeared in Mordecai's attic on the same evening the strange man had appeared on the widow's walk. I knew that Mordecai knew about the intruder and had heard him looking for me in the halls, but I had no idea he had witnessed what I witnessed.

I pictured a wide back in a blue coat swelling over Mama. The sound of skin scraping against sand. A strange man holding me up by the hem of my frock, letting me spin like an insect he had caught and wanted to examine before crushing it.

Mordecai turned away and stood at the rail, looking out over the sea. On the green islands of the archipelago the shapes of buildings began to show through thick trees.

"Captain Tayles, I once heard her call him. I've searched for that name and anything like it in all the logs and journals, and never found anything: Tell, Taylor, Tyler . . . He must have been on some ship that passed through Naiwayonk. Or perhaps she met him elsewhere, I don't know. I only know that it has been going on for years." His mouth twisted and he tossed the glass up and down. "I have my spying places, too, you know. I used to listen to them. I would crouch at the bottom of the rope ladder and listen. They heard me, once, coughing. She leaned over the edge and saw me. That's why she hid me away in the attic. Your mama and that man were afraid I would tell your papa, when he came back. They wanted to make sure I couldn't."

I looked at Mordecai and saw the young man under the pale skin and behind the faded eyes of my tutor. The little boy sent to live in the attic, alone. He felt my eyes on him and stood up straight, clearing his throat. He reached to wipe his brow and felt the stovepipe hat, pulled it off, glared at it, and tossed it to the side of the deck. His hair sprang out of its neat pigtail and blew around his head in the wind.

"Why do you think your mama always walks up there? She's not hoping for your papa to return. She's afraid he will come."

I thought of her walking the boards, night after night. Mama, faithful and abiding. I pulled my knees up and lay my head on them. I closed my eyes. I remembered an entry in a whaleman's logbook that Mordecai had read to me, describing how he and his mates had tapped the sperm's oil. They plunged a great ladle into the dead whale's head, into the vast pool of oil in the case, over and over, until it was empty. I felt as hollowed out as that sperm.

After some time I took up Mordecai's journal again and opened out the chart. I drew Mama's face above her name, her hair coiled tight, her collar buttoned high on her neck. I drew Mordecai's face with its mist of white hair, and my own face, counting out and adding my aunts' hundred braids.

My pen hovered above the place where my missing brother's name should have been. I had Theseus in mind, as he faced the Minotaur; his small, sturdy form and thick hair seemed to me most like the Rathbone men of Moses's time. But my brother wouldn't hold still and pose. The face I drew was too narrow, and the hair would make no firm wave but only floated. It ended by looking much like Mordecai's: not a face to confront the Minotaur. I rubbed the drawing out and started over, this time trying to match Jason's bold profile as he seized the golden fleece from the tree. I sketched in his face and armed him with the sword of Aegeus; I drew the many-headed Hydra, already slain, lying behind him. Jason's eye turned to look at me. He had something to say, but his mouth was only a smudge through which he couldn't speak. Something moved behind him: The children of the Hydra, the skeleton warriors born from its teeth, sprang up from the ground and started toward me with their swords, clanking and clattering.

I rubbed my eyes and looked up. Mordecai was standing by the foremast, his back to me. He had tied his hair, which the wind had been blowing all around, with a length of cord. The cord had passed around a stretch of rigging as well as his hair and he had accidentally tied himself to the fore-mast. He was muttering angrily to himself, trying to get free.

"Mordecai?"

"No more questions."

I glanced over at Crow, riding along beside the ship on the red hat.

"I found something, too." I held out my wrist, turning and turning the rope bracelet. It had been a long time since I last asked

Mordecai about my missing brother or mentioned the singing voice, but I was sure he wouldn't have forgotten.

Still struggling with his knotted hair, his head twisted toward me and he saw the bracelet. He froze.

"Don't you want to know where I got this?"

Mordecai stared at it a moment longer, then went back to working at the knot.

"That's just a common rope bracelet. Your crow, doubtless, dug it up from some bin or other." He sniffed at the word "crow." Though Mordecai was devoted to ornithology, he considered the common crow unworthy of study.

"Have you seen knots like these on a common sailor's bracelet?" I pointed out the little Turk's heads, made from doubled cord so that they jutted up from the otherwise flat bracelet.

Mordecai reached down to the deck and pulled a ribbon from a packet of letters. "Enough," he said, fastening the end of his pigtail.

I sighed. I threw my pen over the side and rubbed my eyes. The wind had picked up and the ropes were rattling against the foremast. I scrubbed at my brother's face with a gum until it was only a faint smear of gray.

The mate cried out from the rigging above our heads.

"Hard abeam! Luff and touch, luff and touch."

We were drawing near the islands. Mordecai and I watched in silence as Captain Avery and his mate made ready to anchor.

Mordecai had taken up the spyglass again and was busily scanning the islands. When a seabird passed overhead, he jerked up his glass, gasping.

"Look, look!"

I jumped onto the bottom beam of the railing, looking all around.

"Is it a sperm? Do you see a whale?"

"No, no, surely it's *Himantopus mexicanus*! The black-necked stilt!"

Mordecai's glass was pointed straight up. I followed his gaze. A white seabird with black-tipped wings glided across the sky.

Mordecai drooped. "No. No, it's only a sooty tern."

I jumped back down, disappointed. "But when will we see the whales?"

"Not just yet. They will not be in among the islands, the water is far too shallow; they will swim in open water, just past the archipelago." Mordecai took his eye away from the glass and looked at me, his thin mouth drawn into a long firm line. "When we find the whales, we will find your father. And I will tell him everything. I will tell him all about your mama and that man." Mordecai smiled bitterly. "I believe that is why the man in blue chases us. He knows what I intend to do and means to silence me."

I considered Mordecai, now standing at the rail, his glass raised to the Stark Archipelago. Had he really considered what would happen if we found Papa? Did he think that Benadam Gale, that any man, would welcome such news about his wife? Did he think that Papa would turn to him in gratitude and be for him the father that he lacked?

I stood and joined Mordecai at the rail. Crow no longer floated off the starboard side; instead we saw a drab shorebird bobbing there. Mordecai brightened.

"A least sandpiper! I wonder that it is so far at sea, they usually incline to the salt marshes. You see how the crest is darker, the legs stouter than the semipalmated . . ."

He looked at me. I was standing at the rail, staring down into the water. He faltered, and stopped.

I felt Crow's weight on my shoulder, water dripping on my gown. The crimson captain's hat dropped to the deck, sodden, its brim scored with beak marks. Mordecai leaned slowly and picked it up, shaking the water from it, turning it in his hands.

"Shall we review the feeding habits of the humpback?"

I shook my head, slowly.

"Perhaps we have had enough of lessons for now."

With his penknife he snipped off a lace cockade trimmed in satin ribbon. He took a paper tack from his box of instruments and pinned the cockade to my breast.

"Felicitations, Mercy, on your graduation from Mordecai Rathbone's Finishing School for Young Ladies," he said with a faint smile.

Chapter Seven:
The Stark Archipelago

*{in which Mercy and Mordecai
encounter the in-laws}*

Late in the day we reached the outer borders
of the Stark Archipelago. We glided through
a scattering of small islands as verdant as
Mouse Island was bare. The sun hung low
over a sea so smooth and glassy that we
might have been floating across a still lake.
In the distance we caught glimpses of long
green lawns and bright buildings on the
central islands toward which we sailed. Far
beyond the archipelago, a hazy coast
stretched into the distance: Long Island, the
captain told us.

Mordecai sat on a crate, bent over a map.
"The main house is, I believe, Captain, just
northeast of the —"

"No need, Master Rathbone, I know my
way."

The mate had been hoisting up crates

from the hold for some time and was now prying one open. Crow was excited at the sight of the crate and tried to assist him, poking at the knots with his beak, but the mate preferred to work alone. Eventually Crow spied something of greater interest among the islands and flew off. I turned to see what had attracted him, spotting a flash of crimson against the green.

I leaned over the rail and gazed down as we passed the first islands. The outermost seemed small enough to cross in a few strides. Though the shallow mounds were formed of the same rough granite as Naiwayonk's shore, they were closely covered in thick grass, with a curiously neat appearance, smooth and shapely. As we passed I saw that the grass had been clipped and rolled to velvety perfection. A man in a gardener's smock kneeled at the edge of one islet, digging away salt-browned sod and laying down fresh strips of grass, creeping around the perimeter. On nearby islands two other gardeners worked at the same task.

As we approached the center of the archipelago, the islands became larger and the channels narrowed. The captain, concerned for his hull, asked for frequent soundings as the brig floated along under close-reefed sails. The mate leaned well over the side and swung his lead, calling out after each drop. "By the deep eight . . . by the mark ten . . . a quarter less ten . . . by the deep nine." His words hung in the still air.

Some islands had not been tamed into soft green mounds but left in their natural, craggy state. Between two such islands stretched an airy footbridge of brilliant scarlet, mirrored in the motionless sea. Structures of Oriental style appeared, like those in one of the colored plates in Papa's atlas: on one peak a pagoda tucked among low twisted trees, on another an open pavilion with curling eaves and pierced screens. Inside the pavilion, two figures dressed in Mandarin clothing lolled on a couch. Above them, a monkey in a tasseled red cap swung from the branch of a stunted pine. The figures — whether male or female, I wasn't sure — at first took no notice of us. It seemed impossible that they wouldn't hear or see our passing. Then one figure raised hand to brow and peered toward us. I could have easily made out their faces if they were not hidden under enormous circular hats that rose to a point at the top. The brig glided on, and the pavilion slid out of view.

We were nearing what appeared to be the

main island, larger than all the rest. Unlike its craggy satellites, the central island was a single low dome of unnatural smoothness, probably filed down by an earlier crew of gardeners and smoothed with sod. A promenade of oaks, their dark crowns struck with crimson and yellow by autumn air, climbed the center of a long green swell of lawn that was as closely manicured as the outlying islands. At the summit stood a large house of two stories surrounded by a high yew hedge. The house's shape was familiar enough, a foursquare Georgian dwelling with a steeply gabled roof. It shared the same sober white clapboard form of many houses in Naiwayonk. But the yew hedge, familiarly clipped just at the sill of the lower windows, here towered above the upper windows, almost to the eaves. Only a few inches of the top pane of glass in each window was visible.

We approached a long, slender dock of the same crimson red as the footbridges, its piers carved with Oriental glyphs. The mate stood at the port rail, holding a long staff to brace against the dock, to keep the *Able*'s hull safe from scraping.

I leaned close to Mordecai and whispered, "Are we stopping here? Is the captain going into that house?" I wondered if we might go with him. I was excited at the prospect, though nervous, having never been in any house but my own.

"Captain Avery has business to conduct here. He tells me there is a wondrous library." Mordecai hesitated. "Also, I believe you may be interested in meeting the locals."

"Master Rathbone, lend us a hand, will you?" Captain Avery called to Mordecai from the helm. "Tie us off on the port side. There's a lad. Handsomely, now."

Mordecai, who had been leaning idly on the rail, staring up at the house, jerked to a stand.

"Oh, certainly, certainly."

He crouched, bracing his legs, holding his arms out rigidly. The captain uncoiled the bow-anchor lead and tossed it as we came alongside the dock. Mordecai lurched and missed, hands grasping air. He snatched up the rope end and began to fumble with it, trying to tie what looked like a strangle snare, ending up with only an unseamanlike tangle. Meantime, the mate had already made fast on the port stern. Now the bow began to drift away from the pier. I seized the rope from Mordecai, tied a quick timber hitch, and in one cast we were moored. Mordecai opened his mouth to make some ready remark, then closed it. He felt the captain's eyes upon him from the foredeck and put his hand up to touch the stiff sailor's cap he had put on again. Captain Avery, with a final glare, adjusted the brim of his own well-weathered cap and turned back to his task, making the foresail shrouds neat.

Mordecai clambered down the ladder and I descended behind him. When I turned at the bottom I saw, between two islands, a painted barge floating in our direction. It was poled by a figure in a peaked hat. A seated figure within, shaded by a parasol, leaned toward us. One of the two occupants of the pavilion; I recognized the jade-green robe.

"Say nothing, Mercy. I have all well in hand," Mordecai whispered into my ear and jerked his head toward the house. A deputation made its way down the lawn, but not to welcome us. Two short men in familiarly plain shirts and breeches (we had not, as I had begun to wonder, drifted into the China Seas) rushed toward us, gesturing with their hands, waving us away. Both had rosy faces, hands dredged in flour, and smelled of warm spices. One man wiped his hands on his apron. As they arrived at the dock, the other man brandished a bunch of greenstuff in a threatening manner.

"The house requires nothing, thank you. No visitors, no visitors. Cast off, if you please, and move on. You'll be better off."

"Should ask your master first, shouldn't you?"

The men looked up to see Captain Avery standing on deck above them, smiling, one raised arm holding a chair aloft by its leg. It was a lavish chair of lustrous black and gold, its curved arms finished with the gilt heads of sphinxes of the Nile. The mate gestured with a sweep of his arm toward a full set of chairs in the same style, arrayed in a line on the deck beside a handsome table with feet ending in claws.

"The latest from the Continent. Mr. Stark would be most disappointed to have missed us. And his daughter, too," said the captain. Behind him, the mate now held up to his breast a gown of pleated white silk and minced along the deck with swaying hips and fluttering eyes.

The two cooks hesitated, whispering to each other. The mate, having tossed aside his gown, suddenly flourished a brace of new copper-bottomed pans. The men's faces brightened. They came aboard and began to rummage through a crate of cookware. Meantime, Captain Avery started to off-load the table and chairs.

185

"Pardon me . . ." Behind me, I heard an unfamiliar voice. I turned to find the man in the jade-green robe hurrying along the dock toward us with long, stiff strides. The scarlet barge was docked behind our brig.

Though the man was not Oriental, he wore wide scarlet silken trousers beneath the jade robe and pointed slippers of embroidered silk whose long tips quivered at each step. Mordecai stood beside me as the man approached. They were of a similar size and bearing, and each boasted a pigtail, one pale, one dark. The man bowed first to Mordecai, pausing for a moment with a troubled look. They might have been two sides to a single coin. He then bowed to me, sweeping off his pointed hat. The pigtail came away with it. Beneath the hat curled a powdered wig. Beneath the wig, a face that made Mordecai seem the fairest of men. It was all sharp angles and harsh planes, the skin rough and pale and faintly gray, though he was a young man. I judged him to be near Mordecai's true age. It was a face that might have been hewn from the granite on the islands that the Starks had worked so hard to smooth. I thought that if I touched his cheek I might slice my finger open.

The man paused before he reached us, stopping next to the *Able* and calling up to the mate. Though I could not quite overhear their conversation, it appeared that he was asking eager questions, pointing at various features of the *Able* and smiling at the mate's responses. It seemed odd that a man dressed as he was and traveling in such a fanciful craft as a scarlet barge would have any interest in a merchant vessel.

"Roderick Stark. May I know your names?"

Though his manner was formal, his voice was friendly. His eyes didn't leave me. They were by far his best feature, a clear, deep blue.

Mordecai bowed in turn. "Mortimer Palmer, at your service. Permit me to introduce my sister, Miss Luna Palmer."

I stared at Mordecai — Palmer? — then dropped a silent curtsey. Mr. Stark bowed again and lifted my hand to his lips. I found it difficult not to shy my hand away. It was not so much the presence of the repulsive as the lack of something essential, a bleak and blasted look.

"I beg your pardon for our unheralded arrival," said Mordecai. "I am penning an article, 'Great Houses of the Atlantic Seacoast,' for *Harper's Monthly,* and it would certainly not be complete without the Stark manse." Roderick didn't seem to be listening; his eyes were still on me. I turned away and tried to look absorbed in the movements of Captain Avery, who headed whistling up the lawn, a chair in each hand and one balanced on his head.

"Might we be permitted to sketch the grounds?" Mordecai was asking, nodding toward the portfolio he carried under one arm. It was tied shut and filled with large sheets of paper, some of which stuck out from its edges. I recognized the corner of a drawing of a narwhal tusk from my lessons and furtively tucked it inside.

Roderick finally turned to Mordecai. "Great houses, you say?" He thought for a moment and laughed, shaking his head back and forth. "I think, actually, that my parents would be delighted. You must stay to tea."

Roderick offered his arm to me and led us up the walk toward the house, Mordecai trailing behind. As we walked along the allée of oaks, I turned to look for Crow and saw him hopping from branch to branch behind me. He dropped down from the last to ride my shoulder.

We entered the house through a narrow arched opening in the yew hedge, directly into a deep, broad hall of double height. The dense hedge admitted little sun. Daylight washed only the top of the room, from the high windows that peeped above the hedge. The room below was lit with candles in sconces along the walls. My eyes adjusted to the low light. If the style of the exterior had held true inside, we would have entered a sober hall of simple solid furnishings, unadorned walls, and bare board floors. Instead the room was awash in furniture. Tables, commodes, armchairs, bureaus, settees of every description, gilded and carved, tufted and swagged, filled the space from wall to wall. Some items were arranged in groupings you might see in any house — divans and chairs facing one another to form seating areas — but with no space between and no one seated. The room was empty of people and had the air of a place not lived in for many years, though the furniture looked well dusted. Stacked side chairs rose here and there in towers; there were shoals of footstools and tea tables, reefs of bookless bookshelves that were crowded instead with bric-a-brac. Though I knew little of the decorative arts, only what I'd learned from a single page of etchings in our dictionary, I recognized several modes from decades past: the lavish curves of the Rococo; the restrained lines of the Neoclassical; Regency floral motifs and bronze chasing. The walls, too, were filled from top to bottom with portraits and landscapes in ponderous frames set hard upon each other and heavy mirrors that sent candlelight glinting along gilt surfaces. Crow surveyed the hall, selected a lofty perch on the frame of a large seascape, and lit there to tuck his head under his wing.

Roderick swept his arm toward the door of a salon far across the hall.

Mordecai bowed. "Too kind. But if I might beg your indulgence and remain outside? I noticed a perfect position from which to capture your magnificent façade with my pen: that charming garden seat among the oaks. And the light just now is perfect."

Roderick bowed, nodding, then turned back to me. Voices and the sound of cutlery on china carried across the hall. With a gesture, Roderick suggested that I should precede him across the hall. I began to struggle through the armoires and hassocks, sideboards and hat racks.

Roderick noticed my faltering step and stopped, smiling.

"I do apologize, Miss Palmer, it's something of a challenge, getting through this hall . . . permit me."

He struck a path, his legs deftly nudging light boudoir chairs and heavy breakfronts out of the way. I started to follow in his wake, but Mordecai held me back.

"I will just have a quick look at the library. You will be fine without me. Engage them in witty banter. Repartee," he whispered, with a flourish of his hand.

"But I don't know them, I have nothing to say."

"Constrict your conversation to the mundane. The weather. Cookery." He considered. "Crustaceans. I will have the merest peek and then we'll be off to see the whales." He cast a hungry look toward the library. "Perhaps a bit longer. Meet me on the east side of the house in, let us say, half an hour." He began to creep away, then stopped and turned around.

"Oh, and by the by, you do know them, in a manner of speaking. This is where your mother's people came from, generations ago. Your mama is descended from the Starks, on her mother's side, and so are you. And I."

Descended from the Starks? I stopped short and knocked up against a tallboy; a porcelain shepherdess and her flock fell from a shelf and shattered. Roderick, not hearing, or used to such accidents, given the ornaments that cluttered every surface in the hall, forged on.

I had never really considered any ancestors but those whose portraits hung on the stair. If asked, I might have said that the first Rathbone was begotten by the sea itself.

In a loud whisper Mordecai called back, "Oh, and this is important: Do not mention the Rathbones. Or Naiwayonk. I'll explain later." He skirted an unstable stack of footstools and scuttled away toward the southeast corner of the house.

I looked with fresh eyes at Roderick as he strode on. His tall, slender form reminded me so much of Mordecai's. I hurried to catch up with him and soon we'd reached the dining salon.

We entered between two crouched dragons of glazed green porcelain, each taller than me. The room and its occupants were in thrall to the same Oriental airs as Roderick. The walls were hung with pale green silk figured with court scenes from an ancient dynasty, lit at intervals by hanging lanterns with garnet paper shades. The floor was cushioned with thick fringed carpets in rich patterns that I thought my great-great-aunts might have admired. In the center of the room a peaked tent of persimmon silk sheltered several low couches around a low black table laden with dishes. The tent was lit by more of the hanging lanterns, whose light shone through the translucent silk walls so that the tent glowed scarlet in the dim twilight, as did the faces of the robed diners who reclined within. Roderick parted a silk panel and we entered into air that swirled with smoke of a heady but pleasant odor. I collected myself, smoothing my braids and the front of my gown, and looked around me. Roderick spoke to an old man on a low brocade settee.

"Grandfather, allow me to present Miss Luna Palmer of . . ."

I thought quickly. "Of Narragansett Bay." Narragansett was many leagues east on the map; I hoped that the Starks knew no one there. I wanted to blurt out who I was and ask a hundred questions, but Mordecai had been so insistent.

The elder Mr. Stark peered at me from under a flat silk hat with long fringes that swung back and forth over his brow. He was just visible through a blue haze of smoke from a long-stemmed pipe lodged in a corner of his mouth. His face had the same harsh cragginess as Roderick's. Was he some old uncle of mine, Mama's great-uncle? He wore a saffron robe over embroidered pantaloons and had a long thin mustache of gleaming black. His eyebrows, plucked into a surprised arch, were the same youthful black, at odds with his aged face. He reached for a delicate teacup, but his fingernails were so long that they curled back in a circle and he couldn't grasp the tiny handle. His nails clicked uselessly against the china for a moment, then he leaned over and slurped directly from the cup.

"From near Newport, are you then, Miss Palmer?" he asked in a thin, quavering voice. I tried not to notice the way his mustache trailed in his tea.

"Quite near." I knew a little of Newport from Captain Avery's chatter. He said it was a summer residence of wealthy city people.

The elder Stark's eye had a wary gleam. I was afraid he saw something familiar in my face, but my appearance would in no way suggest Rathbone to anyone who knew our family, such of it as remained. I was so small and dark compared to Mama and Mordecai.

"Palmer, you say? And your mother's family?"

I lunged for a tea biscuit, stalling, then blurted out: "Have you frequently visited Newport, Mr. Stark? There are so many fine homes on the hills above the harbor, though none surpasses yours."

The elder Stark's sharp look softened. With a gratified air, he turned his attention to a tureen of soup in which a bird's nest floated. I breathed out.

I continued to make my way around the table with Roderick, curtseying at each introduction, wondering if I might be expected instead to prostrate myself, as one does before the Eastern potentates.

"My grandparents, Mr. and Mrs. Percival Stark. My parents, Mr. and Mrs. Lemuel Stark, and my sister, Miss Lucretia Stark." Each nodded his head in vague recognition, then returned to his tea.

There was no doubt that all were of Roderick's family: each had the same grim look, including an infant Stark, attended by a nurse. All wore richly worked Oriental garments and glossy black wigs that only made their faces look more barren. The elder Starks had attempted to adorn their faces with paint and powder, but nothing comfortably adhered; through lead-white the forbidding cheeks still showed, like the guano-laden cliffs west of our docks at home. All were alike but Roderick's mother: She had a fair complexion and wore her heavy golden hair twisted up in a comb, disdaining a wig. She was quite pretty, though nowhere near as lovely as Mama. Clearly it was Roderick's mother who had married into the Stark family. But the mother's beauty had not found its way into any of her three children. In the infant Stark, who was wigless, though in a little frogged coolie suit of blue silk, I saw some faint evidence of the mother's fairness. But a glance at Roderick's sister, near to him in age, showed me that the ugliness had only been lying in wait like an eel in its cave.

Roderick led me to a silk divan. "Please, sit down."

He saw that I hesitated; the seat of the divan was as high as my waist. He hurried out the door, returning moments later with a chair of the correct proportions, fished from the hall. I tried not to mind its childish pattern of nursery figures. Roderick sat close by me, on the silk divan.

"What may we offer you, Miss Palmer?" Mrs. Stark asked, gesturing listlessly at the tea table.

Bowls and dishes of food crowded the table from edge to edge. In the center was a large gilded platter filled with pickled vegetables in glowing shades of ruby and emerald, thinly sliced and cut into the shapes of phoenixes and dragons, arranged around a central mound of steaming meats.

"Perhaps a taste of braised *shih-shih tsu*?"

She speared a thin pink slice onto my plate. It smelled of wet dog.

Roderick leaned over and slid the plate

away. His gray face reddened, and he was frowning. He leaned closer to me and whispered, "I'm so sorry. My family is . . . unaccustomed to visitors." He sat up straight and in a louder voice said, "May we find something more familiar for you, Miss Palmer?"

"Oh. Just a biscuit would be lovely, please."

"Come, something a little more piquant?" Mrs. Stark insisted. She pushed a bowl toward me. Several small jellyfish pulsed in a bed of seaweed dyed jade-green. "Or a taste of Golden Eyes? Burning Brain?"

"Please don't trouble yourself . . . A simple egg?"

Mrs. Stark leaned over the soup tureen and plucked a small speckled egg from the bird's nest that floated there. I recognized it as the egg of a quail, though of a startling cobalt blue. It had scarcely touched down on my plate before it was snatched away by the elder Mr. Stark.

"I'm certain Miss Palmer would prefer a hen's egg?"

I nodded gratefully as Mr. Stark set a plain white egg on my plate; I was by then quite hungry. I cracked the shell with the edge of my spoon and out fell an unborn chick, in its beak a large pearl. I lay down my spoon.

Mr. Stark popped the quail egg, unshelled, into his mouth, closing his eyes as he crunched, his teeth turning blue.

Mr. and Mrs. Stark began to argue about the relative merits of pickled quail and duck eggs, then lapsed into languid sampling of the many dishes at hand. I finally selected a dried sea cucumber and lay it on my plate.

I thought of the dining room in Rathbone House. How different meals were at home. I ate alone, at the great round table in the dining room on the second floor. Larboard brought my unvarying dinner of broth and stewed fruit, while Starboard polished the long rows of plates that ringed the dining room, ranging from the old wood trenchers of ships' messes to bright porcelain to bone china of refined design. There were no arguments. There were no conversations at all, except for those I sometimes made up when I was younger, moving around the table to take each part: "Good morning, darling, I hope you slept well?" Papa would say; "Fine, Papa, and you?" I would reply. Papa would turn to Mama and say, "How are the roses coming along, Verity, my dear?" In truth, there were no roses. Though there had once been formal gardens behind the house, with orchards and box hedges, now only a few tree stumps dotted the barren ground. Sighing, I bit cautiously at the tip of my sea cucumber.

"Pardon . . ." A servant in a crimson silk jacket had appeared at my elbow. He picked up several dishes from the crowded table and set a jade-green plate in front of me. A plain hen's egg, poached, lay on a fanned bed of buttered toast wedges. I looked over to see Roderick nodding at the plate, smiling at me. His face twitched in what I took to be a wink, though it was difficult to read expression on that blighted face. I gratefully began to eat.

Lunch continued in silence, other than the occasional slurp or crunch from a gluttonous Stark. The elder Mr. Stark drew on his pipe; the infant Stark snuffled at a bottle in the arms of his dozing nurse. I felt Roderick's eyes on me throughout. Blue smoke eddied and swirled. I wondered about Mordecai. I saw no clocks in the room and doubted that within their robes any Stark concealed a pocket watch, but certainly the better part of an hour had passed.

As I tried to think of a polite excuse to leave, a servant entered the room, in his hands an ebony footstool that I recognized as one of those from Captain Avery's deck. The elder Starks came suddenly awake.

They leapt from their divans and rushed in a body to the outer hall with shrill cries of delight. Through the door I saw Captain Avery's suite of furniture attractively displayed atop a row of commodes, the captain walking along the row, polishing the legs of his chairs with a handkerchief.

Roderick got up and leaned out the door, calling after his parents, "Mother, please? Father? Not more!"

The Starks ignored him, converging on the chairs, elbowing one another aside to be first to caress each piece.

Roderick, sighing, returned to his seat. "The family Stark, it seems, is about to abandon the mysteries of the Orient for those of the pharaohs." He looked at me with a faltering smile.

I felt more at ease with the elder Starks gone; only Roderick and his sister remained in the dining salon with me. Lucretia Stark was even more lavishly dressed than her elders. Her glossy black wig rose in diminishing tiers, each draped with pearls, topped with a jeweled cricket in a little bamboo cage. Her golden robe, worked with peonies of silver thread, fit closely from throat to hem. Its sleeves were tight at the shoulder and belled wide at the wrist to fall to the floor. She remained slumped on a divan, eyeing my woolen gown.

"How charming your gown is, Miss Palmer. So . . . fresh, so unaffected." She snickered, smoothing the sleeve of her robe, admiring the silver threads shimmering in lantern light. Staring at me, she reached her hand into a bowl of small scarlet sea urchins and began to flick them at me.

Roderick leaned over from his seat next to me and held his arms up to block the little blobs as they flew across the room, but then there was a whistle at the doorway, and Lucretia froze. The striped arm of Avery's mate slowly appeared from one side, draped in a selection of garments patterned with jackals and ibises. Over the last gown the mate lay a broad collar of beaten gold. Miss Stark dashed for the door.

I was left alone with Roderick. He watched me intently as I sipped my tea.

"Miss Palmer, I hope you won't think me rude, but . . . your hair, it's fascinating. Like Medusa's." He looked a little startled, as though he had surprised himself by saying such a thing to me. He hesitated, then continued. "If she'd had your braids instead of snakes, her gaze wouldn't have turned men to stone." He reached to pick a scarlet blob from the skirt of my gown, his eyes still on mine, a half smile softening his sharp lips. "I must apologize for my sister." His eyes traveled up and down my figure. "I think your gown is very charming."

The blood rushed to my face. I had never before been complimented by a man, only by my great-great-aunts.

I glanced at my reflection in a pier glass framed in bamboo that hung behind Roderick. I supposed I was as pleasant to look at as Roderick's mother, though my skin was ruddy, what with recent days spent in the sun, where hers was fair, my eyes a vigorous green while hers were a delicate blue. Roderick leaned toward me, holding out a tray of marzipan. I reached to select one in the shape of a nightingale but before I could grasp it, it was snatched away. The little monkey I had glimpsed in the Chinese pavilion on the tiny island now sat on Roderick's shoulder in its tasseled cap, nibbling the sugared bird. I gripped the chair seat beneath me with both hands. Its gilt carving, damp from the salt air that found its way inside even this enshrouded house, bent off and crumbled in my fingers.

"Are you and your brother on some sort of pleasure cruise?" Roderick asked.

Brother. For an instant I didn't realize he was speaking of Mordecai, and my heart jumped. Roderick didn't seem to notice

Mordecai's absence; his focus was wholly on me.

"Avery's brig seems an odd choice of vessel. Not very comfortable for a young lady, though she's a fine, weatherly ship." When Roderick spoke of the *Able* his eyes shone in his ravaged face.

"Well, yes. Just to take the air for a few days."

"I envy you. I wish I were at sea." He turned his head toward the harbor, invisible from that house.

I thought of the crimson barge in which I had seen him languidly rowing. I couldn't picture him on the open sound. He sighed and pushed a wandering jellyfish back into its bowl.

"I'm home only for a brief visit. I must return to Boston and my studies."

"Oh? What do you study, Mr. Stark?"

Roderick squirmed in his seat, frowning in a way so like Mordecai that I flinched. He must, after all, be a distant cousin of Mordecai's and mine.

"I study the history of the arts. My particular field is the Neoclassical." He turned his cup around and around on its saucer, staring into his tea. "My family's choice, not mine." He glanced down at his clothes and back up at me. "As is my clothing."

"What would you prefer to study?" I asked.

Roderick sat with his elbows on his knees, head in hands. "Oh, I don't know. Something more useful than the significance of first phase Classicism in the Louis XVI style," he said with a weak laugh.

"Well, then why don't you study something useful?"

Roderick looked startled.

"Oh, well, my parents would never . . . That is, I couldn't possibly . . ."

He sat back in his chair and crossed his arms, and lapsed into thought.

"Mr. Stark, I was wondering . . ."

I wanted to ask him what he knew about my family, about our connection, but strident voices came from the hall. I turned in my chair to look out into the hall.

The elder Starks were attempting to bargain with Captain Avery over an ebony armchair.

"Pirate! Not a penny over fifty!" shrieked the elder Mr. Stark, waving his pipe violently.

Captain Avery calmly shook his head.

"Two hundred it is and two hundred it stays," he said, crossing his arms.

"One hundred and fifty! You must take one hundred and fifty!" Mr. Stark clawed at

204

the captain's arm with his long nails, but the captain stood firm.

The women's shrill voices joined in, screeching out figures. The mate, now wearing the collar of beaten gold, ran past the door, Miss Stark running after him. When some heavy piece of furniture, or an embattled Stark, struck the floor, the lanterns above our tea table bounced and jangled on their chains and the flames of their candles wavered. No whale oil was used in this house, I had noticed, only wax. A faint dust of gold from the scrolled ceiling drifted down onto Roderick's wig and into our tea.

Surely Mordecai was outside waiting for me by now; or he might still be in the library. I began to fidget with my braids and tap my foot.

"Shall we take a turn?" asked Roderick. I glanced in the direction Mordecai had gone; I had no ready excuse to escape Roderick. I would try to lead him in that direction and find a way to evade him when we were closer to the library.

We toured the perimeter of the great hall, squeezing along the narrow lane between wall and furniture. The walls were as thick with paintings as the floor was with decorative objects, still lifes, portraits, and landscapes ranging through the same discarded styles as the furniture. Roderick stopped now and then to point out portraits of his ancestors among the crowded ranks. Near the front of the hall the men and women depicted in the paintings looked much like the living Starks, reclining on various couches and settees in lavish clothing, and equally unfortunate in appearance.

Toward the back of the hall, Roderick stopped below a large painting that stood out in its plainspoken style: A robust, handsome man in simple tradesman's clothing stood on a dock, surrounded by barrels and crates stamped with a trademark. Looking more closely, I made out an *S* of rope framed by adzes and chisels. Behind the portrait subject was a busy port scene with men hurrying along docks, a brisk sea, and open sky.

"We were in the merchant trade a few generations ago." Roderick stared up at the portrait. "My ancestors exported timber and fur to Europe and imported spices from the Indies. And before that we were shipbuilders. Perhaps you have heard of the famed Stark brigs?"

The early Stark's face didn't resemble his descendants' at all; its lines were clean and strong, its air purposeful where Roderick's was vague. Flanking the large portrait were two smaller paintings, clearly by the same hand, surely the wife and children of the handsome merchant. The woman was fair-haired and pretty, with a quiet smile and clear gaze; the children, two little boys and a girl, were equally attractive, plump and fair. I stared at the portraits, trying to understand how a family's looks could change so completely. And I wondered, watching Roderick as he gazed with a troubled look of longing at his ancestor's portrait, how the family had so entirely sunken from active and enterprising to slothful and spiritless. I couldn't help but consider the Starks' unhappy progression against that of my own kin.

I looked at the face of Roderick's ancestor. His eyes were bright and clear, the same strong blue as Roderick's. Behind his head the masts of many ships thrust into the sky.

I smiled at Roderick. "Your ancestor looks happy. Maybe you could take up the old family trade."

Roderick stared at me, eyes wide. "Commerce? My parents would die of shame."

"It's only that I noticed how interested you were in the *Able*. My people once sailed the seas, too," I said. "The Rathbones were, I believe, renowned for —"

A shriek cut through my words. "Rathbone! Did you say Rathbone?" I turned to see the elder Mr. Stark halfway across the hall, frozen in mid-descent above one of the new Egyptian chairs, glaring toward me. My voice must have echoed loudly in the lofty hall. He stood up straight, snatched a funerary jar from Miss Stark, and pitched it across the room at me. The jar smashed against a gilt armoire, inches from my head, closely followed by other missiles from other Starks.

"Rathbone!" came the angry cry again. "Out! Get out!"

I glanced at Roderick; he was staring at me with wide eyes and open mouth. A pair of candlesticks hurtled toward me — I felt them skim through my hair before they smashed into a mirror, shattering it. Crouching low, I started for the library, winding as best I could through the maze of furniture. I heard Crow's cry and looked back to see him fly down among the Starks, screeching, lifting wigs, pulling pigtails, plucking the pipe from the elder Stark's mouth and showering him with burning cinders. The Starks fell back, cringing before Crow's flashing beak and tripping over their robes. They stumbled through their furnishings before swarming up the stairs and disappearing, a door slamming shut behind them. Meantime, I reached the library, ducked in, and closed the door behind me.

I stood with my back against the door, waiting for my breath to slow, and listened. No one was approaching; maybe Roderick had not seen me enter the room. I breathed a little easier and looked around me.

The Stark library was larger than the dining salon, though no brighter. Its walls were entirely filled with bookshelves, interrupted only by tall windows with drawn curtains of heavy velvet and an unlit fireplace. Each shelf was stuffed from end to end with books great and small in fine bindings. I couldn't resist walking along the rows to admire the rich array: histories, philosophy, biography, the arts, the natural sciences. One shelf held a few dozen journals in bindings much like Mordecai's treasured log-books. I leafed through one and found renderings of ship hulls covered with notations. Old letters neatly grouped and tied in ribbon filled another shelf. I picked up one sheaf and blew the dust from it. The salutation, in faded blue ink, was too pale to read. Piled on the floor against the rows of shelves were stack after stack of unopened crates of still more books. Furniture cluttered this room, too, though less thickly than in the hall. The chairs and tables smelled of damp paper and mold.

The library at Rathbone House held only a few clusters of books, their spines bleached to pale blues and grays in the sunlight that poured in through curtainless windows. It was furnished only with the crates Papa had shipped home, which stood here and there around the room. The contents of each crate had provided clues to its origin, but there was no word from Papa written anywhere within. I used to trace his path in the folio atlas, lying along its gilt-edged spine and spreading my arms to smooth down each huge page: bleeding madras from southern India; Araby bracelets, brass-belled and tinkling; the heart-shaped pods of the giant komo tree from Madagascar. The paper rippled beneath me, its edges stained as if once lapped by distant tides. There had been other creatures, too, though none fared any better than the little Peking dog: a linnet caged in silver; a hairless cat from Egypt; an ibis egg that neither warmth nor prayer would waken. The last crate came accompanied by my fledgling crows, still living. They flew above the sailor's head as he neared our house, each clutching the end of a rope trailing from the crate, cawing.

I would arrange these objects, those that survived, around the atlas's borders, where they made a friendly ring around me, rising up from the edges of continents. When I lay with head on folded arms, I seemed to see my father's voyage, my eye tracing the curve the gifts made on their way around the world back to me.

I invented reasons for Papa's long absence. I imagined that he and my brother had been waylaid by some South Seas race and made to serve them. They had been marooned on a coral reef, subsisting on algae and plankton. They had joined the emperor of France in his island exile.

"What glories!"

Mordecai's voice startled me. I put away the little book of maps I found in my hand and hurried over to him.

He sat cross-legged in a clearing in the middle of the floor, surrounded by stacks of books. He'd set candlesticks to form a ring of light around him. He paged through an enormous volume of engravings, a rapt expression on his face. I moved closer to see what had so absorbed him and saw a life-size stoat and her young gamboling among the reeds. He looked up at me, beaming.

"A double elephant folio. I never dreamed of such a thing."

"Mordecai." When he didn't respond I put

my hand on his shoulder and shook him. "Mordecai, we have to go. They know I'm a Rathbone."

Mordecai's face slowly cleared. "Oh. Yes. Yes, we must certainly hurry." He showed no sign of rising, instead looking longingly at the nearest stack of books and running a hand slowly along their spines.

The handle of the door creaked. I turned to face it, waving behind my back to Mordecai, hoping he would hide behind a chair. Roderick stood there in the doorway, a troubled smile on his face, turning his pointed hat in his hands. The door remained open. I tried to peer around him but saw no one else in the hall; they must have all fled. The monkey still sat on Roderick's shoulder, now engrossed in a sugared plum.

"Miss . . . is it Palmer, or should I say Rathbone?"

I thought quickly. "I'm not sure I understand. I only meant to say that my family knew the Rathbones many years ago." I wished again that Mordecai had explained his plan more thoroughly to me. Why did the Starks hate the Rathbones, especially if we truly were related?

Roderick seemed relieved, and so was I. I mastered the urge to turn around to see what had become of Mordecai, but Roderick gave no indication of having seen him. I adjusted my position, hoping to block his view of the circle of books, then remembered that he could easily see over my head; I had forgotten, for a moment, my size. I gestured behind my back, pointing vigorously toward the door, hoping Mordecai saw and understood, and began to move in small steps away from the door. I searched for words to hold Roderick.

"Mr. Stark, you've been so kind. Meeting you has given me great pleasure." I wasn't lying; it was quite pleasant to be admired.

Roderick leaned over, so that I couldn't avoid looking directly into his eyes.

The blood rushed to my cheeks. I dropped my chin to hide my face behind my braids.

"Miss Palmer, I'm sorry. I know we've only just met, but . . . may I at least call on you? With your parents' permission, of course."

As Roderick seized my hand, something dropped to the floor — the bundle of letters from the shelf. I hadn't realized I was still holding it. I picked up the letters and stuffed them in my pocket. Roderick, his lips to my hand, didn't notice, but the monkey did. Shrieking, it dropped the plum, hopped off Roderick's shoulder and landed on mine, its claws digging into me.

It thrust a wiry arm into my pocket and began to pull the letters out.

There was a sudden flurry of wings in the doorway and the monkey was upside down in the air, its tail clutched in Crow's beak. Crow struggled to keep the monkey, far larger than him, airborne, while the monkey screamed and pulled at Crow's tail. Roderick, trapped between them against the doorframe, threw up his arms to shield his face. I slipped out and zigzagged across the hall, making for the front door. Mordecai was there, just disappearing through the door, and in moments I, too, was outside, running around the corner and out of sight of the house.

CHAPTER EIGHT:
THE SPERM AND THE STILT

{in which Mercy discovers Papa's true path}

Ahead of me Mordecai's pale head moved down the east slope of the lawn and disappeared past a border of beech trees. Though the twilight was deepening, it was easy enough to trace his path; a trail of books, which I gathered as I went, trickled behind him. I glanced back a few times, but no Stark was following us, and I breathed easier.

Past the border of beeches the ground dipped and a new landscape appeared, a treeless terrain of broken rock, and past it the open sea. I bent to pick up another fallen book and found the ground damp, a wet circle around a few furlongs of dry sand and rocks. At high tide this must be an island of its own.

Where before it seemed I had strayed into the Orient, I now wondered if I had been conveyed to the Cyclades. Against the pale and dusty tract, the sea seemed the burning blue of the Aegean, like the waters into which the Argonauts dipped their oars. From its rim the sun sent a spray of gold across the blue. At the center of the islet, surrounded by parched poplars, stood a small circular temple. I could see Mordecai's shadowy form inside. An olive vine tangled among the columns that still stood; others lay broken among weeds. I climbed the temple's shallow staircase and sat on the topmost step to rest for a moment by an intact column. I felt curiously comfortable. Looking around me, I realized that the temple was somewhat undersized, perhaps three-quarters scale. The altar, a raised dais on which Mordecai sat, appeared too small for sacrifices. A litter of bones lay scattered around Mordecai's feet, the burned limbs of some small, forgotten offering.

Mordecai's portfolio stood propped against a column, bulging at its center, stuffed with stolen books. I handed him those I had recovered from his path, their authors unfamiliar to me: works of fiction by one Nathaniel Hawthorne and a Herman Melville; a volume of birds by a Mr. Audubon; a treatise by K. Marx.

"Uncut. An entire library filled with uncut

books." Mordecai eagerly scanned the spines of the recovered volumes, flipping open a black-clad one. "Look at this one. About an Austrian monk of the name Mendel. He has studied pea plants for years and, based on his findings, claims to be able to predict the traits of offspring, whether plant or animal, from those of the parents." He opened another. "And this Englishman claims we are descended from the trilobite by way of the ape. Can you imagine anything more captivating?"

"Fascinating," I said, arms crossed over my breast.

Mordecai closed the book and brushed marble dust from its dark cover, glancing up at me.

"I am sorry for having abandoned you to the Starks. I didn't want the old ones to lay eyes on me. Had they seen me, there would have been no doubt that I was a Rathbone, and they would not have welcomed me." He hesitated. "And the Starks have, I believe, good reason to hate us." He looked up at me. "I promise, I will tell you more of them in a moment. But this . . ."

He pushed all of the books aside and picked up a large linen-bound volume that lay next to him, *Birds of Stream and Shore.*

"If I had gone with you I would never have

found this."

A book of birds? I looked eagerly between the columns to the sea beyond. Wasn't that where the open sea began, just beyond this island? Why was Mordecai not looking for the whales instead of into yet another dusty book?

I sighed and sat down on a disk of fluted marble and waited. Mordecai knelt next to me and paged through the book, stopping at a large engraved map, spreading over two pages and bearing the legend *"Oceanus Atlanticus."* I recognized the scattered masses of Europe and the great bulk of Africa, familiar from my lessons with all but the shores nearest me, which I'd always neglected in favor of those along which I might trace my father's travels. The continents, pressed to the edges of the paper by the great Atlantic, were represented on the map only by their tips or slivers of their coasts. Anxious over the unbroken expanse of ocean, the mapmaker had here and there along coastal waters tried to divert the eye with fanciful sea creatures (which with their inadequate fins would instantly sink in any true sea). He had been afraid to venture his pen into the uncharted deeps toward the center, a blank span of blue that set off the winding red line to which Mordecai now pointed, a line whose shape looked vaguely familiar. Close to the line a white bird with black markings and a long narrow bill regarded me from a cartouche, its caption reading: *"Migration Route of the Black-Necked Stilt."*

I looked up. Mordecai stared at me expectantly. He drew a folded sheet of thin paper from his breast pocket, opened it, and held it up to the light. I recognized the drawing: It was the map of the sperm's route that he had re-created on the *Able*. He slid the paper into position on the open book over the route of the black-necked stilt. Though there were a few variations in the curves, the shapes of the two maps essentially matched. Mordecai laid the book down and leapt to his feet, kicking out his legs in stiff jerking motions in a dance vaguely reminiscent of a sailor's hornpipe. He tired quickly and sat down, panting, rubbing at his joints. He pointed at the map.

"You see. The migratory routes. They are the same, the very same."

I looked at him, waiting.

Mordecai peered down at the book, smoothing the paper with one hand. "I noticed that the old logbooks always made mention of any notable congregation of fish or fowl. Among sightings of sperm, frequent gatherings of the black-necked stilt captured my attention." He looked up at me and tapped his forehead with a thin finger. "I have long suspected a sympathetic confluence in their routes. As I tracked the sperm, so this worthy naturalist followed the stilt!" He struck the page with his hand. "Such a gratifying corroboration!"

Mordecai peered more closely at the paper. His smile faltered.

"I see, however, that there are a few slight variances. Could I have neglected to adequately account for the equatorial currents? No, no, but certainly this declivity at forty-one degrees and thirty-three minutes north, seventy degrees and ninety-two minutes west may have . . ." He muttered over the route for a minute or two more, pulling a pencil from his pocket and jotting tiny notes on the edge of the map, then looked up, eyes shining. "We have only just missed them! According to my adjusted calculations, the whales are now some fifty-five leagues north of us, no more than sixty. We will catch them up! Surely Captain Avery will not object to carrying us a bit farther . . . ah!" Mordecai jumped up, squinting at the sky. "Could that be *Himantopus* now? I was sure I spied one earlier, this may be a straggler from the flock."

220

A bedraggled gull passed over us. I remembered Mordecai scanning the sky over the *Able* each time any seabird flew by.

Beyond the island, the twilight sky was the color of lead, the sea flat and oily. Not a whitecap was to be seen, let alone a whale. My skin began to tingle and a heaviness settled into my limbs.

Though Mordecai could name any fish or seabird's rank in phylum or species in a flash, I was beginning to understand that he knew nothing of what they swam in and flew over. He did not account for those things that could not be mapped: the vagaries of the wind or a sudden storm that might force a pod of whales deeper, slower; a freak of cold threading up from the deep to send a school of squid spiraling away from the whales, the whales hurrying after, away from Mordecai's precious route. Having lived indoors his whole life, he was so untuned to the sea and its ways. Though I had only rowed my skiff along the shore, I had, I thought, more sense of the sea. I would never believe, as Mordecai seemed to, that a ship would stop and wait for us, would stand still in the sea; that the whales, too, might stop and tread water, waiting. There was one more thing for which Mordecai did not account, which trumped all the others:

221

how a man could choose to leave his family alone for nearly ten long years. Who was to say he was on the sea at all? Or that any whales remained?

It was easy now to wonder how I could have ever believed that Papa was on his way home. I had wanted to believe, allowed myself to believe.

I reached over and picked up the book of birds and looked inside the cover; it had been published in 1836. Maybe whales had filled the sea twenty-three years ago; maybe stilts had flown over them in a shadowing host.

Mordecai opened another book, smiling, marble dust drifting from the temple's ceiling to powder his hair as he flipped the pages. He looked so happy. In his head was a misty picture of Papa sailing straight through gentle seas, a herd of sperm swimming ahead of him in a neat line within easy reach, eager for the lance and the harpoon.

I thought of the last crates my father had sent, which had held only pieces of land-bound creatures: the tusk of a pachyderm born deep in Rhodesia; the wing of a condor that, when spread, covered me. No trace of the sea, no sand, no wisp of kelp. I looked into Mordecai's earnest face.

"Cousin, have you ever considered that

Papa may have given up the sea? Think of the crates. The pachyderm's tusk. The dik-dik."

"Nonsense." Mordecai sniffed. "He might easily have purchased such specimens from other sailormen in his rovings, or in ports. He couldn't, wouldn't, forsake the worthiest of foes."

I looked across the dry little isle. The tide had by then begun to encircle it. I remembered how the latter emperors of Rome had sent their enemies and unruly daughters away to such places as this, accompanied only by one idiot or deaf-mute servant instructed to slowly starve or poison his charge.

The traced map lay on top of Mordecai's stack of books. I picked it up and lay it in my lap, smoothing the thin paper carefully. I thought of the map Mama and I had made in her room, many years ago. Her face had been lit by candles, a softer light than that of sperm oil, which burns a clear, bright white, and the fire had glowed warm in the hearth. She wore a gown of sunlit blue, and her hair lay pale and loose on her shoulders. She pulled my chair close to hers and leaned in to show me a running stitch on the sampler on my knee, patiently correcting my meandering lines of thread. Her skin smelled of sharp lavender and the piney soap she liked. She took me up on her lap and held me close, my back against her breast. I leaned and ran my fingers over what she stitched on her frame: an image of the globe, the kind that is like the skin of an orange, cut and spread flat — glossy continents of silk thread, green and sand and russet, oceans chain-stitched in long smooth waves. She spoke the names of the places to which Papa had sailed.

"The Marquesas."

She took my hand in hers and we pricked the place with her needle.

"New Caledonia. Fiji. Tonga."

On each island we made an *X* of thread.

Mordecai plucked the map from my hand, startling me from my reverie. He placed the map carefully between two pages of *Birds of Stream and Shore* and slapped it shut.

"I will make all of the arrangements. Captain Avery will carry us north. I will need to inquire as to our current speed, but certainly we will make up the lost time in a few days." He shot me a bright, triumphant look. "Then we will join your papa in pursuit of the whales! We will sail with him all the way north, to where the route of the sperm turns to circle back again: the southwest tip of Greenland, just off Qaqortoq."

He slid his stolen books into the portfolio and started to tie the strings.

Watching his hands, I began to see another pair of hands, tying not strings but a rope, large hands guiding my own through the turns of some complex knot. I had always thought the sailors on the dock taught me, but now I was sure it had been Papa. I remembered how I'd sat in his lap, his arms wrapped around me to guide my hands. The hard skin of his palms, brown arms whitened by salt. How he smelled of the salt sea with a tinge of burned tar, and a clean oily smell, like the inside of the empty shells that wash up on the beach. Running my finger along his hand, tracing a deep line on the map of his palm. Now, sitting next to Mordecai, I felt a finger touch my own palm. My heart turned over in my chest. I jumped up, rubbing my hand, and began to pace back and forth in the temple.

I wanted only to be distracted from that touch on my hand, to keep Mordecai talking. "Greenland." I tried to remember the entry in the *G* encyclopedia at home. "Isn't Greenland where the tides race in so fast that ships are thrown onto the rocks and broken to kindling?"

Mordecai eyed me sidelong.

"Actually . . . I believe you're thinking not

of Greenland but of the Bay of Fundy, in the province of Nova Scotia. They are not all that far from each other. Scarcely two thousand miles, a perfectly understandable error. The sea rises from, I believe, 2.4 feet at low tide to 23 feet at high. Astonishing. In fact, during the 12.4-hour tidal period, 115 billion tons of water flow in and out. The indigenous people, the Mi'kmaq Nation, claim that the tides are caused by a vast whale splashing in the water."

My hand was itching and sweaty. I ran down the temple steps, into the trees.

Another image came then, unbidden: the man in blue, chasing me through Rathbone House. I squeezed my eyes shut but there he was. Grasping the collar of my gown, holding me up to examine me. He had gasped at something he had felt while running a broad finger along my spine. The birthmark that floated among the freckles on my back, shaped like a ship. He'd recognized it, because he had seen and felt it years before, on infant skin. He wasn't some strange man. He was my papa.

My legs turned to water and I sat hard on the ground. The bright landscape around me turned to black.

One time when Mama let me undo her hair, when I was much younger, she told me that I was born at night while the owls were out hunting, when Papa was far out at sea. *He was so far away that it was day where he was, and he tried to look beyond the sun, into the dark behind it, to see you.* Later, in the atlas, Mordecai showed me where my father's ship had been when I was born, pointing to two lines crossing in the deepest blue deep of the Indian Ocean, on the far side of the world. I used to dream that if I could have dropped a line straight from my cradle with a lead plumb, down through the center of the earth, that the molten core might transform it into an anchor that would catch his ship and hold it fast, and I could draw him home to me, pull by pull, hand over hand.

I lay down and buried my face in my hands. Crow landed on my shoulder, pushing a soft wing against my neck. That voice in the hall, calling out for me to wait — remembered from a dream, I had thought. Bawling out my name from the sea, as Mordecai and I struggled to get away. I must have heard it at least once before. My father must have visited me, to know the ship that floated on my back, must have spoken my name at least once for me to remember the sound of his voice.

I didn't recognize him that night on the

walk. He hadn't known me either, at first. Maybe he was shocked at the way I looked, not like Mama but like one of the old Rathbones, and thought I was someone else's child. Or surprised that I was so old and still so small.

After a while I walked slowly back to the temple and sat on a step, staring down at the map, which Mordecai had laid aside while he eagerly paged through other books. On the right of the map, across the Atlantic, only a narrow strip of the western coast of all the great expanse of Africa was visible. I wished I could see farther into the interior, could slip under the border and find some dark and coastless place. I wished Papa had gone there and stayed there, far from the ocean, far from the walk where he rutted Mama and left again. And not just once. Mordecai said he had spied on them many times over the years. Papa had been in the house again and again and never stayed, never spoke to me. Why had he come back now? I wished that he had stayed away altogether and found a desert whose dry swells would make another kind of sea, one from which he could never sail again.

I knew then that I must tell Mordecai about Papa. That he had found his uncle after all, not on some distant misty ship but in Rathbone House. I would crush Mordecai's triumph at having discovered Papa's true and noble path.

What would he say when I told him that the man in blue was not some mysterious stranger but Benadam Gale himself? It must have been hard enough for Mordecai to think that Mama had put him in the attic so that her husband wouldn't know of her adultery. But there was no Captain Tayles. I couldn't think why Mama would have called Papa that. Mordecai must have misheard.

Mama had no real reason to have put Mordecai in the attic and left him there, alone. And his uncle Benadam knew and didn't care. Or maybe he was ignorant, since he never visited either Mordecai or me. It was hard to say which was worse.

Mordecai snatched the map away, prattling on again about longitudes and latitudes and the details of his route. Through his drone I heard a clipping sound and saw a movement on the other side of the temple. A man knelt there among the fallen columns, snipping the tufts of grass that sprouted between the paving stones with a pair of shears. Rather than a gardener's smock, he wore a short toga such as the Greeks wore, and on his head a garland woven of mountain laurel. He lifted his face to us and I saw by the white cast of his irises that he was blind.

"Visitors, am I right? I'd know your voices, otherwise. Family never comes anymore, they're usually at that Chinee gewgaw now. This one was always my favorite, so I keep it up. It doesn't take much to keep it in trim." I watched him work. With his free hand he constantly felt what he couldn't see. He didn't clip the tufts of grass smooth but worked to make them more unkempt. After a few minutes he put aside his shears and lifted a basket full of dead leaves, scattering them over the stones. "The Italian Grotto, though" — he gestured with his shears back toward the main island, toward a dark opening in a cluster of jagged rocks near the shore — "I've let that go. Never liked crawling around in them caves. Too damp." He stood to feel along a twist of the vine entwining a column, his fingers running over a few wizened fruits. "Besides, I'm fond of the olives. Though there's few enough I can coax out of this soil, and the birds take most all of them."

"Birds? What sort of birds?" Mordecai's head snapped up.

The gardener jerked his head back over his shoulder, toward a tall poplar nearby; among its branches I could see dark forms

230

and hear munching sounds and low cackles. "Oh. Those." Mordecai snorted and returned to his map.

Crow, who had been napping on my shoulder, was now wide awake and uneasy, shifting from foot to foot, speaking to himself in a low chatter, and flicking his wings. From between the branches of the poplar a large glossy crow emerged, in its beak a fat olive, and stepped onto a low bough that began to bounce. A female, I thought. Crow hopped down from my shoulder, snatched a lizard from a tuft of grass, and flew to an unbroken stretch of pediment at the top of the temple, along which he began to strut, the lizard dangling from his beak.

The gardener clutched his vine. "This is all they've left me. Not even a jar's worth."

Mordecai looked up with an absent air. "It is simple enough to keep them away. You need only scatter the droppings of a natural rival, such as the starling, or the jackdaw, any of the *Gracula,* on the stones, and they will keep well away from your vines."

The man rose, brushed his hands on his toga, and made his way along the columns to where Mordecai sat. He felt for Mordecai's hand, grasped it, and pumped vigorously. "Sir, I'm very grateful. Very grateful

231

indeed." Mordecai, looking a little startled, smiled, then turned back to his book.

Crow flew up to join the female on her branch, whether in hope of an olive or her favors I wasn't sure.

"Beg pardon, I couldn't help overhearing, sir. You mentioned looking for a Captain Gale? I may be able to lend you a hand."

Mordecai waved the gardener away impatiently. "No, no, thank you, there is no need, I have his bearings exactly." He peered closely at the red line on his drawing and poked at it with a dry twig. "Let me see . . . he has by now passed Wellfleet, perhaps is even now looking into Cape Cod Bay." He went back to his map, chuckling to himself.

The gardener felt for my arm and led me down the temple steps, away from Mordecai. "Beg pardon, miss," he said in a low voice, "but Wellfleet ain't in it. Captain Gale, he's on an island just up the coast. Not a morning's sail away."

My heart slammed in my chest.

"Benadam Gale," I said.

"Yes, yes, Benadam Gale. My people live out on the peninsula, a few miles inland from the island. Benadam, that's the name. All the Gales used to live there. My brother mentioned seeing him on Arcady when he passed, let me see . . . a month ago, give or take."

"Arcady?"

I was sure I had misheard. He couldn't mean the island of Mama's bedtime stories.

"Lovely place. Tall bluffs, I remember, rosy pink. Never seen rocks that color before; wish I could see them now. Pine and balsam thick as Eden, and a waterfall springing right off the cliffs into the sea."

He began to scratch out a map on a paving stone with the point of his shears, feeling along the line with his hand, warning me of the shoals and explaining the channels, speaking of how he had known the coast and all the islands from boyhood, before his eyes failed.

"Yes, Gale was there, on Arcady. My brother used to see them, Gale and his boy, coming and going. Whaling. Didn't mention the boy this time, though, wonder if he was along?" The gardener stopped his scratching for a moment and tilted his head up at me. "Mr. Gale a friend of yours?"

A face swam up in the air, so bright I blinked: a young boy's face, ruddy and forthright, green eyes shining, so near I put my hand out to touch his cheek. His lips were moving, but no sound came. The image shimmered for an instant, then wavered

233

and disappeared.

I turned away, my hand over my mouth, waiting for my breath to slow. I felt again as I had felt that first night when I heard his song sound out true and clear. My wrist felt suddenly bare. My hand went to my wrist, but my brother's bracelet wasn't there. I had been wearing it since we left Rathbone House and had shown it to Mordecai on the *Able,* but couldn't remember having noticed it since then.

I questioned the gardener eagerly about the boy he had seen with Papa, asking when he had seen him, what he had looked like, was there anything else he could recall. The old man tried to call up a clearer memory, then shook his head slowly.

From across the water came the soft slap of oars. The dinghy, rowed by the mate, was on its way to fetch Mordecai and me. It was nearly twilight, and the *Able* hovered out in the sound.

"Come, Mercy. Greenland ho!" Mordecai caressed his map, folded it, put it in his breast pocket, and began to gather his things. He had heard nothing of my conversation with the gardener.

Mordecai hoisted his bags and we said our farewells to the gardener. The water that encircled the little temple had grown with the tide from a narrow ribbon to a gurgling stream; we jumped over it and headed back to the main island.

Installed once again on the *Able*'s deck, we looked over the rail, back at the Stark Archipelago, squinting against the sun that hung low in a dusky sky. With the making tide, the temple on its mound had become a true island. The gardener had moved on, to tend some other Stark folly.

I felt Mordecai's eye on me. Glancing up, I found him looking at me curiously. I held the image of my brother close and said nothing. Something about the cant of Mordecai's head reminded me sharply of Roderick and of the elder Starks.

"Mordecai."

"Hmmm?" He was deep in his stack of books again.

"Why did the Starks react that way to the Rathbone name?"

Mordecai, looking up, sniggered. "If the old ones had seen me it would have been far worse. They detest the Rathbones."

"But I don't understand. Why should they hate us?"

He put his nose back in his book.

I pulled the book from his hands and held it behind my back. He started to reach for it, then his eyes drifted to the stack of books he had not yet touched. He picked up the next and was instantly absorbed.

Captain Avery, who had been in the foretop with his glass, slid down a backstay. He pulled a handkerchief from his pocket and mopped his face. Leaning on the taffrail, he looked back at the Stark house and shook his head.

"A handsome family, they were, you have only to look at those old paintings. But all the looks drained out and never came back again."

I looked back, too. The main island was by then shadowy, though the house, high on its hill, glowed in rosy light from the setting sun. Through the trees I saw a movement at a window high up in the house. A curtain moved aside, a tall figure stood looking out: Roderick, watching us sail away. I saw him as clearly as though he were beside me on the deck. He stood stiff and still in the jade-green robe, his powdered wig askew above his pale face.

"All hard to look at. Not like your mother."

I had pulled out Mordecai's journal and was attempting to draw my brother as I now knew he looked, while the image was still strong in my mind. I looked sharply up at the captain's words.

"Captain Avery, do you know my mother?"

Avery looked at me, startled, for once speechless, though only for a moment.

"No, no. That is to say, I've seen her up in the house, just from deck, you know, close enough to know she's a handsome woman." He mopped his face again, then folded his handkerchief and folded again until it was a tiny square, which he popped in his pocket.

I drew him by the arm along the railing, away from Mordecai.

"Was there ever . . . did you ever see her with a boy?" I whispered.

"Boy? Don't remember any boy." Avery rubbed his chin, hitched his pants, and looked up at the rigging. "That topsail could use another reef or two. I'll lend you a hand," he yelled to the mate. He ran up the rigging and passed behind a stretched sail and so out of view.

I went back to Mordecai and bent over the map with him, tracing our route north toward Greenland, a route that would take us past an island with tall pink cliffs.

Something shifted in the pocket of my skirt. I reached in and pulled out the bundle of envelopes I had stuffed in my pocket. I had meant to put them back but in the rush had forgotten. The writing on the outermost envelope was too faded to make out. I pulled out a letter of several pages and unfolded it. The salutation read "Dear Mother." I turned to the last page; the signature, in a tall, elegant script, read "Lydia."

Avery's voice floated down from the foretop.

"Now, let me see . . . the old man, the one with the mustachios, Percival Stark? His aunts, I believe, married into the Rathbones. So that would be, what, three generations back. There were three girls, now what were they called? Lydia. Lydia was the eldest . . ."

Captain Avery talked on. As with my great-great-aunt's account of Hepzibah, it was an incomplete tale, one whose bare stretches I would later weave with all that I found in Lydia's letters.

I called Crow to me and sent him off, over the water.

CHAPTER NINE:
THE GOLDEN GIRLS

*{in which the Stark sisters
meet their matches}*

1800

Lydia Stark didn't at first notice the unfamiliar boat. Her eyes were fixed instead on the dock where her brothers' ship was making ready to sail on the morning tide. The *Venture* had begun loading before dawn. She and her sisters had been watching since first light, leaning over the parapet at the end of the lawn, looking down at the harbor.

The three sisters stood long and golden in the warm light slanting across the water. The skirts of their gowns rustled and crackled in the still air, silk gowns the same hue of gold as their hair. A gift from their brothers, from their last voyage to the Indies, the silk had been sent to tailors on the mainland some weeks before, and the finished gowns had arrived only yesterday. Each time the sisters moved, the silk sent out whiffs of the spices near which it had been stored on the ship: nutmeg and cardamom, bitter mace and vanilla, wafting through the clean air of the rising tide.

The strange boat floated in the little cove below the lawn, under the willows along the shore that stretched their limbs out over the water. Lydia shaded her eyes with one arm against the low sun, but in the shadows of branches could see only dark forms in the boat, hear only the creak of wet wood. She wondered vaguely why it lingered there. The harbor was filled with vessels, all coming or going but for this one. She turned away, back toward the *Venture.*

Stevedores hurried back and forth on the dock, loading the last provisions for the voyage. Sailors swarmed over the rigging against a slate sky. The deep-laden brig, a sturdy and well-founded two-master, rode low in the water, heavy with pine milled from local woodlands. On its next crossing to the Indies the ship would also carry oak and maple from the great forests to the north. Lemuel Stark, Lydia's father, had in recent years made a name for fair dealing and swift passages, and word had spread; traders in timber and fur had begun to bypass larger ports to stop instead in the

Stark Archipelago.

Lydia watched her brothers cut across the crowded dock, each with a crate on his shoulder. It was easy to find them; their fair heads rode high above those of other men. All the Starks shared the same long bones and sunlit beauty. Silas and Caleb had been more at sea than at home since their voices had broken and had taken readily not only to living afloat but to trading. Lydia read in their quick movements and ready bearing their excitement about departing. They would leave not a few girls sighing for them when they sailed. The brothers, crossing the gangway to get another load from the dock, caught sight of Lydia and waved.

Grandfather Stark, too, was there among the hurrying men, his own golden head gone white but still held as high as those of his grandsons. Solomon Stark, tall and straight, walked slowly around the perimeter of the ship, running his hand along the railing, checking seams, gazing up with a critical eye at the masts. He had built the brig himself a dozen years ago, much of it with his own hands, when the harbor was a boatyard and the tight, swift ships were built by the Starks for other men. He leaned over the port railing and gazed at the long sheds that lined the dock. Stacked earlier that morning with corded timber, the sheds were now empty but for the sharp lingering smell of the pine planks, all of which had been loaded on the *Venture*. Solomon Stark remembered when he and his sons and crew had worked the wood in those sheds, had built the great ribs and spars, not passed the wood on to other men. Now ships and harbor alike belonged to the family, but the ships were made in distant boatyards by other men's hands.

Lydia forgot the strange boat for a time, talking with her sisters, comparing their latest beaux — for the Stark daughters were much sought after — and wondering what gift her brothers would bring from the islands this time. Though she already owned a crested cockatoo, Lydia longed for one of the bright-plumed birds that lived higher among the palms: a bird of paradise or a blue macaw. The creak of an oarlock brought her eyes back to the boat. A breeze stirred the branches of the willow and between the leaves she saw green eyes staring at her. Along the side of the hull six oars hung dripping above the water.

Lydia frowned and glared at the boat. It was of a type she had never seen before: small but broad, single-masted, and pointed at both ends. She wouldn't have recognized it as a whaleboat. Her parents had distanced their daughters from the mercenary taint of the sea and, though she had viewed many other types of craft docked below the house or passing through the bay, no whaling ship had ever docked in the Stark Archipelago before.

She leaned and whispered in her sisters' ears; both covered their mouths with their hands, giggling. She pulled a little notebook and a pencil from her purse, scribbled on the paper, tore it off, and folded it.

"Boy," Lydia called out.

She leaned far over the railing, looking down toward the boat, smiling. The light on the water reflected up onto the gold silk, rippled over her face, and lit her hair. She stretched out her arm and held the folded slip of paper over the water, waving it from side to side. In the shadows under the willow the oars all dipped together in one motion and the boat slid noiselessly toward her. The backs of six youths emerged one by one into the sunlight. As they rowed closer she saw that all were small in stature, and soundly made. She wondered if they might be islanders from the South Seas, about whom her brothers had spoken. All wore formal suits of black stuff that were too tight for them. The fabric strained

across their shoulders. On some jackets the
seams opened as the rowers stroked back
and forth. Long dark hair sprang out from
their heads, streaked with sun-white that
glinted each time their heads dipped to pull.

As they glided closer the boy on the seat
in the bow shipped his oars, stood smoothly,
and turned toward Lydia. His skin, browned
by sun and salt, had a coppery sheen. His
eyes did not meet hers. He bowed slightly,
knuckled his brow, and reached up for the
slip of paper in Lydia's hand, but before he
touched it she let it fall, spinning, toward
the water. The boy reached and plucked it
from the air. The rowers lifted their oars for
a moment and the boat glided slowly past,
below the parapet where the sisters stood.
The boy unfolded the paper. He looked
down at the words and then turned his face
up to Lydia. Her heart jumped. His eyes
were of a startling green, unblinking, with
no whites showing around the irises, as
though the sea had filled the sockets. She
wondered if he was not able to read. He
folded the paper and slid it into his breast
pocket, his eyes still on Lydia as the oars
dipped again and the boat gathered speed,
heading for the docks.

Lydia leaned over the balustrade, holding
the little notebook against her heart. "Will

you be mine?" she called out after the boat, laughing. "Will you be mine?" The sisters leaned their heads together, laughing, their hair spilling down, the gold of their gowns pouring out across the water.

The boy holding the note still stood in the bow, looking steadily back at Lydia. His head turned sharply toward the water. He leaned over the side and his arm darted out, in a bright arc of spray, pulling a fat gleaming fish from the water, one finger hooked into its mouth. He grasped it by the tail, beat its head against the side of the boat, and tossed it into the stern.

Lemuel Stark, too, was watching the ship make ready, glancing out the window between bouts of signing bills of lading and relaying last instructions to his sons as they came and went from the house. The door of his office stood open to the great hall at the front of the house. The high-ceilinged space was awash in light from tall windows all around. Sea air gusted through doors and windows, billowing the long white curtains, wafting across fresh-scrubbed floors and over the few simple, solid pieces of furniture that smelled of beeswax and shone in the fresh light. Servants and seamen crossed back and forth, their footsteps ringing, voices carrying clear. Lemuel's wife ran down the stairs clutching her skirts, trailed by a maid carrying stacks of linens for her sons that had yet to be packed in the trunks that stood open by the front door. Lemuel looked up at the sound of his daughters' laughter; three streaks of gold flashed past his office, then the east parlor door slammed. Sighing, he turned back to his ledger and scanned a column of figures.

Lemuel had been proud to provide for his daughters a future free of the hard labor of his own mother's and sisters' lives, lives passed cooking and cleaning for a family of shipwrights and busy from dawn until long after dark. Earlier generations of Stark women had spent their days standing over tubs of boiling potatoes or steaming clothes, patching up gouges from mallets and chisels on their men's hands, their fair faces (the Starks had always possessed great beauty) roughened and red, old too soon. Lemuel's daughters knew no toil but scales on the clavichord or sketching under the eye of a drawing master. Lemuel missed the days when his daughters would not have run past his office but instead run to him, to be hugged and praised. Perhaps it was only that they were older. It was natural that they would be less attached to him, seeing him so seldom in recent years, what with his busy days. But when he was with his daughters, at dinner or in the parlor, he sometimes felt a cool, disapproving eye on the way he held his knife or how loudly he laughed. His daughters had grown from sweet, biddable children to haughty young women. These days he was more relieved than disappointed when they ran past his door without stopping.

Putting aside his papers and rubbing his eyes, Lemuel stood from his desk and looked out at the *Venture*. The crew had completed watering and ballast, and the decks were cleared. His sons stood by the wheel, leaning over the binnacle, studying their charts. He was proud of Silas and Caleb, pleased with the profits that had been growing modestly but steadily for the past five years.

Lemuel had shifted the livelihood of the Starks from shipbuilding to trade five years ago. He had made the decision after a visit to Boston, to deliver the ship that he and his crew of shipwrights had spent the previous year constructing. He had been well satisfied with the new design: three-masted, square-rigged, carrying more canvas than any he had built before, trim and fast. He was eager to log its sailing time to Boston.

The voyage that usually took a full day and night in fine weather, with the cutter's prow driving the sea high and white along its flanks throughout the passage, had this time required, in equally fine weather and similar winds, only seventeen hours. He had proudly reported the time to the cutter's buyer as he signed over its papers, and the man had been most pleased to hear it. As Lemuel strolled the Boston docks all that afternoon, waiting for the far slower sloop that had followed the cutter to take him home, he watched the loading and unloading of great shipments of goods: crates of cocoa, sugar, tobacco, barrels of molasses arriving from the Indies; salted cod, baled lumber, and textiles on their way abroad. On one dock vast blocks of ice breathed out a cloud of cold, waiting to ship to the West Indies — to cool pretty girls under swaying palm trees, the man who loaded it said with a laugh. When Lemuel heard the prices such goods were fetching in distant ports, he began to grasp the true value of fast ships such as the one he had just built. But it was not in the ships themselves that Lemuel saw his future; it was in the swift passages they enabled, the quick wits with which fortunes were being made in months, rather than the long years his trade required. He had never been wholly at ease as a shipwright, had always felt an urging toward bolder, brighter endeavors, and on the Boston dock that day he saw his chance. He determined to lay down his mallets and planes and take up bargaining and bills of lading. Now, sitting at his desk, he scanned the bill he held in his hand, well pleased with the list of figures he saw.

His mind touched on the *Challenge,* captained by Ephraim, his eldest son, due in from northern waters with a cargo of seal skins. The furs, in high demand for capes and chapeaux among the ladies of Europe, might prove his most lucrative shipment yet. Soon he would be able to complete the landscaping around the new house, plant box hedges and a fine allée of sapling oaks. With the proceeds from the *Venture*'s next voyage he might even be able to purchase a third brig, and tear down the last of the old boatbuilding sheds to build a new warehouse.

Deep in consideration of a fruit-tree orchard, he failed to hear a knock at the door, and when he looked up a young man was standing in front of his desk.

Lemuel assumed the lad was looking for a position on the crew; many such had been turned away in recent weeks, from fishing villages farther up the coast, though none had been as likely-looking as this youth. Lemuel noted with mild regret the boy's compact body and sure stance; he looked to have the makings of a capital bosun or master's mate. He looked, in fact, like Lemuel himself at that age, sun- and salt-toughened. It was a pity he hadn't arrived in time to be hired on. The boy's arms and hands were scarred from harpoon line and blade; Lemuel looked at his own hands, well groomed but still bearing the marks of chisel and mallet. The young man stood politely, eyes down, hands behind his back, shoulders and legs straining the seams of the suit he wore, sewn for some more slender boy.

Lemuel leaned back in his chair.

"Son, I'm afraid you're too late for this voyage. Come and see me in a month or two. I'll have something for you then, when the *Challenge* is back."

The boy made no reply. He leaned and hoisted up three fat sacks of soft sharkskin, and from the first poured out a stream of gold coins that covered the desk, spilling onto the floor.

The Stark sisters always spent their mornings in the east parlor. Since finally moving into the big new house, after having lived with an aunt on the mainland for months while it was being built, they had quickly chosen their favorite haunt. The room was full of fresh light and faced the new green lawn that rolled away to vistas of the scattered islands of the archipelago, away from the harbor that stank of fish at low tide. After months in their aunt's small, smoke-darkened house and, earlier, years in the cramped saltbox their grandfather had built, they loved running through the bright and airy rooms. Most of the house was as yet only sparsely furnished with the fine old spindle chairs and benches of hickory and oak that early Starks had hewn from trees on the property, when the bitter winter cold kept them out of the boat sheds, furnishings that had been more than adequate in the far smaller saltbox. The east parlor boasted a new spinet and window hangings of heavy linen. Delicate slipper chairs of carved and painted wood with petit-point seats stood on a thick carpet around the fireplace. Here the sisters had their music lessons, played piquet, and gossiped over their embroidery frames. They hurried in that morning to practice their lessons at the spinet; their tutor was due to arrive and none of the three had practiced enough, having given over the

251

early hours to their brothers' departure. They ran into the parlor, arms linked, laughing and arguing about who would be first at the keys. It took a few moments for them to notice that they were not alone in the room. The girls stopped short and stared.

Two of the boys from the strange boat sat on the sisters' slipper chairs by the fire. Their tight black jackets, each held closed by one strained button, were worn over striped seaman's jerseys. Sturdy bare ankles showed between stretched breeches and stiff new boots polished to a high shine, gaping wide at the tongues, too narrow for the boys' broad feet. One boy didn't look up, intent on a small block of wood he was whittling. Pale curls of wood flew; something round was shaping from his blade. The other sat erect and motionless, staring directly at Priscilla. He clutched a small white box between his hands. The whittling boy's legs swung back and forth; neither boy's boots reached the floor. Their thick dark hair, though freshly oiled and combed, leapt in waves from their heads.

Lydia strode to the hearth and stood before the boys, glaring at them.

"Who let you in here?"

The whittling boy didn't look up; curls of

252

wood continued to fly. The boy with the box glanced at Lydia, then returned his gaze to Priscilla, who colored and hid her face against Miriam, giggling.

"If you have some business with our father, you may wait in the yard until he is free." One hand on her hip, Lydia pointed with the other to the door. The boys didn't move.

Lydia turned away, smoothing down the skirt of her gown and breathing deep. She strode back and forth in front of the boys, eyeing them up and down. She stopped and turned to her sisters, a smile now lighting her face.

"Sisters, clearly these gentlemen are envoys from some foreign state. Those must be the newest fashions that they wear. I had heard that a closer-fitting silhouette was all the rage on the Continent this season but never dreamed to see it so soon!"

Priscilla and Miriam stood turned away from the boys, laughing gaily behind their hands, glancing back to see the boys' reactions. The whittling boy held up his wood to the light from the window and turned it back and forth, one eye squeezed shut, the other appraising, then returned to his work. The boy with the box continued to stare at Priscilla.

"Prissy, does he not remind you of your Phineas? Though Phineas hasn't this person's knack with pomade." She gestured at the whittler's gleaming head. "Nor his aroma." Her sisters burst into open laughter.

A screech came from the corner behind the settee. Lydia's cockatoo normally presided there on its tall gilded perch while the girls were in the room. The bird was there now but a large crow was muscling it along the rod, shouldering it sideways until the rod ran out and the cockatoo fell off the end with a screech. It flapped to a distant curtain rod and hunched there, shivering. The crow lumbered back to the center of the perch, settled its wings, and regarded Lydia.

The boy with the box rose and walked to Priscilla with a rolling gait. His head, when he arrived, reached only to the bottom of her chin, which she now lifted higher. Seen so close, he was clearly older than his size implied. Though his cheeks showed no stubble, his hands were broad and sun-dark and scarred with white. He held out the little box to Priscilla. She covered her mouth with a hand, giggling, then glanced at Lydia, who looked at her sternly and motioned *no* with her head. Priscilla hesitated, then snatched the box. It looked to be carved out of ivory; the flukes of a sperm whale were scribed on its lid. She opened the box. Inside was a lump of waxy gray matter the size of a fist. She poked it with one finger. Its surface sprang back like flesh.

The whittling boy, without getting up, put down his block of wood and knife on the floor, reached into the breast of his jacket, and pulled out a bouquet of beach roses, crushed and sodden, smelling of wet wool and low tide. He held them out to Miriam.

Besides the fishing smacks and luggers, and the usual weathered little bumboats that one might expect to see in any coastal town, that day the big island was ringed with seagoing ships at anchor: trim frigates, smart barks, and brigantines from the north. While the Stark sons and their crew hurried about, readying the *Venture* to depart, a few-score tradesmen and locals from the mainland lingered on the dock, finishing their paperwork or parading up and down the pier, enjoying the pleasantly warm morning before returning to their vessels. Young merchants from the north, city swells in swallowtail coats, their business with the Starks completed, smoked thin cheroots and sauntered along the dock or began to pack up their wares.

Few noticed the six boys in black suits, or if they did, vaguely wondered if the boys were members of some strict sect. The practiced eye of one man, a tailor, recognized their clothes as home-sewn; Patience Rathbone had made a dozen of the suits some thirty years ago for a younger, less muscled set of Rathbones to wear to Sunday mass, before she knew that for a Rathbone a ship was the only church. Eventually she'd put the unworn suits away in a trunk, where they had rested until Bow-Oar retrieved them for this excursion.

Bow-Oar's eyes ranged past the stacked goods on the pier, over the townsmen and merchants in their fine suits, the trim frigates with sides fresh-painted in stripes of crimson over gray or white on gleaming black. Though he had sailed five seas and viewed the verdant or barren coasts of distant continents from the deck of the *Misistuck,* he had seldom stepped ashore, all his mind and body devoted only to the whale. Nor had he visited his own country's great eastern ports, with their teeming harbors towering with trade goods. In all his years at sea, Moses had never permitted men from other vessels to board Rathbone ships. He did not want his sons tainted by the ways of other whalers.

Naiwayonk, though it lay halfway between Boston and the city of New York, might have been hidden deep in a forest or stranded on a vast and empty prairie, so little did its men interact with the world.

Bow-Oar stared at a few strolling swells in their cutaway jackets and buff waistcoats. They wore tall shining boots and doeskin gloves. His brothers had meantime stopped at a table full of bottles of pickled fruits and vegetables, boxed teas and tinned biscuits. Third-Oar lifted a string of sausages high and took a cautious nibble, then began to devour it link by link. His brothers snatched strings of their own and stuffed sausages into their mouths. When Third-Oar lay a gold eagle down in payment, the man behind the table widened his eyes at so large a coin; he began to count out dollars in change.

Bow-Oar continued along the dock, taking it all in. Until that day, the only items he had ever purchased were those ship's supplies not made by the family or found in the sea: tools to shape the wood shafts of their spears, sturdy boots, hemp for the rope walk. Now he saw barrels packed with bolts of fine cloth of every hue; pallets filled with furniture of oak and mahogany, stacks of dishes, glass, silver. He felt a hunger he had never known before. He began to buy.

Lydia burst into her father's office, the ivory box in her hands.

"Father. You must come this instant. There are . . . people in the parlor who do not belong there. You must come and put them out of the house."

Lydia's father wouldn't meet her eye. He was pushing something quickly into the drawer of his desk, something gleaming. When she moved close, he sat back in his chair. His eyes darted to the corner of the room. The boy from the boat, the one she had given the note, was slouched against the wall, hands behind his back, one leg crossed over the other, looking out the window as Lydia spoke.

Lydia stared at the boy, then back at her father. She didn't know what had passed between them but she felt uneasy. She couldn't have understood. She had not been there to hear the boy speak to her father about what he could do with the bags full of gold brought that day, with more to follow. She was not there when, as the boy spoke, his voice low and rhythmic, her father's face changed as the words took hold. He spoke of things that Lemuel realized were already in his mind. The boy had only found them and drawn them out where they wanted to be, but once in the air they grew. Lemuel's mind slowly turned to grander plans: He would be able to furnish the house as his wife wished and better — yes, he thought, as was proper for a man of his standing. He could dredge and widen the harbor and build larger ships with deeper drafts. Not the mere three he had dared dream of but a fleet of ships that would enable longer, more profitable voyages. Voyages as far as the Orient. He would buy, too, the last of the islets that made up the archipelago, so that all of the chain, which until then had been known by the casual names the sailors gave them, names suggested by their shape or size or what grew on them — Little Cedar, Black Cat, Flea Bite, Bilberry, Willow Rock — would bear instead the name Stark.

Lydia looked slowly from the boy to her father. Lemuel would still not return her gaze. He turned back to the window. Lydia looked out, too; the *Venture* had weighed anchor and was skimming eastward, all its canvas aloft.

When she looked back at the boy, he was fingering a piece of paper in his breast pocket, staring at her with those too-green eyes. She recognized her notepaper, pale blue with gilt edges. She began to understand, though she didn't yet believe. She looked down at the ivory box in her hands, opened it, pulled out the gray lump, and flung it at her father. It struck his chest and fell to the floor. He leaned and picked it up, turned it in his hand. He had seen fragments of ambergris before, washed up on the strand or brought back from the open sea by sailors, but never of such a prodigious size. It was said to be vomited up by the sperm whale in its death flurry and was prized by perfumers for its fixative properties, by vintners for its flavor, and by spinsters for its potency in love elixirs. The lump in his hand was worth, ounce for ounce, more than the gold that now filled the drawers of his desk.

Lemuel looked out the window, to where his sons' sails were edging over the horizon. When the ship was hull down, he turned to the boy. The boy moved from the corner to stand in front of Lemuel's desk. Lemuel wrapped the lump of ambergris in his handkerchief and stuffed it into his breast pocket. He wiped his oily palm on his waistcoat, reached across the desk, and took the boy's hand.

By the time the boat was out on the full

blue circle of the sound with no land in sight, Lydia's sisters fell quiet. When they had traveled far enough so that the boat, seen from shore, would have been only a dark smudge against the bright rim of the sea, and still her sisters sobbed and struggled, the boys had bound them.

They hadn't needed to wait so long. Lemuel was not watching his daughters disappear. He would later tell friends and business associates, when questioned, how his daughters had been sent to study abroad. He would instruct his wife to refer all such questions to him. In a few months he would host a dinner party to commemorate the christening of the first of his new fleet, a fine two-hundred-ton frigate purchased straight from the yard at Bath. In the months and years that followed, Lemuel's friends and their wives would ask after the Stark daughters less frequently, would be told the girls had stayed abroad and married, and eventually, busy with their own interests, forget them. The friends' sons would remember the daughters longer but settle in the end for drabber girls from inland families.

Lydia's father had made no attempt to reason with her. He had told her, standing in his office that day, that her future was his decision alone, that her mother of course agreed with him, that he should not have spoiled his daughters so. She had been too angry to listen then. She felt no real fear until the shore disappeared and her stomach began to rise and fall with the waves. She had never been on a boat of any kind. Now, standing in the stern, staring back toward her house, shame rose up and overcame her seasickness, shame for her sisters' craven behavior. As the eldest, she was used to setting the example for Priscilla and Miriam, and proud when they followed it. But though she had said nothing as the boat pulled away, determined to give nothing away, her sisters had begun wailing before they left the house.

The boys had trussed Miriam and Priscilla head to foot, taking seven turns around each girl as they did with their hammocks to keep them neat and out of the way while they chased the whale. Each sister lay in front of the boy to whom she had been allotted, tucked crosswise between bench and bench. Bow-Oar had brought the length of rope Moses had kept on a peg by his high blue bed; each brother had wound the rope around his girl's hand and his own, as Moses had always done with each of his wives.

Miriam had fallen asleep on the boards beneath Second-Oar's feet; Priscilla lay and stared, her eyes following Third-Oar's arm as it stroked back and forth. Their gowns formed golden pools in the bottom of the boat, drifting in sea spray and bilge water, among coiled ropes and bailing buckets. After they were finally quiet the boys had loosened the ropes and freed their hands. The sky, clear when they set out at mid-morning, had thickened with cloud, the sea gone dark and rough. Miriam's boy had draped his jacket over her and swathed her head in his striped shirt to keep her fair skin from the sun. All the boys had taken off their jackets and shirts and boots, and their broad bronze backs moved now with ease, their toes spread wide to grip the boards. Third-Oar murmured to Priscilla, hummed a low song, now and again letting go his oar to pet her hair. He wore a clamshell on his face, tied around the back of his head with strands of sea jerky, over the place where his nose had been before the thrash of a fluke had taken it. Lydia watched Fourth-Oar reach forward, toward Priscilla's breast. Third-Oar turned and slashed at the hand with his oar.

Lydia's legs ached from standing, trying to balance on the thickening swells, though her stomach was settling. She stood in the stern, just behind Bow-Oar. Each time he drew his oar in a stroke he leaned back and upset her balance. Finally she sank down and sat in the hull. She was afraid, but her sisters' stronger fear helped steady her. She wouldn't let these boys overpower her. She wouldn't think about how easily her father had let her go, how he'd waited until her brothers were well away. She looked forward, to where Bow-Oar stood. Rather than row as his brothers did, all facing her, he stood in the bow, never turning his head to look at her, always facing their destination, still invisible over the rim of the horizon. He had not stripped off his shirt like the others and wore, she now noticed, a different suit of clothes; he must have bought it from someone on the docks. It was a suit somewhat like those her father wore, of fine blue twill, though her father's were soft and this one was new and stiff. It fit the boy well across his deep chest and around his strong legs, and his trousers were of a correct length. His thick dark hair was sleeked down and caught in a neat club. His smooth cheeks shone. She caught a drift of witch hazel on the breeze.

Lydia couldn't see where they were headed, sea and sky having merged into a cold gray mist. It began to rain. She looked down at her gown. The rain didn't matter; the silk had already been drenched by salt spray, and had great dark spots of oil from bilge water. Among old wooden tubs full of coiled rope, lantern kegs, and floats were stacks of fresh packages tied with paper and string and wrapped in oilcloth to keep them dry.

Bow-Oar pulled another such package from the inside pocket of his jacket and unwrapped it. He drew out a gleaming arc of metal and mirror that made his brothers murmur, backing away and shaking their heads. A harsh croak sounded from above; from the mast top a crow swooped down and tried to seize the glittering object, to which Bow-Oar held fast, swatting away the crow with his free hand. The crow veered off, cawing, and winged away ahead of them, up and into the clouds. Lydia had seen her own brothers use such an instrument, raising it to the horizon on the *Venture* and marking down measurements; a sextant, she thought it was called. Bow-Oar now turned it in his hands, examining its parts, adjusting. Soon he was holding it up to the horizon toward which they sailed.

Moses Rathbone lay in his high blue bed,

his head turned toward the light where he knew the *Misistuck* was docked. He saw only its ghost through once-bright eyes, their green scorched by sun and sea to nearly clear. His sun-browned skin, though still smooth, had stiffened so hard that if struck it might have clanged or rung as hollow as a sea-turtle shell. His limbs waved slowly, barely stirring the blue blankets. His breath came in slow gasps.

Moses had not sailed in eight years. Though he was a man of only fifty-odd years, his long exposure to sea and salt, wind and whale, had worn him down to a twist of driftwood. He had poured forth all his strength into his sons and had little left for himself.

One day he mistook the rising sun for the disk of the moon, it seemed so pale and cool. Another day he'd remarked on the constancy of the fog to one of his sons, who replied in surprise, "Why, Father, we've had nothing but sun." The boy had clapped him on the back and laughed at his joke. Though his vision was failing, he got by easily enough; he knew every part of his ship, the *Misistuck,* without his eyes and knew his boys by their voices and smell and the way they moved. When the lookout spotted a sperm, Moses had no need to see its spout to know where it breached and where it would sound again; he might have easily sent the harpoon home with his eyes closed. But his limbs were too stiff; his arm would no longer answer.

He lay thinking of that day long ago when he had killed his first whale. He had envisioned a single ship, manned by his sons, a fine brig with a full set of sails. Enough sons to be sure that no whale would be lost, no villager would go hungry or be cold when winter came.

But one ship had not been enough for his sons. The wives produced a steady stream of boys, enough so that, though some didn't return from sea, many were left to vie for places on the whaleboats. All were reluctant to be left behind on the ship or, worse still, left at home, waiting out the months until it was their turn to sail. The sons clamored for more ships, and more ships Moses had given them; there was gold in plenty to buy more. On and off, staggered between voyages, Naiwayonk harbor held a pair of brigs — the *Sassacus* and the *Misistuck* — and a square-rigged bark, the *Paquatauoq,* all deep-drafted vessels capable of ever-longer voyages, to the Pacific Ocean, the Caribbean, and the Indian Ocean. In the Thousand-Barrel Years some thirty sons slept in Rathbone House.

But the whale was always honored, as Moses had planned. Once the oil was rendered and the barrels filled, the body stripped of all that the men could use, the carcass went to the sharks. At the end of the hunt, Rathbone ships always lingered one last night at sea, to give thanks for the hunt. A great iron try-pot filled with the whale's blood and organs boiled on the deck, the fire lighting up the ship as if it were burning — red and gold, the sails white flames above. By the whale's light the men sat in a circle and, first setting aside Moses's portion, cut up and shared the whale's raw heart, big as a man. They raised their voices to the sky and to the dark waters around their ship, and gave thanks for a successful hunt, the flames a beacon of their arrival.

Moses had been expecting the arrival of the *Misistuck,* aware of its approach long before it was finally seen, hull up on the horizon, the night before. There was no fire, no beacon; the decks were cold and dark. The ship had docked early that morning after a voyage of eighteen months, its stern trailing a mile of weed from weeks becalmed in the southern latitudes, its hold two layers deep in sperm oil, every barrel filled. Moses was impatient for news of the voyage. He longed to see Bow-Oar, the *Misistuck*'s captain, and to find out why no fire had been lit. But no sooner had the ship docked than Bow-Oar left again. While other brothers streamed into the house, laughing and jostling each other up the ladders and through the door, eager for fresh food and dry beds, Bow-Oar was setting off in one of the ship's whaleboats with his boat crew, none of the six having set foot on dry land, though all had been a year and a half at sea.

Bow-Oar had been less attentive to his father in recent years, in those few weeks when he had been home between trips, but Moses knew that his son was busy with his many duties. He had always been Moses's favorite and closest to him in skill. Like his father, Bow-Oar could kill a sperm with one strike of the spear. Other sons could occasionally kill with one thrust, but not every time as Bow-Oar did. As the surviving eldest, many older brothers having gone to the whale, he was responsible, too, for overseeing the training of green whalers. Moses knew that he had not come ashore with the rest of the returning crew and had been absent all day. He was pleased to finally hear Bow-Oar's step, more so because none of his other sons had paid their respects since returning nor had they brought any offering of the whale.

Heavy steps approached along the hall. When Moses turned his head, Bow-Oar was standing at the foot of his bed, something long and golden draped over his shoulders.

Maybe here, at last, was his offering. Bow-Oar stepped close to the high blue bed; Moses craned over the edge and reached to touch Lydia's dangling arm.

The girl didn't feel right. She was not like the other wives. She had no mineral tang, no whiff of sulfur, and no salt at all. Her eggs were not fat and thickly bobbling but lay in slender yellow threads.

He beckoned his son close, so that his voice, a hoarse whisper, could be heard.

"This pale thing? This is what you have brought me?"

Bow-Oar stepped back, clutching Lydia tighter at wrist and ankle.

"No, Father, this one is for me."

Moses drew his arm away and sank back in his bed.

"Where is my offering, my proper portion?"

Bow-Oar hesitated. It wasn't too late then. He could have chosen to explain it all to his father.

He had driven his men hard all the way home. The whaling grounds of the South

Atlantic were thick with sperm, but before the *Misistuck*'s two thousand barrels were all filled with oil, Bow-Oar had decided to start north. He planned to fill the remaining empty barrels — a hundred or so, a few whales' worth — on the voyage home. They had been at sea for sixteen months, and Bow-Oar longed to get back.

He could not wait any longer to claim his golden prize. He had first spied Lydia and her sisters nearly two years ago, on a trawling expedition for fresh wives. He had glimpsed them walking on the grounds of the Stark house — from a league away with his keen eyes — and had thought of little else since. He would go back for them the moment the *Misistuck* returned from this voyage.

But the ship met with no sperm on the way north. Though Bow-Oar knew that the whales were always scarce in the North Atlantic at that time of year, he thought they would have luck enough; the sea had always answered him. When they were two or three days from Naiwayonk and still had found no sperm, he began to worry. No Rathbone ship was allowed to return without every barrel filled; none ever had. Finally, a day away from home, the *Misistuck*'s lookout spied a small pod of sperm: three young

271

whales. Bow-Oar stared out at the spouts, considering.

Moses had taught his sons to always leave two whales alive in any pod, however small, and to take only mature sperm, leaving the young ones so they could make more whales. But these three sleek young whales, coursing smoothly along not a league away, were easy picking; they should yield just enough oil to fill the last of the barrels.

What would it really matter? If he stayed at sea, looking for a larger pod, for older whales, it could take weeks. And Moses wouldn't know. If he still came on board when the ship docked, as he used to do, and checked the barrels, Moses would have sniffed out the difference, smelled the clean light oil of the young whales threading through the heavier oil and known what Bow-Oar had done. But not anymore. Moses never left his bed.

Bow-Oar could not wait. He would drain a herd of too-young sperm if it meant reaching the golden girls a minute sooner.

He went out with his crew to kill the three whales, himself harpooning the first. Instead of lingering one more night at sea, the men towed the dead whales to burn in the great shed, unused since whaling ships had begun to carry their own tryworks twenty years ago. By the time the *Misistuck* docked, her brick hearths had long been cold and swept clean. The men, busy with the whales, had lit no beacon of arrival. No whale's heart had been set aside and shared out. The ship had docked, and Bow-Oar had hurried away to the Stark Archipelago.

Now, standing in front of his father, Bow-Oar could have chosen to confess. But he was ashamed of killing the three young whales, ashamed of lighting no beacon and bringing no offering.

If he had confessed, Moses would have chastised him, probably punished him, how would be hard to say — no Rathbone son had dared disobey his father before. But, after his anger abated, Moses might have given his son a chance to redeem himself; he loved Bow-Oar enough to forgive much. Bow-Oar might have felt relieved and grateful, and returned, chastened, to the old ways.

But Bow-Oar did not confess. When Moses asked for his offering, his son said, "I have it, Father. I will get it for you."

Bow-Oar walked out into the hall, carrying his burden carefully. Lydia hung from his shoulders as though dead. She had, in the end, given in to seasickness, barely stirring when Bow-Oar hoisted her and slung her from his neck as they docked. The whaleboat in which they had arrived only a few minutes ago was already all a-tanto, hung from davits on the deck of the *Misis-tuck,* swabbed, and flogged dry. A fresh crew was moving about the deck silently and efficiently, stowing the hold, splicing and knotting rigging. A pair of men hung over the starboard side on a platform, painting onto the sober gray hull of the ship a bright band of scarlet, which Bow-Oar eyed approvingly. He admired, too, the rack of new harpoons along the rail, their iron shafts gleaming dully. Moses had never permitted iron harpoons on his ships when he sailed. Each son was required to make his own weapon from what he found in the sea: a sharpened shell, a shaft carved from driftwood. But Moses would not see the new harpoons. And the new harpoons would strike deeper and harder. Even those few men who had not always killed with their first strike would kill now.

Bow-Oar raised a window and called down to the crew.

"Send me up the chum bucket."

A heavy wooden bucket rose on a pulley in the rigging outside the window. Bow-Oar leaned well out, reached inside, and felt around among the odds and ends of fish, used by the crew on calm days to fish over the side for the mess table. He lifted out a dripping piece of dolphin. Returning to Moses's room, he found his father dozing in the high blue bed.

Bow-Oar gently took the old man's grasping hand and closed it on the piece of dolphin. Moses woke and sniffed at the lump. There was no smell of smoke. And no hum of the whale at all, only a weaker beat.

"It doesn't smell right. It's not right."

Bow-Oar settled the old man back in bed.

"It's all right, Father. It's sperm. We had rough water coming in, and the fire was doused."

Moses held the lump in his hands and tried to sit up straight in bed. He turned his face toward the sea and held up his hands, murmuring. He bit into the lump, chewed a few times, then his jaw slackened and he fell back, soon asleep.

Bow-Oar turned, carrying the bucket in one hand, Lydia still draped across his shoulders, and moved back along the hallway. He stopped at the first window he came to, lifted the bucket to the sill, and tilted the chum into the sea.

Lydia struggled up from sleep, her head pounding. At first she wondered if she were still in the whaleboat or instead on some larger vessel; the house seemed to shudder under her and she still heard the sea and smelled it. Her stomach heaved, though it was by now empty. She didn't remember the end of her trip across the sound or being carried into the house. She realized that the pounding was not in her body but at a door, and that she lay on a bed in a dark room. She shook her head to try to clear it. The door cracked open and in a shaft of light she recognized Bow-Oar's silhouette, his leaping hair. He started to enter, then turned to someone outside, blocking the doorway with his sturdy body. She heard him speak in a low tone, heard answering voices.

"But what about us, brother?"

Their voices were pleasant, laughing. When Bow-Oar didn't move from the door the voices turned hard. The door lurched inward and Bow-Oar leaned against it to keep it shut. He stood there for a minute or so, listening; then the voices, grumbling, moved off.

A flint was struck, a lantern lit. In its flame Lydia saw that the bed on which she lay stood in the middle of an otherwise empty room that stretched away on either side into darkness. The wall behind Bow-Oar wavered in the lamplight, in places a pale gleaming blue, in others only raw joists and bare boards. She smelled the sharp scent of freshly cut wood. Though it was deep night she thought she heard the sound of saws somewhere under her, and again the house seemed to tremble. Cool air poured in at the window frames; no glass hung there.

Bow-Oar stood at the foot of the bed, holding the lantern high, looking at her. He bent and set the lantern down on the floor and began to shed his stiff blue suit.

Lydia couldn't know that Bow-Oar had seen her and her sisters out walking months before he brought them back to Rathbone House. That once he had seen the long and golden Lydia he had lost his appetite for fishermen's daughters. She didn't know that he'd singled her out from among her sisters, the tallest and brightest of the three Stark daughters. She only knew that he leaned over her now, his body taut and gleaming in the lantern flame, smelling of clean sweat and salt, his green eyes steady on hers.

Lydia no longer felt confused, or queasy, or ashamed. She thought of the young men who had courted her, none of whom had ever done more than kiss her hand, of their soft white skin, faintly scented with sweet talc. They seemed now a weak wash in comparison to the man above her, though he looked little more than half her length. She laid herself out on the big bed, wet from the rain. He hauled her up and peeled away her crackling gown to find the sweet pink meat beneath. He probed her secret parts, searching for the pearl, and when he found it, plucked it until she gasped. He turned her over, mounted her long body, and rode her like a fin, his dark hair tangling with her gold. Rain slanted in, rain and salt spray soaking their bodies, the raw-wood walls, salt from their skin and the ocean soaking the bed so that they might have been making love in the sea itself. They rocked in long slow waves until Lydia dropped, exhausted, into sleep.

Toward dawn the door opened and a woman came quietly in, a toddler balanced on one hip. She was Trial Rathbone, fourteenth of Moses's wives, mother of three fine sons. She swaddled the little boy closely, laid him on the floor at the end of the bed, and began to crawl on hands and knees toward the top. Bow-Oar, without turning, pushed her off the bed with a foot. Trial stood up, brushed wood shavings from her muslin shift, picked up the baby, and left the room.

The black squares of windows began to

gray. Lydia woke to faint light, cold, and damp. She pulled a cover over her legs and looked around. The room was larger than it had seemed in the dark. It stretched from east to west, the windows at either end showing scudding cloud in a pale sky. A thin rain drifted through the open frames. She saw that the only furniture in the room was the bed. The raw-wood smell came from the unfinished planks of the floor and the unplastered joists of the walls. The bed was large and finer than those in her father's house, with gracefully curved headboard and footboard and four tall turned spindles of dark polished wood. She recognized the spindles, she had seen them in the bottom of the whaleboat, their finials protruding from a sheath of oilcloth. One long wall had been plastered and papered in blue silk moiré; it was this that had gleamed pale blue in the light the night before. She wondered if the paper, too, had been in the bottom of the boat, hung by unseen hands sometime during the night. In the wet air the blue strips were peeling from the top, sinking slowly down. A few had just begun to slip; some were slowly curling down the wall with a wet sucking sound, some lay heaped on the floor. The smell of wallpaper paste mingled with those of spilled seed and salt

279

spray. The golden gown, spread beneath her and Bow-Oar, seemed a faint blue in the sodden air.

Lydia turned to look at Bow-Oar, who was still sleeping. His bright bronze skin had dulled down to cold metal. She had been afraid to look at him when she first woke, afraid that she would begin to feel again the fear she had felt on the boat. Instead, when she looked at him she felt the same strong surf she had felt the night before.

She heard a faint voice; it sounded like someone was calling her name outside. The sawing noise of the night before vibrated through the house. She crept quietly from the bed, wrapped herself in her limp gown, and leaned out the window. The light drizzle was dispersing, blown away by a wind off the sound. The voice again; there was Priscilla, leaning from a distant window along the side of the house, toward the water. Behind her, Miriam's head appeared at another window, then both were snapped back inside and she heard sobbing. Near Lydia's window, the sawing and pounding sounds were loud; around and above her, boys were clambering over the house, mallets tucked into their belts, levels balanced on their shoulders. She had not, being half conscious, noticed much about the house on her arrival. She now took in its stance on the long pier, on pilings high above the surf. She felt dizzy, looking down at the dark water below. The room in which she stood was part of a second story that was perched, half built, atop the long low bulk of the house. Closer to land, more rooms like the one she stood in were framed in timbers against the sky, their walls not yet in place. Far below, in the half-light, men were bent over great stripped logs in long rows, chanting together, heaving to shove the logs under the house, which stood on blocks above the long dock. At the end of the dock the *Misistuck* floated, silent and dark, all its sails furled tight to their masts, rigging taut and creaking.

Against the western sky, Lydia saw a great black building at water's edge. Its tree-high door was rimmed in red, smoke seething into the sky from its edges. In the dark water a fleet of darker shapes floated slowly leeward, the three young whales that the *Misistuck* had towed. Atop one a boy stood, driving a long blade into it. On the others seabirds clung, gorging. Along the shore thin stands of pine barred the paling sky.

Lydia felt a deep creaking and the floor under her groaned and jolted. The house began to move beneath her. The stripped logs under it screeching and rumbling, the house headed up the hill, breaking branches off trees with loud snaps. She unwrapped the golden gown from around her, shivering, leaned out, and dropped it to the water below. She watched it twist on the surface in the lightening green sea, then sink.

CHAPTER TEN:
THE GOLDEN WIVES

*{in which the Rathbones
overreach their grasp}*

1801

Bow-Oar paced the dock, smiling in satisfaction at the neatly furled sails and fine new flemished rigging. He had commissioned new suits of sails for all the Rathbone ships from a Boston sailmaker, to replace the dozen home-sewn sails that had long served each whaler: full sets of thirty-seven sails, of finest No. 10 canvas, every studding sail, every staysail, skysail, and spanker. He'd trained the men, who had always navigated by observing the stars or by dead reckoning, to observe the sun at noon with a sextant to find their latitude, precisely timed with a chronometer. He watched the men move around the deck and up and down from the hold; they were due to sail the next morning on a cruise to the South Seas and the men were making ready. As he walked along the dock, Bow-Oar put out a hand to caress the hull of the *Misistuck,* now painted in broad stripes of scarlet and gold, and admired her new stern chasers of gleaming brass. The *Sassacus* and the *Paquatauoq* had been fully refitted, too, and were both away, whaling.

Bow-Oar was anxious to sail, to watch the fresh white sails climb into the sky like clouds. And he missed the whales. His arm ached to hold the lance, to feel its weight and balance, its smooth iron. But he ached more for his long and golden wife. He wasn't ready to leave her to go to sea. He turned at the end of the dock and, glancing at the position of the sun, quickened his step and headed for the house.

Rathbone House now stood well away from the sound, on the highest point of land. The pines that once thickly clothed the ground down to the sea had been clear-cut when the house was moved, so that it stood exposed on all sides to sun and wind. Below the house, deep ruts — made by the great logs on which the house had been rolled from dock to hill — could still be seen, though covered in thick green grass. Each spring the ruts were filled with new earth and planted with grass seed; each summer the earth sank again and filled with salt water. The first floor of the house was unchanged from its original form, the wharf-long lodge of rough pine built by Moses two generations ago. It squatted, smoke-black and pine-pitched, beneath the second floor built by Bow-Oar and his brothers when they brought back their golden brides.

If Lemuel Stark had seen Rathbone House from a league's distance, if he had stolen away and sailed to Naiwayonk a year after he sold his daughters, regretting his bargain (and who can say he didn't?), he might have been startled at the resemblance of the second floor to his own house: the same mellowed red brick, the same pediment windows shuttered in deep gray. As the distance decreased he may have become uneasy about the details: six panes where there should have been twelve, moldings with neither egg nor dart, details foggy and uncertain, as though he were moment by moment more distant rather than closer. Bow-Oar had modeled the new second floor on the appearance of Lemuel Stark's house from afar, to provide his bride and her sisters with familiar comforts. Though none had eyes keener, Bow-Oar's had been focused, when he and his crew rowed past the

Stark islands, not on the house but on the girls for whom it served only as a dim backdrop against which they glowed.

Bow-Oar hurried up the granite steps that climbed from the beach and through the front door. He could hear Lydia's light step somewhere above, and the voices of her sisters. At the top of the stairs was a bolted door. Next to it a grizzled sailor sat on a stool, smoking a pipe.

"Good day, Bemus."

"And to you, Bow-Oar."

Bemus got up from his stool and pulled a key chain from his pocket. He unlocked the door, lifted out the heavy slab of wood, and opened the door, nodding to his captain.

Bow-Oar ran up to the second floor, calling out as he headed toward the bedrooms.

"Wife, are you ready yet?"

The rooms into which the golden wives had settled were, like the exterior, a foggy copy of those in which they had been brought up, each room radiating off the circular central hall that Bow-Oar now passed through. The floor's crude parquet pattern mimicked the floors in the Stark house, but without their gloss; Rathbone floors were swabbed and flogged dry each day by a crew of sailors, always clean but dulled by water.

Intended to make the wives feel at ease, the rooms had instead confused them. The parlor and hall were similar in scale to those in the Stark house but with different proportions: a ceiling too high, a chair rail too low. In their first days in the house, the wives wandered among the rooms as though half asleep. Priscilla walked the perimeter of the central hall and found herself stooping to look out at the sea. Though twelve tall windows pierced the wall as at home, all were smaller and set lower. Miriam woke in the morning and swung her legs over the side of her bed to step into her slippers and instead tumbled to the floor; the beds, like that of Moses, were twice as high as those of the Starks. Though covered in fine cloth and with rich hangings, the beds were made less with the wives in mind than their husbands, who preferred high berths that afforded them the longest view over the ocean. Each night, after coupling with their wives, Bow-Oar, Second-Oar, and Third-Oar returned to the bottom floor to sleep in their narrow cots.

Bow-Oar opened the door to Lydia's bedroom and leaned in, squinting against the morning light that streamed in and bounced from every surface. The blue silk paper, unsuccessfully hung on the walls when Lydia and her sisters were first brought back, had been replaced with sheets of thin beaten gold so that the wives' glow, in these rooms, never dimmed.

Lydia sat at her dressing table, holding a swag of pearls across her breast, regarding herself in the mirror. She frowned and dropped the pearls onto the table, into a tangle of other necklaces. She next drew a strand of amber to try against the bodice of her topaz silk gown. A dozen other gowns spilled from her closet in shades of lemon and daffodil, goldenrod, bright copper, and pale gold.

Lydia glanced up at Bow-Oar.

"Only a moment more."

She dropped the strand of amber and picked up a choker of filigreed gold.

Bow-Oar sighed and walked to the window. The gardens behind the house were nearly complete. Fruit trees and shrubberies were laid out in stiff symmetries, copied from a design on a pamphlet from France. Espaliered pear trees spread their branches among box hedges trimmed into cones and spheres. Gravel walks progressed to marble benches where the wives would soon be able to stroll on long summer days.

"Which do you think looks best?"

Bow-Oar went to his wife, pulled the

strand of amber from the snarl of necklaces, and fastened it around her throat. He leaned, hands on her shoulders, to look at her reflection, which glowed as brightly as when he had first seen her, the amber a deeper gold against Lydia's honey skin. Her eyes met his in the mirror and she smiled.

In the year after he brought Lydia and her sisters to Rathbone House, Bow-Oar's attention had turned away from the sea. He had stayed ashore for a full year with his bride, a honeymoon on which he traveled only to her golden cove. He had urged Second-Oar and Third-Oar to return to sea in the *Sassacus* and the *Paquatauoq;* none of the other men were as capable of commanding. But they, too, preferred to continue to sleep beside their brides, and other brothers had captained the *Sassacus* and the *Paquatauoq* on their latest voyages.

Bow-Oar had taken the *Misistuck* out on a training run a month ago with a crew of novice whalemen. As they passed other ships, he noticed that the captains' spyglasses were always focused on the *Misistuck*'s fine rigging. He could see, too, what the captains wouldn't have known he could discern at such distances: envy written clearly on their features, envy not only on whalemen's faces but on those of captains of loftier vessels, of swift clippers and elegant barks. Bow-Oar longed to see such men's faces when they beheld not flemished ropes but golden tresses. And tonight they would. He kissed his wife and went off to dress for the party.

Miriam and Priscilla appeared in the doorway, arm in arm.

"Aren't you ready yet?" They pulled Lydia up from her chair, laughing.

The wives stood together in the hall, chattering about the party. Miriam and Priscilla, in gowns of pale gold silk chiffon that floated around them as they moved, were as lovely as Lydia in her topaz.

"I can't wait to see! Let's peek." Priscilla giggled.

"No, we promised. We don't want to ruin the surprise," said Lydia.

Lydia had the invitation list in her hand. Miriam and Priscilla crowded close, eagerly scanning the names, as they had so often in the days leading up to the party. The invitations, ordered from Boston and engraved on heavy cream stock, had gone out three weeks ago:

"Do you think the Packer boys will come?" said Miriam.

"I'm sure of it! You don't really think they could have fallen out of love with us so soon, do you?" said Priscilla. "They'll be so jealous!"

Lydia smiled at her sisters. She was excited to see who would be at the soirée, but she didn't really care if any of her old suitors came. She hadn't wearied of Bow-Oar's embraces; she relished them more with each passing week. Priscilla and Miriam felt the same about their husbands. If only her mother were there to see how happy she was. She had written to her mother once a month since leaving home. Her mother never wrote back.

Down the hall, groups of men were stomping up the stairs and into the parlors and dining hall. The wives heard grunting and heaving, the sounds of heavy furniture being moved. In the weeks before the party, the sounds of hammer and saw thrummed through the rafters, making the golden wives briefly wonder if the house was about to move again.

"I can't wait to see the new settees! Do you think they used the cream silk or the brocade?" said Miriam.

"And the dining table, and the chairs. The mahogany will be even more beautiful than the table at home," said Priscilla. She looked wistful for a moment but was so excited about the party that she quickly forgot. Always the most praised of the three sisters by their erstwhile drawing master, Priscilla had been encouraged by her sisters to make the careful drawings they gave to Bow-Oar, for the Rathbone shipwright to use as models for the new furniture. The table was similar in design to that in the Stark house but grander in scale. The chairs were modeled on an etching Priscilla had seen in a periodical from the Continent: dark and lustrous mahogany, lyre-backed, with graceful, tapering legs, even more fashionable than the fine walnut chairs in the Stark dining room.

"Chestnut soup!" Lydia said, smiling.

"And roast pheasant in port wine," said Miriam.

"And Bavarian cream!" said Priscilla.

Lydia laughed and hugged her sisters. The

wives had passed many a happy hour in the weeks before the party in planning the soirée. The harpist who had taught the Stark sisters was to be hired for the evening, to play her classical repertoire. There would be saddle of venison with puréed root vegetables, and citrus ices, and wines ordered from Boston. Lydia had given Bow-Oar a list of the ingredients necessary for cooking such a menu. She had worried about whether the old ship's cook would be able to manage such elaborate dishes; he usually made only simple chowders or boiled fowl for the wives. Bow-Oar had smiled and told her not to worry.

As the wives chattered about the menu, the bell at the top of the stairs suddenly clanged and they all jumped, startled. They laughed and hurried arm in arm down the hall.

They entered the dining room and fell silent. The room was blindingly bright, lit by sconces set into the walls all around, candlelight doubled and trebled by the golden walls, glaring off the new furniture. The dining table and chairs were made not from the fine-grained mahogany or burled walnut of their models, but from the yellow pine and white birch at hand, in the woods behind the house — all finished in marine varnish rather than wax, so that the wood glared rather than glowed. When the wives moved closer they saw rough cross-hatched lines scribed on the wood's surface, along the edges of the seat, and along one side of each leg. The shipwrights had mimicked the strokes of Priscilla's pen, taking her pen's suggestions of shadows for part of the design. The wives lowered themselves cautiously into the new chairs. When they stood again, the scribed lines caught at their gowns and loose threads floated, shimmering, around them.

A score of whalemen stood at attention around the perimeter of the room, wearing not the white shirts and pale-gray waistcoats Lydia had ordered but starched watch coats of bright blue, with flaring lapels and large gold buttons. Near the dining table, rather than the harpist, a fiddler and a fifer tuned up and began to play. Lydia recognized the melody: a lively minuet by Bach. The notes stumbled, then faltered. The rhythm changed and the lively minuet became a brisk sailor's jig. As the music shifted, a crow perched on the fifer's shoulder scrawked loudly and started to shift from foot to foot. The sailors around the room began to smile and tap their feet, then remembered themselves and adopted again the stern expressions they wore on watch at sea.

Lydia and her sisters walked all around the dining table, staring down at the steaming dishes that crowded the polished surface. A great basin of soup, green and pungent, stood at the center, served in an enormous turtle shell of mottled green and black. A bright red chain of boiled lobsters, linked claw to tail, encircled the turtle shell. Vast platters of salt pork and plum duff sat among bowls heaped with glistening suet puddings. The table was set with a service of bright porcelain, edged in ultramarine with lavish swirls and swags of gold, and golden tableware. Crystal stemware banded in gold shone from each setting.

Bow-Oar and his brothers entered, dressed not in the black serge jackets their wives had ordered but in thick gold brocade, fashioned into tight waistcoats and long swallow-tailed coats, with ruffled stocks of white silk at their necks. They smiled at their wives and, checking their pocket watches, began to pace the hall, taking slow, stiff steps in the tight brocade.

Rathbone House glowed so brightly that passing ships that night mistook Naiwayonk for some larger coastal town. Mates quickly checked their charts to make sure they had not strayed off course. But no ship or skiff or sloop approached the Rathbone docks.

The evening wore on. The fiddle and fife played to an empty hall. At two bells in the last watch, the men on duty around the perimeter were replaced by a fresh watch. At four bells, the candles in the sconces, twice replenished, guttered and burned out. Bow-Oar and his brothers continued to pace the hall; the wives dozed in their chairs. At six bells the wives retired. At eight bells, Bow-Oar and his brothers left the hall and, rather than joining their golden wives, descended to the barracks.

During the night a group of young Rathbones climbed up from below, carried away the platters of salt pork and plum duff, and feasted below in the dark.

Chapter Eleven:
Little Absalom

{in which Lydia fails to understand}

1803

"Absalom, where did you get that? Bring it to Mother."

The little boy glanced up from the carpet on which he sat surrounded by toys: a tumble of building blocks, a wooden top, a hoop for rolling. Primers and picture books lay scattered on all sides. But the boy was ignoring his favorite toys and instead was bent, absorbed, over a toy Lydia had never seen. Absalom stood up, green eyes bright in a rosy face, and walked on chubby legs toward Lydia, the toy trailing behind him on a string, wheels squeaking. He dropped the string to hold his arms out to his mother, who hugged him close, then sat him next to her.

Lydia picked up the toy and turned it in her hands. It was a little wooden boat, an ark made of birch, its rough white bark streaked with black. It was filled with carved animals: a crouching wolf; a bear rearing up on its hind legs; a deer with little antlers of horn, and its fawn; a pair of crows. Absalom squealed and stood up, grabbing the ark from Lydia's hands. He clutched it tight and waddled to the window, thrusting the ark up onto the sill. He rocked it back and forth, a dark shape against the bright sky and water, as though it rode on the sea. His white-gold hair shone in the sun, springing in bright waves.

Lydia sighed. When she had begun to swell with her first son, she was determined to keep him near her. She wanted Absalom to live upstairs, to play at his mother's feet in the high bright rooms, to learn his letters, to study mathematics and Latin and rhetoric, as her brothers had. She had cajoled Bow-Oar until he agreed to allow Absalom to stay with his mother for five years. And his cousins, too: Priscilla and Miriam had borne golden babies of their own, little Jeroboam and Ezekiel. Lydia had thanked Bow-Oar and kissed him. She kept to herself her hope that, once little Absalom and his cousins had been five years upstairs, Bow-Oar would relent and let them stay.

Before the golden wives came, the Rathbone boys had always spent little time with their mothers. On the day he began to crawl a Rathbone boy was plucked from his mother's breast and set before a bowl of sailor's burgoo. No sooner was he weaned than he began to pass the greater part of each day with the men. At first he only toddled along the chain of rooms, where the off-duty crew, having no task ashore but to restore their strength for the next voyage, slept or honed their weapons, or ate at the long tables that dropped down on pulleys from the ceiling beams every six bells, laden with spotted dog and toasted cheese, with salt beef and dried peas and figgy-dowdy. A cousin would lift the baby onto his knee to bounce and give him a piece of squid jerky to gum, while his tablemates sang a soft chantey. When a babe's stance was sturdy and his walk sure, he spent part of each day on the sandy shingle with other small brothers, supervised by a retired seaman. At two, a harpoon was put into his hands, its shaft short, its blade small but keen-edged, fit to slay crabs and slow fish. On the tail of a dead mackerel he learned, at three, how to cut a neat hole, as he would later cut the whale's tail to tow it. He and his young mates floated in a stove-in whaleboat that rested on the sandy bottom in the weak surf of low tide, bailing with small piggins, learning how to wet the harpoon line to stop it from smoking when the line ran fast and hot as the wounded whale tried to escape. At five, he hurled the log and counted off the knots. At six, he could reef and hand and steer. At seven, he was off to sea.

Lydia wanted her son's life to be different. She wanted to send him away to a boarding school, where he could meet sons from good families and make useful connections, where he could learn some cleaner, drier calling: barrister, or minister, or a merchant like her father and brothers, though if he chose to be a merchant she hoped her son would choose to conduct his business in a city, somewhere far from the shore.

Bow-Oar had been whaling only once in the three years since the golden wives came to Naiwayonk. Lydia was relieved when he told her that he would soon set off on a long whaling voyage, that he would be gone for at least a year. She was pregnant again and looked forward to having her bed to herself in the coming months. Priscilla, too, was with child again.

Lydia could no longer bear the smell of the ocean — not just the fetid odors of dead fish and rotting weed at low tide but the bracing freshness of salt air on a bright, windy day. She hated the sound of the surf on the rocks below the house, a sound that never stopped. She hated the sight of her husband when he came into the golden rooms during the day, his skin stinking of old burned oil, a smell that never left the men or their ships. She hated most that she could still not resist her husband when he came to her bed, which he continued to do every night. In his arms she still felt the same great waves of pleasure. She wondered if one night when he thrust into her she would burst open and drown.

Little Absalom was born not in the dark below but in a high bright room, his first view not the rigging of a ship but the lovely face of his mother. Absalom was swaddled in white linen and laid not in a swinging hammock but in a pretty cradle. He was bathed and changed not by a worn wife in the dark nursery below but by Bemus, the old sailor who guarded the stairs at night. Absalom's aunts sat at the spinet to play him lullabies. He lay in his cradle looking up at them with his father's bright-green eyes, his arms and legs waving to the rhythm of the songs. When he was old enough to understand, his mother read aloud to him each night, tales of woodland princes and of kings who reigned in great cities far from the sea. Absalom had lived happily upstairs for nearly three years.

But lately Absalom had been restless. There was still a worn wife in the nursery below, still fresh Rathbone sons in residence. Humility, the fifteenth wife, had succeeded Trial, who departed the year before, leaving three little boys behind. All told, a dozen whaler boys lived in the barracks below. When Absalom heard them shouting outside, he ran to the windows and craned out to see. Jeroboam and Ezekiel, a few months younger than him, were still content to spend their time playing with their mothers, but Absalom would stand at the window for hours at a time, watching the men busy at their duties when a ship was in port or gazing at the horizon when no ship was docked.

In the past month the boys who lived below had climbed the stairs a few times and knocked, asking for Absalom to come out, until Lydia told Bemus to turn them away.

The whaler boys began to come instead silently at night, leaving gifts for Absalom outside the door: slices of sea pie, bowls of spotted dick or lobscouse; a baleen whistle; a little cage of whalebone.

Lydia watched Absalom playing at the

window with his ark.

"Come, darling, time for your breakfast."

Absalom turned around and smiled at his mother, then set the ark on the floor. He ran to the table for his porridge and milk, and spent the day making block castles with his cousins.

The next morning Lydia woke to find the window open and Absalom gone. A grappling hook hung from the sill; a knotted rope swung in the breeze. When Bow-Oar came to her room that night, Lydia pleaded with him to bring Absalom up from below, to send him back up into the light, but Bow-Oar shook his head.

"You have had your chance. Now he is ours."

CHAPTER TWELVE:
THE WEAKENED ONES

{in which the Rathbones' sea legs stiffen}

1814

The three boys slowed down as they neared the last room. Though it wasn't yet dawn, the hall of beds was empty; all of the men were already at the docks, readying the boats for the trials. The door to the little room at the end was always closed, and no one but Bemus ever went in there. Now he was behind them, herding the boys down the dark hall toward the room at the end, whispering in their ears.

"He won't see you, but he'll know you're there all the same. Just go in and wait for him to speak."

"But why do we have to go? No one else ever has to go," whispered Ezekiel.

"He's never asked for anyone else," said Bemus. "You should feel honored."

The boys stood in a bunch outside the

door, shifting from foot to foot in the cold air, each clutching his harpoon. They had all heard the men tell stories of Moses, but the boys had never seen him. They'd only passed the little room on their way in and out.

"He breathes through gills." Absalom elbowed his cousins.

"I heard he sleeps in a great big tub of water," said Ezekiel.

"No, he sleeps on the rocks with the seals," said Jeroboam, stifling a laugh.

Bemus slapped the top of Jeroboam's head and pushed him toward the door. Jeroboam hesitated, then knocked softly. All three boys edged slowly into the room.

Once inside, they went quiet. It was so dark they couldn't see Moses at first, only heard him breathing above them: long rattling breaths, each with a click at the end. Moses, propped against pillows at the head of the high blue bed, leaned forward, far enough so that the boys saw a glint of white eyes, a tangle of silver hair. A hand reached out and beckoned. Absalom rolled his eyes at his cousins, then climbed up and knelt at the end of the bed.

Moses ran his shriveled hands over the boy's hair and face, over his shoulders and down his body, prodded his belly and groin.

Absalom stiffened as Moses poked and grunted, then felt his body relax under the old man's searching hands. When Moses had finished he pushed Absalom away, then inspected Ezekiel and Jeroboam in the same way.

Moses fell back against the pillow. He lifted a hand to wave the boys away and they ran from the room, laughing only when they were out the door and on the dock, in the lightening day.

The three boys stood in the prows of their whaleboats, far out in the sound. At first darker silhouettes against a dark sky, then limned by the sun as it began to mount, they faced south, their backs to the shore. The boats rocked on a chuff sea. Clouds scudded high and swift above them.

From the end of the dock their fathers watched, staring out to where the boats and their crews hovered along the horizon. Bow-Oar, Second-Oar, and Third-Oar stood unconsciously in the same posture as their sons, legs braced, arms stiff, harpoon hand tensed to clutch, each ready to reach for the blade that stood not by him but by his son. Each approved of the angle of his son's arm. Each knew that the boat in which his boy balanced had been readied to perfection:

ropes coiled, blades honed, fittings polished, hulls and oars sanded and varnished. Each crew was trained to the keenest pitch. The boys shone among their dull cousins at the oars who, had they been standing, would have stood only chin-high to the golden three.

Besides the boys' fathers, four older Rathbone men were on the dock that day. Maimed by the sperm years ago, they had long since been set ashore, reduced to pulling hemp in the rope walk or to household tasks. There was room for them and more on the wide dock where the house had stood in Moses's time. The wood had weathered in the fourteen years since the house had been moved up the hill so that the place where it stood, at first dark and grimed from decades of smoky fires and scuffing boots, was now nearly as silvery and worn as the pilings beneath the dock. Though the April air was mild, a few of the older men had built a fire where the hearth had been, the place now only a patch of scorched brick. The men crouched or stood nearby, though no one lay any offering on the flames.

Bow-Oar glanced at the vacant moorings along the dock. The two Rathbone ships that still sailed were away. The *Misistuck* had been gone for two years, the *Sassacus* nearly three. On those now distant days when they had set sail, he had not felt confidence in their captains. Not that the two mates he had raised to captain were not good men, but they were well into their middle years, among the only Rathbones to have survived so long with no loss of limb or faculty. But those faculties were slower now and the men less resolute. Bow-Oar had hesitated before sending them back out to sea, but what choice did he have? He and Second-Oar and Third-Oar were needed at home to oversee the proper training of their sons, for without their sons the Rathbones had no future. Four young Rathbones — sons of Humility and Trial (the most recent worn wife, Silence, had produced nothing) — trained along with the golden sons, but Bow-Oar placed little hope in them. Their older brothers, already at sea on the *Misistuck,* had proven fainthearted.

Though in the last generation Moses's wives had continued to produce infant whalemen at a steady rate, fewer had survived to adulthood in the years since the golden wives arrived. The younger Rathbone men no longer felt the deep sympathy with the sperm that was so natural to their ancestors.

If you had asked any of the older Rathbone men when the tide had turned, they would have told you, in low voices, behind their hands: on the day Bow-Oar and his brothers brought home the golden girls. Some would have said the true turn began when Bow-Oar fooled his father, giving him not a portion of the whale's heart but an indifferent gob of dolphin; when he tilted the chum into the sea — that he might have done as well to tilt Rathbone House itself and tip all the men into the sea, so much did Bow-Oar, in ending the old ways, choose to fall from grace.

Mama would have said who knows when any tide turns? It's as impossible to tell as where one wave ends and the next begins.

But ever since Bow-Oar had killed the three whales on a fall day fourteen years ago, more men were flung overboard or mauled beyond repair. They lanced the whale too soon, not waiting for, or no longer knowing, the precise moment when the whale had tired just enough, and the whale, instead of sinking, turned and smashed the boat to pieces. Some men suffered no bodily harm but, after encounters with whales that didn't easily yield, whales that towed a hundred fathoms of line from the boat and still swam on, whales that Moses would have met with his blood singing, they showed fear

309

in their eyes, and their crewmates saw it. Once marked, such men were not wanted in any boat.

The two remaining ships were only thinly manned by Rathbones, their crews filled out by hired men. Including the captains, just twelve of Moses's sons still whaled, split between the *Sassacus* and the *Misistuck*. The Rathbones stood thigh-deep in blubber after the hunt, hooking slabs up into the hold, and filled the benches on the whale-boats as second oar and third oar and fourth oar, but they no longer served as harpoon-ers. That role was filled by sailors from distant ports: Gayheads from Massachu-setts, Portogos and Fiji Islanders, men who knew little of the family and cared less, as long as the disks of gold were promptly counted out into their hands. These were men who struck the whale with spear and harpoon unafraid, men whose lives were still wholly connected to the sea and all that swam in it, though they couldn't, like earlier Rathbones, kill in one strike. The second harpoon, or the third, might hold well enough; the whale might tire after a long chase and finally succumb to a dozen lances. Just as often no harpoon held or the line snapped and the whale swam away.

Though it had seemed, in that brief period

after Lydia and her sisters came, that the family, so long secluded, would become connected to the wider world, they'd retreated yet further after the failed soirée. Bow-Oar and his brothers turned their full attention back to the sea. The scarlet stripes on their boats were allowed to bleach in sea and sun to a dull rose. Shining chronometers and bright sextants tarnished to black in their cases. Bow-Oar continued to rig the ships in the full suits of thirty-seven sails that lent the craft such great speed, but when the sails wore thin his own men stitched new ones, using the frayed sails as patterns. It wasn't that the Rathbones couldn't afford ready-made sails — they could rig a dozen ships and provision each for a voyage around the world — but Bow-Oar hoped that, in bringing back the old ways, he would bring back the whales.

Local seamen had kept clear of these waters, having heard tales of passing mariners being pressed into service by the Rathbones to crew their whaleships.

The whales had long since learned to skirt Rathbone territory.

So the sighting of a pod of fledgling right whales at first light that morning, far out in the sound, had been greeted with joy. Though inferior to the sperm in speed and oil quality, they were considered adequate to serve in the trials, which had been delayed for weeks in hope of just such an event. If the right whales had not appeared, a gam of narwhals or a shiver of nurse sharks would have had to suffice, but wouldn't have served to fully test the mettle of the novice whalers. The right whale, though slow, was known to breach frequently, its tail-slaps powerful enough to cleave a careless whaleboat. The crews were hurriedly assembled: the four sons of Humility and Trial, ranging from nine to fourteen in age, were enlisted to man oars, with local fishermen's sons, hired for the day, filling out the crews, six boys to a boat.

The golden sons all knew that the trials would determine their positions on the whaleboats: Harpooner; Boatheader; First-Oar, Second-Oar, Third-Oar, Fourth-Oar. Everyone knew that Absalom would earn Harpooner, and his cousins Jeroboam and Ezekiel would, too. In the weeks before the trials they had cleanly killed every sunfish and marlin they had practiced on. Today, the first boys to cleanly kill their whales with one thrust of the harpoon would earn places on the *Misistuck* and the *Sassacus.* When the ships returned to Naiwayonk the outsiders hired to fill the crew would be replaced with true Rathbones. Absalom and his cousins couldn't wait. When they were nine years old, they had all been to sea on the *Sassacus,* on a six-month voyage to the north. They had served as topmen, their days spent climbing high above the ship in the rigging, trimming the sails at each change in the wind. But they had been at home ever since, training with their fathers while the ships were away, whaling. Each longed to be out on the open sea again, to take his first sperm.

Bow-Oar had not speared a whale himself, nor been close to one, since the day the three young whales had been killed. He had been the first to lose his bond with the sperm, when he wielded the harpoon that day. He would not have admitted it. He would have made other excuses for never joining a whaleboat crew anymore: He was the best navigator and needed to stay at the helm of the *Misistuck,* or he was needed at home to train the boys, reasons which were true enough. But he felt the absence of what he had lost. He knew that if he had ever raised his blade again, it would never have flown true or sunk deep. He could call up pictures of every whale he had killed before that day; its length and shape, how many barrels of oil it had given, how much bone and blubber. But how each had given over its life, in a last leap from the water, arcing up to crash down again or sinking silently, he had forgotten. He couldn't remember the feel of the living flesh under his hand or the beat of the whale's blood in his ears, though the sound had once echoed the beat of his own heart.

Bow-Oar sometimes wished he could go back to the time before the golden wives. He wished that, when his men had rowed past the Stark Archipelago on that long-ago day, he had asked the men to tie him to the mast, to blindfold him and stop his ears with wax so that he wouldn't see the long and golden bodies of the Stark girls. Though he was busy with the training and wanted only to fall into a cot in the barracks at night, he was still drawn to Lydia like sea to sand, still rocked her each night until he sank exhausted into sleep.

But she had given him such beautiful sons that he couldn't truly regret having married her. Sons as long and golden as their mother and as strong as their father. Besides the three boys on trial, Lydia and her sisters had given their husbands five more boys in as many years: Lydia bore Parmenas and Philo one after the other, then came Miriam's twins, Lanman and Layman, within a month of Priscilla's little Silas.

Bow-Oar couldn't keep his heart from leaping at the thought of the next voyage of the *Misistuck*. Whereas the whaleboat ranks would be determined by the trials, Rathbone ship captains were chosen by vote, and Absalom had already been voted in as next captain of the *Misistuck*. The ship had made do without a captain since Bow-Oar had come ashore to supervise the training. Absalom, who led his two cousins in the trials that day, would soon turn thirteen. He would be joined the next year by his younger brother, and in the years to come by his youngest brother and cousins, all in training. The crews would be replenished in the coming years and the Rathbones' primacy restored.

The three boys blazed with beauty. The early sun that struck gold on the sea suffused their skin and hair. The light seemed to spill off them into the water. The boys drew back their arms. They held their arms high, angles exact, sinews taut. Gulls gathered and wheeled above, among them a black bird, a crow that dropped and lit on the mast of Absalom's boat. Though the whales were not yet visible, their voices began to sound over the water.

■ ■ ■ ■

"There's Jeroboam," said Miriam.

Priscilla leaned out farther.

"No, that's my Ezekiel. Do you think I don't know my own son?"

Lydia squeezed between them and held her hand over her eyes.

"There's Absalom, at the front. He still holds his head that same way."

The golden wives stood at an open window, watching the trials. Their whaleboned gowns bumped and scraped as they maneuvered for space at the open sash on the seaward side. Their shawls snapped like signal pennants in the stiff breeze. They were still slender and just as lovely when seen from a certain distance. They wore gowns of silvered bronze and dull pewter and mercury, in styles long out of fashion.

"Are you sure that's him? A year. It seems even longer since we've seen them. Look how tall they've grown!" Priscilla leaned out, squinting at the glare of sun on water. It was difficult to focus on such a distant point, her eyes being used to the near at hand: to the point of a needle, to spinet keys, to the dimmer rooms at the rear of the house where the wives passed their days.

"One year and nine days," said Miriam.

Priscilla blinked and rubbed her eyes. "I don't understand why we can't see them more often."

Lydia smiled and squeezed her sister's hand. "They'd grow soft. Don't you listen to your husband?"

"Just for a few minutes, now and then. On their birthdays . . ." Priscilla returned to staring out the window.

If they could have seen the boys more clearly, the sisters could still not have easily told which son was whose. Though the boys had been living at home all this time, they never came upstairs, and the wives were not allowed to visit them. Only when ships departed or returned, or during the spring trials, did the men and boys gather on the dock, only then did they stand still long enough so that the sisters could catch more than brief glimpses: bright heads hurrying down the hill to the docks; hurrying back again when the dinner bell was struck below; rowing far out in the sound with their cousins. The sons in the boats that day, the eldest sons, looked much alike in any case, all born a few months apart, thirteen years ago. Still, the golden wives squinted at the horizon, trying to match their scant memories with what broad gestures were visible from so far.

The golden wives would no more have thought of descending to the lower floor than they would think to wield a harpoon. Lydia had tried a few times, long ago, in the first months after Absalom had gone down to live with the men, had pleaded with Bemus, but he only shook his head. Bemus still held his post at the top of the stairs, sleeping each night in his hammock strung across the door.

Lydia still remembered those nights, before Absalom was born, when she woke to the sound of voices outside the door, like the voices she had heard outside the bedroom on her first night in Rathbone House. Bemus had spoken in a low voice, and the men had moved away. Once, when the voices raised in anger, she heard the thud and crash of a body tumbling down the stairs. But no man had tried to climb for many years.

Occasionally the wives did descend the staircase halfway to the landing. A door on that level led outside to the gardens at the back of the house. They walked outdoors on fine days, though no trees shaded them and no roses scented the air. A few of the older seamen continued to prune and weed the few hardy bushes and the tough little beach roses that persisted; the flowers and fruit trees planted for the golden wives' arrival had died long ago from too much salt air and water. The house stood on the highest ground of Naiwayonk, but the sea found its way up through the earth like a spring. The empty furrows of the garden's formal geometry had become a watery maze along which fish swam.

The wives passed much of their long days with needlework, stitching delicately petit-pointed signal flags and braiding satin lanyards for their husbands. They sewed clothes copied from catalogues from abroad that found their way to Naiwayonk, already years outmoded, from such fabric as made its way there too. Bow-Oar and his brothers wore waistcoats and frock coats and breeches of thin Indian paisley in which they shivered, or thick felted wool from some northern climate that, once wetted by whale's blood, never dried. The wives walked the golden rooms not in the fresh Regency on display in city salons north and south but in tired Empire silhouettes.

Lydia stared out at her son, standing strong and sure in the whaleboat. She thought she saw the bright head turn, caught a glimpse of his pale face. She reached her arm out the open window and waved. If her son returned the gesture, she couldn't see it.

She no longer felt the great pain in her heart she had suffered when Absalom had first gone to live below. For her two younger sons, who had descended to live with the men at six months old, she felt a similarly diluted love. It may have been the distance at which she always viewed him or the long intervals between sightings. Whatever the cause, she was grateful to feel that day only a thin wash of pain. She looked down at the girl who stood beside her and hugged her.

"Besides, I have you, dearest, don't I?"

After the boys had all descended to their lives below, after the wives had begun to sigh at the empty cribs and quiet rooms, each began to swell one more time. Three more golden Rathbones were born, and this time they were daughters, the first girls to grow up in Rathbone House. Lydia and her sisters, whatever they knew or did not know of the fate of girls in earlier generations, would not have suffered their daughters to be spirited away. Bow-Oar and his brothers did not object. After their sons were taken from them, the wives were less unhappy with their daughters for company, less troublesome to their husbands. The girls, now all in their ninth year, stood by their mothers at the window, looking out at their brothers. Their hair, in infancy the same shade of gold as that of their mothers, had paled to a shade nearer white. Their names were Claudia, Julia, and Sophia.

Claudia looked up at her mother. Her eyes, Lydia's soft blue when born, had lately shifted hue and brightened to a vivid aqua.

"Mama, I want to go with Absalom next time."

Lydia smiled, and hugged her daughter close.

"Why would you want that, dearest?"

"I want to talk to the whales."

The wives all laughed.

"And what would you say to them?" asked Priscilla.

"I would ask if I could swim with them."

Priscilla and Miriam smiled at their niece and looked at each other, laughing.

"Claudia, you don't want to swim with any smelly old whales."

"Papa says I shall marry a fisherman."

Lydia smoothed her daughter's pale hair.

"No, my darling, you shall marry a prince."

The sun rose higher, light spreading across the water and striking the dock. The fathers raised hands to brows; the golden wives squinted through their fingers. At the edge of the sea a line of spouts rose and shimmered. The boys crouched lower. They raised their arms as one. The harpoons flashed out together and in a single swift arc the blades struck home.

Three whales, their smooth glide checked, churned the water with their heads, thrashing the sea with their flukes. The whales soared straight up and dove down again, disappearing under the surface.

The men on the dock roared. The women at the window clapped their hands. Bow-Oar and his brothers didn't move at all, or take their eyes from the place in the sea where the whales had sounded.

Such a seemingly small thing: the distance from minor valve to major artery, barely the span of a man's hand in a body of forty feet from end to end. The difference between a slow trickle of blood and a deluge; a huge heart that pumped on, only nicked, and one that burst and emptied into the sea. The women didn't know, nor did the younger Rathbone men, the significance of that small difference.

Bow-Oar, watching his son, tried to find excuses for that hand's span of error: a freak of wind; a slippery hull. But deep within he knew, if the blades had struck where they should have, just above the root of the left fin, that the whales would have breached in a fount of spray and blood and died within moments. Instead they rose smoothly to the surface, their backs bristling with shafts, their pace unchecked, lines loose and trailing, and surged away.

Katurah finished spooning the thin porridge into Moses's mouth and set the bowl aside. She knelt on the end of the bed and stripped down the sheets and blankets, then turned Moses over to change his soiled bedclothes. He was by then light as hollowed bone. She remade the bed with fresh sheets, tucking them neatly under Moses's chin, and sat next to him. She smoothed the blankets over his shrunken body, and sat looking down at him.

It had been five years since she'd come to Rathbone House. She had stayed longer than any of the other barren wives. Those who had not become pregnant within a year of their arrival had been replaced. But Katurah, though she had borne no children, had been allowed to stay on to keep the old man company and, in the last few years, to take care of him as he grew frail. Caring for Moses, she thought, as she wiped a drool of porridge from his chin with a corner of her apron, was little different from tending to an infant. She was glad that she had borne no sons of her own. She had seen enough men die at sea.

Katurah had grown up in a fishing village to the south. Her brothers and father were lost at sea in a storm when she was a young girl. Five years ago, she had, like Hepzibah, like Euphemia and Beulah and all the sixteen wives before her, seen a whaleboat one morning — the same long slim hull, oars flashing in unison against a bright sky. She had, like her predecessors, reached for a boy's hand and stepped in and glided away. But unlike so many previous wives, she felt no irresistible urge. She was compelled not by fresh boys in blue middies, bright ties flying, but by necessity. There were few men left in her little town. The plentiful cod and haddock in the sound that had sustained them for generations had thinned in recent years. Some men had joined the merchant marine to feed their families, while others moved inland to work in the new factories there. She and her widowed mother lived off their kitchen garden and shellfish gleaned from the shore. When Katurah saw the Rathbones rowing toward her, she knew who they were. Even the smallest, most isolated villages knew by then about the Rathbone wives. She had already decided to go with them. When she stepped into the boat, she was not, like the wives before, in thrall to bright springing hair, to hypnotic strokes or rippling brown backs. The Rathbone boys' hair was now more greasy than gleaming, their strokes less than perfectly matched, their broad backs narrower. They had by then lost that unity with the sea that shone in earlier Rathbones, and no bright haze obscured them from Katurah.

She looked down at the frail old man and thought how much harder her life could have been. Other than watching over Moses, she had only to lay with a few of the men in the barracks now and then, which was easy enough.

There were no babies in the nursery to care for. The youngest had already been taken to live in the barracks with the men before she arrived. So had the sons of the women who lived upstairs. Now and then, on her way to Moses's room down the long passage, she looked out a window and caught a glimpse of one of the women, staring out an upstairs window.

They were pretty, of course, the women upstairs, and Bow-Oar and his brothers must take pleasure in bedding them, but

they were of little other use that she could
see. They would do better to walk along the
shore, she thought, and take the sea air,
such pale, jittery things they were, cooped
up in the house all day. They must have
come from some inland place, where people
didn't understand the sea. And their boys.
She had seen them in the barracks and
watched them training out in the sound.
There was something not right about them,
though they were as pretty as their mothers.

Moses was restless next to her. He had
begun to moan and click, and turn his head
from side to side.

From its peg on the wall Katurah took
down the necklace that had so long hung
there, a whale tooth strung on a length of
braided hair. Lifting Moses's head, she put
it around his neck. His breath slowed and
steadied. She searched among the sheets for
the length of knotted rope that was always
close by and lay it in Moses's hands. His
fingers found the knots and stopped twitching. He turned his head away from the
window.

"All gone," he whispered.

Katurah looked out. Three whaleboats
bobbed in the sound. In each boat a tall
golden son stood, staring out to sea.

"They're still there, safe and sound," she said.

Moses shook his head.

"The whales, the men. All gone."

He closed his eyes. The right whales had rejoined their pod and moved off. Nothing larger than a school of tuna stirred in the sound. The herds of sperm were all distant now, the water far less alive. The trying fires on the ships had not been lit for many years. The whale's heart was tossed into the sea for the sharks.

Moses knew that Absalom, Ezekiel, and Jeroboam wouldn't succeed that day. He knew that the blood of the golden wives had thinned the Rathbone veins, had stiffened their sea legs and bled their dark strength to white. He knew that in their next session the boys' aim wouldn't improve, that instead their harpoons would fall shyer of the mark each time. The harder the boys tried — for they would never lack the will or the courage — the more their strength would wane. Their fathers would drive them on from pride, but after three such seasons, would finally tell their sons to give up the sea. The boys would nod their heads, not meeting their fathers' eyes. They would secretly vow among themselves never to stop. In the summer of their fifteenth year Absalom,

Ezekiel, and Jeroboam — and their five younger brothers, who wouldn't be left behind — would take out a boat forbidden to them one morning. They would swear they saw a sperm, just out of reach over the horizon. They would row away one last time, harpoons in hand, never to return. Whether they would sink in one final struggle with the whale or meet some less glorious end, Moses couldn't see. But he knew that their fathers would never recover. They would return to sea and become reckless, or forgetful, and find quick mariners' fates of their own. Second-Oar would become entangled in a line during a chase and be dragged under. Third-Oar would slip on a slick deck and split his head on the fluke of an anchor. Bow-Oar would climb to the crosstrees to which he had climbed a thousand times before with no misstep and fall silently into the sea.

Moses turned his head back to the boats. His bones ached. They always ached now, but today a deeper pain pulsed along his arm and down his spine. There was a whale out there, after all. A sperm, far out in the sound, moving smoothly toward him through the dim water. His arm reached up for the harpoon that still lay in its rack above him, then fell back.

He knew this whale, he realized. He had known it in the time before he came to Nai-wayonk, when he was a boy. He had never thought of the whale again, until now. It was not the spring whale on which the village lived all year. He had come upon it by himself one day in the autumn before that last whale, when he was swimming far out where he liked to swim, on the wide circle of the sea with no land in sight.

He had been stroking steadily along and was out of breath. He had stopped to rest. The water was still warm from the summer, and the sea had that golden cast it always had before the chill air of autumn cooled it to blue. He floated easily on his back with eyes closed, rocking on the smooth surface, weightless. He wasn't aware of the moment when the whale rose under him; it was just there, under his back, his own body sud-denly heavy. He rose and fell with the whale's long, slow breaths, his hands resting on the smooth gray skin. The whale drifted, half asleep, and Moses drifted with it, for how long he didn't know. Once, the whale blew, showering Moses with warm drops. When he finally opened his eyes the water was cold around him. He was shivering, and the whale was gone. He swam home and never told his father, or anyone in the village, about the whale.

Now it was coming, swimming toward him across the sound. Soon, he knew, he would feel again that same sun on his face, that warm blood streaming along the whale's body under him, beating in its great heart. He felt his own heart swell, throbbing against the walls of his chest until, enormous, it burst.

Katurah crawled across the high blue bed. She pressed Moses's eyes closed. She lay his body straight, arms close along his sides, and stroked the blankets smooth around him, tucking them tight and seamanlike. She reached up and grasped his harpoon by the blade. Lifting his head away from the pillow, she turned it to the side and neatly sliced away his pigtail. She coiled the long white braid, tucked it in her pocket, and left the room, closing the door behind her.

Katurah passed no one as she walked back down the hall of beds — the house was still empty of men. She looked around the room, the same room in which Hepzibah had first stood more than thirty years ago, the room in which all the worn wives had lived. In the back, the line of infants' hammocks swayed empty in a breeze from an open window. She lifted the patchwork quilt that covered the bed, the quilt to which each

Rathbone wife had added her name, seventeen in all. She ran her hand over her own name, chain-stitched in white thread — *Katurah, 1809* — on a square of faded calico. She folded the quilt carefully and tucked it under one arm.

Katurah opened the front door and stood looking out. No one noticed. All eyes were still pinned to the horizon, over the edge of which most of the men expected to see the boats with whales in tow, and where now instead the boats were creeping back, harpoons unblubbered, spermless.

She walked across the lawn and climbed down the boulders to the little beach where a few small craft always rested. She chose a skiff, ran it down the sand, and pushed off.

As she rowed out, heading southeast, away from Rathbone House, she looked west along the long crescent of beach to the point. Past the headland, tucked in a deep cove, a hull, dismasted and lifeless, rocked in slack water. Katurah could just make out the name in faded paint on it side: *Paquatauoq.* Past the ships stood the dark sheds, with their tryworks, the cauldrons unused since Bow-Oar burned the three whales many years ago. The smell of cold old blubber wafted across on a breath of air. She looked back at the docks, emptied now of men, except for the three figures who still stood there, watching three boats head slowly home.

She rowed on. She passed no fresh wife, as there were no more to come. No outsider would enter Rathbone House for many years nor would any woman journey from there.

Katurah had, when she set out, meant to head for home, for her village. But as she rowed she thought about what it would be like to return there, what welcome she might receive, after these five years, after her life in Rathbone House. She stopped rowing and stood up. She pulled Moses's pigtail from her pocket, unmade its braid, and strewed the long white strands on the water. When she was halfway out on the sound, she changed course and headed for Mouse Island.

EUNICE *m.* 1785   FELICITY *m.* 1788?   BEULAH *m.* 1792   EXPERIENCE *m.* 1793   DESIRE *m.* 1794   TRIAL *m.* 1798   HUMILITY *m.* 1801   SILENCE *m.* 1806   KATURAH *m.* 1809

MIRIAM   3RD-OAR *m.* PRISCILLA

SON   SON   SON SON SON TWINSONS SON SON   SON SON SON SON TWINSONS SON

LAYMAN   SOPHIA   EZEKIEL   SILAS   JULIA

THE RATHBONES

CHAPTER THIRTEEN: HALCYON DAYS

{in which Mercy and Mordecai
sail through golden waters}

"An adolescent humpback!"

Mordecai leaned out over the waves, pointing to a plume of white on the horizon. He was in no true danger. The mate had, with his permission, lashed Mordecai's lower half to the topmast with several turns of a stout backstay around his waist so that he could enjoy his perch in safety, as he had done every day since we had left the Stark Archipelago. He still wore my aunts' salve against the sun on his face and hands, and his blue spectacles.

I had noticed a few minutes earlier that Mordecai's humpback was only an oversize sturgeon, its plume of spray just a wave dashing against a distant reef, but kept it to myself. He seemed so happy. The wound on his arm had finally healed, and the dark

336

bruises had faded. Late each afternoon, as the sun began to drop in the west, Mordecai ascended, the mate climbing the rigging behind him, guiding his feet and pushing him through the lubber's hole at the top. The sky had been full of birds, gliding and wheeling, ever since we set sail, and the sea full of fish. While Mordecai watched his birds, I sat below with the captain and he told me all he knew of the Rathbones and the Starks.

I glanced up to make sure Mordecai hadn't noticed what I was doing. I had borrowed his journal and was adding more portraits to the chart as the captain talked. Mordecai was still protective of his long-cherished journal, though its secrets had been revealed. Each afternoon, when Captain Avery returned to his sailing duties, I had read Lydia's letters. Between her notes and what the captain told me, the story of my family began to come clear.

On the chart, under Moses and his many wives, I drew Bow-Oar, Second-Oar, and Third-Oar. I dressed them not in the fine clothes they had tried to adopt but in their comfortable sailors' shirts and caps. Next to each man I drew his wife: Lydia, Priscilla, and Miriam in their golden gowns. By Priscilla I drew the ivory box that Second-Oar had given her, its lid open to show the lump of ambergris within. Under the wives, I drew their eight sons, all crowded into the boat on which they finally sailed away; and next to the sons I lightly sketched the faces of the daughters, little Claudia, Julia, and Sophia.

Now the captain sat mending a sail, pulling a long curved needle through the canvas.

"I never really knew the men, mind you. Except for Bemus, a little. Just what I've heard over the years, picked up in Stonington and Mystic . . . and selling to the Starks, of course. The Rathbones didn't like outsiders, even a pleasant fellow like me." He smiled at me, rubbing his whiskery chin.

Mordecai's excited voice came from above.

"Oh! No. No. Just a storm petrel . . ."

I thought it couldn't hurt to let him believe for a while longer that Papa still followed the sperm. Papa was, I now knew, much closer than Mordecai thought him to be, or had been only a few weeks earlier, when we fled Rathbone House. I couldn't help but wonder about the island the old gardener had described. It had sounded so much like the Arcady of Mama's stories; maybe it really did exist, though without its giants and their beds of gull down.

The wind veered two points to the north, and a cool current wound through the warm air. We had been sailing for five days on our passage northward, running at a smooth, unhurried pace. We were headed for the Davis Strait, off Greenland, some seven hundred miles north-nor'east. Or at least that's what Mordecai believed. In fact, I had taken Captain Avery aside, before Mordecai could make his request to carry us all the way to Greenland, with a request of my own: to not tell Mordecai our true route. The captain had given me a sharp look, then chuckled and said, "Well, miss, I'm sure you have your reasons," and nodded his agreement. We were in fact sailing northward, but only as far as New Bedford, where the *Able* would turn south again on its customary route, stopping to trade at every little port with sufficient draft to anchor. Mordecai was dimly perplexed that the captain would agree to take us so far but spent little time puzzling over it, staying busy with his observations and notes. Before we reached New Bedford, when the moment was right, I would gently tell him the truth about my parents. I had put it off again and again, trying to understand why Papa and Mama had hidden him away in the attic for all those years.

As I finished sketching little Claudia under her mother, my eye went to the faint gray smudge next to me on the chart, where I had erased my brother. I now tried to draw that bright face I had seen so clearly when the gardener told me about Papa and his boy. When I had finished, I held the page away from me and squinted at the drawing; he looked much like me.

"If you ask me, they should never have married those girls . . . no offense to you, of course, miss." The captain tipped his hat. "Greedy, they were. That's when things started to go bad for the Rathbones. And for the Starks. They sold all that beauty away and have been trying to buy it back ever since. Cursed, is what I'd call it."

"Nonsense." Mordecai's voice floated down from above, startling me. I hadn't realized he was listening. He waved an open book at me. "I've been reading more of this Austrian fellow, Mendel, and his pea plants. The Starks look the way they do because of inborn characteristics that emerged, not the workings of fate." He sniffed and turned back to his book.

"But what about the Rathbone daughters? What about Claudia and Julia and Sophia? What happened to them, Captain?"

The captain considered, finishing a seam

and knotting it off. He tugged at the brim of his hat.

"I suppose one of them must have been your grandmother. Not sure which one, though. You'd have to ask your mother."

"Captain Avery, do you know any of my family . . . of my living family, that is? Have you met my mother and father?"

I was sitting next to the captain as he mended the sail. He looked down at the seam he had just finished and ran a thumb along it, then looked up at me. His sharp mariner's eye softened and he laid a hand on my head.

"No, Miss Rathbone. No, I don't know them."

He seemed to want to say more but didn't. He stroked my hair for a few moments, his eyes staring off. His arm was warm against mine, smelling of wet wool and pipe smoke. He straightened up and, briskly patting my head, folded his mended sail and went off to his cabin.

I sat watching the mate at work in the rigging. The weather was fair, the cold autumn winds that had wound through the Stark Archipelago having given way to some warmer surge of the Gulf Stream from the south, and the mate whistled as he clambered spiderlike over the lines above me.

He moved so easily in his cotton shirt and wide sailor trousers, leaping from mast to top or running up and down the lines. I watched him for a while, then descended to the hold, to the little cabin the captain had curtained off for me, returning with a thick woolen jumper the wives had woven for Mordecai.

"Mr. Beebe? Mr. Beebe, wouldn't this look well with your trousers?" I held up the jumper, a deep blue, by its sleeves. The mate paused in the middle of winding a line around a clamp and slid down the main-mast. He pulled his cap off and nodded at me, one eye on the jumper, the other on Crow, who sat, as usual, on my shoulder. The mate didn't like Crow. He said it was unnatural for crows to go to sea, that they feared the ocean, but Crow had shown no signs of discontent. He had, in fact, become as deft a marksman as the seabirds that wheeled around the ship, plummeting straight down and pulling up at the last instant a squirming herring or mackerel in their beaks.

"Call me Zeke, miss." The mate grinned and ran a hand repeatedly over a cowlick that only popped up again.

"Mr. Beebe, would you be willing to make a trade with me?" I pointed to his trousers of salt-softened blue duck.

The mate began to unlace the front of his trousers.

"No, please . . . don't you have another pair?"

He shrugged and made his own trip down to the hold, returning with a clean pair of ducks. I held them up against the skirt of my gown; he was somewhat taller than me, and the legs of the trousers were several inches too long and far too wide.

"May I, miss?" The mate pulled a piece of chalk from his pocket, squatted, and marked several quick lines on the trousers. He straightened up, produced needle and thread from another pocket, and dropped cross-legged to the deck. He stopped for a moment, considering something, then jumped up and ran to the hold, returning with a spool of red ribbon. Then he sat again and in a trice he had hemmed the legs higher and neatly taken in the seams, at the same time sewing along them lengths of the ribbon, which gave them a more feminine air.

I thanked him and went below to change into the trousers and a light calico shift that I normally wore under heavier gowns. Back on deck, I stood looking up into the mainsail, curving away in a great white arc, the blue shadows of a thousand lines and shrouds webbing it. Above, the topsails and topgallants filled the rest of the sky, a vast, many-layered dome of white stretching up and up.

Free of my bulky skirts, I ran up the swaying stairs of rope as easily as though they were solid wood. I was soon sitting on a yard, one arm around the mast, among the sails themselves. Below me, the captain stood at his wheel. The mate moved about in the rigging, changing the trim of a sail, adjusting a stay, both men alert to every creak of rope on wood, every minute shift in the wind. I stayed up until the last light faded and stars began to prick the sky.

The next day I was up the foremast at first light. I ran straight up a ratline, balancing easily on the single thick cable stretched taut from deck to mast, past the foretop, up and up to the fore-topgallant yard. Sitting on the yard at the front of the *Able*, feeling the sway of the mast under me and the wind streaming on my face, I felt like a figurehead placed too high. The *Able* was under a full press of canvas, cutting a fine strong furrow through the waves.

I sat there, plaiting and replaiting my hair, naming all the sails I could remember: "Foresail, mainsail; fore-topsail, main topsail; fore-skysail, main skysail —"

"That sail's a royal, Miss Rathbone. No skysails on the *Able*." Captain Avery's face appeared above the yard, smiling. "Know a thing or two about ships, then? You climb like a sea monkey, at any rate." He eyed a rope bolt on the yard and gave it a rub with his sleeve until it shone. "Maybe I should hire you on, I could use an extra hand." He winked and, clutching the nearest backstay, slid down to the deck.

That afternoon, I found a spare length of line in a dinghy and sat tying all the knots I could recall. I made a bowline and a cleat hitch, sheet bend, eye splice . . . I couldn't help but think of Mama as I tied, of all those nights when I practiced my knots, lying on her bed. I wondered if she missed me. I wondered if she had even noticed I was gone. But it was easy, cutting through the sea on the *Able*, to soon put Mama out of my mind. When the captain came by, I presented him with my knotted rope and made the small speech I had rehearsed.

"Captain Avery, would you consider teaching me how to help? You'd be gaining an extra hand at no cost. And I hope that I'd be repaying you a little for the kindness you've shown in carrying us."

The captain's eyebrows shot up, and he

put a hand to his mouth to cover a smile. But he saw that I was serious.

"Well . . . maybe you could learn a few tricks. Maybe I could teach you how to hand, reef, and steer? Then you'd know enough to run off and join the Royal Navy and be rated able. They'd have to take you then." He winked.

"I could try."

"Well, well." He chuckled. "Maybe we will, maybe we will." And with that he returned to his duties.

I lingered on deck that afternoon, watching the sky. I felt the weather changing, and soon the wind shifted a point to the north and blew harder. The captain and Mr. Beebe climbed to the topsails and began to shorten sail on the main topgallant. I came up beside Mr. Beebe, took up the end of the sail, and neatly secured the reef point. I had watched the two men do it a few times before and it was easy enough. The mate gazed openmouthed at me and looked over to Captain Avery, who shrugged and smiled. After the mainsails and topsails were reefed, we climbed higher and furled the topgallants tightly to their yards. The mate scowled at me as I slid down a line; the captain only laughed.

In the days that followed I was entrusted

with a few minor tasks: swaying the lead and paying seams with slush. Eventually, as the days passed, and the captain came to trust my abilities, I vied with the mate over weightier tasks. I could trice up the tack and scandalize the mainsail faster, fish anchor to cathead neater, and polish a head-nut brighter, feats about which the mate seemed less than pleased. Mr. Beebe, besides his other duties, served also as cook, and he now tended to short my porridge and served me only salt horse at supper, and no plum duff for dessert.

Mordecai, when not engrossed in his observations, proved useful, too, assisting Mr. Beebe in the galley, a dab hand at jointing seafowl and shelling shrimp — skills acquired from his long hours of dissecting in the attic.

When I was not busy, I ranged along the rigging or crawled out along the bowsprit and clung there, riding above the waves, savoring the spindrift that soaked me.

Having had until then only Mordecai's limited vision for comparison, I now realized how acute my own sight was, for not only could I see farther and more clearly than any man on the ship, but I also had a certain premonitory knack. I often pointed to some imminent sight — a flock of birds, a storm front — and met with a blank look from the mate or captain, followed by a look of perplexity when the flock or storm became visible to them, too. One day the captain asked me to take a watch, an honor I didn't treat lightly. When the mate had some trouble with his stomach for a few days, I kept double watches, and stood through a squall one long night, only coming down on deck when the sea had calmed with the dawn. Mama might have been proud of me. I, too, could wait.

I learned the nameless equations of water and wind, cloud and light. I soon knew before the captain when and how the wind would shift and the clouds form. I sensed the presence of sea creatures large and small. I felt the friendly rise of dolphins far astern, the lively spark and twitch of blenny and hake, and the slow, heavy swirl of plankton deeper down.

I wondered if what I saw and felt was what Moses had felt and seen, and Bow-Oar and his brothers, before they lost their sympathy with the sea. I had never seen a living whale, only its bones. I had never paid much attention to Mordecai's careful diagrams, those dry and scratchy depictions of a creature I had heard described only at second and third hand. Now I wondered if

I'd ever be lucky enough to see a live sperm.

One calm clear afternoon, I joined Mordecai in the crow's nest. Our sailing had been so smooth that day that there was little to do, and even the captain and his mate were taking their ease, leaning back in chairs on deck, each with a pipe in his mouth, while Mordecai and I swayed high above the wide blue world.

Mordecai had shed his headgear altogether. His white hair billowed behind him, perhaps not quite glossy but with more of a sheen than before — doubtless from all our healthful exercise in fresh air. He exclaimed at some new sight every few minutes, for there were, besides mistaken whales, other wonders correctly identified: flying fish arcing over our stern; immense schools of shad and silverside split by our bowsprit and streaming down our flanks. However deep in such pleasures, Mordecai still glanced now and then at a particular point on the horizon, straining, I thought, to see in the pattern of waves the path Papa had taken, repeatedly consulting his migration map.

"Soon now, Mercy, you will see the whales streaming northward. You will witness not mere humpbacks but the great sperm himself in grand profusion." He swept an arm across the horizon, as though it was all his to offer.

I listened silently, nodding. It pleased me to see him so lively and taking such an interest in living creatures after his long preoccupation with the dead and desiccated.

I tried to imagine the Far North toward which we sailed, tried to remember that page of Papa's atlas, but could recall only the southernmost tip of Greenland, a brief protrusion of icy blue at the top of the Atlantic, cut off at the top of the page. I pictured the sea stiffening as we pushed northward, the ship slowing, crunching through crystals of ice until we were trapped in a trough between two frozen waves, our sails yearning northward, timbers straining, going nowhere.

But for now the air was warm and soft. It was that hour of early evening when the sky quiets to a blue that might be either dusk or dawn. I was weary from an afternoon of shifting ballast in the hold and leaned, drowsing, in a corner of the crow's nest, chewing a strip of cuttle jerky and absently mending a tackle block. Mordecai still eagerly scanned the horizon with a spyglass, borrowed from the captain and chained securely around his neck. He took great pleasure in viewing the world through an uncracked lens.

Mordecai collapsed his glass and I untied him from the mast, discreetly attaching a short lead from his ankle to mine for safety. He folded his long legs and sank beside me. He had clearly been rummaging in his bag again; the squid eye that usually accompanied his reveries had been replaced by a relic of the Arctic: not the crudely carved walrus tusk that I had seen in the attic but the silky white fur of an ermine, its lush tail tipped with black. Mordecai spread the skin over his knees and stared to the north, where the blue sky was draining to white.

"Above the sixtieth parallel nothing ever thaws. I remember the log of the *Houqua* . . . she was driven off course in a storm in the year eighteen and eight, and happened upon a whaleboat frozen into an ice floe. All hands were frozen at their oars, shrouded in snow. The captain wrote that an old mariner had told him that such a boat had gone missing from a whaler thirty years earlier." Mordecai draped the ermine skin around his neck and began to stroke it, eyes still lifted skyward. "Whalers never used to venture so far north, not until the herds close to home began to thin in your father's time." He slipped lower, arms folded behind his head, staring at a fleet of fat gray clouds riding above the horizon. "The log told of how the night sky shimmered with fractured light. Of mountains of floating ice that glowed like turquoise or jade. The polar bear challenging the ship from his icy throne . . ."

I looked up sharply from my mending. Mordecai's description was so vivid, he might have sailed there himself.

"The polar bear was observed by Palliser to be a retiring creature, without the fierce aspect with which he is endowed in popular literature." Mordecai tossed the end of the ermine fur over his shoulder, eyes shining, and raised his hands like fearsome claws. "But no, oh no, not when threatened. He reared, like this, half again as high as me —"

Mordecai leapt up, lost his balance, and fell off the edge of the crow's nest. In the moment after he dropped, the moment before I, still tethered to his ankle, plummeted after him, I realized that he had read no log, that he had been on that ship himself, had himself beheld *Ursus maritimus.* But before I could challenge what he'd said the deck hurtled up to meet me. I closed my eyes, bracing for the impact. But the ship tilted a point in a breath of wind, and instead I struck the sea. Icy cold pierced me. I shot gasping to the surface, just long enough to take a gulp of air and to see Crow spinning in circles above me, and was jerked back down.

I was pulled deep and deeper. The rope at my ankle burned, the water froze, and the light above me shrank. I looked down, through icy water, to see Mordecai sinking straight into the dark below me, boots flailing, arms spinning, with me whipping along at the end of the tether. I wanted to gasp at the cold and had to force myself not to draw breath. I steadied myself as best I could and pulled myself along the rope stretched between us until I could grasp Mordecai's shoulders. I put my hands to his face and tilted it toward mine, trying to calm him. His eyes were wide, his hair a nimbus of white. A thick stream of bubbles poured from his mouth. I turned my back to him, wrapped his arms about my neck, and began to struggle up toward the surface with him in tow. At first, still flailing, he only dragged me down, but soon I felt his body relax and lighten, felt a surge as his legs kicked out behind us, and in a few moments we burst to the surface. I kept him close — grateful for the air, which was much warmer than the sea, and took in several great breaths. Then I ducked below the surface to sever the tether between us with my dirk (a welcome gift from the captain, which I kept tucked in the waist of my trousers). I was afraid Mordecai would panic again. But instead, though he still took long rasping breaths, his eyes shone through plastered hair, and he smiled wide. He kicked his boots off, turned, and dove back down into the cold sea. I drew a deep breath and dove after him.

When we came up for air, we spotted the captain and mate at the rail, not far ahead, calling out our names; as soon as he realized what had happened, Captain Avery had turned the *Able* into the wind and eased the mainsail.

"It's all right!" I shouted, treading water. Mordecai bobbed up beside me, sent a spout of water high into the air, and laughed. The captain watched us doubtfully for a minute before going back to his chair and pipe. The mate stood there longer, then turned away, shaking his head.

We swam together through the deep. Mordecai stroked confidently through the water. He swam smoothly, powerfully, so unlike the way he moved on land that he seemed a different person. We swam and swam, until it was nearly full dark, and we called to the mate to put a ladder over the side. We climbed up with our teeth chattering, laughing.

We swam each day after that, staying under longer each time. The captain indulged us, since we didn't slow the ship down — not that she was hurrying. We matched the *Able*'s leisurely pace, a steady two to three knots on a long sea under a pure sky. We stroked side by side through brisk swells, then lay on our backs and drifted in the ship's wake. Though the deeper sea was bitter cold, a warm band lay just below the surface and we swam along in it slowly, savoring all that we had not seen in our first plunge. Some days it seemed like all the creatures in the ocean congregated around us. Sea worms and comb jellies danced close to the surface, while larger companions escorted us below: great hosts of tuna, streams of mackerel and cod, haddock and hake. We witnessed the cichlid spitting out her new-hatched young and the king of the herrings leading his column, a host that streamed behind him for many leagues. We passed through colonies of glowing polyps clinging to reefs. We plunged into the half-lit world below, where the moray peered from his watery cave. Once I felt a larger presence, and thought that, at last, I was about to see a whale, but it passed so far below that I couldn't see it clearly, only feel its size, before it slipped into deeper water.

Mordecai grew more agile day by day, and though I sometimes couldn't keep up, I felt my stroke stretch longer as the days passed. Sometimes I locked my fingers around his neck and lay along his back and we swam along as one. The joint pain and swelling that had troubled him earlier on our journey eased more and more each day. It was strange to feel his body below me. He had never seemed to even have a body before. Now his back moved under me, long and sinewy, the bones of his shoulders poking into my stomach as he stroked through the water. I recalled a broader back, a stronger neck; it must have been Papa's back I remembered clinging to, Papa teaching me to swim. I wanted to stay beneath the waves forever. I wanted to gallop with the sea horses, to scuttle sideways with crabs, to sleep on the seabed.

When the *Able* sailed closer to shore, in shallower water, we skimmed along reefs, stopping to gather what bounty we could carry. We came up streaming seaweed, our hands fat with mussels, scallops stuffed between our toes. The mate smiled to see us and added our offerings to the stewpot.

We sat in the crow's nest after our swims, drying in the sun. The mate whistled, busy in the rigging around us. The captain chattered companionably below. Mordecai suffered me to brush out his hair and tie it back in a manly queue. I would hold up the chronometer I was polishing so he could see himself in its shining case. He would turn his head from side to side, admiring my work. He looked reconstituted, as though our plunges in the sea had swelled his veins, and his skin had acquired a faint golden sheen.

"I look a right jack-tar now, eh, me matey?" he asked, and the mate, passing by, rolled his eyes.

But soon the mate had less to roll his eyes about. Before our long days of swimming, I had relied on Zeke to climb behind Mordecai as he crawled cautiously up the ladder to the crow's nest, to guide Mordecai's feet so that he wouldn't fall. Now Mordecai could skip up the ropes almost as quickly as me. One day as I was climbing aloft I saw Mordecai and the captain on deck, chatting together like old shipmates. I moved nearer and saw what they were leaning over: a chart unfamiliar to me, a complex pattern of swirling lines and dense notation. In the days that followed I would sometimes see

Mordecai standing at the wheel, guiding the ship, his hair blowing back, a proud smile on his face. Captain Avery would hover behind him, making furtive course corrections when Mordecai was distracted by some fish.

At night our bodies glowed from the phosphorescent creatures we had swum through. I wondered what wan beacons we two made, lying on deck in the dark. When I stretched out on the sun-warmed wood my muscles felt pleasantly sore from so much swimming, and my bones ached. We slept in each other's arms under a wherry, like Mordecai's attic in compact form. Small chinks in the wherry's planks were like the worn knots in the rafters, admitting, rather than shafts of sunlight, the beams of stars. Under its dome we slept soundly.

On one such night we lay on deck in the last dogwatch, watching the moon empty out, staring up at the stars' slow wheel.

"The seas move like that, too," said Mordecai, swirling his finger at the sky, "in great gyres. They are all one vast body of water, you know, they are all connected, though we give them separate names. The North Atlantic Ocean to the Arctic; the Arctic to the North Pacific; the North Pacific to the

Indian Ocean; the Indian to the Southern Ocean . . ."

I sat in front of Mordecai so that he could comb out my hair and rebraid it. Where before I wouldn't have let him near my hair, now he could deftly weave the hundred braids my aunts had first plaited, adding along their lengths new knots he had learned from the captain.

"Where would you sail to, if we could sail on forever?"

Mordecai looked up at the sky. "I would stop at each speck of land and gather two of each creature. I would be a new Noah." He traced the shapes of those constellations formed like animals: the Greater and Lesser Dogs; the Sea Goat; the Winged Horse; the Two Fishes. He sat quietly for a moment. "I should sail with your papa through all of the seas and back again. I shall sail with him this time. And with me he will miss no sperm . . ."

Mordecai hesitated, then reached into his ditty bag — he kept it around his neck all the time now, with his precious migration map inside — and carefully withdrew another piece of paper. I recognized the chart he and Captain Avery had been poring over.

"The original is back in my attic, but I knew your papa would want to have this as soon as possible, to augment his pursuit of the sperm. It is my wind and current chart of the North Atlantic. With this, any sailor may harness the might of the ocean's currents and winds to speed his passage — considerably, I might say, with all due modesty." Along with his plotting of the whales' migration, Mordecai had pored over his collection of old logs and assembled data on currents and winds in all weathers.

If the old gardener was right, my father was only a few leagues away. We might very soon achieve Mordecai's dream of finding him, and in so doing destroy it. If Papa was so near, he was far from any sperm.

I wondered if he had come after me, not Mordecai, when he swam after us that day. Maybe he had wanted to try to explain. But I could think only of all of the times he had been at Rathbone House, times he could have seen me, been with me, and yet had not.

"And you, cousin? Where would you sail to?"

I compared Mordecai's dreams of sailing with Papa to my own far less ambitious fancies: Papa reading with me in the library, one more populated with books; dining with Mama and my brother and me at a table laden with homely fare. Papa's mere presence in the house while I slept was dream enough when I was a child.

I considered the kingfisher we had sighted earlier that day, bobbing along in her nest on the open water. She was said to have the power to charm the waves and winds into calmness — on the peaceful water the hen-halcyon then builds her nest and hatches her young. I watched the clear horizon that receded as we advanced, unchanging, a serene circle. I wished only that I might add my own charm to the kingfisher's and linger here forever.

CHAPTER FOURTEEN: THE SINKING ISLAND

{in which Mordecai too begins to founder}

One mild evening a few weeks into our voyage, the *Able* stood in for land. We had until then kept well away from the coast, clear of reefs and breakers, sending the mate ashore from time to time in the bumboat to trade with merchants in the towns we passed.

I had secretly been tracking our route each night during the last watch, studying the ship's charts under the binnacle light. I knew we were nearing the island that the gardener had spoken of as Arcady. Maybe there were several Arcadys. Among the many little islands within rowing distance of Naiwayonk, I knew of three Belle Isles (none of them, I thought, particularly belle) and at least four Gull Rocks, generally free of gulls. Nevertheless, I found myself scanning the sea for a high piney island, pink in hue. I took Captain Avery aside and asked if he knew of the island.

"Who told you of such a place?" the captain asked.

I explained about the old man pruning weeds in the Starks' temple. I didn't mention Mama's story.

Captain Avery chuckled. "Why, that's old Enoch. He'd say anything to keep a body talking, lonely old fellow. Loony as a blue booby. Probably told you how he used to sail, too?" He saw by my expression that he had guessed correctly, and nodded. "Blind since birth."

I thought I was ready to be disappointed but was surprised by how my heart sank. It must have been merely coincidence that some of the details of the old man's description had matched Mama's, if they truly had. I began to doubt my own memory, wondering whether I had heard what I wanted to hear to make Arcady real.

The *Able* had been for some time approaching a rocky point. The captain cleared his throat and began to rub at his beard.

"Well, look at that. We're nearly to Esker Point. Maybe I'll pull in for a bit. Just a small delivery to make. Won't be long. Would you mind taking the wheel for a minute or two, miss?"

As soon as I had my hand on the wheel,

the captain hurried off below. The mate had disappeared earlier. Many minutes later they emerged, scrubbed and dressed in clothing that fairly shone compared with their usual dingy ducks and jackets. Captain Avery wore a fresh white shirt with a frill, tucked into laundered trousers. He took the wheel from me with an embarrassed air. The mate wore my great-great-aunts' woolen jumper over clean breeches, and both had shaved their whiskers so that their jaws were raw and pink. They kept sliding their eyes toward shore as they made ready to anchor, avoiding catching my eye.

It was a soft night, the weather having held warm for the season, with light breezes. Plump, rosy clouds gathered around the setting sun, and the sky overhead was deepening to indigo. Along the darkening coast the scattered lights of a village winked, and as we sailed closer I heard laughter over the water and saw a cluster of docked boats — dories and baiters, other small craft — silhouetted against the sky. The *Able* approached the dock faster than seemed prudent to me; the mate's always carefully preserved paintwork scratched as we bumped alongside the dock, but he seemed not to notice. In a wink he had splashed the bower anchor home, leapt onto the dock, and was trotting toward town. The captain checked his reflection in the polished brass of the binnacle.

"Just keep an eye on those forecourses if the wind rises." He dropped down the side after the mate, as brisk as a boy, and hurried away.

I leaned over the poop rail and watched the lights of the village, my eyes adjusting to the deepening dark. A particularly brightly lit house stood close to shore, a small seaman's dwelling of weathered planks on which hung a multitude of lobster traps and glass buoys. I could make out a line of men, starting at the door and winding around the house. There was a sudden flash of light and a pair of men shot out the open door, ejected, and fell sprawling in the street, greeted by hoots of laughter. In the doorway, limned by the light, stood a woman, hands on hips. Her shape was like the plumpest figurehead in Mordecai's attic but considerably less stiff. Breasts bared, hair streaming, she turned her head to and fro as she reviewed the line of men. She chose a new brace of sailors, hauled them in by their neckerchiefs, and slammed the door. I caught sight of Captain Avery and the mate near the end of the line. I couldn't help but picture the inside of the little house and wonder how the woman accommodated the seamen, and where. I pictured Mama, stretched out on the floor of the walk.

I hadn't thought of Mama in many days. Now, standing there in the dark, it felt like our carefree hours were ending. The captain had told me earlier that day that Mordecai and I must give up our swimming, as we had entered waters frequented by sharks. I sighed. At least the captain and his mate were in good spirits. And Mordecai still had his dream of finding Papa. Perhaps I would find my missing brother yet. The old man may have made up Arcady, but he had no reason to lie about his brother having seen a boy with Papa.

I walked the length of the ship to the stern. The mate had strung a dinghy astern to tow behind the ship as we sailed so that Mordecai could view the riches of the sea at close hand. Though Mordecai was by now a useful hand on the *Able* — plotting charts with Captain Avery or splicing rope or reefing sails — he still loved to sit in the dinghy, looking down into the water, studying what fish passed by. I usually joined him in the early evening, after I had fulfilled my shipboard duties.

I dropped down the companion ladder, ran down the line stretched taut from stern to bow over the water, and stepped into the dinghy. Mordecai was fast asleep, his head tucked into the point of the prow. I meant to wake him so that we could have our dinner together, but he looked so peaceful, and I was fairly sure that it would be some time before the captain and mate returned to the ship. I curled up beneath the bench, under Mordecai's knees, and called Crow down from the mast to join me. A light breeze sighed among the sails, bellying the fore and mainsails in soft swells, making them strain against the masts, creaking the stays. Soon I, too, slept.

The lively pitch and roll of the hull woke me, along with Mordecai's voice.

"Mercy. Are you certain you secured the lead line?"

I sat up. A league or more of sea now lay between us and the little town. Its lights were far astern and blurred by rain. Ahead of us only blackness and stronger squalls of wind, the rain thicker. The lead rope that had tied us tautly to the *Able* lay slack in the bottom of the boat. I pulled it up to find its end frayed, though I had secured it myself earlier that day in a stout bow hitch. I turned to where Crow perched on the tip of the prow behind Mordecai's head. His beak was deep in the fresh mackerel he clutched in one claw. I noticed that the torn flesh of the fish was strewn with little fragments of rope.

I jumped up, suddenly fully awake, and began to struggle with the sail, my braids snapping in the wind, stinging my face. I was grateful that the little vessel was equipped with a stub mast and sail, such as it was. With only oars, we would have soon foundered in such strong winds. Mordecai pointed to the tiller and took hold of the sail so that I could steer.

I tried to bring the boat nearer to the wind, but each time I tried she threatened to broach to and capsize. All my newfound seaman's skills were not equal to the buffeting wind and the sail blew clear out of its ringbolt. Mordecai leapt up to snatch it, but it had already sailed high away. All I could do was keep my hand on the tiller and try to hold steady through sheets of rain, driven by the wind, hurtling through the dark.

I didn't realize for some time that we had stopped. The wind continued unabated. There had been no grinding, no sudden lurch when the boat met land, but somehow we were still. I strained to see in the darkness, tuned my ear to the wind and heard it drop a tone, and another. Crow nipped at my neck. The moon slipped in and out of a dark scrim of clouds that showed me only the gleam of his eye, a faint gloss of feathers.

"Mordecai!" I called out.

"Cousin, I am here," came a muffled voice close by.

I stepped from the boat, Crow on my shoulder, onto a thin, rippled strand of sand, scarcely wider than our craft, Mordecai beside me.

Crow had led us there, I knew. Though I couldn't be sure how far we had scudded along in the storm, I could calculate fairly well. The wind had been roughly north-nor'east, and, factoring in time and speed, I knew that we must be at or near the coordinates on the map that the old gardener drew. At the coordinates, but clearly not Arcady, only a flat, empty strand. It would have been hard to conceive of a place more unlike the high pink island, verdant and teeming with life, of Mama's bedtime story. It was the wrong island, but surely the right one was nearby. Maybe we would be able to see it from the other end of the strand.

The firm sand in which we walked quickly deepened and softened. Soon my ankles ached from struggling through dunes shaped by the sea into high, billowing drifts. We had walked for perhaps half a mile when the terrain began to alter. The sun was by now nudging over the horizon and the air was keen, blown clear by the wind.

"Remarkable. I had no idea sand could be such a color."

I had been so intent on what lay ahead that I hadn't looked down. Mordecai was standing behind me, straining sand through his fingers. Pink sand.

"Coral exoskeletons, ground fine? Or perhaps iron deposits in the underlying stratum?"

It couldn't be. I looked back the way we had come, and ahead. The shape, the footprint of the island was essentially right, long and thin, though far, far smaller than the island the gardener had described, and seemingly lifeless. But there were those coordinates. And the sand was pink.

We continued on. It felt as though we were walking uphill, though it was hard to judge, the high drifts having smoothed into long swells that rose and fell under our feet. Here and there, among the rounded ridges of sand, square edges began to appear. I soon realized that I walked through a cluster of dwellings, hewn of stone, sunk deep in the sand, and set in a rough circle. The square edges were the tops of roofless walls; whatever roofs had protected these rooms had blown away or lay buried elsewhere in the sand.

Between the sunken dwellings, what I at first took for pieces of driftwood proved to be the silvered limbs of trees that, though dead, still stood where rooted, their topmost branches stretching just beyond the sand. Next to one house, the upended bow of a fishing smack protruded from a drift, pointing skyward. I walked around the smack, running my hand over the planks; the hull was still sound, though sun and sand had worn away all but a few patches of its red paint. A stand of what looked like sedge grass sprouted through the sand. What I at first took for blades of grass were in fact slender poles of wood. I took hold of one pole and pulled; the wood, dried and hollow from its sleep in the sand, snapped in half. It was a fishing rod of finely whittled pine, a broken line trailing from its eyelets.

One dwelling, near the center of the circle, stood higher than the others, its walls jutting up from the sand so that the tops of window and door openings could be seen. From this house I heard Mordecai calling to me. As I approached, the house seemed to gather girth and heft. I walked off the length of a wall and measured it as thirty feet end to end. Around the house stood a broken circle of fencing. Coming closer, I found the pickets to be made not of wood but from the broken-off spears of swordfish, jammed in the sand side by each, their sharp tips pointing up. Crow scrawked, launched off my shoulder, and skimmed through the empty window. I stepped through a wide, low doorway whose bottom half was submerged in sand, bending over to avoid bumping my head.

I stood inside a single large room. The dunes had drifted through the doorway and window openings in foot-thick walls of rough stone. A sea of sand filled the room. Here a skeletal perch seemed about to leap, there a swirl of kelp traced the pattern of a wave. I wasn't sure whether the sand had risen — it looked too deep to have only drifted in — or whether the house was sinking.

Mordecai stooped in the far corner of the room, his head bent under a beam of worked stone. He leaned to extract abandoned belongings from the dry swells: a crumbling book, a tin coffeepot that poured a stream of sand. A few chairs jutted up at odd angles from the sand, as though bobbing in the sea. The top of a brick chimneypiece showed where the hearth had once been.

At the far end of the room four finials thrust through a drift of dried seaweed, the posts of a bedstead sunk beneath. I lay along the sand above the bed and stretched my arms high, my legs long. Two of me might easily have slept end to end.

Captain Avery had told us of the great cities where men melted not the flesh of whales but metal in vast cauldrons, and with it built new cities. Fishermen of some kind had lived here, judging by what remained. But maybe they had suffered like other local fishermen when the once boundless fish had dried up along with the whales on our coastline. Maybe they had chosen to leave the homes of their ancestors and go to the cities to work in dark iron and cold steel in a dry world, a world in which nothing shifted under their boots. My great-great-aunt had spoken of the families that tried to compete with the Rathbones in the early years of whaling. This island might have belonged to such a family.

I lay on my bed of sand, braiding two strands of sea palm, staring out the window at the dunes. It may have been only the way the clouds were gliding slowly to the west, but it felt as though the island were drifting eastward. Crow dropped down and stalked about on the bed, plunging his beak at intervals in the sand, prodding for clams. I spread my arms and legs on the sand to make a larger me.

"Mordecai."

"Yes, Mercy." Mordecai sat cross-legged on the sand above the spot where the chair was buried, his nose in a tattered book. I pulled a clamshell from the sand next to me and with it drew circles on the surface.

"What will you do when we find Papa?"

"I shall sail with him, naturally. I shall take my place by his side." He looked up at me keenly, patting the ditty bag around his neck, which held his wind and current chart. "I will be his navigator."

"And what about me?"

"You shall be lookout, of course." Mordecai smiled at me.

I looked around the sunken room and out the window at the long strand of sand. Maybe Benadam Gale really had been seen here by the old gardener's brother. Maybe this really was the island of which the gardener spoke, with thick woods and high bluffs, and it had dried up along with all the fish in the sea around it. He could have stopped here to rest in his pursuit of Mordecai and me. It was not impossible that he had lived here, in those years when I'd pictured him far away on the sea, though what few objects remained in the house had clearly not been used for many years. The roofless house would provide poor shelter against rain and wind, and nothing grew on the island. He would have had only fish to eat. If Papa had been living here, I'd been right about one thing: He had, after all, chosen a desert.

The wind sighed through the empty windows, bringing with it a swirl of sand.

"Mercy."

"Hmm?" I had been half asleep on my bed of sand. I turned my head to find Mordecai still staring into the book he had found.

"I believe we know someone with the initials 'B.G.'?"

I sat up straight. Mordecai came and sat next to me, handing me the book.

It was a clothbound logbook of a common type, with leather corners and marbled boards of a dull green, with the initials "B.G." lettered roughly on its cover, the ink blurred by seawater. I opened it eagerly, holding it so that Mordecai and I could read together.

The logs I had seen in Mordecai's collection began with a title page of some sort: *"Journal of a Voyage to California by Charles Stoddard, 1837"* or *"Remarks on Board the Bark Houqua."* Some included an invocation for a profitable voyage in verse, such as: *"Let Neptune keep from us Unkind Gales, Let our Harpoons spear many Fine Whales."* The logbook of B.G. began with no such formality. On the endpaper inside the front cover was a crude painting in watercolor of a sperm swimming in a green-black sea; from its spout spumed a cloud of blood.

The pages of the journal proper looked much like other whalemen's journals, with brief entries on date, activity, winds, and heading. Wide margins to the outside of each page carried the stamped images of whales, used to mark those days when a chase had been successful. On one such spread we read:

Remarks on board Feb. 26, 1846. These 24 hours begin with light winds from the west. At 4 p.m. saw sperm. Struck, killed, and took him alongside. At 10 p.m. got through cutting and took in sail. Sixe hands employed in boiling thus ends these 24 hours.

I flipped quickly through the book from front to back, scanning the text for some mention of my brother. But there were no names mentioned at all, only details of sailing, and weather, and whales. I handed the book to Mordecai and lay back on the sand. Mordecai bent eagerly over the book. I closed my eyes, listening to the pages of the logbook turning and the soft swish of sand outside in the dunes, while Mordecai read.

"Cousin." Mordecai's cool hand touched my shoulder, and I sat up. He looked stricken. His mouth trembled. He took a deep, shaky breath.

"I am not quite sure how to tell you this, but I have been much mistaken about your papa. You must brace yourself." He moved closer and put a rigid arm around my shoulders, his fingers cold and damp against my neck. "He does not follow the whales, after all. He has not followed them for some time. He is no more to be found now than he ever was." He took his arm away. "Our expedition is at an end."

With a grim nod, he handed me the logbook. I didn't know whether to feel relief or guilt. I could almost have laughed at Mordecai wanting to protect me from what I had so long known, so long avoided telling him.

I began to page through the journal more carefully. Other records that I had seen usually included only a scattering of whales over the course of a voyage, with many blank days. In B.G.'s journal the early pages were thickly populated with whales, jostling so closely that there was little space left to write. Often, only dates accompanied the crowds of whales; the hours of their deaths went unremarked, their boiling uncelebrated. I thumbed through the book quickly, so that the stamped whales flashed past, seeming to live and swarm on the pages: now stamped in blue ink, now in black, lapping one over the other. Some pages were sprinkled with blood or splotched with oil, so that whales from the pages underneath shone through the translucent paper. About three-quarters of the way through, their numbers diminished rapidly and trailed to nothing. I turned back to the beginning: The log entries began in the year 1842. The final entry, scant as all the latter entries, recording only date and wind bearing, was in 1852. Seven years had passed since ink had marked these pages. After the final entry were a few dozen pages barren of any writing.

I looked up. Mordecai was standing in the doorway, staring out. He turned to me, eyes bleak.

I told him, then, what the old gardener had said, about his brother seeing Benadam Gale not a month ago on this island — Arcady Island.

I wondered if all of the questions that followed for me were in his mind, too: why Papa wasn't still pursuing the whales; why he hadn't come home, if he was so near, instead of to this dead place. Mordecai turned his head to me, a faint smile on his lips.

"It need not be his," Mordecai said. "B.G. It could be the log of a Bartleby Greene. A Barnabas Grimwell. Brendan Goforth . . ." He turned away again.

I hadn't realized how much I had relied on his dream, the way a drowning sailor relies on a cracked buoy, knowing he will sink but hoping, hoping. Even if I had long since given up on Papa, I never expected Mordecai to.

The wind sighed through the empty windows, bringing with it a swirl of sand. I suddenly felt like I would smother in that great bed, as though the ceiling were about to collapse, the whole house about to sink deeper into the sand. I left Mordecai to his book and went outside.

The morning mist had burned off, and I looked down the strand to see the *Able*'s dinghy, drawn safely up, well above the tide line. Captain Avery would be worried about the boat by now, and perhaps about us. My eye fell on the buried smack jutting from the sand, a few houses down the strand. It appeared seaworthy enough. I would leave the captain's dinghy here and find some messenger to let the captain know its whereabouts so that he could retrieve it; maybe Crow would consent to act as carrier pigeon, a note tied to his foot. It was time to give up our false quest. I turned and leaned into the doorway.

"Mordecai, come help me."

Mordecai seemed at first not to have heard. Shoulders slumped, eyes dull, he looked now like my tutor of old, not the hale and hearty Mordecai of our halcyon days. He followed me out into the thin light.

We retraced our steps to the buried smack and together we hauled it from its berth and let it drop down. I examined the hull carefully; its sandy sleep had cured rather than rotted the sturdy oak planking, and its oars were equally well preserved.

We pushed the smack down to the sea. Crow stationed himself in the point of the prow, a small figurehead of lacquered black, suited in size to our vessel. I took the first stint at the oars, pulling us through the choppy surf as I looked back at the island. It may have been the angle at which I viewed it, but the village of stone seemed even lower in the sand than before, the sand itself lower in the sea.

"Mordecai, is it possible for an island to sink?"

His voice was toneless. "Islands formed by volcanic activity have been observed to recede beneath the surface, leaving behind only their coral reefs. Also, those located along some perilous divide between tectonic plates of the earth's crust have been known to . . ." His voice trailed away, and he stared off vaguely.

I looked to the north, to the point of the compass from which Mordecai had expected the whales to come, and in their wake my father. No matter the time, no matter what else he was doing, Mordecai had, until now, never failed to glance in that direction every few minutes since we had been traveling northward on the *Able.* To the north was only the same unbroken gray sea, and a light mist hung in the air.

A movement on the island caught my eye. Not a movement so much as a presence, for the shape I saw was that of a man, legs apart and firmly planted, arms held stiffly at his sides, motionless, facing my way.

My body knew before I did. A hot wave spread through me and I jumped up, dropping the oars. My spine thrummed and my skin twitched as though he had just reached out and touched me. Papa.

He seemed to stand on the surface of the ocean itself — our boat must have come far enough for the curve of the earth to hide the island, or the island was sinking as we rowed away.

I knew him now. I hadn't recognized him that night on the walk, but now I did. I knew now that we were alike, both bound to the sea. I felt its pulse as Moses had felt the whale's.

But that was all that connected us. No days spent together, no stories read or dinners shared — none of the simple stuff of life that would have bound daughter to father. I would never have abandoned my family as he did, never have chosen to hide on this dried-up island in a house of sand. I would have chosen instead a death like Bow-Oar's, who climbed to the crosstrees of his ship and fell silently into the sea. I would rather have drowned, with the fish swimming through my bones at the bottom of the ocean.

I didn't wave, and I didn't call out. I wanted nothing to do with him. I only wanted my brother. But no smaller silhouette stood next to Papa. I told myself that he only lagged behind, that he would come running to join his father in one more moment. But as I stared, hoping, hoping, Papa, still alone, faded from gray to white in the thickening mist and disappeared.

I glanced at Mordecai. He lay slumped in the hull, staring off, away from the island; he had noticed nothing.

I was unsure what heading to take, and the wind was boxing the compass in weak gusts. I let the smack drift into the current, south by southeast, rowing only to stay far enough from the coast to keep clear of shoals and breakers. I looked back again at the nameless island as we rowed away. You might never know a village had ever stood there, it rode so low in the dunes. Soon, I knew, it would sink altogether.

CHAPTER FIFTEEN: CIRCE

*{in which Mordecai
succumbs to a siren song}*

Our fishing smack was weatherly, if not swift, built for patient trawling along the coast. Judging by the map I found in Mordecai's bag, Naiwayonk was perhaps a three-day sail, though the trip would take longer in our little vessel.

"Well. What do you say, Mordecai? Shall we go home?"

Mordecai was hunched in the stern, trawling a hand in the water.

"We could go to Mouse Island. My great-great-aunts will teach me to weave. You could continue your study of the sheep."

Mordecai ignored me.

I considered and quickly discarded the Starks. Though I thought Roderick would welcome us, I didn't think we would find a haven in that house. I fished in one of

Mordecai's bags and found the sailor's cap he had affected earlier in our travels. I wound my braids tightly around my head and pulled the cap down tight.

"Maybe I'll join the merchant marine or the navy of some foreign power."

The cap popped off my head and my braids sprang out. I sighed and put the cap away. Mordecai had not looked up at all.

We made slow progress southward. On our starboard side I kept in view a rocky coast topped with pines, the branches of some lightly dusted with snow, under a lowering bank of cloud. The weather here held true to the season, for we were now deep into autumn. We anchored that night in a cove, dining on a few handfuls of crumbled ship's biscuit from the bottom of Mordecai's bag. Neither of us slept well in the chill air, huddled under tarps in the little smack.

On our second day of sailing the coast began to change in character, its rocky forms now softened with verdant green. The wind, too, softened and pulled us always leeward, no matter the trim of our little sail. The placid sea on which we rode, a clear and plangent blue, showed no treacherous shoals or sandbars, and I allowed the smack to sail closer to shore.

The air was ever warmer. The water warm, too, when I dipped a hand over the stern. Though the sun shone strong and low in a soft sky, it didn't account for the unseasonable November temperatures.

Mordecai, who had been dozing in the stern, wrapped in oilcloth, lifted his head slowly above the rim, squinting over his blue spectacles toward the coast. We were sailing past a little cove of white sand. I leaned over the side and reached to the shallow bottom, taking up a handful of sand and letting it run through my fingers. It was made up of finely crushed shells of every kind I had seen and some I had not. The fragments were all rounded, as though they had turned in this same gentle surf for many years. Above the pale crescent of beach, against a backdrop of slim white birches, rose a terrain of rocky crags pierced by caves, softened by lichens and mosses. From their dusky recesses came the sound of trickling water, not a rhythmic sea-like sound but the sound of fresh water, in intermittent tinklings and drips.

As we sailed past, a loud whooshing sound startled us both. From the dark caves came pale flashes, flutterings of white — wings rising, then as suddenly sinking down again, out of view. Crow left his post as figurehead to fly toward the flashes of white and was soon lost to view in the dark landscape.

Mordecai half stood, shielding his eyes, looking eagerly toward the rocks. In a moment he had scrambled over the side and was hurrying across the cove and into the gloom.

I dropped anchor and followed. My boots crunched on the strand of shell, then stepped soundlessly on the thick moss that coated the rocks that rose all around, obscuring the sky. As I clambered up, a cavern, thirty or forty feet across, opened before me, its roof lost in darkness, its rear wall receding in a deep curve. Light, from some opening farther in, filtered through moist air. Rivulets of water trickled down the cavern walls, echoing. I stood waiting for my eyes to become accustomed to the low light. The whooshing sound started again, and I could now see large white birds, dozens of them, rise perhaps a foot in the air then drop to the moss that covered the floor of the cavern. The floor was covered with birds. Where they didn't stand or mill the rock was white with their droppings. Among the white was one black form. Crow strutted among the flock, all taller than him, turning his head to nip now left, now right; the birds twitched at his nips and moved aside but didn't startle or scatter.

Mordecai stood among the birds, an ecstatic look on his face. He leaned and lifted one. The bird suffered him to hold it in his arms and gently stroke its feathers. Though I had not seen such a specimen before in the flesh, I knew it well from Mordecai's map: the black-necked stilt. Here, then, were the birds that should now have been, according to his calculations, winging northward to Greenland with the whales, closely followed by Papa. But these birds had winged nowhere; their wings were scarcely larger than their heads. No wonder they couldn't rise beyond the lowest branches of the birches. They had, besides, a complacent air, more of the domestic chicken than a wild, man-wary creature; a dull eye; an unassuming beak. I recalled the stilt's plumage in the tinted engraving as a rich black and white, its legs as quite long and bright red in color. This bird trailed legs of only moderate length, a faded pink in hue. Its plumage didn't have the stark division between dark and light of its depiction on the map but rather a mottled appearance, a gray and white like the lichens clinging to the rocks among which the stilt's companions huddled, emitting low and infrequent *kip-kip-kips.*

Mordecai gravely stroked the bird, which lolled in his arms, gazing vacantly into his face.

"At least I have found my stilts." He smiled dimly. "Though not where I expected. It seems I have been wrong about everything."

Something moved in the dark recess behind him, something larger than the birds: a slender shadow, a curve of long pale hair. I wouldn't have noticed if the figure hadn't moved slightly, it was so similar to the pale-barked trunks of the birches that sprang here and there from the mossy floor of the cave.

A voice from the dark recess; the figure moved again. This time Mordecai saw and started. A high, soft voice, a woman's.

"Kip-kip-kip."

I would have thought the birds had made the sound if I had not seen her mouth move. The stilts all began to shuffle excitedly toward the woman.

"Kip-kip-kip. Kip."

We moved closer to the figure in the cave. She was, in the dim light, attractive, with a slender figure and a pale smooth complexion that didn't suggest any nameable age. She looked so like Mordecai that I caught my breath. Her whiteness, though, was of a different variety, not dried but moist in a fungal way. Her pale hair was long and sleek. She was clothed in a soft garment of a mushroom hue.

"Kip-kip-kip."

I cleared my throat and dropped a curtsey.

"Excuse me, may we introduce ourselves? This is Mordecai Rathbone, and I am Mercy Rathbone. May we know your name?"

The woman didn't look directly at us, though I believe she tried. Her eyes traveled tidally, rolling high in their sockets then sinking down like waves on a beach, never stopping. The birds were thick around her; most squatted down and drowsed, those nearest stretched their beaks up to her. In her lap lay a cluster of garden snails. As we watched she placed one on a large flat rock beside her, cracked it with the small rock in her hand, and dropped the meat into a waiting beak.

"What lovely birds. Do you take care of them all yourself?" I said, nudging Mordecai.

"Yes, yes, what fine . . . robust specimens of *Himantopus mexicanus* you have here. I congratulate you."

The woman only replied in the language of the stilts. I thought at first that she understood us and was trying to respond, but the sounds she made seemed after all directed at her birds, not us.

As my eyes grew used to the gloom, other, smaller creatures took shape on the rocks around the woman and in the crevices. Each was familiar and yet altered. I recognized several small *echinoderms;* clumps of agarum and sea palm; the sand dollar and the sea urchin, leached of their color and clinging not to a reef but to a tuft of moss; the brittle star become pliable; the horny sponge moistened. When Mordecai, too, could see them, he bent and lifted them close to his eyes, examining first one then the next, exclaiming softly as he turned them in his hands.

We ventured farther into the grotto. Smaller caves were here and there worn in the rock, lit by wan shafts of light from openings in the rock above. In one such recess was the woman's sleeping place: A fine bedstead of the early colonial era stood, somewhat unevenly, on the rocky floor, its crewelwork hangings still bright, protected in the dim cave against fading. I thought I saw, farther back in the cave, the end of another bedstead, though the light was too dim for me to be certain. In another recess stood a carved chest on which were stacked a few porcelain dishes and candlesticks of pewter. Other niches held baskets. I dipped my hand in each and held it up to see: tree nuts, some kind of twisted root, late berries. My stomach rumbled; the berries were tempting. I had not tasted anything land-grown these many weeks. The *kip-kip* came again; I turned to see the woman gesturing and nodding toward the baskets, smiling. I grasped a handful of dark, prickled berries and ate gratefully.

Mordecai, meantime, tried to slake his thirst at a thin trickle of water running down one wall, pressing his mouth against the stone with little success. The woman, watching, gestured eagerly toward a small pool just behind her, fed by some underground stream or spring. Mordecai knelt at the pool's edge and sniffed at the surface, dipped a finger, and tasted. His furrowed brow cleared and he put his lips to the pool and drank thirstily. Crow left off tormenting the stilts to join Mordecai at the pool, plunging a greedy beak and drinking deep. Refreshed, he took up a perch high on the cave wall and used it as a base to dive upon the stilts, snatching snails from their beaks. After several dives, the woman called to him. He first approached her as she beckoned gently, then retreated, sidling nearer by degrees until finally he hopped in her lap and allowed her to stroke his head.

My skin began to creep in the dark and humid space. I picked my way across the rough cave floor to get outside, to light and fresher air, Mordecai following behind me. When he stooped to pass through the low entrance, he struck his forehead against the roof of the cave with a loud smack and a howl. Wincing, he lowered himself slowly to sit cross-legged on the rock, hand to head. When he pulled his hand away I was relieved to see that he wasn't bleeding, but the blood had jumped under his skin to start a great dark bruise already. I burrowed in his bag and found his bandanna, knelt beside him, and gently bandaged his head. Mordecai, grimacing, pressed his spectacles closely against his eyes, drew up his knees, and sighed. We both stared out to sea.

I knew the woman's eyes were on us. Without turning my head, I leaned close and whispered, "Who is she, Mordecai?"

Mordecai looked down at his hands. In them he turned a sand dollar, not one of the stiff disks with which I was familiar but a soft and spongy circle.

"I believe she may be a relation." He smiled.

Around us wandered a few stilts, fresh

from the cave, blinking in the sun. Mordecai gathered one up as it passed close and cradled it in his arm. He examined, tenderly, its scanty wing.

"They do not need wings here. How admirably they are suited to their environment. Note the beak variance, fully two inches longer than the species mean and angled to adapt to the land-bound snail. Such a beak could no longer pry the recalcitrant sea mollusk. But these stilts no longer need the sea. It looks to me as though they found plentiful sustenance here, stayed and built their nests, and over time lost the power of flight. They had no need to strive further." Here he patted his bag. "Though I have it on authority that they did once fill these skies." He looked off, over the water. "And, beneath them, the great herds of sperm filled the sea."

He cracked open his satchel. Though it had looked moderately old when we started out, the bag now told its true age, its brittle leather bleached and cracked. He took my hand in his and with his other hand reached into the bag, then slid the woven bracelet onto my wrist. I had realized it was missing back in the little temple on the Stark Archipelago, that I hadn't seen it since showing it to Mordecai our first day on the *Able.* It felt tighter, whether by salting or because my wrist had grown larger, or perhaps both.

Mordecai leaned back against a rock and closed his eyes against the sun that now seemed so bright after our time in the cave. He appeared to be suffering from the same drowsiness that afflicted Crow. He reached up and pulled my bandage lower on his face so that it shadowed his eyes. His skin, golden in our days on the *Able,* was starting to burn, and his eyes were as sensitive to the sun as they had ever been. When he straightened his legs he winced, as though the joint pain that had vanished with all our swimming had returned.

"It is so warm here. I do not like the cold, it does not agree with me. Though I didn't mind it then . . ."

His mind was wandering, I thought.

"What do you mean, 'then'?"

He leaned forward and looked at me groggily.

"Did you know, Mercy, that the northern whalers used a barrel nailed to the crosstrees for a crow's nest, to shelter the lookout from the cold? Though it provided little protection in those latitudes."

We had not spoken of that northern voyage since the day Mordecai fell overboard. I had been startled by his vivid description of the polar bear, certain that he had seen *Ursus* not in starry form but in the flesh, rearing against the Arctic sky. So I had suspected then what he told me now, though not all.

"I rode up there, in the crow's nest, once or twice. Your papa carried me up himself, wrapped in furs of *Ursus*. I didn't care how cold it was then." He leaned back against a rock, closing his eyes in the sun. "I beheld the aurora borealis. I observed teeming populations of the *Aptenodytes* penguin filing toward true north." Mordecai swept his arm across the sky and lost his balance, falling to one side. Righting himself, he slowly smoothed down his wandering hair. "At night great swarms of migrating herring shimmered beneath the ice. If such life thrived so far north in turgid waters, I could scarcely bear to contemplate the glories of maritime life that awaited me to the south." He paused, drawing his legs up and leaning his chin on his knees. "But it was not to be. I was not to train for whaling, nor to serve in any useful capacity aboard your father's ship."

"But Mordecai. You told me Papa didn't know about you. That Mama and the man in blue hid you in the attic."

"Did I?" His eyes were unfocused behind the blue lenses. I glanced back at the cave.

Crow slept soundly in the woman's lap, while she continued to feed those stilts who were not themselves napping. Most had gathered their legs beneath them and settled to sleep. I was glad that I had not drunk from that pool.

"Why weren't you allowed to sail again, a second time?"

"I was . . . superseded." Mordecai turned up a corner of the handkerchief and squinted up at me with a wan smile.

I felt suddenly very cold.

"What do you mean . . . 'superseded'?"

Mordecai sighed and waved me away with a limp hand.

"You need not concern yourself for my feelings, Mercy. I will be comfortable here, as much as anywhere. I shall stay here, and study the stilt and his companion creatures. I shall classify them. A crustacean shall be named after me. Perhaps record my own learnings, produce my own volume. Something worthy to gather dust in the attic."

Stay? That wasn't possible. I searched for something to say.

"But Mordecai. We have to find Papa."

He lay back again on the rock and turned his head away.

"We both know that will not be."

I clutched his arm and shook it.

397

"But you can't stay here. You have to help me find my brother. And make Mama tell me what really happened." I clutched my braids to stop my hands from shaking.

Mordecai sat up slowly. He reached deep into his bag and pulled out one more item. I knew before he laid the folded linen napkin in my lap what it was. I couldn't bear to look.

"He's been properly treated. I had wanted to cast him for you in plaster, but there was only enough to repair your skiff . . ."

From the cave came, again, the woman's *kip-kip-kip.* Those few stilts that had wandered out into the light turned and hurried back toward the cave. Mordecai lurched up and followed them. He trod into the cave like a sleepwalker, knelt beside the woman, and lay his head on her knee. She began to stroke his hair; soon he lay beside her, his head in her lap, next to Crow's. Mordecai looked as like to her as a twin. He appeared to have fallen asleep but then he opened his mouth and started to sing, his voice slurred and off pitch.

"Father, Father, sail a ship,
Sail it straight and strong.
Mother, Mother, make a bed,
Make it soft and long . . ."

398

My mouth went dry.

"Didn't you hear it? The song?" Mordecai asked.

I got up from my place in the sun and approached the cave, stopping where bright sunlight abruptly ended and the dark began.

"Don't you remember, Mercy? The barrels?"

"Barrels? Do you mean the crow's nest?"

"No, no, the bed your mama made. A bed in a barrel . . ."

Mordecai was confused. He couldn't know what he was saying.

"He was in the way, you see. Of her . . . recreations." Mordecai turned over, stilts shuffling out of his way, so that he faced away from me, his voice muffled. "Your brother. Gideon. She stuffed him in a barrel and left him there . . .

"For it was Father sailed the sea,
For it was Mother murdered me . . ."

He fell silent and his head dropped back into the woman's lap.

"Mordecai!" I screamed.

The woman smiled at me, her eyes executing a slow somersault, and petted Mordecai's head. He didn't stir again.

I had to wake him, had to get him to

explain. I rushed up to him and pushed and prodded and slapped his face again and again, but nothing would rouse him. Crow lay languid and uncaring among the woman's soft skirts. One glazed eye opened. I snatched him up and ran out into the light. Slinging Mordecai's bag over my shoulder, I headed for the boat. I looked back once more, despairing. I didn't know what else to try. I didn't want to leave without him but I couldn't stay. I had to get away from there.

I ran to the cove and set off across the little lagoon, rowing across its glassy, windless surface, rigging my sail only when I reached open water. I sat on the stern bench, took a deep breath, and started to cry.

Crow crawled from my pocket, stretched his wings, and hopped to the top of Mordecai's bag, which lay on the bench beside me. He cocked an eye at the opening, where a peak of white cloth showed, and with his beak tried to pry the opening wider. I gently pushed Crow away and pulled out Mordecai's journal. I opened it to the chart and stared at the drawing I had made only a few weeks ago. I'd had such a clear, strong picture of my brother in my head as I drew and was so pleased with the likeness. Now I saw only a vague jumble of line and shadow.

I had, at least, at last, a name. Gideon.

My brother. After all this time. Mordecai had lied, just like Mama. I tried to grasp that fact, while my mind ran ahead: Stuffed in a barrel? Mordecai was delirious; it must have been the bird woman's water.

I slammed the journal shut. I tried to picture my brother the way I always had, until Mordecai and I ran away. I imagined my favorites among the images I had used to assemble him. I chose his head from among the bronzes of the Greeks. I tried *Victorious Youth* and *Ephebe of Marathon,* their curls turned verdigris by the sea. I tried my favorite, *The Charioteer of Delphi,* with his thick bronze lashes, the bright whites of his eyes startling in seagreen flesh. I chose a marble, the *Torso of Miletus,* for his body, and tried to attach each head to it, but none would stick.

I wiped my eyes and stood to trim the sail. Cold wind whipped my calves; the hem of my gown now rode above my ankles, no longer soaked by the sea when I stood in the bow.

Why hadn't Mordecai ever admitted I had a brother? Why? He had heard the song, too. He had spoken for so long in half-truths that I didn't know what to believe. I was little better; I had dawdled as long in lies small and large. I had loitered on the *Able* and delayed going home. If I had known what I would find there, I might have begged the captain to sail on to the Davis Strait after all, and beyond, to that point so far north that the ship would have halted, frozen between two waves. Or I might have returned to the Stark Archipelago and found the jilted grotto of which the gardener had spoken, and become another Circe, attended not by many snowy stilts but by one dark crow.

A flash of white caught my eye; a single sail, on a familiar craft — there was the *Able*'s dinghy, not a mile behind me, bearing west toward Circe's cove, with Captain Avery at the tiller. I was glad that he had already recovered the dinghy, but surprised to see him in these waters, miles south of the *Able*'s northward course; then beyond the dinghy, a mile or so to the north, I saw the *Able* herself anchored off a point, saw the glint of a cable curving down into the sea.

I was not far from the dinghy; I waved, but the captain didn't notice, intent on his destination. I changed course and tacked back, until I was only a few boat lengths away.

"Captain Avery!" I shouted.

He whipped around, his mouth dropping open. I ran the smack neatly up alongside and tossed out a line; he automatically reached for the line and made it fast, but said nothing, only stared at me.

"Captain, I'm so sorry about the dinghy. We never meant to leave the ship. The wind came up and Crow had chewed through the line and . . ." I faltered and stopped. I steeled myself to be reprimanded. But instead he reddened and began to chatter.

"Never you mind. Found her all snug and sound." He patted the side of the dinghy briskly. "Wasn't hard to guess which way you went, I knew the wind was north-nor'east, and there's no other landfall for miles and miles. Never you mind, she's fit as a fiddle." While holding my eye, he fumbled behind him for something: a canvas tarp, which he was trying to spread over a group of crates that filled the dinghy. There was also a woven basket full of vegetables and another of apples. Nestled among the apples were a few smaller baskets filled with the same dark, prickly berries I had seen in Circe's cave.

"Is she my aunt, then?"

The captain's hands froze on the tarp; his mouth opened and closed. He stood up, heaved a deep sigh, and nodded.

I thought of the second bed I had glimpsed in Circe's cave.

"Are there others?"

The captain slowly pulled the tarp off the crates and folded it.

"There were. She's the last of them. Name of Limpet." He sat on a crate, lit his pipe, and pulled his collar closer around his throat. A keen little wind had sprung up; the hulls of the boats bumped against each other. He looked sidelong at me.

"Limpet? How did you know that?" I asked. In my mind I had named her Circe, though the Circe of the Greeks had charmed Odysseus's men not into stilts but swine.

"Maybe I did visit Naiwayonk a time or two. And I might have known Bemus, a little."

"What about my mother?"

He shifted on the crate. "Well, now, her I never knew."

I realized I was shivering. I pulled my shawl tight and looked toward the island; the white cove was just visible, and behind it the dark rocks.

"Captain, why didn't you tell me about my brother? When I asked you, back at the Starks'? I know about him now. Mordecai told me."

Captain Avery looked keenly at me, then

looked down at the hull and sighed again.

"Well. I don't know anything much, miss, really I don't. I'd heard there were two youngsters up at the house, twins, and that the boy disappeared along with his father. There were a few stories about what happened to him. Just gossip. Nothing that would do you any good to hear." He glanced up at me. "He's just gone, has been a long time."

I was tired of all the questions, tired of asking them. I gazed across the water, toward Circe's cove.

"Don't worry, I'll keep an eye on him." The captain winked gravely at me. "Going back?"

I nodded. He took up an empty bucket and put in a few apples from one basket, carrots from another. From his breast pocket he took a flask and, unscrewing the top, tipped it into his mouth and took a couple of long drafts. He rinsed it over the side and filled it with fresh water from a cask, then put it in my hand.

"Best to keep a good two miles or so off Napatree Point on your way back, the shoals there . . ." He looked up at me, chuckling. "But then you'll not have any trouble handling a boat, will you?"

He cast off my line and leaned to push

our hulls apart, then stopped and reached out for my hand. When I put my hand in his, he pulled me close and hugged me.

"Try not to think too poorly of her."

"What do you mean?"

The captain sighed and looked out across the water, toward Naiwayonk.

"Perhaps it's time you knew about the rest . . ."

I pulled Crow close to me and stroked his feathers, and felt his strong pulse of warmth in the ever-colder air. He struggled from under my hand and launched off and away.

CHAPTER SIXTEEN:
THE WHITE CHILDREN

{in which Lydia again fails to understand}

1819

Lydia looked up at the clock, then returned to her letter. She had already read the response from Miss Marylbone's Academy earlier that morning, but she reread it with satisfaction and relief. The school's answer to her first inquiry had not been encouraging.

March 3, 1819

DEAR MRS. RATHBONE,
Thank you for your inquiry regarding your daughter, Claudia Rathbone, and your nieces, Julia and Sophia Rathbone. At present we anticipate few openings for the autumn for our freshman class, and we must fill those from our extensive waiting list. Moreover, we regret that we

are not familiar with the Rathbone family. We are certain you will understand and, indeed, acclaim our practice of scrutinizing the background of any young lady we invite to join the daughters of New England's preeminent families. Have you, perhaps, relations in the Boston area with whom we may be acquainted and who might provide references on your behalf?

Regards,
Miss Edith Marylbone

Lydia folded and unfolded a corner of the letter. She had no relations in Boston who could satisfy Miss Marylbone's curiosity. Her mother, even if she had answered her letters, would have been able to offer little additional claim to social standing of an ilk that would satisfy Miss Marylbone. Lydia had occasional news of the Starks from Bemus, who had it from some merchant who visited the archipelago from time to time. Though the Starks' wealth continued to grow with their thriving maritime trade, they had climbed no higher in society's ranks, having squandered their most valuable social currency on the sale of herself and her sisters, who might well have married into the very preeminent Boston fami-

lies that would have impressed Miss Marylbone. The Starks had, with their growing
wealth, lured a few young ladies of good
family to marry Lydia's brothers, but the
offspring of those unions were so alarm-
ingly unattractive that their grandparents
and aunts, one of whom did in fact live in
Boston, were reluctant to present them in
society, let alone invite them home for the
holidays.

So Lydia had spoken to Bemus, and a
cutter had sailed up to Boston with a heavy
satchel, returning a day later with Miss
Marylbone's reply.

April 9, 1819

MY DEAR MRS. RATHBONE,
   I am delighted to inform you that three
places in the freshman class have unex-
pectedly become available, with a fine
suite of rooms in the dormitory. I have
taken the liberty of reserving the rooms
for the Misses Rathbone. I look forward
to personally welcoming the daughters
of your distinguished family in September.

Kindest regards,
Miss Edith Marylbone

Lydia was relieved to have the girls' future finally settled. The three girls — her own Claudia, Miriam's Sophia, and Priscilla's Julia — had been without a tutor since early the previous winter. She had considered advertising for a new teacher, but the last one had been such a disappointment. Few tutors of good credentials were willing to leave positions elsewhere to accept a situation in a private home, especially one so far removed from the more stimulating life of the towns and cities. Mr. Phipps, a bachelor of late middle years with excellent credentials, had arrived at Rathbone House in the late spring. Previously a master in a boy's boarding school to the north, he had answered Lydia's advertisement and accepted her offer in the happy expectation of light duties with biddable young ladies (after the rigors of many years of teaching willful young men) and anticipating healthful walks along the shore. Lydia ordered books and instruments for the girls' studies and had Bemus ready one of the golden parlors as a schoolroom. Mr. Phipps would teach French in the mornings, mathematics and music in the afternoon.

Mr. Phipps was installed in a comfortable room at the north end of the house, far from the women's quarters and the schoolroom, all of which were near the great hall at the south end. The tutor thought it pleasingly courteous of Bemus to stand outside his door each morning, waiting to accompany him to the schoolroom. For his morning walks on the beach, he could have easily found his own way outside, but Bemus accompanied him downstairs and out of the house, and was always waiting on the front steps when he returned.

Lydia was at breakfast one morning a few weeks after the tutor's arrival, listening with pleasure to the sounds from the schoolroom: the girls' light voices conjugating French verbs, the tutor's deep, grave voice praising and correcting. She was surprised to hear his step, much quicker than his usual measured tread, coming down the hall. He rushed into the dining room, breathing hard, face flushed, tie askew.

"I . . . regret that I find this position unsuitable."

From the schoolroom came a burst of laughter.

"Kindly accept my resignation, effective immediately."

Lydia sat back in her chair, staring.

"But Mr. Phipps. Whatever is the matter? Are the girls not applying themselves? Are they not progressing in their studies?"

The tutor guffawed. He tugged at his collar and ran shaking hands through his hair.

"Ha! Yes, yes, they are certainly progressing." Mr. Phipps looked wildly at Lydia. "Prodigies, madam. Prodigies!" he yelped. He turned on his heel and half walked, half ran down the hall to the door to the stair, and stood knocking until Bemus came up to let him out. Mr. Phipps left then and there, leaving his trunk and books behind him.

Lydia couldn't account for his sudden departure. When she asked Claudia and her nieces about it, they only smiled secretively and shrugged.

So Lydia had decided to send the girls to school in the autumn, though she would have liked to keep them close a little longer. Having taught them reading and writing before the tutor ever came to stay, she took up as best she could where Mr. Phipps had left off, working through her rusty French grammar and watching over the girls at the spinet. But as winter moved into spring the nieces applied themselves to their lessons less and less, arriving late, fidgety and sullen. Between lessons she could hear them running up and down the halls. Once she had caught them with a crow that had somehow gotten inside; they had tied a string to its tail and were chasing it through the house, the bird flapping and screeching just ahead of them, trying to get away.

It was time for them to acquire the polish that Miss Marylbone's would provide, time for them to meet daughters of the families into which they would marry.

Besides, Lydia disliked having a man, however respectable, live in such close proximity to her daughter and nieces, especially with Bow-Oar gone. He had been dead for more than a year, Second-Oar and Third-Oar longer. There were, of course, the handful of Rathbone men still living on the first floor. They cooked the women's meals and laundered their clothes, though it was still only Bemus who was permitted on the second floor, to dust and polish and otherwise take care of Lydia's housekeeping needs. Lydia's daughter and nieces took no notice of the men downstairs.

Or so Lydia had thought. Lately she was not so sure. As she passed the schoolroom one day, Lydia had glanced in and seen the girls all leaning out the window, calling to someone below. She pushed between them and looked out.

Two ships rode anchor along the dock. Lydia seldom looked in that direction and observed little when she did. She would not have noticed that, though the *Sassacus* was swept and swabbed daily, its canvas was worn thin, its racks of harpoons rusted. The *Misistuck,* though, wore a good suit of sails and her rigging was in trim: The only Rathbone ship still in service, she would leave the next spring on a voyage to the Arctic. Since Bow-Oar had died, the *Misistuck* had been captained by Steersman, one of the last of the old Rathbones. The *Paquatauoq* was moored in a cove to the west and hadn't sailed since a few years before Moses died.

Lydia did notice two young men on the near end of the dock, one slowly coiling a rope over his arm, the other stretching a spear across his shoulders. Both stood grinning up at the window until they saw Lydia, at which they hurried away down the dock.

"Aunt Lydia, who was that?" asked Julia. "He's so handsome!"

"I claim the one with the curly hair!" Claudia laughed, shouldering her cousin aside.

Lydia stiffened and put her hands to her hips.

"You'll have nothing to do with either of them, any of you! They're just dockhands, not fit for any niece or daughter of mine!"

"Oh, Aunt Lydia." Sophia rolled her eyes and frowned. Claudia shrugged, and the three girls ran giggling out of the room.

Lydia sighed. Now it was April, and though her daughter and nieces were a handful, she was sad to think they would be off to school in just a few months. The girls were all on her shoulders. Julia and Sophia were always with Claudia, hardly ever visiting their own mothers. She didn't really blame her nieces; Priscilla and Miriam had never recovered from the disappearance of their sons nearly three years ago. Every night since Absalom, Ezekiel, Jeroboam, and their five younger brothers had sailed away, Priscilla and Miriam had sat by the windows in their rooms, staring out to sea. After their husbands died — soon after the sons were gone — Priscilla and Miriam kept to their rooms all the time. Lydia tried giving them busywork, simple tasks to keep their minds from darker thoughts: mending the seam on a shift or darning stockings. But the shift would be returned with long, wandering stitches; the white stockings darned with rough red wool. Or the tasks would not be completed at all, the needles having dropped, forgotten, from her sisters' hands. It had fallen to Lydia to watch over the three girls.

She glanced again at the clock, then stood and began to pace back and forth.

Unlike the schoolroom, which was crowded with furniture and books for the girls' studies, the music room, where Lydia spent most of her day, was sparsely furnished. A spinet stood near the windows, a harp by the hearth; the settee on which Lydia reclined and a small tea table were the only other furniture. The curtains were faded and in places threadbare, the petit point on the settee frayed, though its wood was polished to a high luster. The golden walls still glowed, untarnished, cool north light from the windows reflecting off the gold to bathe Lydia in soft light as she walked. She finally heard her daughter's light step in the hall.

"Claudia, dear, where have you been? I've been calling you this hour past, it's time for your practice. Where are Julia and Sophia?"

Claudia sidled into the music room. At fourteen, she was even lovelier than her mother had been at that age. Her hair had a fine living spring, her movements a supple grace. She wore a simple Empire frock of white muslin. Her hair, palest gold, nearly white, was clasped in a thick coil at the back of her head.

"They're still at breakfast, Mother."

Lydia stood and sleeked down a loose strand of hair on her daughter's head. She watched Claudia sit at the spinet and begin to flip through the sheet music, then picked up her embroidery frame and bent to her needle. She was stitching a pillow cover for Claudia's new room at school, a pattern of asters against a field of ivy.

Claudia plunked out a few notes but didn't begin her scales; instead she twirled on the stool, holding her legs straight out. Lydia looked up.

"Darling, please . . ."

Claudia ignored her and started to spin faster. Her hair sprang from its coil and streamed out in a bright circle as she spun. When the stool slowed, she put a slippered foot down and pushed off strongly to spin faster.

Lydia stared. That movement, that particular angle of Claudia's leg, her smile as she spun, all so like Absalom. Claudia, Lydia realized, was now nearly the same age Absalom had been when he disappeared.

"Please stop that this instant."

Claudia slowed down and came to a stop facing the keys. She began to pick out a song. Lydia half listened, holding up two strands of embroidery floss to the light to choose from. She didn't recognize the melody.

"What is that you're playing?"

Claudia paused before replying. "It's Haydn, Mother. Mr. Phipps taught me."

Lydia listened for a few more bars. She was not familiar with Haydn — his music had not been in vogue when she was learning to play. But the music didn't in any case sound like any of the composers she had learned as a girl. The melody was simple and repetitive; it reminded her of the songs she sometimes heard the men singing out on the docks while they were working.

The melody slowed and stopped. As Claudia began to spin again, a strong odor billowed into the room. The hem of her frock stood stiffly out into the air in a circle, wet and heavy. It smelled of salt and low tide.

Lydia stared.

"Love, where have you been?"

"Only in the garden, Mother."

When the girls were younger, Lydia had often watched them splashing in the watery maze behind the house. After the shrubberies died, the men of the house had lined the maze with smooth stones from the shore, so that when the sea rose up each spring it traveled along a neat waterway. The girls were forbidden to play on the beach. Their movements were restricted to the gardens, which were surrounded by a high hedge that was tough enough to withstand the sea.

"What have you been doing to get your skirt into such a state?"

Claudia slowed and stopped. She turned back to the spinet and plinked at the keys; the song again, now slower.

"Catching tadpoles, Mother."

"Darling. At your age? Really."

Claudia looked around to meet Lydia's gaze.

Bow-Oar's eyes stared up at her. When had her daughter's eyes changed from aqua to bright green? Claudia's irises had expanded so that only a sliver of brilliant white now showed to either side, where Bow-Oar's eyes had been green through and through. Lydia could still see them now, staring up at her from the whaleboat that first day. The note fluttering down, *Will you be mine?*

She had not thought about Bow-Oar in so long; she had tried not to think of him. Now she felt again that same surge she had felt the first time she lay with him and had felt for all her years with her husband, every night until he died. It had always felt like drowning, her body first floating, then pulled deeper into wave after wave, sinking, the weight of the water on her, lungs ready to burst, wanting to open her mouth and take in a great draft until all went black.

The blood came into her face; she put her hands up against her hot cheeks. Claudia's eyes were still on her, and she was smiling. She turned back to the keys and began playing the same strange melody, singing:

"This bone once in a sperm whale's jaw did rest
Now 'tis intended for a woman's breast."

Pain shot through Lydia's finger. She had pricked it on her needle. She sucked her finger to soothe it, tasting blood. She looked down at her embroidery. Her asters looked like starfish; the curling ivy like strands of seaweed.

Bemus woke in the dark one cool night in April, sure he had heard something. He lay still, listening, but all was quiet. His hammock bumped against the door with a soft thud. Maybe it had been a draft that had woken him. He was accustomed to such drafts, having slept at the head of the stairs since the day Bow-Oar and his brothers brought the golden wives to Rathbone House. The dogwatch was for a time taken by a withered bosun, until he was found peering through the keyhole in an attitude that showed him less withered than Bemus had supposed. So Bemus kept all the night watches now. Though the golden wives and their daughters slept behind the door, Bemus had never felt any stirring, having been unmanned in an encounter with a sperm in his youth.

He heard the sound again, this time more clearly: a click, then a soft bumping sound, from outside. He had checked the locks not an hour ago, as he did each night, and all had been secure. It had been many years since any man had tried to climb up to the golden rooms; the last to try broke both legs on the rocks below when Bemus pushed him off the wall. He sighed and heaved himself up from his hammock, peering out the window and down into the dark.

The door to the barracks was at the bottom of the stair; a second door, on the landing halfway down, led outside to the gardens at the back of the house. No one was on either stair or landing, and there was no movement at either door. He leaned out a window and looked down. There were no ropes, no spikes, no evidence at all of someone trying to climb. He waited, holding his breath to better hear those soft bumps, but heard only the dry rasp of cicadas, faintly, from the distant pines, above the shore and well inland.

Bemus climbed back into his hammock. He drifted, half asleep. He still heard the cicadas, now louder, and with them the soft swishing of the pines. As a boy, he had been as stirred by females as any Rathbone, but now when he dreamed it was not girls he conjured, it was always the woods and shore of his boyhood. He and his brothers used to play in the pine wood that marched thick right to the edge of the dunes, in the time before the trees were cleared. They'd spent hours chasing hares through the trees; hiding among the rocks to watch foxes as they slunk in and out of the dappled light in the woods. Climbing the tall pines to watch for the whales, seeing them rise one by one, blowing. His neck began to ache; he must remember to ask Bow-Oar for a cot to replace the hammock. His hip had begun complaining in damp weather. It's remembering the clench of my whale's jaw, he thought. But no, he had forgotten again that Bow-Oar was gone. He closed the window, lay down heavily, and was soon deep in sleep.

The sounds outside began again.

■ ■ ■ ■

October 9, 1819, Boston

Dear Mother,
I am happy at the school. Julia and
Sofia also are happy at the school. The
teachers are very nice with us. We are
studying French and also the mathemat-
icks. We will stay here for the holidays
because we need to do more study.
Your daughter,
Claudia Rathbone

Lydia folded the letter and continued
walking around the hall. She had been so
happy to know that Claudia and her nieces
were safely established at Miss Marylbone's.
She had watched them go one morning late
in August. Bemus had taken them across to
New London, to catch the ferry that would
take them up to Boston. She had watched
them step off the dock into the trim little
cutter, handed down by Bemus, so lovely in
their new gowns and hats, chattering,
excited. She had longed to hear of their
daily lives, but Claudia hadn't written until
now. Her daughter had always been an
indifferent writer, impatient with grammar,
but this letter sounded odd, and something

about the hand was off . . . but surely she was imagining things. She had written Miss Marylbone to ask after the girls' progress but had not yet received any reply. Perhaps Bemus could run up to the school in a cutter to inquire; but he wouldn't be able to tell what was wrong. Lydia should go. She must go. But she had not left the grounds of Rathbone House since she arrived, nearly twenty years ago.

With her sisters shut away in their rooms, mourning their sons and husbands, with neither daughter nor nieces as companion, there was little for her to do. To fill the time, Lydia began to take long daily walks in the garden, following the path of the maze, stopping to pick shells from the gurgling stream. She passed many hours on needlework for Claudia and her nieces. She had sent all the girls off with fine wardrobes for school, from a dressmaker in Providence: muslin and calico for everyday clothes, three silk gowns each for social occasions. Now she embroidered the collars and plackets of three fur-tipped pelisses to send for the winter to come. Lydia had herself for many years worn simple, unembellished muslin or wool gowns. The rich gowns she and her sisters had worn when they first came to Rathbone House had long been packed away and had, anyway, lost their sheen and grown thread-bare.

In November she began to dream a troubling dream, always the same. Claudia swimming along the narrow waterway of the maze, her arms tight along her sides, hair sleeked back, shift plastered to her small pointed breasts, rippling through the water like a seal. Her cousins swam in line behind her, jackknifing deftly around the sharp corners of the maze.

Lydia began to sleep in the music room on the stiff settee, hoping that the dream would not follow her, but still it came each night. She woke in the dark to cries like an infant's, wondering if they, too, were imagined, or if she had made the sounds herself. One night she thought she heard Claudia's laugh. In the mornings she sometimes smelled nursery burgoo, which hadn't been cooked in the house since her daughter was a baby. Her mouth watered at the scent of warm oats and brown sugar. She woke in the night and paced around the perimeter of the hall, looking out the windows that faced the sea as she passed them, watching the moon's silvery track along the water, now smooth, now broken and glittering. Once, as she passed the door to the lower floor, she noticed that it was open a crack.

Through the crack she glimpsed a round pale shape: a little head. She hurried to the door and jerked it open, but there was only the dark staircase leading down.

One morning in January she woke again to crying sounds. She lay still. The sounds came again, not from her but from outside the music room. In the hall she waited, listening. The cries were coming from her bedroom, strong and clear. She leaned slowly into the room. In the corner by the window, in the fine crib that had for so long stood empty, lay four infants. The Rathbone men had crept up in the night, this time not to steal away babes but to give them back.

Lydia moved closer. Four naked infants, arms and legs waving. At first glance they looked so much like her own children had that she caught her breath.

Twin boys lay side by side. They looked like thinner, paler versions of her own sons, but something wasn't right. She looked more closely. In each small, narrow face one eye was a little higher than the other; each jaw misaligned, as though the hand that formed it had been unsteady, had stretched it too long then tried to push it back, or formed it from stock that was too soft to hold its shape. The infants cried feebly, heads wobbling from side to side, eyes

426

unfocused. A third little boy, though pale and narrow as the others, had regular features and lay with his eyes closed, breathing quietly.

The fourth infant was a girl. A rosy little girl with a tuft of pale-bright hair, round-cheeked and perfect. She could have been Claudia at the same age. She looked straight up at Lydia with bright-green eyes and reached a fat fist toward her.

Lydia put her hand to her throat and backed away, out of the room, looking all around for Bemus. She ran to the music room and pulled the bell cord, but there was no answer. She drew a deep breath and walked over to the door that led downstairs to the men's quarters. She had never been in the rooms on the bottom floor. Once or twice she had found the door open and had stood by it, listening. She'd never had more than a passing interest in the men below. Now she tried to think of how many there were, what cousins, brothers, uncles of Bow-Oar lived below. Lydia knew that the last of the women had left five years ago when Moses died; she had asked Bemus. She wouldn't have known that, besides four grizzled oldsters who survived, eight younger Rathbones remained downstairs: Humility's four boys, fourteen, fifteen-year-

427

old twins, and eighteen; Trial's eldest, twenty and twenty-one; and Desire's twins, twenty-five. She stood on the landing, looking down into the darkness. Cool, dank air rolled up. A spider crab ran across the toe of her slipper and scrabbled down the stairs.

"Bemus?"

Lydia crept down two more steps. There was a crack of light at the foot of the stair. Through the door came the sounds of men's voices, the clank of cutlery. The door wafted open a few more inches. Through the crack she caught sight of a slice of long table lit by a hanging lantern that cast a warm light. She saw dark heads along either side, lowered over their plates. Platters of food steamed on the table. She smelled pork fat and oily fish, and the hot sweet odor of burgoo. On the back of one chair a crow perched. A man across the table tossed a gobbet of meat high and the crow caught it neatly, gulped, and rasped its beak against the chair. Lydia crept farther down the stair. A bright shape flitted across the dark. A slender white arm encircled a man's neck. She heard Claudia's high, bright laugh. Saw Claudia pulling the pins from her hair and shaking it out in a long stream of white, wrapping it around the man's neck and hers. Claudia's sea-green eyes looked up at Lydia.

If Bemus had woken again, that night months ago, and looked up rather than down when he leaned out the window, he might have seen something after all. He didn't consider that, besides that thin stuff that trickled through the golden wives, Rathbone blood coursed in the golden daughters' veins. He didn't dream that Claudia, Julia, and Sophia, at fourteen years, would slip out of their rooms and unlock the windows. That they would hike up their skirts, climb out, and clamber down the wall as nimbly as any Rathbone male on a mast. That they would willingly, eagerly, be passed from bunk to bunk, from boy to boy, from man to man. Neither Bemus nor the girls' mothers knew that the golden daughters so descended every night, returning early each morning before the sun rose, climbing back into their golden beds, brimming with Rathbone seed.

Lydia ran up the stairs, closed the door, and stood with her back to it. Someone knocked; she jumped and put her hand to her throat.

"Ma'am? Just come for you," came Bemus's voice. A letter slid under the door.

December 14, 1819

DEAR MRS. RATHBONE,
We are deeply grateful for the generosity of the Rathbone family. We do not understand, however, why you have not responded to our repeated inquiries. We regret to inform you that, unless we hear from you by the end of the month, we shall be forced to release the three places we have been holding, as there are so many young ladies on our waiting list.

Kind regards,
Miss Edith Marylbone

From her bedroom the cries began again. Lydia walked slowly back to the crib. The little boys were asleep; the girl stared up at her. The infants had kicked off the blankets in which they had been wrapped. The window was open and the room was now cold. Lydia started to pull the blankets up over them, then stopped. She left the blanket where it fell, halfway up their legs, and went out of the room.

Bemus found Lydia on the beach the next morning. A golden gown eddied in the surf around her, its faded cloth restored to brightness by the sea.

CHAPTER SEVENTEEN:
ERASTUS AND VERITY

{in which we meet Mama and her brother}

1837

"Wait for me!"

Verity was two rooms ahead of Erastus, though they had started out together only moments before. She looked back at him, laughing, and ran through three more rooms before darting aside and disappearing. Erastus, looking down as he ran, didn't at first see where she had gone. When he looked up, the hall was empty. He slowed down and limped along the chain of rooms until he found her, lying facedown on a bed in a corner. She was propped on her elbows, swinging her legs up and down, scarcely breathing hard, watching him. He reached the bed, dropped down next to her, panting, and closed his eyes. Verity turned on her side, head on her outstretched arm, scowling.

"That wasn't even a hundred feet. You're like an old sea cow." Her scowl softened as Erastus lay there, still wheezing. He struggled to sit up, grimacing, reaching for his knees.

"Lie back."

Verity pressed his knees gingerly, watching his expression, then began to massage his joints, first knees and ankles, then shoulders. When he was breathing evenly, she got up and went to the door, looking back along the chain of rooms. Morning sun, thin and sharp, slanted through the long row of windows and lit her hair to a white blaze. She wore one of Lydia's old gowns, bronze silk shot through with gold thread, the worn elbows patched with darker silk from some other old gown.

She stood, listening. There was no sign of Conch or Crab; they would soon realize where their brother and sister were and come looking for them. Surf boomed on the rocks below. Wind gusted seawater up and sprayed it through the windows and into the corridor. Verity looked the other way, toward the front of the house. A crow flew past the windows toward the sea, its shadow flickering along the corridor. Near the end of the hall, someone crossed from room to room: Steersman, a leeward twist to his torso, wearing an old middy and nothing below. He held up a lantern as he walked, calling out *Six bells* in a cracked voice, *Six bells*. No one slept in any of the beds. Out the window opposite, Verity saw old Fourth-Oar in the rigging of the *Misistuck,* inching along the yard toward the mainmast, gray pigtail wafting out behind him in the wind. She winced; Boatheader had fallen from the top yard a few months before. Now only Steersman, Fourth-Oar, and Bemus remained of the old Rathbones. Rathbone House was otherwise empty; Miriam and Priscilla had died a few years ago, one after the other. Never having recovered from their husbands' deaths, they had barely noticed Lydia's passing and finally faded away altogether. Where her mother was — who her mother was — Verity didn't know, nor Erastus. Bemus would never say.

Behind her, Verity heard Bemus's shuffling step. He moved past her into the room, a stack of clean sheets on one arm. He began to strip the sheets from the bed across from Erastus.

Verity went to her brother's bed and lay next to him. She reached behind her head, pulled her hair up, and spread it over the pillow and all around her face, thick and pale. She began to fan herself with the bed curtain. Its heavy wool was patterned with fish, swimming in rhythmic streams across the cloth.

"Watch. If I move it just so, I can make the marlin swallow the cod."

Erastus opened his eyes and smiled absently. He sat up and watched Bemus finish making one bed, then move to the next and begin to strip the sheets.

"Bemus."

Bemus didn't look up from his work.

"Bemus."

"You know he can't hear you, leave him alone."

"Oh, Mother . . ." Erastus called to Bemus.

Verity sat up straight and stared hard at Erastus, frowning.

"Well, he's the closest we've got, isn't he?" Erastus smiled slightly.

He lay down again and pulled a narrow book with soft green covers from his waistcoat pocket. He flipped through, then ran a finger along one page.

"Bemus, would you like to know what your name means in Greek? Here it is. 'Bemus: *foundation.*' A worthy name. Solid. Strong."

Verity rolled over and looked at him.

"That's not really his name, you know."

"What do you mean that's not his name?"

"It just sounds like that. His name is Beam Ends."

"Beam Ends?"

"He told me, once, years ago. It's because of the way he walks."

Erastus looked at her blankly.

"Beam ends. When a ship lists, she tilts on her side. On her beam ends. His whale took part of his thigh, when he was fifteen. He said he used to walk straight enough before . . ." She looked at Erastus and her voice faltered.

He closed his eyes and smiled.

"Perhaps that should have been my name, too."

Verity stared down at her brother. Making herself smile, she grasped an end of the bed curtain and drew it across Erastus's face. He brushed it away and she drew it across again.

"Tell me."

"Tell you what?"

"What do I always ask you to tell me? About Moses."

"Ask him to tell you." He gestured at Bemus, who had just finished making the second bed. Bemus straightened up slowly, hand to his back. First looking vaguely around the room, he bent over and began to strip the bed again.

"He won't remember anymore. Please."

Erastus sniffed, frowning. "Aren't you ever tired of those old stories?"

"Just one more time."

He sighed and swung his legs carefully over the side of the bed, then sat looking out at the sea. His hair, as pale and long as Verity's, was tied neatly back. He wore a thin white shirt and old buff breeches cinched in with a belt.

"All right, if you must hear it."

Verity lay back on the bed, her hands behind her head. She could just see the edge of the sea out the windows, rough with whitecaps, deepest blue under a clear gray sky. She closed her eyes as Erastus began.

"It was always Moses who spotted the whale, not the lookout in the tops but Moses, down on deck. All the men could see far enough, and most of them could sense the whales, knew when they were close, but none could see in the way that Moses could. He saw them swimming beneath the surface. He watched them rise slowly from the deep. He knew just where each whale would breech, how high his spout would blow. He knew how many sperm were in each pod, and which was heaviest with oil.

"When they gave chase, the harpooners in other boats stood with a leg braced against the thigh board, but Moses jumped up on the bow, right up on the rim, balancing like it was dry land. His spear shot out so fast it set the line afire; the crew kept a bucket ready to douse the flame."

Erastus raised his arm and mimicked the thrust of a harpoon. Bemus caught the movement and turned from his sheets. His face brightened and he made his own weak thrust toward the sea.

"He never missed his mark, no matter how far he threw. Just as Moses knew the whales, the whales knew Moses. When a sperm, fleeing from the boats, looked back and saw Moses standing up there on the bow, harpoon poised, it would stop in the water and wait for him, knowing it could never escape."

"How many spears did he need to kill the whale?"

"One. Only one."

Verity was silent, her eyes bright.

A door opened and closed at the far end of the corridor, loud in the echoing space.

Verity hurried to the doorway and peeked around the corner. Two tall pale youths were walking toward her from the end of the hall. They wore faded sailors' slops that rode high up their legs and arms. Their jaws preceded them, and their heads wobbled on thin stems as they walked. One held a pair of Erastus's boots and a polishing cloth. He saw Verity and began to hurry, holding the boots out toward her, his tongue working in his jaw but making no sound.

Verity seized Erastus's hand, pulled him up and out into the corridor, down to the end of the hall, and into Moses's room. She latched the door behind them and stood with her back to it, Erastus panting beside her.

There was a flurry of knocks on the door, then the footsteps moved off.

Verity scrambled up the side of the bed and reached down to help Erastus up. They lay side by side on the high blue bed. The blankets were damp and smelled of mildew. She unlatched the porthole window and opened it, hinges creaking. There had been no window in the little pine room until a few years ago, when Verity asked Bemus to put it in, so that she could watch the sea from there. A soft breeze moved across the bed. On the pine walls, bleached and dull, the pegs were empty. In the rack above the head of the bed a harpoon rested.

"You'd think they'd get tired of following us everywhere," she said.

"They're just trying to help me pack."

Verity looked up at the ceiling. Watery reflections rippled across the pine, brightening and fading as the wind pushed clouds across the sun.

Erastus reached to touch her hair.

"Your hair is wet. Have you been swimming already this morning?"

She moved away and pulled her hair around from her back to her breast. Her back was wet where her hair had been, a dark patch on the bronze silk.

"Yes, but I want to go again. Come swim with me."

"How amusing you are today, Verity."

"I'm sorry. Truly I am," she said. She leaned over and began to massage his legs again; he winced and turned away. She took up his hand and held it to her cheek.

"The packet leaves at noon from New London. Fourth will be getting ready to go, and I can't be late."

She let go of his hand and turned to stare out the porthole.

"I don't understand why you have to go."

"Yes, you do. You know you do."

He flipped through the little book again.

"I've read all the books, all ten of them. I know all the stories; I'm sick to death of them. There's no one to talk to, nothing to learn, nothing new to see or hear or know. Nothing but this house and the sea. I'd do anything just to get away from the sound of the sea."

He reached for her hand.

"You could come with me."

She turned around with a half smile, then turned her back again.

"We'll start in London. Then cross the channel to Paris and head south to Venice, then Florence and Rome. And finally Athens. We'll stand together on the Acropolis, surrounded by the temples of the gods." He flipped through his book, tilting it toward Verity so that she could see its small engravings. "We'll see the Erechtheum. Its roof is held up by giant maidens of white marble, so straight and strong." Erastus's eyes shone. "Everything in Greece is like that. Clean and straight and pure."

"You know I couldn't leave the ocean."

"This isn't the only ocean, you know. The Aegean isn't green like here, it's blue. It's bluer than the bluest sky you can imagine . . . I have to go now, while I still can."

Verity, still turned away, began to braid her damp hair.

"I wish Moses still sailed. I wish . . ." Verity reached up and pulled down the old harpoon, and turned it in her hands. "You have to stay."

"All right, I will." Erastus took the harpoon from her and ran a cautious finger along its dulled edge. "I'll become a new lord of the seas. I'll kill two sperm with every cast to Moses's one. The whale will dance around me in a great circle before he dies."

"Don't leave me."

"You won't be alone."

"You can't be serious."

"This isn't right. I have to go."

The harpoon fell from Verity's hand. She threw back her head and howled. She twisted around and wrapped her arms and legs around Erastus. He buried his face in her hair.

After a while Verity let go. They lay side by side, looking up at the light rippling across the ceiling. She reached over the side of the bed and picked up the harpoon, and lay the shaft lightly across their bodies. She moved closer to Erastus and ran a shaking finger over his pale arm, along the thin blue veins.

"The sea is in you too, you know. You say you hate it, but that's like saying you hate me."

Erastus began to sit up. Verity grasped the harpoon tighter and held it down across her chest and his.

"Tell me again. What Erastus means."

"It means 'beloved.' "

"And Verity?"

"*Veritas.* Truth."

"Stay. Stay."

CHAPTER EIGHTEEN: THE SEVEN SUITORS

{in which Erastus's plan goes awry}

1841

On a spring morning soon after Erastus Rathbone returned from the Continent, seven crews of carpenters congregated on the lawn of Rathbone House. They shuffled their boots uncomfortably on the broad expanse of smooth green, checking the edges on their tools and glancing up at the windows of the big house on the hill, waiting for instructions. They had come from as far as Baltimore and Providence, having seen the oversize notices with gilt edges that Erastus's agents had posted in guild halls and taverns all along the coast, promising fat purses to crews willing to leave within the week, seasoned crews who had built the solid merchants' houses that lined those cities' harbors. A few men had abandoned half-built houses, unable to resist the money, substituting second-rate crews or leaving angry merchants high and dry.

The town of Naiwayonk had no carpenters of its own; there was little business for them. The few fishermen who still lived there had built their own ramshackle houses of rough pine and tar paper, and what little furniture they owned they had knocked together themselves. Though the carpenters were told by the fishermen that other large houses had once stood on the hills above the harbor, only Rathbone House remained, on the highest hill, its original builders long dead. The carpenters wondered what sort of craftsmen those men had been, looking at the low, dark wood lodge that formed the first floor, and at the second story of red brick, not wholly unlike those their fathers had built but oddly unfinished — windows without pediments, gables without dormers — a house seen through fog.

The men stirred as two figures made their way down the lawn. They were at first confused; they had been told they would meet with the master of the house, a young man of twenty-two, but the figures approaching both appeared to be aged. Erastus walked with a rolling gait unrelated to the rise and fall of ships at sea, his back bent, leaning heavily on two canes. He was accompanied by an old sailor in faded middy and ducks, holding a parasol to shade Erastus from the sun. Though bent, Erastus was still taller by a head than his companion. He wore an embroidered waistcoat over pleated mole trousers, and slender polished shoes. His white hair was trained with pomade into a wave that sprang from his forehead.

With a brisk smile and a general nod to the men, Erastus unfurled and laid on the lawn a large set of plans. A crow dropped down from a tree onto the plans and stalked across them, claws clicking on the paper, until waved away by the sweep of a long arm. The carpenters squatted around the blue-inked drawings, murmuring and scratching their chins. A few stood and squinted against the sun or looked down toward the dock, where neat stacks of seasoned lumber stood ready.

The next morning, on the empty pier where Rathbone House once stood on its pilings above the sea, seven cottages began to rise. The structures grew at impressive speed; the first crew to finish would earn a handsome bonus. Enough whaling gold remained from the glory days of the Rathbones to build seven mansions, little having been spent since Lydia's time and so few

Rathbones left to spend it: the surviving sons of the worn wives, Bemus, old Fourth-Oar, and Steersman; Erastus and Verity; Conch and Crab (later known as Larboard and Starboard) — the white children, grandchildren of the golden wives.

Sturdy oak framing was cut, set, and joined in a few days, drawing the outlines of the cottages against the sky. Clapboarding of white pine was lapped and hung; plaster of crushed oysters and sand was mixed and troweled on. The carpenters eyed their competitors' progress as they worked, and wielded hammer and saw faster, calling out jokes about whose timbers were stiffest, whose hammers harder. In two weeks' time the buildings were complete.

Each cottage stood square to the sun, precisely three fathoms apart. Each had the appearance of a small Greek temple of the Doric style, its peaked roof supported by fluted columns. Each wore the name of a sea god inscribed in large capital letters above its portico. Proteus and Triton stood closest to the house; Poseidon and Oceanus trailed toward the open sea. Though built of clapboard rather than stone, their walls were painted with coat after coat of bone-white brightened with mica to mimic marble from a certain distance. When the sun struck them full on the front at eight bells in the first watch, the most squint-eyed old sailor would have been blinded. Tucked just above the cornice on the back side, one small window broke the smooth perfection of each pediment.

The cottages were a few feet narrower than the dock, their fronts flush with the edge that faced the open sea; along their backs was space enough for a narrow pathway. Their doorways were accessible only from the sea side. At high tide the water lapped the second step of the stairway that dropped from each door into the water; at low tide each stair ended in empty air. If a whaler out in the sound had sent a wherry to collect its crew, each man would have had only to step off, still yawning, losing no time in making the tide.

Erastus inspected the buildings, declared his satisfaction, and saw the men off as they headed home. Some had come by sea in dories and skiffs, others by land in horse and wagon. Some of the carpenters returned soon enough to make up for lost time or to salvage jobs gone awry in their absence, so that their employers never knew they had been gone. A few stopped in towns on their way home to buy shawls for their wives and sweets for their children. The Boston crew, having finished first and spent its bonus on rum and whores in Stonington, capsized halfway home in heavy seas off Newport, the bonus of gold gone with them.

The morning after the carpenters departed, Erastus stepped into his sleek new schooner, the *Argo,* a two-masted vessel of thirty feet. Built in Mystic to his specifications while he was abroad, the slender fore- and aft-rigged vessel sliced through the waves at twice the speed of the larger Rathbone ships. It was crewed by half a dozen hired men in crisp white middies and billowing trousers. The *Argo* sailed east, skimming along close to the coast.

That evening, the fishing fleet of a hamlet some leagues east of Naiwayonk coasted into harbor at dusk. As they approached the dock, the fishermen saw a strange cutter moored at the end. Its snowy sails were neatly lashed, its crew standing at the ready, hands clasped behind their backs. The fishermen stared at the tall, pale young man swaying slowly along the dock in a frock coat, leaning on two ivory canes. They felt his keen eyes on them, watching as they hauled in the last load from their nets and poured streams of gleaming fish into baskets and crates to carry ashore, where their wives waited to clean the catch and ready it for market. When the men had stowed their gear and made ready to go home, Erastus beckoned to them, smiling and gesturing with one of his canes. The men looked at one another, laughing uncomfortably. They dipped their fishy hands in the water and wiped them on their slickers, then climbed up on the dock and shook Erastus's dry white hand. Erastus looked each man attentively up and down as he made pleasant conversation about the weather and the day's haul. He drew one man, taller and burlier than the others, aside and stayed talking to him on the dock after his fellows had gone home. The next morning, that man failed to appear on the dock and was seen instead, by an early fisherman, seated in Rathbone's slim, swift cutter as it sailed away.

In the days that followed, the cutter was noted by locals at ports farther east and far to the north, all along the curve of the great cape, its benches filling with men. Duffels stowed neatly beneath their seats, the men shifted restlessly as the cutter glided along, legs bouncing up and down, hands twitching for something to do, unaccustomed to being passengers.

A week after the Naiwayonk cottages were completed, smoke spiraled above seven chimneys. Seven fishermen stood in their doorways at first light, staring out to sea. From where Erastus surveyed them, installed in a chair on the curve of the lawn, under his parasol, the men were as like to one another as the cottages. Most were local men, others itinerant whalemen he had found lingering in coastal towns between trips. All were brine-tough and sun-dark, large and strongly made.

Erastus stood on the lawn, watching, as the men rubbed their eyes and stretched and stood awkwardly at their doors, gazing out over a morning sea. The sky was a pure, clear blue, the air chill and bracing.

He turned his gaze from the seven cottages to the west harbor, where the remains of the Rathbone fleet were moored. The *Paquatauoq,* first of the ships to be abandoned when the whales began to disappear, had sunk years ago in a cove, its rotted hull coming to rest on the sandy bottom. At high tide only the stump of its mainmast was visible, tilting above the water; at low tide its drowned deck rose just above the waves, only to drown again at turn of tide. The *Sassacus* huddled nearby, masts struck, decks drifted in weed and sand. Only the *Misistuck* still sailed, manned by no Rathbones, only hired men, and bringing in just a trickle of oil the last time it docked three years ago. Erastus envisioned the ships clearly, raised from their disgraceful state and restored to their first glory, fresh spars and yards soaring, sails of blinding white billowing, breasting the sea once again.

Surveying the seven men standing in the doorways of their cottages, his eye dwelt longest on the young man in the farthest cottage, who outshone all the others.

Erastus had found the young man yesterday, on his way back to Naiwayonk. He had signed on two men, bringing the total to six, though he had hoped to reach his goal of seven that day. Anxious to put his plan into action, he would select only men who were clearly superior in form and skill, and had left behind several who didn't meet his mark; he would, he thought regretfully, have to continue his search.

But Erastus had found his seventh man after all. Late in the day, as the *Argo* headed back to Naiwayonk, a sudden squall had whipped the smooth sea into tall waves and sent the cutter off course. As she tacked back against the wind, an island came into view, one that appeared on no Rathbone chart, a long, verdant isle above which hovered a single lush cloud of the same shape. The island, perhaps a mile long and a quarter as wide, at first appeared uninhabited. No dwellings showed, no smoke rose through the branches of the trees that lined its shore. Silvery stands of birch shone through thick trunks of oak and elm that spread their leafy crowns high above the island. Among the trunks Erastus saw a herd of white-tailed deer wandering. In the branches of one oak a sleeping bear lolled. The forest grew, seemingly unbroken, from a high base of granite that fell away sharply to the sea. Erastus at first thought that the rocks, a pale, rosy tone, were tinged by the warm rays of the sun that rode low in the sky, but as the sun continued to drop and the light cooled to blue, the rocks didn't lose their pink cast.

As the cutter sailed past, a spit of bare rock came into view at the southern tip of the island, and on it stood a young man. Erastus had no need, as with the other men he had gathered, to assess the boy's skills at a remove; he witnessed his prowess first-hand. Although Erastus couldn't tell his true height without something to compare it to, and the bare spit of granite thrust well beyond the trees, he could easily see the boy's mass and girth. Within that generous chest might have beat the hearts of two men.

The boy, who looked no more than seventeen, stood on the spit, above surf that broke high on the rocks, sharp against the darkening sky. In his raised hand he held not a harpoon of steel but a wooden spear, a tapered shaft as long as three men. The spear flashed out quicker than Erastus's eye could follow. There was a flailing far out in the water and white spumes of sea, then the boy dove in. A swordfish leapt up in a long curve, its great dorsal fin split by the spear; on its back was the boy, clutching the fin, the sleek silver-blue body between his thighs. The swordfish thrashed from side to side and spun in circles, trying to shake him off, but he held firm as the fish dove and surged up and plunged again, the arc of its body lower each time. Finally, its energy spent, the swordfish turned on its side, scales heaving, its tail giving now and then a weak thrash. The boy grasped the swordfish by its blade and, swimming one-armed, towed it behind him. He reached the rocks and clambered up the sheer face with his burden. Erastus watched him climb to the top and drop the great fish. Now that it was free of the water, he saw its true size; it must have weighed more than the boy. Its scales gleamed silvery in the cooling light. The boy stood looking down at the swordfish, breathing hard, then knelt on the rock, head bent.

He pulled a knife from his belt and sliced swiftly across the fish. Standing straight, he held the bony sword high. He drew it across his own chest. In the faint light Erastus could see dark blood welling along the slash, and the scars of older wounds.

The *Argo* drew near the tip of the island, now a long black shape against the darkening sky. A fire leapt and crackled, and the smell of roasting fish drifted over. Erastus had in his travels abroad dined on many a subtle dish and delicate sauce; now his mouth watered at the strong, oily odor.

He called out to the boy, his voice carrying easily over the water.

"Ahoy! Ahoy there!"

The boy looked up from the fire, his face bright with the flames. He grinned and waved.

"Come join me! Plenty for all!" he boomed, pointing the crew to a safe cove in which to anchor.

When they reached the fire, the boy stood up, wiping his hands on his legs. Erastus was startled afresh by his size. Two Erastuses tied together might not have matched the width of his torso.

The boy reached for his hand and pumped it up and down, still grinning.

"Benadam Gale."

He wore duck trousers tied at the waist with a piece of rope. His feet and chest were bare. In the firelight, Erastus could clearly see the healed welts of other swordfish slashes on his chest and arms, parallel cuts like the gill slits of a fish. His body shone with sweat. His long hair was a tangle, sun-bleached. He brimmed with the life that had leaked from the Rathbones.

Benadam welcomed all the men, asking them to sit. He cut slabs from the steaming swordfish and handed them around, using elm leaves for plates. After the crew had eaten their fill, Erastus sent them back to the cutter to ready her for sailing on to Naiwayonk. He sat by the fire with Benadam, talking. The boy told him about the village, deep in the trees, where his family and a dozen others lived, all of them fisherfolk. Erastus could see the lights of the houses winking through the trees.

"I've never seen a fight like that."

Benadam shrugged. "Always done it that way." He spoke lightly, but Erastus heard the pride in his voice.

"Why don't you just spear them, from farther away?"

"That wouldn't be very fair to the fish, would it? He can't throw his sword at me." Benadam was smiling, but Erastus could see that he was serious.

"Of course it would be different with something really big, like a whale."

Benadam, stirring the fire, looked up sharply at him.

"Have you seen them?"

Erastus shook his head.

"I used to see them, when I was a boy. The big sperm whales. Twice a year they would pass, north in spring, south in the fall, ten or twenty at a time. Never near enough so I could get to them in time." He was staring out at the dark water. "I'd try, though. Once my uncle's little brig was docked when I saw a whale, and we set out, but the wind was blowing wrong that day. Sometimes I tried rowing after the whales in a dory, my friends and me taking turns at the oars and rowing for our lives, but we never came close, the whales were always long gone before we were halfway across the bay."

"How would you like to chase them again? From a ship, a whaleship."

Benadam stared at him, openmouthed. Erastus began to talk. The two sat long over the fire, the boy's eyes shining as Erastus offered his bargain. At some of the details the boy frowned and hesitated; after a long silence, he stood and grasped Erastus's hand.

Now, the day after he had brought the men back to Naiwayonk, Erastus watched them begin to settle into their cottages. His eye went again and again to Benadam. He was not like the other men Erastus had gathered; he had not been very interested in how much gold the bargain included, like the others had. His eagerness was all to do with details about the ship and about going after the whales. Though Benadam stood idly in his doorway like the other men, looking out to sea, Erastus regarded him uneasily.

There had been little for the seven men to do since they arrived. Rathbone House was swabbed spotless each day from top to bottom, its floors slippery not with the blubber of whales but with fresh polish. Conch swabbed in broad strokes, Crab following behind flogging the wood dry. The new cottages were equally well maintained, though by Fourth-Oar, not Conch and Crab; they were afraid of the sea and would not go so near it.

Each cottage was provided with furniture in the reborn classical mode, shipped from Philadelphia: oval tables of polished mahogany with slim, fluted legs; narrow chairs with backs carved like lyres; beds anchored at each corner by slender mahogany columns and piled with snowy linens. Each cottage was fitted with beautifully joined cabinetry built flush into the smooth plaster walls by the crews of carpenters, cabinets in which the men's meager clothes took up little space. No sooner had each man risen from his bed than Fourth-Oar made it up. No sooner had he seated himself at table than a hearty breakfast appeared, to fortify his flesh for the tasks ahead, cooked by Bemus: basins of steaming burgoo, stacks of toasted soft tack, platters of grilled smelt.

When the sun sank low and the sea calmed to a smooth sheet of silver, Erastus, who had retreated to the house during the brightest part of the day, returned to his chair on the broad lawn overlooking the water and seated himself, eyes on the horizon. Behind him stood Bemus and Fourth-Oar, watching too.

In the red disk of sun on the edge of the sea a dark speck grew. A whaleboat glided on light airs toward Naiwayonk harbor from the southwest. The boat moved slowly, its sail barely stirring, aided by the oars of the boatman. It moved in a series of jerks, favoring its starboard side, before at last gliding onto the shingle.

A group of girls stepped from the boat onto the strand. Steersman stepped out after them, his twisted torso accounting for the craft's irregular rowing. Enough light remained for Erastus and the men to see them, silhouetted against the sky: seven females, all tall and pale, in gowns loomed of undyed wool. Their skin was not white but rather the pearly colors of shells found in dimly lit water or trapped beneath a reef. If he had not known them, Erastus would have been hard-pressed to guess their ages. Their faces had a watery, shifting appearance and a faint abalone sheen; their bodies were all slender in the same ageless way, though Erastus knew them to range in years from nineteen to twenty-one.

Some were Erastus's cousins, some his sisters — which were which, he didn't know. Eleven infants all told had been born in the barracks of Rathbone House. They hatched in clusters each winter, like cod. They were brought upstairs in batches to the cradle in Lydia's room, where Bemus looked after them all. Lydia had named Verity and Erastus — the only two babies she could bear to look at — before she drowned. Bemus had named all the rest: the twin boys were Conch and Crab; the girls Abalone, Wentle, and Limpet arrived the next winter; followed the next winter by a third batch: Scallop, Periwinkle, and the twins Cowrie and Coral. Their mothers were Claudia, Julia, and Sophia. Who their fathers were, Erastus didn't know, other than that they were his uncles or cousins.

The young women trod slowly up the beach with different degrees of lurch and sway, their gaits as varied as their hues. They moved as creatures might who lived far under the sea, where the pressure is great. One girl's stride matched that of the sailor who accompanied her. She shared the same leeward twist, though his infirmity was due to an encounter with a whale, hers an outcome of inbreeding. Still, each girl was pleasing in her own way: one with thick white lashes and a smooth skein of pearly hair to her waist, another whose skin had a coral tinge that complemented her rosy irises.

The last two girls stepped from the rear of the boat, trailing behind the others. They wore long capes with hoods that shadowed their faces. Their skin was pied, like dappled light on water. Erastus was not sure whether the mottled appearance of their skin was caused by the clouds now scudding past the rising moon or whether they were more sea tortoise than girl. He hoped it was only nervousness that caused the judder of their eyes, the tremor in their steps as they crossed the sand.

Bemus, who had been busy in the house until now, went down to greet the girls and walked with them, giving one his arm. A few other girls cried out and clung to him; he petted them all, smiling. He was fond of them, though they had been so much trouble as infants — always fretful and ill, slow to walk, slow to understand. Though Bow-Oar had decreed after the birth of his golden daughters that henceforth all Rathbone girls would live, Bemus had been sorely tempted to revert to the old ways. The first batch had been different. Erastus and Verity were quick, healthy, no trouble at all. The twin boys Conch and Crab were a little slow but not difficult. Their mothers had had nothing to do with any of the children, staying downstairs with the men. After the third batch was born, Bemus had realized he couldn't take care of any more. He'd put Claudia, Julia, and Sophia on the packet to Boston one spring morning, their purses full of gold, and they hadn't been seen since.

As the babies grew, Steersman and Fourth-Oar glimpsed them on the stairs or in the garden, and began to grumble to Bemus. They were afraid of the white children. They began to whisper about a curse. Fourth-Oar said it had all started years ago, when Bow-Oar and his brothers brought home those Stark girls.

Bemus decided to move the girls out of the house. He thought of a little cove on the coast a few miles west of Rathbone House, tucked out of the wind and out of easy sight from sea or land, with a freshwater spring among its rocks. When Bemus was younger, the Rathbone ships had sometimes stopped there on the way out to sea to gather eggs from the nests of the white birds that sheltered in the caves that pocked the rocky cove. He moved the girls there and hired a woman from Stonington to help care for them. When the girls were older, and the more capable could take care of the less, the woman had gone back to her village, and Bemus had visited the cove once a week, bringing what the girls needed, or sent Captain Avery in his stead. The first, healthiest batch — Verity and Erastus, Conch and Crab — stayed at Rathbone House.

Erastus glanced back at the house, at the windows on the top floor, but all were dark. Verity had not known about her cousins for as long as he had. The girls had all been moved to Birch Rock when Erastus and Verity were still babies themselves. The girls had been a secret for many years before Erastus, when he was ten or so, caught Bemus off guard one day. Bemus was loading supplies in a boat to take to the island, and Erastus had made him tell the whole story. Verity had not known about them until she was fourteen. She had seen Bemus pressing a dozen linen shifts, too small to be her own, and had made him tell her, too. She had wanted to bring all the girls back to Rathbone House and wouldn't listen to any of Bemus's arguments; the girls wouldn't have liked it, he said, in the bright house, after the quiet and dark of the caves; they had everything they needed and were quite content; they would miss their birds. Verity begged to at least be allowed to visit the girls, but Bemus was afraid it would be far too upsetting for them.

Verity had tried to get Erastus to help her convince Bemus to bring the girls to live in the house. "They're your cousins," she had said, crying. "Some of them are probably your sisters." But he had felt little. He did not know them at all. Any more than he knew his own mother, whichever she was of the three. He had no memory of any of them. Verity had pleaded with Bemus for months, but he wouldn't be moved.

As much as she had wanted the girls to come home when they were younger, Verity had refused to come down to greet them now that they had finally returned. She wanted nothing to do with Erastus's plan, and had not left her room since morning. A wave of doubt ran through him. Maybe it would have been better to leave them on their island. But no. This needed to happen, before it was too late.

Now the seven suitors leaned out from their doorways over the water, straining for a clearer view of the girls in the sinking light. Instead of their normal jerseys and corded trousers, the men were all dressed in fresh white shirts with brocade waistcoats and moleskin trousers, with hair brushed neatly back, beards trimmed. Each held a nosegay of beach plum and glasswort. The seventh suitor, Benadam Gale, wore his work clothes of old blue cotton bleached by sea and sun; none of the clothes Erastus had ordered were large enough to fit him.

The seven girls, weaving their way across the lawn, were briskly herded by Steersman into a neat line facing Erastus. Bemus, in a guernsey frock, gray pigtail freshly braided, trolleyed a tea tray across the lawn and offered a cup to each of the girls. They stood

464

quietly, sipping from their cups, nibbling at ship's biscuits. A few turned their heads to stare at the suitors in their cottages. One, tired from her short journey, sank to sit on the lawn. Erastus rose and greeted each girl, taking her by the hand, speaking a few words of welcome, regarding each thoughtfully. He took a frail young woman with coiled white braids by the shoulders and gently moved her from the end of the line to a place between the coral-tinted girl and the taller of the two in capes.

"Welcome, Limpet, Abalone, Wentle, Scallop, Periwinkle, Cowrie, and Coral, welcome."

One girl smiled, her eyes rolling back; the others only stood quietly.

Erastus examined the line of girls once more. Finally he moved one, the sturdiest in appearance, to the ocean-most end of the line. She stood straight and still, though her gaze wandered. Bemus followed as Erastus went down the line of girls, indicating to each to bend her head, placing on each a chaplet woven of sea oats and sandbur. Erastus studied the gowns in which the girls were dressed, which Bemus had ordered from Mouse Island. They were made from plain, undyed wool but finely crafted. Erastus briefly regretted not ordering true chiton robes, such as the temple virgins wore in the friezes of ancient Attica, but it would have taken longer than he wanted to wait. He was, however, pleased that his timing had gone according to plan, so that the suitors would first behold their brides in the gentle light of a fading day.

Bemus led the line of girls back to the whaleboat on which they had arrived and helped seat them on the benches, in the order determined by Erastus. Steersman pushed off from the beach and the boat turned to glide alongside the dock, toward the cottages. Dusk was falling. In each cottage a lantern had been lit; each of the seven doorways glowed warm against a violet sky. As the boat reached the first cottage, Steersman lifted the first girl to her suitor, who was waiting on his steps. The tide was full; each man, standing on his top step, stood a few inches above the sea. The boat, not stopping, moved on to the next cottage, and the next. In a minute or so all the girls had been delivered and all the doors closed.

All but the last. The seventh suitor stood in his doorway, so large that he blocked the light of the lantern inside. The boatman began to hand up the seventh girl but Benadam held up a huge hand. The girl faltered back into the boat. The suitor looked straight at Erastus and pointed up at Rathbone House.

Erastus turned to follow his gaze. Though the bottom of the house lay in shadow, the top was lit by the long warm rays of the setting sun. Another girl, an eighth girl, leaned out a window.

If the seven brides had been whole and healthy, had their thin veins swelled, they might have resembled Verity Rathbone. She was the bright counterpart to the girl who swayed back into the boat, who could have served as her shadow: tall, slender, her hair not white but of the palest blond, her skin a healthful pink. Anyone who saw her would have thought her flawless. Her eyes were as green as Moses's in his prime.

The seventh suitor, still pointing at Verity, said in a clear, loud voice, "That one."

Erastus lurched from his seat and began to thump with his canes back and forth along the dock. He frowned, shook his head slowly, and stopped, looking keenly at the seventh suitor.

"No, Mr. Gale. She wouldn't suit you. Would you care, perhaps, to trade with another man? Your neighbor's bride has a more pleasing form by far."

The seventh suitor only kept pointing.

Erastus paced, removing his hat and running a hand through his thin white hair.

"The fourth maiden, what of her? Surely you observed her lovely coloring."

The seventh suitor shook his head and kept pointing. Erastus stopped pacing and sat down again, folding his arms across his chest and speaking firmly.

"You have signed, you know. It's too late."

The seventh suitor didn't move.

Erastus leaned forward in his chair and called out in a loud whisper that carried across the water. He need not have worried that the other men would hear or, if they did hear, in the now-dark cottages, would care.

"What if I were to double the gold? Triple it?"

The seventh suitor still pointed.

Erastus looked up at the window and back at Benadam. He sank into his chair. He shook his head.

Benadam slowly lowered his hand and stared at Erastus, his arms held tense, his body still. He stood in thought for a long moment, then looked toward the skiff that still hovered nearby, the rejected maiden sitting quietly in its stern. He held out his hand. Steersman brought the skiff neatly alongside. The girl placed a timid foot on the step and, when she was sure that she wouldn't again be expelled, gave her hand to Benadam. Together they entered the cottage and the door closed behind them; a moment later, the lantern was doused. Bemus and the other old whalemen headed up the hill to the house, whose windows now glowed with lantern light. Erastus sat for some time in his chair, his eye on the seventh cottage. Then he, too, headed for the house. The sun sank, the dock was silent, and dusk deepened to dark.

In the morning six doors opened in six cottages; six men stretched and yawned; six brides kept to their beds. The door to the seventh cottage didn't open. The seventh girl, her mysteries unplumbed, lay alone. Erastus's sleek schooner, the *Argo,* was missing. Benadam Gale, the seventh suitor, was gone. And so was Verity Rathbone.

Summer came and went. A brief autumn flared among the trees in the thin woods above the shore, then faded; the air grew chill. The six suitors stayed in the cottages with their brides, though they were ill at ease in the cool white rooms, away from their boats and tackle. They treated their dwellings with the deference of man to virgin, perching on the edges of fragile chairs, carefully scraping their boots on the shells at their thresholds, reluctant to enter their own houses. When it came to their wives, however, the men didn't falter. They relished rocking back and forth on their pale brides, eyes closed, dreaming of being at sea. Erastus, who had kept to the house in the weeks after Verity disappeared, emerged at last to patrol the dock, craning up to peer through the little windows at the white girls laying on their beds or lingering at the sea doors, their bellies slowly swelling.

As winter came on, the men wearied of the cold white walls of their cottages, a white that, against the hot blue Mediterranean sky, would have served as relief. Hungry for color, they stained the walls with what they could find, with fish blood and sea cows' milk, with blueberries from a nearby bog, so that their rooms grew rosy, or creamy, or the blue-white of the skin of the fifth wife. Though nervous at first (their bargains with Erastus included strict confinement to the cottages), the men soon realized that Erastus was not keeping close watch; he spent little time outdoors in the sunlight. They slipped out for driftwood, scavenged for timber in the dwindling pines above the shoreline, and passed the time building rough chairs and sturdy bedsteads to replace the delicate furniture in their

470

rooms. Over time, the cottages began to resemble, rather than the temples of Greece, the fishermen's cottages of those islands. In the early mornings the men stood in their doorways and looked longingly out to the few small craft that trawled the shoals, their fingers itching to be at work.

As the brides' due dates drew near, Erastus called back a few of the crews of carpenters who had built the cottages to add a third story to Rathbone House. Above the Georgian red brick of the second story, in the ever-cooler autumn air, rose a top floor like a Greek temple, with fluted columns and capitals of the Doric order. Along its front, under the peaked cornice, a man perched on a scaffolding wielded chisel and mallet, carving a frieze of Poseidon. The sea god wielded his trident above the waves, his great scaly tail curling behind him, his Nereids leaping and gliding about him, though somewhat stiffly, being carved not from fluid marble but from sturdy oak by a Boston man renowned for his ship figureheads. His nymphs resembled tavern trollops more than a god's handmaidens, Erastus thought, but he was pleased with the austere white of the painted wood. Erastus never knew that the original friezes on which his were modeled had been as brightly painted as any ship's figurehead, and the temples within which they stood, too. Within the shining white walls, all along the perimeter, the carpenters began to frame out a series of rooms. As the work progressed, Erastus would stand at the top of the landing, turning in a circle, envisioning each of the small white rooms as it would look when finished, each with a crib, each crib with slats like thin white columns and soft new quilts stuffed with the down of young gulls.

Meantime, the six men were becoming impatient. Their contracts with Erastus called for berths on the *Misistuck,* contracts to be fulfilled as soon as she returned to port. The agreements included a generous lay, enough gold to keep each man and his family — for a few of the men had wives and children waiting at home — comfortable for many years. But through three seasons no such ship appeared and no rumor of any, until a New Bedford brig finally passed with the news that the *Misistuck* had passed them six months earlier, not homeward bound but headed for the Azores, on the far side of the world.

In warm summer, the men all left, leaving behind six swollen brides in the cottages. In the seventh cottage the abandoned bride abided, intact.

At the beginning of the ninth month, the brides were moved to the main house. Since the third-floor nursery was not yet finished, all were installed in the room at the back of the first floor, that same room where all the Rathbone boys had swung in hammocks, watched over by the worn wives. Five more beds were moved into the room, and all were spread with newly loomed linens from Mouse Island. By the first bed, Conch and Crab were stationed, dressed in clean white cooks' slops. Though the room, like all the others, was always clean and shipshape, Conch and Crab, excited about the new life on its way, had redoubled their efforts. The floors were swabbed and holystoned twice daily; the brides were offered every comfort, pressed with offers of fresh banty-hen eggs, of new white bread and warm milk.

As the time drew near, the brides' attendants timed their contractions and tried to hold off those whose birth pangs didn't coincide with the striking of the bell at noon. Bemus assisted, distracting one bride with a soothing chantey, calming another with sips of rum-laced tea. The team stood by ready to haul the line. When each squalling head breached its mother's thighs, Conch hauled and heaved, then Crab neatly cut the cord and tied it in a square knot and duly noted down the time in the log. The brides all gave birth in a wave within two hours of one another, between one and three bells in the first dogwatch, on the last day of the year.

When they were finished, a weary Conch and Crab opened the door and beckoned to Erastus, who had been waiting outside throughout the last watch. He walked slowly into the room, his heart racing, his hopes high for this infusion of new blood into tired Rathbone veins. He had long waited for this moment: the birth of a new generation of strong sons, sons who would reestablish the Rathbones' mastery of the sperm and of the sea.

Conch and Crab stood aside, avoiding his eye. Erastus stepped close to the hammock in which the six infants lay, swabbed and swaddled. The infants did display a closer relationship to the sea than any Rathbone had in three generations, but not in the way that Erastus had hoped for. They looked as though they would have been more at home in the fluid with which they arrived than breathing the air. They gasped at each breath. Their limbs and features showed no symmetry, as though viewed through a fathom of water. They resembled more a spill of shell-less shellfish in a net than human infants. One boy's flipper-like arms, waving feebly, might have served him well in the sea. The skin of one infant girl sparkled, scaly, and from her spine rose a vestigial fin.

Erastus stared at the hammock, now swaying in a breeze. His fingers fumbled at his waistcoat pocket and pulled out a folded piece of paper; he opened it to look at the list of names he had chosen. He refolded it, put it back in his pocket, and left the room.

Conch and Crab fussed and fretted over the infants while the mothers, exhausted by their labor, lay sleeping. They fought over how to fold the diapers, deftly changing them in pinless fashion, plying the babies with bottles and tucking them snugly into their hammock. But in the same order in which they came into the world, within minutes of one another and on the same day they arrived, the babies all departed. Fourth-Oar and Bemus, whispering, returned them to the sea.

The carpenters were sent away. The unfinished third floor remained unfinished, lifting its white columns against the sky. The cottages were torn down. The brides, emptied, sailed back to the island in the west, to the caves and to the birds that had bred there each spring, birds with long red legs, with white plumage and glossy black throats.

CHAPTER NINETEEN:
WEDDING WALK

{in which Mama and Papa measure no miles}

1841

The minister stood in the crow's nest of the *Argo,* one hand clutching the rail, the other pressing his Bible to his breast. Three sturdy men, Benadam's friends, hoisted him there, placing his feet on the rope rungs, pushing him from behind. From time to time he dipped a hand in his frock-coat pocket to trade his Bible for a handkerchief to mop his brow, keeping one hand always on the railing and his eyes on some distant point of the horizon to avoid looking down.

The crow's nest was decorated with swags of sea bladder, studded here and there with rosy starfish. A thick garland of braided seaweed spiraled around the mainmast. From each strand of rigging, bow to stern, flew all the cutter's pennants, gaily flapping.

The minister opened his Bible, smoothing

its damp pages with a shaking hand. He coughed and shifted his feet, and began to read, directing his voice out into the air.

Verity stood on the yard at the top of the mainmast, her arms wrapped around the thick pillar of pine. She wore a plain white gown of muslin, her hair in a loose braid down her back. Her gown, wet from salt spray, dried quickly in the sun. Below her the main top-gallant sail swelled, bellied out and back with each fresh breeze, its white blinding her. She closed her eyes and lay her face against the warm wood of the mast. She heard the ropes creaking. Seabirds dipped and lifted above the ship, calling.

Benadam balanced on the fore-topmast. He wore a red tricorne hat, his old coat of brown twill, new buck breeches, and boots polished to glass. The ship tilted in a sudden sharp gust; he balanced, needing no mast or line to stay him; he grinned and held his arms out to Verity.

She laughed and let go of the mainmast. She began to walk along the yard; it was wide enough, and if she began to lose her balance she had only to put out her hand to find a rope, there were so many. She kicked her slippers into the sea and tightrope-walked her way out. Her arms tilted back and forth, themselves yardarms, trying to balance; she didn't, wouldn't grasp a line. She moved easily, as though she were born to it.

The minister cleared his throat and began to read. Verity didn't look into the distance, didn't see the prismatic spout of a whale that was just passing out of view over the horizon. She saw only Benadam, and he only her, between them the distance of a few strides, the length of a yardarm, between them only a stretch of wood, no distance at all.

MOSES *m.* THANKFUL *m.* PATIENCE *m.* CHARITY *m.* AMAZIAH *m.* CONSTANCE *m.* HOPESTILL *m.* HEPZIBAH *m.* EUPHEMIA *m.*
m.1761   m.1765   m.1768   m.1772   m.1773   m.1775   m.1781   m.1784

BOW-OAR *m.* LYDIA   2ND-OAR

ABSALOM   PARMENAS   PHILO   CLAUDIA *m.* (?)   JEROBOAM   LANMAN

BENADAM GALE *m.*   VERITY   ERASTUS   CONCH   CRA
                                          (LARBOARD) (STARBO

MERCY   GIDEON   MORDECAI

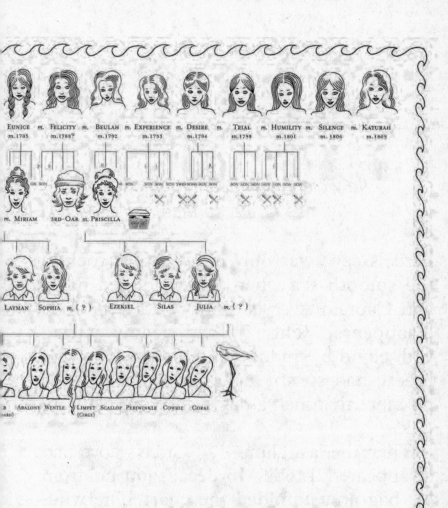

EUNICE *m.* FELICITY *m.* BEULAH *m.* EXPERIENCE *m.* DESIRE *m.* TRIAL *m.* HUMILITY *m.* SILENCE *m.* KATURAH
m.1785   m.1788?   m.1792   m.1793   m.1794   m.1798   m.1801   m.1806   m.1809

m. MIRIAM   3RD-OAR *m.* PRISCILLA

LAYMAN   SOPHIA *m.* (?)   EZEKIEL   SILAS   JULIA *m.* (?)

B   ABALONE WENTLE LIMPET SCALLOP PERIWINKLE COWRIE CORAL
(BARD)   (CIRGE)

THE RATHBONES

Chapter Twenty:
The Little Sailor

*{in which unpleasant memories
rise to the surface}*

Circe's cave was only a low jag of rock in the smooth sea when I next looked back, and Captain Avery's dinghy had long since disappeared. The sky had deeply settled with cloud by midday, and a good following breeze had sprung up. I judged that I was no more than half a day's sail from Naiway-onk.

When the last glimpse of Circe's cove had disappeared, I took Mordecai's journal from his bag and unfolded the chart. The wind picked up its edges and rattled them against the bench. I smoothed the pages and held them flat against the wood. There were Moses and his wives; under them, the long row of sons, with my little portraits of Bow-Oar, Second-Oar, and Third-Oar, each next to his golden wife; then all of their sons, crowded into the boat on which they sailed away, and the roughly sketched faces of Claudia, Julia, and Sophia.

I could fill out the fourth row now: Verity and Erastus; Conch and Crab (Larboard and Starboard); and all the shell girls. I didn't know how to arrange the names, though. Was Claudia the mother of Verity and Erastus, and so my grandmother, or was Julia? Did Sophia join with a cousin or an uncle to produce Abalone? Were Coral and Cowrie twins, or only born at the same time to two of the sisters? Who were their fathers? Next to Coral's long white face I added a stilt, its head tucked under a wing.

The thread of Captain Avery's story disappeared when Mama and Papa ran away together. Only Mama knew the rest.

I was grateful for the tasks of navigation, for the many small corrections my course required. I didn't want to think any more of Mama, or of my brother, or of any other Rathbone.

It was past midday; the sun had begun its slow descent in a sky thick with cloud. The air was chill but not yet cold, and the sea rose and fell in low smooth swells beneath my hull. As the hours passed, I regretted not asking the captain for more water; his little flask was long empty. I was thirsty, and tired, and struggled to concentrate on keeping to a true path along the coast, far enough away to avoid submerged rocks, close enough to avoid my little craft getting swept out to sea by strong currents.

I must have let my attention wander for some time. I rubbed my eyes and was surprised to find that the sail was slack and the boat scarcely moving, the sun far lower in the sky than when I had last noticed. The coast might have only been veiled by the thin drizzle now falling, but I felt that it was far away. I looked over the side and all around and saw that I was becalmed in a sea of weed that stretched as far as I could see on all sides. Mordecai had once told me of a vast region of floating algae in the middle of the Atlantic, but I was certain it was at least a thousand miles farther east. When explorers bent on the New World had entered that region, after many months afloat, they had thought themselves nearly at landfall and become excited, only to suffer disappointment when they realized they were only halfway across the ocean. Abandoned ships were said to be trapped here and there among the weeds, from a distance seemingly skimming along, when in fact their decks had dried to dust and their hulls rotted. Or they hung suspended under the surface of the sea, caught in the weeds, never sinking to the bottom.

Though my rudder was not tangled, the sea beneath me seemed itself to have slowed. The wind had died entirely. I secured the tiller with a stout line so that I would stay somewhat on course if the wind revived, and leaned over the side.

Long fronds of sea palm waved among delicate sea lettuce and crusted coralline and other varieties unknown to me. In the still air I could hear the air bladders of algae popping. If it were not for the shallow breath of the sea, its slow rise and fall betraying what lay under the skin of green, I might have been tempted to step over the side as onto a meadow.

Crow had finally shaken off the spell of Circe's cove and now flew low over the weeds, snapping here and there at sinuous black lines that drew themselves along the surface. When one came near the boat I could see that it was a great black eel coiling slowly along. Shimmering jellyfish quivered and pulsed among the weeds, clear moon jellyfish and pinks, and the bloated crests of the man-of-war bobbed above the algae. I recognized a colony of rare obelia by their trailing green tentacles, and thought how pleased Mordecai would have been at my erudition. I reached farther over the rim and tried to part the weeds with my hands. What water I could see was of a pale clear green, light-veined. The weeds were studded with fish, trapped and straining to free themselves or floating motionlessly, caught in final positions of struggle. Besides common haddock and halibut there were fish not native to those waters, brilliantly colored, with frothy fins. Flotsam and jetsam traveled with the weed: a long cuffed boot, on which a sleeping turtle perched; a crushed crate; the stave of a barrel.

I reached and pried the stave from a mat of sea moss. Its wood was soft and nearly rotten, sodden black, its slight curve like the rib bones of the sperm that Mama carved. I hung over the side and stirred the water with the stave. Below the thick layer of weeds, I could see only green. I tried to think about what Mordecai had said about the game with the barrels. I was no longer thirsty, but my head felt as though it might float away. As I stirred the water I felt the woven bracelet bite tight on my wrist. The air around me went black and cold. I twisted the bracelet and stared down.

I move down a dark corridor, running my hand along a thick rope bolted to the wall. The ceiling is low and crossed by heavy beams. Little windows with bars of iron pierce one stout wall; outside, a red sun falls into the sea. Along the other wall runs a row of cupboards. I open the door to each as I walk and feel what's inside with my hands: neatly coiled rope in this one, boxed nails and brass fittings there, and bolts of stiff cloth. I reach the room at the end of the hall. The door is low and has a rope pull. A big knot forms the handle. It smells dank and cool inside. It's dark, only the iron bands of the barrels that fill the room in neat rows gleam in thin light from the hall.

I know he is in here, my cousin, hiding. If I find him before sunset, he has promised me a surprise. I walk slowly along the row of barrels, lifting a lid here and there, careful to make small sounds as I go, so that he'll know I'm searching. I turn back, and open and close the door as though I'm leaving, but I stay inside. I stand motionless against the wall and wait. There are small rustlings among the barrels; a rat winds through and disappears. Then a faint sound from the back of the third row. I move as silently as I can down the line, push aside each lid and peer into each barrel.

The first two are empty but each tells me what it held. The lid of the first feels sticky; the smell of soured molasses wafts up. To the staves of the second, small soft feathers cling.

The lid of the third will not yield; as I struggle with it a pale cloud rises from the fourth barrel and Mordecai unfolds, smiling, holding out to me a little figure: a sailor made of metal, missing only one leg.

I'm in the room with the barrels again. A dusky sea of blue stretches before me, the skirt of Mama's gown. On it great dark roses bloom all the way around. She stands with her back to me, doesn't know I'm there, crouching between two barrels behind her, peering through the gap, my face close to her skirt. Her skirt smells wrong. The roses are not flowers but huge blooms of mildew; she must have sewed her skirt from the bolts of indigo stored too long in the cupboards.

Mama is breathing in long ragged breaths. There's another smell and something leaking on the floor. She holds something heavy in her arms, she's putting it in one of the barrels. She sways back and forth. Something drags between her legs. Something white drags behind her.

Now something blocks my view — Mordecai's there, putting his arms around me, pressing my face tight against his chest.

I jolted back from the rim of the boat. My braids, which had been trailing over the side during my reverie, had come undone: My loosened hair whipped back, spraying water over my face and soaking my gown. Something not water moved in the mass of my wet hair; I put up a reluctant hand and pulled away a long wriggling strand, the color of flesh: a ribbon worm. Shuddering, I tried to fling it away, but it was tangled in my hair, so long that no matter how much I pulled it wouldn't end. Crow was suddenly there. He gripped the worm firmly in his beak and flew backward until, with a loud, unwholesome snap, the worm broke free of my hair. Crow, already glutted on black eel, flung it into the floating weed.

I tried to shake away what I had just seen and felt. I was still dizzy, and tired, but even so, I knew that what I had just experienced were not foggy imaginings but memories long pressed down.

The leaking smell came again and my stomach heaved. I remembered it now, the room on the bottom floor with the barrels, where Mordecai and I had played when I was a little girl. I hadn't been near it for years. I seldom went to that part of the house; it had made me uneasy to walk along that line of rooms with their empty beds, long before the man in blue chased me there. Now I wondered if my unease had come more from that room than from anything else. I leaned over the side and splashed cold water over my face until my head stopped swimming and my stomach steadied.

I stood up, my arm around the mast, and took a deep breath of cold air. The bowl of the sky was pricked now with stars and bluing down to meet the sea, the shore a long curve of dark between. A shore I recognized. There was the western point, and beyond it Naiwayonk.

Chapter Twenty-One:
A Bed in a Barrel

{in which Mercy returns to remember}

The arc of the bay broadened as I approached, and at its back, at the farthest point, a light flared. I wiped my eyes and wondered for a moment if I had strayed into Hepzibah's time. Was that light, pulsing and ever brighter, coming from the cauldrons in the sheds? Had the fires been lit after so long? I scanned the long curve of beach out to the point; the great hulks were dark and silent as ever. The light was coming from the widow's walk, far brighter than any that had burned there before. I thought at first that the walk itself was burning, but no, there were no flames, only the light. The dome burned bright as a lantern held up by a dark hand.

I squinted to see the house beneath the glare and remembered how, when Mordecai and I had sailed out of the Stark Archipelago, I had looked back toward the Stark house through the trees and seen Roderick standing at a high window, staring out after me.

I turned my smack in to the bay and was carried forward in the making tide. She moved so fast that I had to furl the sail and man the tiller to keep her from broaching to and overturning in the rush of water. Though roiling beneath, the surface of the sea was calm, and from the dark water all around me I now heard splashing and other, smaller sounds: a whistling on my starboard side, a bark on the larboard. Straining my eyes, I could just discern darker shapes moving in the water around me. I leapt out and ran the smack onto the sand, halfway along the shore between the house and the western point. Crow clung to my shoulder, hunched and sullen.

The dark shapes that had accompanied my boat had come ashore with me, and the beach was thick with them, limned by the light from the widow's walk, some of them moving, some still. Cautiously approaching the nearest, I recognized the glistening form of a dolphin, chirping faintly. I ran my hand along its smooth side and found it up to its flippers in sand; it had plowed a deep furrow and was stuck there, gasping. Besides the dolphin I could make out an exhausted manatee wedged between two rocks. I tried to help the dolphin get back to the sea, but though I pushed with all my strength it wouldn't budge nor would the manatee stir. I grasped a brace of twitching haddock and flung them into the surf; they struggled back to shore and lay wheezing on the sand.

I left the panting array of sea creatures, regretfully, and walked east along the beach toward the house. A long beam of light from the walk marked my path. When I arrived at my little cove I thought for a moment that my old skiff had returned from its ocean grave, but as I drew near I saw that in its former place was an overturned boat, a long craft pointed at both ends: a whaleboat. Whatever name had once been painted on its stern was worn away to a shadow. I touched its seaweed-slimed hull and found it wet. I climbed up my boulder stair and crossed the lawn, my own breath now coming short and my heart beating hard.

I didn't know what I would say to Mama. I didn't want to think about it too much and lose my nerve. I would find my words when I found her.

The house was dark and silent as I entered. I stopped just inside the door and lit a lantern that stood on the hall table. Even here, at the bottom of the house, the glare of the widow's walk intruded from above. The air smelled stale, brackish. I didn't linger below but started up the wide stair.

As I climbed, I passed the portraits that hung along the stair. There were the waxy profiles, now better known to me: first Moses Rathbone with his tangle of hair, then Bow-Oar in his top hat; Lydia's handsome young Absalom and unlucky Erastus. As I moved up the narrowing spiral I might have been climbing up the throat of a sperm, the house was so hollow and damp. I thought of that picture in Mama's room, tucked in her mirror, its image of the drowned world that lay at the bottom of the ocean. Maybe all of that land had once been green mountains and thick forests, and the sea had risen to reclaim it. Or it had all sunk, like Arcady.

I had not been gone long enough to account for the changes I saw around me. Mold and mildew once restricted to the foundation had crept high into the house, here repatterning wallpaper, there splashing wood as though with mud. The plaster on the walls was damp and cracked, and in places looked encrusted with barnacles. I reached the top of the stair, turned, and headed toward the front of the house.

When I neared Mama's room a dark shape on the floor outside flickered in the glow of my lantern; Larboard lay curled on the floor in his faded blue linen, gently snoring. Starboard, I thought, must have finally shriveled away while I was gone. I had never seen one outside Mama's door without the other. I passed on tiptoe and came to the hatchway of the walk, then stopped there, listening. At that hour Mama was always to be heard pacing back and forth above. Maybe she has only paused, I thought, and waited, but all remained quiet. I eased open the hatchway and leaned in to look. Light flared and guttered on the sides of the well; I heard from above the faint hiss of burning oil, but still no other sound. I closed the door and peered around the corner, into the dark behind the hatchway.

I stood in the hall, at a loss. Where could she be? Crow, still and sullen before, now paced back and forth across my shoulders, catching his claws in my braids, pulling my hair from my scalp, until in exasperation I caught him up and threw him, squawking, into the air. He flapped for a moment above me, then flew off, back down the hall.

The door to Mama's room was slightly ajar. I stepped carefully over the sleeping Larboard, slid through, and closed the door

gently behind me. Looking around, I saw
with fresh eyes the room's familiar details,
edged in white by the moon. At one end the
tall spindle bed, its hangings woven in the
pattern of a fleet under full sail, the pale
ships bobbing in a faint breeze from the
window. In the middle of the room the long
black table with the boat of bone at its
center. The straight-backed chair by the fire.
The basket of bones, no longer filled with
ribs but scattered with a few gray teeth and
splintered jawbones. Mama's plain pine
wardrobe still stood tall in the corner, its
door ajar. I opened it and ran my hands over
the dark indigo gowns that hung there. I
put my face among them, smelling cedar
and salt, cold cinders from the fire.

I looked down at my own gown, its vivid
green darkened by the surf I had struggled
through. It now rode high above my ankles.
I peeled the sodden fabric away from my
skin and stepped out of it, then drew one of
Mama's gowns over my head. I ran a hand
across the soft, warm wool, and thought of
that day when I had tried one of her gowns,
and she had sliced the buttons away. That
gown had fit me precisely across the shoulders and through the bodice, as this one
did, but where before the skirt had pooled
on the floor, it now hovered an inch above.

I had grown. From Mama's dresser I picked up the mirror whose frame she had carved from the spinal disk of a sperm and, moving the lantern close, looked at myself.

I might have been looking at Mama but for my color. Never as fair as hers, my skin had browned to bronze these weeks past. My hair was streaked by sun and salt nearly as light as hers, if you didn't part it to look beneath. I unbraided it and brushed it out. It coiled around my neck. Crow flew in at the door, back from his brief exile, and landed on my shoulder. He cawed at his image in the mirror and began to preen his tail feathers.

From a hook in the wardrobe I took one of Mama's wide white collars, boiled and bleached, starched and pressed, and tied it around my neck, where it made a stiff sail smelling of lye. I laced the front of the gown as tightly as I could, but a narrow gap remained where my shift showed. If I had worn Mama's corset, the edges of the gown would have met. The chair by the window where her corset stood sentinel each night was empty but for a single long sliver of white. I picked it up; a stay from the corset. Mama had removed one more bone.

I moved my lantern to the dresser, where a little chest of ebony wood stood open, its interior glittering in the moonlight. The chest was full of jewels that Papa had sent in the crates those past ten years. I grasped a handful, held them up, and turned them in the light — bracelets of amber and coral; carved jade rings of every shade of green from pale as milk to nearly black; a long string of enormous pearls. She had never worn any of them, only the necklace of three bones strung on a silver chain.

I returned the jewels and closed the chest, putting up a hand to restrain Crow from plunging in a greedy beak and carrying a gem away. I felt Gideon's woven bracelet on my wrist, now so tight that I wouldn't have been able to tug it off if I'd tried, and remembered how the crows had brought it to me that night. Why shouldn't Crow have a jewel of his own? I opened the chest again and selected a little bracelet of faceted black jasper that looked handsome against his blue-black wing and offered it to him. He canted his head and regarded me warily, then snatched it in his beak and flew off. I stood looking into the chest, considering, then lifted the heavy strand of pearls high into the moonlight. The lustrous spheres graduated in size, the central pearl as large as a plover's egg.

I lifted the strand over my head and

looped it around my neck, and looked in the mirror. The moon entered into each pearl, taking up the gleam of my teeth, the sheen of my eyes. I turned from side to side in the mirror. I looked out at the sea, at the bright path the moon made along the water to me. I lowered the pearls, clicking, into the box and shut it.

When I turned to leave, something caught my eye on the long black table; among the broken pieces of scrimshaw was one round, whole object. Though I had never actually seen it before, I recognized it by its description, something Mama once said while she was carving. "For your papa I chose a section of sternum and modeled a compass that always points to me." He carried it with him on his travels, she said, keeping it always in his pocket. I picked it up and stroked the smooth ivory of the case. It looked to have been fashioned from cast-off pieces of other devices: the glass face, its edge beveled, was from a barometer; the dial once a watch face; the needle pulled from a clock, too large for the case. Its point rasped against the glass, quivered, and pointed west. I tilted the compass in my hand; the needle held at west, trembling, then shot around to east by northeast. I doubted that Papa had ever carried this compass anywhere. I put it back down, looking up at the boat of bone; it was nearly complete. Mama had planked it while I was gone, so that what had been only an outline was filled with the long, curved sperm ribs that had filled the basket on the hearth, fitted together and honed into a smooth white hull.

Crow flew in from the hall and dropped down to hover behind me, his wings whooshing loudly in the quiet room. He nipped at my hands and pulled at the strings of the collar, flying out the door and back again, urging me away.

I walked down to the second floor, stopping now and again to look into the drawers and cupboards, many of which stood open. They had been emptied of their meager cargos of rope ends and candle stubs, the contents of others spilled on the floor. From one bin that had been left ajar, seeds were sifting in a thin stream. Crow hopped down from my shoulder to stand with an open beak under the stream, swallowing. I leaned into one of the golden rooms. The circle of light from my lantern should have set the room ablaze; instead only a weak and wavering gleam greeted me. The gold walls had tarnished. Crow, having finished gorging himself on the stream of seeds, flew on.

I knew where Crow would lead me. We descended to the bottom floor. As we rounded the newel post at the bottom of the stair and I saw the little black door to the storeroom, tucked under the stairs, I began to feel seasick, as I never felt afloat.

I opened the door slowly and peered in. The storeroom, long and low, was filled with rows of iron-strapped barrels full of once-fresh water, faintly damp in the dark, readied for some voyage and forgotten. The brackish smell that I had noticed on first entering the house, ever stronger as I had walked, was overwhelming here. I was instantly back in the boat, seeing again what I'd seen then. Something that Mordecai wanted to hide from me. Mama dragging something white.

Crow flew to the barrel at the end of the nearest row. He circled its rim, scrawking softly and fixing a bright eye on mine. His claws clacked loud against the barrel's lid.

It was easy for me to weave, once I started, to see what Mordecai had seen.

Mama's white collar, its strings loosened by Crow's tugs, drifted down and it all flooded in.

She didn't look dim or hazy but un-naturally bright, like dry beach stones plunged in a jar of water, their parched grays returned to vivid hues, their soft outlines suddenly sharp. There she was, walking slowly along the row, in her indigo gown with its great blooms of mildew, her tread heavy, the something white dragging behind her, between her legs. She was breathing hard, pulling someone whose legs trailed between hers. I moved closer, until I was just next to her. There, lolling on her arm, was my own face. No. It was the face of my brother.

She stopped and stood next to the barrel at the end of the row, the one on which Crow had been walking. Crow was gone, the lid of the barrel was off, and the brackish smell was coming from inside — not a scent but a great sour wave of brine that filled the little room. My stomach lurched and I turned away. Behind me I heard Mama grunt, heard the barrel heave and slosh. I didn't want to look. I turned around.

Mama had stuffed my brother into the barrel, folding him to fit. I stood beside her and looked in over the edge. His hands and feet pointed up at me, his face turned up to mine. I didn't understand why he was so white. He looked frozen. As if he'd been doused with powder, dredged in flour. I moved closer. The barrel was full of brine.

He was encrusted with salt. The white crystals sparkled, his skin and hair dark beneath the glitter. His eyes were open, green glazed with white. I touched his cheek. His body swayed and bobbed, his hands signaled stiffly.

I jumped back and threw an arm over my eyes, my skin burning as though I, too, bobbed in salt.

I sank down on the floor, pulling my knees up to hide my face. When I opened them she was gone. My eyes stung less; the vivid colors returned to dull. The floor was dry, but the smell of brine still hung thick in the air. Crow was back, circling the rim of the barrel as before.

Now I remembered what Mordecai had said, back on the island, his head cradled on Circe's lap. About my brother. About Mama making him a bed in a barrel.

I stood up and nudged Crow off the barrel. I tried to pry off the lid with my hands but it wouldn't yield. I thought there must be a tool to lift these lids somewhere in the storeroom; I looked all around and spied an old marlinspike, rusted but stout, leaning against a barrel across the room. I hurried there and back, and began to pry the rim of the barrel lid, the wood squeaking and groaning as I worked my way around. At last the lid popped off and clattered on the floor. I moved slowly closer and looked in. The barrel was dry and empty. I leaned in with my lantern and breathed deep; a strong waft of salt. Close to the top a rough line of white ran all around, marking where a tide of brine had reached. In the white crust a hair curled, dark at its root, white where it met salt.

CHAPTER TWENTY-TWO:
SEVEN SUITORS REDUX

{in which Mercy selects her own suitor}

I woke hours later when the moon looked in at me. I had gone up to my little room after opening the barrel and lay down to rest for a moment. The room had seemed so small, as did my bed; when I lay down my feet hung over the end. I couldn't remember when I had last slept, other than drifting in and out while stranded in the weeds. I felt drained, my head hollowed out. A wind pushed against the wavery panes of my window and the cold light of the moon faltered across my blanket. I sat up, rubbing my numbed feet.

He was in the way, you see. Of her . . . recreations.

I thought of the sailors who would come to Rathbone House with crates from Papa. They came hurrying up our walkway, shouldering those heavy crates, eager to make their deliveries. They left much later, often late in the evening, not bowed down but stepping jauntily, as often as not whistling a cheerful tune. Mama had looked, if not happy, less sorrowful on the mornings after those visits, a mood which I attributed at the time to the arrival of the crate, not its carrier. On such mornings she could be found in the laundry, standing over Larboard as he stirred a big kettle of boiling water and lye and bleach, head bobbing on its thin stem, tossing in her collars. Later she watched Starboard as he starched the collars, then pressed them smooth with a flat iron.

Other memories came nudging back. The time she had sliced the buttons from my gown, scribing my skin with a long pink line, a line that I now saw might have easily split me from throat to belly. The time she had so coolly regarded her own blood welling up from her wound when she had cut herself. How she had not even looked at me when I hung spinning in the air from my father's fist that night on the walk.

Someone knocked, far below, a sound odd enough in itself, since we never had visitors, and doubly odd at that late hour. I leaned and pressed my face close against the window. I could just see down to the front door. Two men, strangers, stood on the porch in the moonlight. They stood awkwardly side by side, not looking at each other, waiting for someone to answer. Though the moonlight was not strong enough to let me read their expressions, I could tell from their stiff stances that they weren't pleased to be in each other's company. It was too dark for me to see much, only enough to know that they weren't seamen. One wore a broad-brimmed hat and heavy boots, which he stamped on the porch against the cold. The other wore dungarees with straps whose brass clasps caught the light. There was a sound of gravel crunching and the men on the porch both turned to see a third arrive, walking along the path that curved around the back of the house from the inland road, a man wearing a suit of city clothes and a black derby hat. I knew why he was here, and the others. Mama's corset was one bone lighter. Another year had passed since Papa had left. It was the tenth anniversary of his disappearance. The men were here for Mama, to compete for her hand. And, though she was still beautiful, they were here for the gold.

They were all mistaken: Papa was not dead. But he was to me. There was only a man named Benadam Gale, who from time to time came to the house to sail his wife across the walk and return the same night to a greater sea.

I woke Crow, who was still asleep on a bedpost, nudging him onto my shoulder, and slipped out into the hallway. At the top of the stairs I stopped and listened. I heard two, three pairs of footsteps, climbing from below. I continued as quietly as I could, restraining Crow, who flapped his wings and threatened to launch off and down the stairs, with a firm hand. Through the knocking, which continued at intervals, I heard another sound, toward the end of the hall: chair legs scraping, polite coughs. I stopped about twenty feet away, from where, peering around a column, I could clearly see the end of the hall, with the door to Mama's room to one side and the hatchway straight ahead, well lit by a line of sconces on either wall. A row of chairs had been arranged there, backs to one wall, and on them sat five men. A sixth arrived and sat as I watched. One chair, the one farthest from Mama's room, stood vacant.

None of these men had come by sea, or if they had they must have come as passengers. Though Rathbone House had seen few visitors these ten years past, word had clearly gone abroad of the fortune that languished in Naiwayonk. I crouched close enough to know that these men smelled not of the sea but of forest and field and plain: a loamy farmer with hay still clinging to his limbs; a woodsman whose heavy boots were fringed with mud and leaves. Another man's face, though well scrubbed and rosy, had a black tinge beneath that spoke of coal. Besides the merchant in the derby, there was a man in shop clerk's garb and one wearing wide trousers of leather, turning a large felted hat in his hands, who looked as if he must hail from the western territories.

My eye went back to the fourth chair, to the man dressed like a shop clerk. He had taken a pipe from his pocket and was packing it with tobacco. The gesture was so familiar. He raised his head to light the pipe, and I saw that it was the captain. Captain Avery, in a fine new bowler hat and a wool suit, courting Mama. My mouth fell open.

At the end of the row of chairs, between Mama's room and the door to the walk, sat Starboard on a stool, not dead after all. He bent over a small writing desk, on top of which stood an inkwell and an hourglass. He was making notes in an open ledger, his head wobbling on its stalk. The door to the hatchway was cracked open. Starboard consulted his pocket watch, turned the glass, and jerked a thumb at the first man in the row. The coal miner stood, smoothed his suit coat, producing a faint puff of coal dust, and passed through the hatchway door, closing it behind him. The other men, prompted by Starboard, all moved down one chair.

After a few minutes a familiar sound began above. The sound of Mama walking back and forth, I had once thought, but now I knew it for what it was. By their reactions, I judged that the men had not expected to take part in a contest that evening. A few looked at each other, eyes wide and blinking; one glanced up at the ceiling with a puzzled expression, then his brow cleared as he recognized the source of the sound and he turned his gaze quickly down. The men must have expected a more formal interview. I glanced at Captain Avery; he was busily packing his pipe, stuffing it with tobacco until it spilled over.

The minutes passed. The sand sank in the glass and the rhythmic sounds from above continued. The woodsman consulted a note in his hands, first running a finger along the writing, then closing his eyes and mouthing the words. The farmer stroked a runtling sow that lay in his lap, its neck encircled by a ribbon. Captain Avery began to tap his foot and kept glancing back down the hall, toward the staircase. Now and again sand sifted down from cracks in the ceiling, where light from the walk also burned brightly.

The sounds above abruptly stopped. A minute later the coal miner slid out the hatchway door and hurried down the hall past the men, head lowered, continuing down the stair past where I crouched behind the column. I pressed back against the wall, but he didn't look up as he passed. In a few moments I heard the front door quietly open and close. Starboard, having observed the miner closely as he passed, scratched vigorously in his ledger and turned the glass, though its sand had run only half through. He again jerked his thumb.

The woodsman stood, laying aside his ax and hiking his trousers, and strode through the hatchway. The sounds from above started again. The runtling sow began to squeal loudly. The farmer cuffed it across one ear, at which it fell silent. The four men who remained, looking increasingly troubled, neglected to move down one seat. They attempted to train their gazes on the wall across from their seats or on the floor, avoiding their neighbors' eyes. The sound above was less steady and forthright than it had been with the coal miner, and the waiting men looked alternately pleased or worried by the faltering sounds.

I waited on the landing with Crow, as the men waited below, trying to understand why Mama had arranged this gathering of suitors. Papa was still alive, as she well knew. Or maybe he had drowned that day when he swam after Mordecai and me, after all, and the figure I had seen on the sinking island was only a shadow, a shade come back from Hades.

I watched Starboard at his desk. When the sand had nearly run out I heard the rope ladder creaking behind the hatchway door. The second suitor, the woodsman, was descending. Starboard had by now laid his heavy head on his ledger and fallen asleep. The woodsman snatched up his ax and hurried away. When he had disappeared down the stairs I stood straight, smoothed my skirts, and walked down the hall, Crow firm and steady on my shoulder.

The four remaining suitors looked up. Captain Avery's face went red and he jumped up, snatching off his hat.

"Miss Rathbone, I didn't . . . I couldn't . . ."

His face went slack and he looked down at his feet. He took a deep breath and looked up at me. "I always fancied her. Not that she ever talked to me, I only saw her now and again when I was visiting with Bemus. I thought that now, maybe . . ." He shrugged and smiled. He held a hand out toward me, then snatched it back.

"Sorry, miss."

He put his hat back on, tipped it at me, and walked slowly off toward the stair. What had he called out from the boat? *Try not to think too poorly of her . . .* I stared after him.

When I looked back at the row of men, I found them all staring at me. A few appeared to be confused, looking at the door where their competitors had entered, then back at me. Others seemed to be reconsidering their choice.

The two suitors nearest me stood. The cowboy put his large hat on the empty chair next to him, spit on his hands, and slicked back his hair. The farmer rose and offered me his pig.

Though I couldn't, in the windowless hall, see where the tide stood on the pier, I could feel that it was on the wane. But I didn't suffer like Mama from the ebb and flow of the sea. I felt strong and unafraid.

I smiled and curtseyed. Nodding to each as I walked by, I slipped through the hatchway.

CHAPTER TWENTY-THREE: MAMA'S SONG

{in which Mama's bones will not break}

At first I was blinded. Every light in the house shone on the walk. Lanterns hung in clusters from the seams of the dome and from the spokes of the ship's wheel; lamps stood on the floor all around and crowded on top of the trunk, their glow doubled and redoubled by the glass on all sides. Crow shifted to and fro on my shoulder, blinking, nudging his beak under my collar to try to cover his eyes. It was at first too bright to see anything clearly, but gradually, as my eyes adjusted, I could make out Mama's silhouette. She wore what she always wore, an indigo gown and white collar, like those I was wearing, but the skirt of her gown was sodden and heavy with sand. The hem twinkled here and there with shards of crushed glass among the grains of sand. On the floor by her feet was the hourglass that had always stood in her room, broken. Her hair hung half loose down her back. She faced away from me, leaning against the side of the dome, her head turned to the sea.

She hadn't heard me come up, and I waited, my heart thudding. I had no need of rehearsing my words, I had said them often enough to myself. They were the questions for which I had so long wanted answers. Why did Papa come, only to go away? Why did you abandon your nephew? Why didn't you love me? Even those questions fell away before the figure of my brother in the barrel.

In the hall below, one of the three still-waiting suitors cleared his throat. Mama turned toward the voice, her movements weary, her face blank. Then she saw me. I opened my mouth to accuse her.

"Mercy. Mercy."

I have sometimes wondered whether I imagined the joy I saw in her eyes then, the welcome in her arms as she stretched them out toward me. I saw what I had so long thirsted for. I faulted myself, afterward. But in the end I think there are few who wouldn't have, as I did, run into her arms.

In those moments, in her embrace, I made for myself acceptable answers to my questions. Papa hadn't stayed away by choice:

He had been conscripted by some distant army and was allowed only short leaves; he had learned to breathe water and could live only in the air a little at a time. Mordecai had not been abandoned, only mislaid. And I was not, after all, unloved. For Gideon's end, I had no answer; I skipped it over.

Mama's skin smelled of coal and hay. Her hair was dank, her breath foul, but I didn't care. I don't remember just what she said to me. She asked me where I'd been, told me how she had missed me, exclaimed at my size. She stroked my hair and held me close. I wanted only to lay my head against her, to listen to her murmur into my hair.

The rope ladder creaked.

Her head turned. Her eyes opened wide. Her arms, so warm around me, went slack.

For a moment it was that last night on the walk, when Papa's hand had held me spinning in the air and my crow lay crushed in the trunk, when Mama had looked up, but not at me, called out, but not to me. She had reached only for him. And now, again, she set me aside, to reach for whoever was next on Starboard's list, whoever's head was now rising above the rim of the well.

The cowboy stepped up into the walk. He pulled off his hat and stood there, blinking in the glare of the lanterns, clutching the rim of his hat in both hands. The silver spurs on his boots jingled faintly. He looked from me to Mama and back again. His mouth dropped open and he began to back away.

If I had stopped to think only a little, I might have a different story to tell. I might have realized that Mama wanted no cowboy, no farmer, no landsman at all. She only ever wanted to lie under the wide blue back of the sea. She only ever wanted Papa. But I didn't stop. And though the route might have been different, the end would have been the same.

I felt suddenly calm. I didn't think or decide what to do next, I only did it.

I walked to the cowboy, took the hat out of his hands, and tossed it onto the floor. I started to unbutton the long row of buttons on the front of my dress, from the top down.

Now Mama wanted to hold me. She pulled me away from the cowboy, who had backed to the edge of the well, as close as he could get without falling in, and was frozen there. He looked down at the rope ladder up which he had just come, then doubtfully toward his hat, which was out of reach.

Mama clutched at me and tried to wrap my arms back around her. She struggled with me, but I was her match. Everything I wanted to say came flooding back, all my questions rushed out. I poured them in her ear as we struggled. Crow shrieked and flapped his wings in her eyes, darting his beak between us, jabbing at her face. He flew to the trunk and, hovering, took the clasp in his beak and flung the lid up. Something leapt and clattered inside. The cowboy's head, hatless, retreated down the well. Then Mama's sodden gown was twisting all around my legs, and I was falling. I must have struck my head on the edge of the trunk. Mama was still there, above me, moving slowly, her mouth making the shape of words I couldn't hear.

I wasn't unconscious. Though I can't say that I saw all of what followed, I saw, and heard, enough. It was best, I later thought, that a fog came between me and what I witnessed; it was easier to bear. But I have sometimes since wondered if the reality may have been easier to bear than what I remember seeing.

A scuffling sound came from below. Chairs scraped and clattered; footsteps retreated rapidly away, down the staircase. Another voice sounded through the house, a voice that belonged to none of the departing suitors. It boomed up the well. The rope ladder went taut; in a moment he was up. The man in blue was back.

I had never seen him so clearly before. A face smeared with blood as I dangled from the end of his arm; a pair of arms pushing through the sea, swimming after my skiff; a shadow standing on the sinking island staring after me who, even from that distance, had looked larger than any other man. Now, as I lay on the floor, looking up at him sideways, his body blocking the glare of lamp and lantern, he seemed a giant, he was so tall and broad.

"Verity."

He didn't see me, lying there next to the trunk, bright though it was. He saw only Mama. His face was split dark below and pale above, where his hat sat at sea. Veins beat high and blue on his neck. On his forehead and cheeks were fresh scars, beak-shaped.

From below, outside the house, came the last sounds of the suitors, their footsteps hurrying, fading along the path.

Papa stood there next to the well. His body was so wide and full of heat. His breath came fast. He held himself still, his arms stiff; his hands were shaking.

He stood that way for a few more moments, then his body slumped and his

519

breath blew out. He unbuttoned his coat and yanked it off. He unlaced the front of his breeches. In one stride he reached her and lifted her. She pulled the skirt of her gown up and over her head. She was naked from the waist down. He put his hands around her ribs and lifted her high, then ran her down hard, and up and down and up again. She rose and fell, her boots tapping against his thighs, her head lolling, her pale hair falling over them both. After a while he lifted her off and lay her on the floor and on they went.

Something scraped inside the trunk, behind me; I jumped, jerking myself up from the floor. Kneeling, I lifted the lid of the trunk and felt for Crow. My fingers closed on him and I eased him out — with him came a spew of bones, clattering to the floor.

I reached slowly down and picked one up: not a whalebone but an ulna, slender, s-curved. Its twin was there, too, and a pair of femurs. Crow, perched on the edge of the trunk, leaned down and tugged at something, struggled with the weight, dropped it back into the trunk with a soft thud. I moved closer and looked down at a rounded bundle, wrapped in muslin, nested in a bed of kelp. With shaking hands I unwrapped a skull, its jaw and teeth intact. Between the rows of teeth poked a fan of finger bones, a second smile. When I dropped the skull, it fell softly into the kelp but the fingers popped out, chattering.

I slammed the lid down and scrabbled away backward, taking great gulps of air, until my back hit the wall of the walk. I held Crow close against my breast and pulled my knees up tight, dizzy, the walk spinning around me.

Mother, Mother, make a bed, make it soft and long . . .

She had made a bed for my brother in the barrel, but it was not his final resting place. Those were my brother's bones in the trunk, on top of which I had curled, hiding, as I spied on Mama and Papa. My brother had been there all along.

The glare of light on the walk, at first blinding, started to dip. In the minutes that followed the lanterns and lamps began, one by one, to gutter then go out.

Mama and Papa looked just as they had the first night I'd watched from inside the trunk, his blue back swelling over her, her body rocking; the scraping sound as her skin ground against sand. But there were new sounds now — not the sounds of pleasure but of something creaking, something grating and harsh. Where before I couldn't see Mama's face, only her skirts and her lifted thighs, her boots moving back and forth, now I could see her face, and she was looking at me. Her mouth was open, her eyes huge, staring. Her skin drained to white.

I'm not sure when I knew what was happening to her. I used to think that if I had realized sooner, if my wits had been keener, my head clearer, I could have stopped it somehow. But I have come to believe that whatever I did wouldn't have mattered.

Her hand went to her throat, to the wide white collar, crushed and wet with sweat. She pulled out the chain, the little trio of bones. She looked like she was trying to speak. Her eyes were still on me. The creaking sound went on, a ship in heavy seas, timbers grinding one on the other.

I hadn't noticed the difference in Mama, between that other night and this. That from the waist up she was fully clothed. That her breasts didn't roll on each rise, her corset was not cracked open but laced tight, tighter than before by one bone. The whalebones bent with her own as she arched under the man in blue, but they wouldn't break. She couldn't breathe. Still he plunged on. Mama didn't push him away. She made no gesture to let him know that she couldn't breathe.

I don't know how long he rocked Mama before he realized that she was dead. He didn't seem surprised to discover it. He pulled away from her and kneeled over her. He pulled her skirt down over her body and smoothed it, tenderly. He turned to look at me. It was then I realized that he had known all along that I was there. I thought he was going to speak, but a moment later he had dropped down the ladder and was gone.

I looked at Mama from across the walk for a while, then went and sat by her. Her head was turned toward the sea. Her eyes were open, the horizon there in each iris as always before. I closed them. I lay my head against her. Now I could leave it there for as long as I liked.

The last of the lanterns went out. The sky was thick with cloud, the moon hidden. The clean hot smell of oil hung in the air.

When I finally looked up, a white shape was drifting up the dark well. Just before I lost consciousness I saw that it wasn't my dead brother. It was Mordecai.

CHAPTER TWENTY-FOUR:
BUILDING MY BROTHER

{in which Mercy meets Gideon}

Crow flew them down to me one by one. I sat on my bed and lay each bone among the sheets, then looked up to watch Crow again turn the corner at the end of the hall and fly toward me. He began with the larger bones, his path wavering and dipping with the weight, flying low to place each bone before me, then circled around the room to head back to the walk. Panting, he dropped the pelvis into my lap; next the spine, disk by disk, then femur and humerus, working his way toward the extremities. He grasped a clavicle in each claw; the kneecaps required two trips. He beaked the smaller bones in batches, faltering for a moment as he passed the window under which his nest hung. The slender metatarsals seemed suitable to lend extra strength to a bird's bed against winter gales or to fill the space where his companion no longer slept, differing little from the thin twigs and dry straw that lined the nest.

As he neared the end, Crow's wings dropped lower. The final bones, unbalanced, scraped the floor, chalking thin lines along the planks. The last phalanges fell into my hands, and Crow dropped to my knee, breathing hard, to rest for a moment before lifting off for his final trip. I dropped my head and drifted for a while, then heard a dull clattering and looked up to see him flying toward me, bumping a bundle wrapped in white cloth along the floor, slung from his beak. He dropped the skull into my lap. Mama's white collar drifted down onto my gown, boiled and bleached, starched and pressed.

I gathered the bones and started to build my brother, allowing a small space between them — no cartilage remained to soften the shock of joint on joint — so that they spread out, a constellation of bones in the dark. I knew how to map him. Mordecai had used the skeleton of a spider monkey to teach me how the bones fit together. The parts were much the same. I first lined up his spine, placing the pelvis at the base. It formed a shallow bowl that held what light there was from the sky and reflected it back into my face. I arranged his ribs in parallel lines, docked at his sternum. I made his legs as straight as I could, though with no cushioning flesh the long femurs keeled over, curving outward, so that his legs bowed. In the end they were all there except those of the ring finger on his left hand. I lay myself along the bones and stretched my arms and legs along the same lines. Had I found his bones before I fled the house that night months ago, they would have matched mine in size. Now my limbs stretched farther.

I sat up and ran my hands over Mama's collar, lying across my lap, smoothing the linen to lie flat along my thighs and across my calves. It had fit tight about her throat, like a baby's bib, then flared far beyond her shoulders, curved in a wide white crescent, narrowing to fine strands of rope that hung down her back, the ends weighted with ivory. I tied the ropes to my bedposts, the collar stretching between them to form a small hammock, a cabin boy's size, at the foot of my bed. I hung it as high as I could so that he would be able to see the harbor, and pressed my hand down in its center, to see what weight it would bear: Enough, I thought. I kneeled and gathered the bones. I stacked them in my arms, kindling for a cold fire, and lay them in the hammock, side by side, skull facing the sea.

Crow climbed into the hammock and it swung gently to and fro, as though under sail on a soft sea. I sat on the end of my bed, one hand to the hammock to rock it, and began to sing a lullaby. When the bones were set in motion they started to tell their story.

CHAPTER TWENTY-FIVE: THE BONES TELL THEIR STORY

{in which Gideon sails three times}

First Voyage March 15, 1849–August 7, 1849
The first time we were gone for nearly half a year. Mama didn't want me to go but Papa took me anyway. I was four. I remember you watching us leave from the dock, and Mama looking after us from way up high. I remember you getting smaller, and the dock, and the town just prickles of light, and then there was only the dark sea.

I didn't sleep at all the first night. Papa strung a hammock for me next to his, in his cabin. I liked how it swayed, the creaking sound the ropes made, and Papa's deep breaths. I crawled out of the hammock and climbed up onto the long seat under the windows that stretched across the stern. The wake behind the ship was like a big white fan under the starlight. The ship lifted and tilted under me. I clutched the harpoon

Papa had carved for me. In every wave I saw the shape of a fin or the curve of a fluke.

I woke the next morning to bright sun and salt spray on my face, the crew hurrying and shouting around me. Papa had hoisted me on his back, wrapping my arms tight about his neck, so thick my hands could only just clasp together. He kept one hand there to hold me safe and then we were running up the shrouds of the mizzenmast. He climbed with only one arm but so fast and smooth that I hardly bounced as we went up. I looked down at the water, farther and farther away and at the same time bigger until all I could see were green water and white waves. I caught glimpses of the deck far below, through the stays and sails that surrounded me. When we reached the crosstrees he slung me over to the topman and slid down the ratlines, back to the deck, then straightaway he went into the whale-boat that was being lowered over the side, the crew already clambering in. I leaned from the safety of the topman's grip to watch the boat splash down, the long oars slicing into the water. Half a league off the starboard bow I saw a fountain of spray and under it a great long shine of gray.

Papa was standing in the bow, one foot braced on the rail, both arms raised. He held a long slender wooden spear in each hand. He looked like a statue made of metal, so still and bright under the sun. The whaleboat moved fast across the water, the oars flashing out and cutting through the long swells. Already the boat was almost within striking distance of the whale. It was a sperm, the first one I had seen. Papa said they used to swim thick in our own bay, years before. This sperm was nearly as long end to end as that row of rooms downstairs, the one with all the beds: seventy feet from blowhole to flukes. He lay in the water, holding his great blunt head up high, not swimming away but lying there waiting, breathing and blowing. The boat was only a cable's length away from him. The oars all lifted together and hung over the water. The whale lay there a moment longer, its head turned toward Papa, waiting for him. Papa stood like before, both arms raised, motionless except for the rise and fall of the sea. Then the whale slowly turned in the water and began to swim away.

The water between the whaleboat and the *Verity* was so bright in the sun but still I could see everything sharp and clear: the long wet curve of the whale's back as it swam just ahead of the boat, Papa's arms lifting higher; the first spear flashing out, then the other at almost the same moment. The flukes burst from the water, twisting, slapping down into the sea, spinning one man out of the boat — his foot caught in a coil of rope and he was gone under. Then the whale was sounding in a surge and swimming away, the jet of white spray now a bloody mist, the rope streaming after it, the men leaning hard on the oars. Through it all Papa stood solid in the prow, urging them on, faster. Suddenly it was over. The boat slowed, the great gray body bubbled up and slowly turned over. The crew hooked on and they towed the whale back to the ship.

The *Verity* was manned with a full crew, all from Arcady. There were three whaleboats with six men in each boat. But Papa would allow only one boat in the sea with the whale, and no one but him held the spears. The men all clamored to be chosen each time a whale was sighted, all wanted to be with Papa. My favorites were Jim and Peter, who crewed in the first boat that day. They said they wanted to take me to Arcady when we got back and we would go nest-hunting up in the cliffs.

Each time Papa chose a fresh crew, driving them hard, urging each man to row faster and stronger than the last. The chase sometimes lasted for two glasses, or longer with a fast whale, though once in range Papa never missed his mark. The men were so tired they slept all the next day after a chase, but if a whale was sighted the next morning Papa was out again with a new crew. And the boats tired, too; one or another was always under the carpenter's hands, stove-in planks being repaired or bent davits straightened. Papa needed three boats to be sure one was always at the ready. The men didn't mind; they all knew they would have their turn soon enough, and they were kept busy cutting up the whales and melting them down.

No sooner had one whale been harvested than another would appear. Some days we saw pods of thirty or forty, all swimming together alongside. I would lay along the yard and look down at them running close to the surface, so that the light dappled on them and the water ran gleaming off their backs. The calves would travel in the middle of the pods, their bodies sometimes covered by the little fish that rode on them. They blew their plumes of spray up at me and clicked and called to me. Some days I saw right whales, their double spouts making rainbows. Or humpbacks blowing rings of bubbles, trapping big columns of fish in the rings to feed on. But we were after only the sperm.

Each day I took my place in the crosstrees. On quiet days when no whales were in view, I pointed out other things I could see from my perch. A distant flock of gulls glutting on an endless stream of haddock. Once, a storm that made a waterspout go spinning along the surface. But I stopped pointing when I understood that no one else on the ship could see such things. The men would roll their eyes and chuckle when I claimed to see such distant sights. I had always been able to see far, but on the *Verity* I realized that I was different. It was not only distant things that I could see clearly. I could see well under the surface of the sea, deeper than our draft. I knew what the soundings would be before the mate made them. I felt reefs and shoals coming up and tugged at Papa's coat to warn him. You know what I mean, sister. We both have Moses's gift.

We sailed through the warmer waters in which the whales traveled on their way south, going for weeks without sighting land, only sea from rim to rim. The men all said they had never known such clear sailing: a steady wind always on our beam, the *Verity*'s best point of sailing, no matter the compass point, as though, the men said, the wind shifted just for us.

I swam each day with Papa when the weather was fair, which was most all the time on that first voyage. Each day, before beginning his watch, Papa put me on his back and dove deep off the stern. We swam alongside the ship in the warm water. Swarms of fish parted around us, passing so close that I felt their smooth scales.

The weather held fair all through the summer, and no week passed without its count of sperm. The men called me their lucky charm. It had always before taken at least a twelvemonth, sometimes twice that, to fill the barrels. By the time we turned for home, early in July — a month from Naiwayonk — the oil of sixty-two whales ballasted the ship. The *Verity,* heavy with the oil, rode through the sea as steadily as Papa stood in his whaleboat. With no more empty barrels, no more need to hunt, Papa passed the weeks of homegoing pacing the quarterdeck, front to rear and back again, wearing a path in the wood. He called out never-ending orders to the men, making them change the trim of the sails without rest, to be sure each breath of wind would help speed us home.

All through the last leg of the voyage Papa manned the wheel himself, a full night and a day. I stayed aloft all that time, too, higher than him, first carrying up a blanket and filling my pockets with biscuits. I looked down at him, walking back and forth. Each time he reached the foremast and turned to walk back again, he took a compass from the breast pocket of his jacket and opened its case to look at the braid of hair he kept there, pale woven with dark. He forgot I was up there, or he wouldn't have let me stay so long. I saw Naiwayonk come into view long before Papa, though he'd kept watch all those hours. I know I saw Mama long before him. She stood on top of the house, her shape black against the sky where the sun was setting, glinting off a curve of green glass; a dome was being built there, behind her, supported by a scaffolding of posts and planks. She was holding on to the scaffolding, looking toward the *Verity* as it sailed toward Rathbone House.

Second Voyage October 7, 1849–February 21, 1850

The whales were boiled at night. Some nights I watched. Down below in the dark Papa would stand on the edge of the pit. The trying fires flared on his face and lit up his teeth. He swung the big hook over to where the whale hung along the side winched in a great sling and stripped down the first fat coil of blubber. His boots squelched in oil when he turned, swaying the long spiral down to the mate in the pit. From the coil the mate chopped a wide chunk and held it in one hand, skin-side down, slashing along it with his blade so the thick pieces splayed open like a book. He said the oil came faster that way. The mate called them Bible leaves. He dropped them into the big pots where the boys stood and stirred, thigh-deep in blubber, flame-bright.

I hung up high on the mainmast, slung from the yard in a ditty bag, an extra one; the sailor it belonged to had gone to the whale. Papa thought I was asleep in his cabin but some nights the cook brought me up there when I asked him to. He knew Papa wouldn't like it, but he also knew that I would find him the biggest fish in the morning and plenty of crabs to sweeten his stew.

It was our first whale in two months. The men whispered and wondered what they would live on that winter. We had been out for four months and our hold held the oil of only three whales. Some of the men were saying that the whales had all been fished out, others that the whales had grown wise and had found different waters in which to swim. They began to grumble about hunting with only one boat. They wanted to go farther out, they wanted to use easier ways to kill the whale, like other whalers, pikes and spears made from sharp steel. But Papa wouldn't allow it. He said that the whale, having himself no metal, must be met by only one man and only with wood or there was no honor in it.

One night, after the men had taken a fifty-footer, I watched them take off the head. The wind was shifting, swinging me away from the yard, and when I swung I saw the men crawling along a line between head and body and together they began to slice. Farther out and far beneath the dark surface of the sea silver points began to grow, the first sharks started to rise.

The wind shifted again. Behind the ship the water burned green — the sailors say it's called phosphorescence. In the bright wake I watched the sailors' white trousers wave, bleaching in the brine, nipped at by fish. I wanted to dip my hand down into the wake to see if the green fire hurt.

Onto the deck the men lowered the whale's head (the sphinx, they called it), laying it to rest along the cut edge. Soon the men would stand on the head and break into the case, dip into it with their long ladles for the oil.

I swung in my hammock and saw below me the mate and the men bent over the Bible leaves with Papa, murmuring. The sailors skimmed the whale's own skin from the pots and fed it into the fire to make the flames soar high. The whale cooked best that way.

Above the deck I swung between mast and mast and turned my face up to the sky, to the stars beginning to spill from a great gash of light in the black. Papa would have been able to see me if he looked up. He said that I was too young to do what he did. Next year, he said, next year.

Over the rail the sailors stopped beating away the sharks. The ship tilted to starboard as the sharks bit into the stripped carcass, slopping water over the rail and into the pit to make the fires hiss.

On deck in the dark the whale's head waited, looking up to the sky like me.

Third Voyage February 23, 1850–April 12, 1852

I wasn't meant to go the last time. Mama had made Papa promise to leave me at home after the second voyage. I had turned five at sea.

We came in one evening from the second voyage, having been more than four months at sea, just before dark. Before we rounded the last point, before Rathbone House came into view, we anchored offshore.

We only came back, Papa said, so that we could swap crews and let the men go home to Arcady. They wanted to stay with him, they said, but they had to feed their families. They would go to the cities to look for work. Papa sent the whaleboats off to Arcady to take the men home, asking them to spread the word on their way.

I asked Papa why he had anchored so far from the house. He said he couldn't let me go inside. He said if I went in Mama would never let me go again. He needed me with him, his lucky charm, he said. We had to go farther this time, we had to find the whales. But he went to the house himself that night, rowing away in the dark, rowing back the next morning just after dawn.

By midmorning enough men to man the *Verity* and more had sailed or rowed from villages nearby, and Papa signed the best of them. Most had crewed on some other whaleship; a few were only fishermen that Papa had liked the look of and taken on, saying they'd be easy enough to train. Though all the men had heard that the *Verity*'s last voyage had not been successful, they had heard, too, that he was offering not a lay but a set sum, and a large one, no matter how many whales they harpooned.

With the turn of the tide, late that morning, the *Verity* weighed anchor and started to sail away. I was busy in the tops with the rigging and didn't look back at Rathbone House until the ship had begun the turn around the western point. Mama was not on top of the house as she had been when I sailed away twice before. She was in the sea, far from shore, swimming after the ship, her gown streaming behind her, a dark streak on the gray sea. She was still there, her white face turned up in the water, when we rounded the point and left Naiwayonk behind. I don't know if Papa looked back.

We sailed farther than on the earlier voyages, which had taken us only a few hundred miles from home, usually running north and south, within easy hail of the coast. This time we headed east by southeast until we lost all sight of land. Papa said we were going to the big whaling grounds in the middle of the ocean. But whatever luck I had brought before had gone away. I once glimpsed the V-shaped blow of a bowhead many leagues off, and once heard the song of a pair of blue whales running deep below, but nothing nearer, and no sperm at all. The weather was queer besides. Papa said the southerlies should have been pelting us with rain in those latitudes, driving us on so that we made two hundred miles from noon to noon. Instead there were only weak gusts of wind from no particular point of the compass and no rain at all. Within a month our fresh water ran low and we had to drink the tarry water we had gathered in sails and funneled into barrels during earlier rains for just such a drought, and we washed our clothes in seawater so that our skin went rough and raw. Not only were there no whales but the fish had thinned out or changed their routes. I felt almost nothing beneath the ship, only a few scattered dogfish and bloodmouths. The sky was empty of birds. There was little for them to feed on.

Papa paced the deck for hours, wearing a path in the wood until it gleamed. Other times he took the wheel himself, though it didn't take much to keep the ship on course, the winds were so weak. He stood as tall and broad as ever, but it was like he was empty, like all his oil had poured out. The men kept to their duties, which were light without any whales to flense and boil: mending line, polishing fittings that already gleamed. Sometimes, as the air grew warmer, they just dozed under the whale-boats.

I was posted lookout now officially, though I had long served as such. I stood two watches, sometimes three. Papa didn't object, though I think it shamed him to see me stay awake so long. He knew I was his best hope.

The day I finally saw the whale, we had just crossed the thirtieth parallel. The sea, for days a low, choppy gray, now showed patches of bright green, smooth and still. A cool wind came from the northwest, billowing our sails enough to make the water sing along our sides and put the men in a happier mood. I leaned out from the mainmast top and looked down into the sea. I knew from the mate's charts that at this parallel a cold stream from the north was turning in a great loop beneath us to return home. The cold was surging up to the surface and bringing with it creatures from the deep, pale, formless things without names. But I felt something larger among them, caught in the churn. I saw a huge dimness rising slowly from far below and I called down to Papa.

I knew he wouldn't let me go with him. I knew he had promised Mama that he wouldn't let me go into a whaleboat until I was twelve. I think Mama hoped all the whales would be gone by then. I think she knew I would never have the chance to do what Papa had done.

By then the whale had surfaced, a few ship lengths ahead. He didn't breach, only rose and lay there, just breaking the surface with his huge head. I could hear his long slow breaths from my perch. Papa looked up at me once, his face shining, then he was over the side, into the boat. I waited until it had splashed down and pulled well away, then slipped over the side, from the stern, where no one was watching. All the men were pressed against the rail on the port side, all eyes on the whale. I swam just behind the whaleboat, in its wake. I knew none of the men in the boat would see me. They, too, were bent on the whale, only the whale. I kept my head low and stayed close. It was hard to breathe in the churn of the wake, but if I swam in smooth water the men would see me and tell Papa. I swam well, keeping up easily.

The whale didn't at first seem to know the boat was coming close, it didn't change its pace. I felt its body pull me closer. I turned away from the boat's wake and let the smooth surge of water pull me along beside the whale, close to its flank. I reached out and clutched the edge of a great fin and rode along. It was an old whale. I could see in the clear water the places where its skin was scarred in circles by the suckers of giant squid and scored by shark teeth and jagged reefs. I could feel the surge of its heart under my hands. I didn't know why Papa, why anyone, would want to kill such a thing as that whale. I would have been happy to swim with it forever. I felt the long smooth curve of the whale's motion as it turned; I knew it was turning to face the men. The whale opened its long, long jaw and drew in a deep draft of sea. I saw, just before I was swept with startled fish down between the rows of teeth and into the dark, its little eye turn in its socket to look at me.

Papa must have seen me, or one of the men saw and told him. By the time the whale was speared and dragged and Papa had pried open its jaws and come in to find me, I was already dead. The whale had not chewed me, I had simply drowned. Papa pulled me out in one piece.

The men were silent as they rowed back to the ship, the whale in tow. Papa sat in the bow with me in his arms. When the boat had been winched up and the men were out, he lay me on the deck and smoothed the hair away from my face. He called the mate over and spoke to him. The mate leaned over the stern where the men were securing the whale with tackle and line. Cast it off, he said. Let it go. The men hesitated, then untied their knots and hauled in their lines, and the whale began to drift away, north by northwest, its head turning into the wind. They all stood at the taffrail to watch it go, so they didn't hear the splash on the lee side when Papa dove in. They didn't see him swim away, eastward. After they realized he was missing and had searched the ship, they thought he had drowned, and headed for home. But they must have had bad luck somewhere on the way, for the *Verity* never returned to Naiwayonk again.

Do you understand yet, sister? Mama didn't put me in the barrel. She was only welcoming me home. She had made Papa promise never to lose her son at sea. So he told the mate to salt me, lest I spoil on the long journey, and sent me home. You have misjudged her, as I misjudged the whale who swallowed me whole.

CHAPTER TWENTY-SIX:
MORDECAI'S LAST LESSON

*{in which Mercy teaches Mordecai
all he needs to know}*

I woke to the sound of a boy's voice singing. At first I thought I was dreaming, or
that I was reliving that night months ago
when I had first heard the voice. That I
would look up to see both my crows on the
bedposts and go downstairs to find Mama
carving in her room. But Crow slept on one
bedpost and the other was empty. I wondered if I had only dreamed of Mordecai,
too, rising in the well of the walk like a
ghost.

Then the voice came, the song, not strong
but clear and true, and I knew I was awake.

"Father, Father, sail a ship,
Sail it straight and strong.
Mother, Mother, make a bed,
Make it soft and long.

Sister, Sister, listen close,
Listen to my song,
For it was Father sailed the sea,
For it was Mother murdered me,
Sister, Sister, come and see,
Come see and sing with me."

Crow woke. He was stiff from his labors of the night before. He dropped from the post onto the bed, trundled across the spread, grasped its edge in his beak, and dragged the cover down.

Neither of us wanted to follow the song. I would rather have crawled back under the blankets. But I got up, and we started along the hall. The house was dark, with no hint of light at any window; it was still deep night. I stopped along the way to take the stub of a candle from one of the cupboards, the lanterns having all served to light the walk the night before. The song was not coming, as before, from the walk, or from Gideon's bones. It came from the back of the house and higher up. I started for Mordecai's attic.

I made my way along the hallway that led to the final stair, the narrow switchback that led to the attic. I walked fully around the perimeter at the base of the square tower where the stair was, Crow muttering on my shoulder. I wondered if I had made one turn too many and retraced my steps, but the door didn't appear. I thought I must be confused by the previous night's events, and my stub of candle provided such a scant light. Finally I heard the voice once more, thin but close at hand, and turned a corner I was sure I had turned at least twice before to find the stair. The door stood open, and a faint light washed down. I tiptoed up. Though Crow had always refused to enter the attic before, he now stayed with me, hopping from my shoulder to the top of my head.

I couldn't at first see Mordecai, it was so dark. A few thin beams of starlight angled from the knotholes in the hull above, wavering on the bare wood. A wind was picking up outside, making the hull shudder, and the sea sounded against the rocks below.

He was seated at his worktable, his journal spread open before him. He must have found it in my room. He worked by candlelight, with his books and papers in slovenly stacks on the table around him. I wondered how he got back to the house, then realized that Captain Avery must have brought him.

As my eyes adjusted to the low light I noticed closed crates standing about the attic. Mordecai's cherished relics, normally in positions of prominence on tables and shelves, were no longer there: his collection of cast fingers, the prelate's heart. Only a few nameless crumbling specimens were strewn among his papers on the table. I looked up. Even the rafters were bare of their busts but for one. Crow flew up and perched on the bust of the woman. Without her red hat she had a chastened look.

I dipped my flickering candle into the flame on Mordecai's table. He was looking up at me; I tried to allow no expression to cross my face. His forehead, where he had struck it on the ceiling of the cave, was swollen as though he had just struck it — it had been two days since I had seen him, though it seemed longer. The dark bruise had spread across his forehead and down one cheek, blotched black and purple; I couldn't help but think of Erastus's mottled sisters. He was otherwise as pale as he'd ever been before our journey. He had been so alive during our time on the *Able,* when we swam together, as though the sea itself had cured him of all his ills. Now his irises had washed nearly to white. His cloud of hair had flattened to a few thin white strands. He leaned heavily on his arms as he wrote, his pen rasping against the paper.

He looked up at me briefly, with a slight

smile, and continued writing.

"I was not sure you would find your way here," he said.

"The song."

His pen stopped. He sat up straight, then slumped back in his chair, his eyes turned up.

"Oh yes. The song. How does it go again? 'Father, Father, sail a ship . . .' "

Mordecai sang an octave higher than his speaking voice, in the high thin tone that I had taken for a boy's, for Gideon's. He sang the song, staring up at the hull over us, from start to finish. It had been Mordecai all along. I reached for a chair and sat heavily down. I waited to speak until I could keep my voice from breaking.

"Why? Why did you pretend to be him?"

He continued to stare up for a few moments more, then sat straight, picking up his pen, leaning again over his journal.

"Oh, that I could never do, Mercy." He smoothed open the chart in the center of his journal, unfolding it so that it draped over the edge of the table and hung to the floor. "I did try, though. I was not permitted on the dock or on board to learn the necessary skills, but I studied them as best I could, in my books." He picked up a seaman's manual from the pile nearest him and

550

flipped through its pages. Dozens of pictures of ships flashed by. "I knew the name of every part of the ship, each piece of rigging. I knew more of navigation than Gideon, as much as your papa, though I was never given the chance to employ it. I was not granted the advantage of invigorating exercise in fresh air, as was your brother, but I could have become as hale and strong had I been given opportunity." He drew himself up and gave me a defiant look. "Captain Avery permitted me to handle the *Able*'s dinghy on the way here. Certainly it is no three-master, but nevertheless I am not entirely without skills." I wondered how the captain had managed to let Mordecai think he had handled the boat.

He really believed that he could have thrived, given the chance. If he hadn't, he couldn't have flourished so in our time on the *Able,* however short. And I had half believed it myself. I'd believed he'd sailed with Papa to the Arctic and back.

"But when we were with Captain Avery, and you spoke of the icebergs, of the polar bear . . . I was sure you had been there yourself."

He smiled, shaking his head, then grunted and put a hand gingerly to his forehead. "I begged and begged your mama to be allowed to go to sea, on those rare occasions when she came to the attic. She always denied me." He cleaned his pen on a napkin and lay it down. "And Uncle Benadam clearly did not consider me seaworthy."

Mordecai's journal slid to the floor. He stared down at it, leaned stiffly and picked it up, and slowly closed the cover.

"I sometimes believed that I had been on every voyage, so clearly did I imagine them. I experienced each mile more than did Gideon, though he was the one who sailed, he the one who took each trip for granted, who knew nothing of waiting and wanting." Mordecai pushed away his books and pens and lay his head on the table, his face turned away.

I sat next to him and took his hand. It felt fleshless, dry and hot.

"Mama didn't mean to hurt *you,* Mordecai." I let go of his hand and looked away. "Or my brother."

Mordecai turned his face slowly back. "What do you mean?"

"Don't you remember what you told me, back in Circe's cave?"

He looked at me blankly.

"Back at the cave. You told me my brother was in Mama's way. That she had made a bed for him in a barrel. She had stuffed him in a barrel, you said."

"Oh, Mercy." Mordecai's face sagged first, then his body followed. He slumped, defeated, over the table. "I should never have drunk from that stream." He hesitated, then reached for my hand and awkwardly stroked it; his own hand was trembling. "I didn't want you to ever have to find out. I tried my best to keep it from you, I thought I had. I thought I got you away before you saw."

I stared back at him. Mordecai crossed his arms over his chest and squeezed them tightly, as though he were cold, and closed his eyes.

"I saw her. I see it all the time, your mama, standing in front of that barrel. Your brother's face, staring up out of the brine. She put him there. She killed him."

"No. No. She was taking him out."

Mordecai's eyes sprang open and he stared at me.

I reached into the pocket of my gown and held up the last thing Crow had flown down to me from the walk the night before. A packet of oilcloth, which I unwrapped to reveal a small thick book, sheathed in whale ivory.

"This house still hides a few mementos you haven't discovered. I found this one under the bones, at the bottom of the trunk."

Mordecai gazed at the little book covetously. Its covers were made from thin sections of a sperm tooth, tapering to a point. The pages had been trimmed to the same shape. It was hinged with soft, knobby gray leather — the whale's skin — and on its smooth face nothing was graven. Mordecai reached out for the book; I snatched it back and put it in my pocket.

I told him how Gideon had been salted and sent home. Not on Papa's ship; the *Verity* didn't return then, and never had since. The barrel had been passed to a merchantman at sea and delivered to Naiwayonk by a few of its crew, in a jolly boat.

I told him how, after Mordecai had taken me away, Mama had pulled Gideon out of the barrel. I didn't know how she had gotten him up to the walk; perhaps Larboard and Starboard helped, though she was always so strong, she might have carried him herself. She did not describe every detail, but I could picture it all easily enough: Mama hauling my brother, grunting, from the barrel. The brine sloshing; a thud and a wet slap. Mama sitting on the floor in a pool of brine, my brother lying across her legs, wrapped in a length of cloth. Her hands are busy and she speaks to herself. She is sewing, stitching the cloth in a long neat seam up the front of my brother, with an awl and a length of line. At his feet, two round lumps under the cloth — two cannon shot Mama has put there to weigh him down, as men are weighted for burial at sea, so that their bodies will sink. The two shot must have remained at the bottom of the trunk on the walk, too heavy for Crow to carry down to me along with Gideon's bones.

Mordecai sat back, sighing. He sat quietly for a while, fingering the rope on a crate that stood nearby, avoiding my eyes.

"Perhaps . . . perhaps I wanted to think your mama had killed Gideon. And wanted you to believe it, too." He pushed a drift of hair from his eyes and looked at me. "She didn't murder Gideon, but she murdered me."

Crow squawked from his perch on the bust's head, one yellow eye fixed on Mordecai. Mordecai felt among his papers, found a dried plover egg, and tossed it up to Crow, who deftly beaked it and swallowed it whole.

"I was happy when he drowned, happy to see that barrel, to know that he would spend his days whitening in a box as I have all these years."

He had begun to shiver. I pulled off my

shawl and draped it over his shoulders. He lay his head back down.

"Mama did care for you, Mordecai. I know she did."

"Oh yes. She held me in such high regard that she never troubled me with her company."

I pulled a shriveled starfish from beneath a book and twirled it between my fingers. "Don't you remember walking along the beach and playing in the surf when you were small?"

He raised his head a little from the table and squinted at me.

"Certainly I remember. One of the old ones used to take me. Bemus, I think."

"It wasn't Bemus. It was Mama. She walked you along the beach every day, when you were very young. She would have worn pale blue in those days, and she held a black parasol over you against the sun."

A different light came into Mordecai's eyes. I could see him reluctantly casting back, trying to remember. He wanted to hear something good about Mama, and yet he didn't.

Mordecai turned his head and stared up at the hull. His expression had lost its wary look, his eyes had softened. The skin around the sockets was drawn and dark. He looked as old as I had once believed he was.

"I have a lesson for you, Mordecai."

Without lifting his head, he looked up at me with a wan smile.

"The sperm's favored diet?"

I smiled back, no more brightly than him.

"Squid and skate are preferred . . . No. A different sort of lesson. Are you sure you want to hear?"

His eyes flashed a little. He remembered, too, when he had asked me that question, when he had first told me about the man in blue and Mama.

"It would be better if I read to you."

I led him to his berth and helped him lie down, tucking him tight under the blankets. I set a beaker to boil for tea. Then I pulled a chair close and settled myself, smoothing the skirt of my gown and pressing the little book open so that it would lie flat in my lap. The pages were closely covered in indigo ink, in Mama's long, impatient hand, the words slanting off and away, sometimes leaping off the page altogether.

I called Crow down from the bust to my shoulder, where he folded his wings and tucked his beak. I flipped through the diary and chose a few entries, and began to read.

April 12

When I lean out the window the sea is
right under me, far down. It's nearly
twilight. He'll be back soon. I can smell
the pines, they grow right up to the
house. The cliffs are pink in this light,
with the sun setting. There are birds
nesting in holes all along the cliffs, swallows. They lift and drop on the wind,
looping and diving, so close I can almost
touch them. He's been gone since first
light. He said he couldn't miss a day of
fishing, not even for me. I knew he
would come for me. He didn't tell me
his name until last night. Benadam. It
was all I could do to wait until E. went
to bed — was it only two nights ago?
When Benadam walked in the front door
I was waiting at the top of the stairs with
my cloak on, my trunk packed. There
are the boats now. He's coming.

April 16

He lies on top of me so that I can't
move, barely breathe. I love how heavy
he is on me. How straight and strong.
His blood runs right under his skin, it
streams along those thick blue veins. I

can hear his heart in every part of his body, wherever I lay my ear.

April 18

He fills my every gap. He swells my every sea. He splits me apart. I don't care. He stitches me together again.

April 22

The sea is warmer here, and the fish — the water is thick with them just past the surf. So many more than back home. Yellowtail and flounder, great crowds of cod, spiny dogfish and rosefish. Sometimes a school carries me with them out and away, deeper down. I almost forget that he's not with me, when I'm out swimming. When the boats return and he comes home, he strokes my hair and pulls strands of weed from it, and shards of coral from the reef. He laughs and says he wonders it doesn't turn green to match my eyes, with all the time I spend in the sea.

May 7

The whales came today. They never surfaced, they were far below me, far from shore, swimming north, three of them. I felt them coming. I knew they were sperm from the old stories, their great blunt heads, pushing slowly through the water, one after the other. The last turned on his side as he passed under me, opening his long jaw to take in a stream of little fish, then sank down until he was swallowed by black. My stomach twisted when he opened his jaw and I felt like I was sinking, too. Benadam ran down to the point as soon as I told him. It was full dark already, I knew he would see nothing, but he's still down there.

May 8

He said the whales used to pass by the island twice a year, close in to shore. He's still down at the point, standing there with his lance, scanning the water, as though he could reach them. There are at least twenty, strung out for miles. They're still passing but they'll be gone soon. None of them has breached since first light, they're all well down. Too far for him to reach, with no ship.

I asked him why he didn't just keep E.'s cutter. He sent it back, right after the wedding. He said he wouldn't sail any ship of my brother's. And that the *Argo* was too small, anyway, not suited for whaling.

I wonder if I should have told him about the whales.

If he hadn't seen me and brought me here, he would be out on the *Misistuck* by now. He would be in a whaleboat now with his lance, not standing down there on the rocks, staring.

I know what he's thinking. He can't forget what E. described, what E. never saw or felt himself — the boats, the chase. He wants to face something stronger than him. He wants to know what it feels like to be afraid.

It's what I've always wanted, too. For it to be the way it used to be. I knew it the moment I saw him, that he could meet the whale the way Moses did. And now he has me instead, and the whales swim on and away.

July 2

One of the women, Hannah, is teaching me how to clean the fish and to cook a little. At first I was impatient with the work. I only did it to pass the time until Benadam comes home each night. But more and more I like spending time with the other wives and the children. We talk of common things: the weather, the children's health, and such things . . . but I like it. I never would have guessed how nice it is just to sit among other women, peeling apples or mending a smock or braiding a girl's hair, light voices and laughter all around me.

The men all fish, from the little boys to old Nate, who turned eighty-three last week. There are a dozen houses, each with a family. Nine children, the youngest Hannah's baby, a fat little girl with red ringlets, Sarah. Hannah lets me hold her.

Little Sarah is not much older than Mordecai. She's so plump, and laughs all the time. I told Hannah about Mordecai. I told her about E. and me. She hugged me, and said I couldn't have known any better.

I glanced up at Mordecai. He stared at me, then turned away to face the wall.

September 6

Benadam says M. can come live with us. But it's so bright here, I could never make our little house dark enough. He always cried whenever the sun shone on his cradle. Outside, no matter how well bundled, how cloudy or bright, the sun found his skin and burned it. I thought heavy curtains would work, in the darker rooms, but he always made his way to a window and tried to crawl out, or stole out a door. After I found him down on the docks that day, chasing crabs, his skin blistered black, that was the last time he went outside. He can't come here. It wouldn't work.

October 28

The sea is cold now, I'll have to stop swimming soon. The fish are moving into deeper water, too deep for me. I swim now with only kelp for company. I hope Bemus has remembered to bring up the quilts to the attic for Mordecai. I hope E. does not think of me too much. Conch and Crab will keep busy, taking care of him. They will have forgotten me. I'm sure the girls will have everything they need, Bemus never forgets.

March 9

I should have known. I should have felt it. Bemus's writing was so shaky, I wasn't sure I was reading it right at first. E. tried to hide it from me, how bad it had gotten, but I knew, he could barely walk when I left. He would have been twenty-five next week.

April 10

I should have stayed. I should never have left him.

April 16

It's mine, now. The empty house, the rotting ship. The gold.

He wants to go back. He wants to re-build the *Misistuck* and go whaling. He says we can do what E. tried to do and failed. Renew the family. Regain the sea.

If he had kept E.'s bargain and married Scallop, he would be whaling right now, he said. I told him what Bemus wrote to me, that the *Misistuck* never came back. I told him about the six wives and the six babies.

He didn't listen. He said he'd buy a new ship.

I told him what I've realized, living here. We already have the sea. We have our house and our garden and our life here, and the other families. Our children can grow up to be fishermen like their father. Not like the Rathbones. Once you kill your first whale you will never want to stop, the more you kill the more you will want to kill, until there isn't a whale left in all the seas.

Now that I have you, I said, I don't want you to go after the whales. I only want you to stay here with me.

May 2

I haven't told him yet. There will be two,
I know.

October 8

They came just after dawn yesterday. A
boy and a girl. The women were all
there, helping me. Heather gave me a
cuttlebone to bite on for the pain.
They're perfect. Fine fat babies with
thick heads of hair and pink skin. Their
eyes are bright and steady, their limbs
strong and well knit. Benadam looked
so happy. But tonight he is back out on
the point, looking for the whales.

December 11

If we went back in the spring, I would
see Mordecai. And Conch and Crab,
and I could go visit Periwinkle and
Cowrie and all the girls at Birch Rock.
Benadam would be busy with fitting out
the ship for months. And he would have
to find men up the coast who know how
to whale, to train the islanders, that
would take time. He would be with me
at least through next winter.

February 23

It's still so cold . . .

I said I'd go back.

I made him promise never to take Gideon to sea.

I closed the little book and looked at Mordecai. He lay quietly among his pillows, staring up into the hull. No starlight shone; instead, a dull red glowed in the sky behind the knotholes, though it was, I remember vaguely thinking, too soon for dawn.

"She didn't know that what she and Erastus did was wrong, Mordecai. Who was there to teach her?"

Mordecai turned his head away.

"Maybe Erastus did know, maybe that's why he went away. But he came back. He couldn't help himself."

I picked up Mordecai's journal and unfolded the chart. I looked at the fourth row of faces: Verity and Erastus, the twins, the seven shell girls. Under them, in the last row, Gideon and me. And floating off to the side, Mordecai. I picked up a pen and drew a line between Verity and Erastus, and connected it to Mordecai. I drew a line from

Mordecai to me and from me to Gideon.

"You were the real reason she finally agreed to go back to the house."

Mordecai shot me a look filled with bitterness, and turned away again.

"I would be lying if I said that she was not also relieved to have you . . . aside. But she did care. Before Papa was gone all the time, before she stopped seeing what happened around her. Before she began carving."

Mordecai turned from the wall. His voice was low and hoarse.

"She could have been kinder to you, too, Mercy." His eyes softened. "Sister."

My hand strayed to an open crate that stood next to my chair and fumbled with the excelsior that spilled from it.

"I was so like Gideon. She didn't like to be reminded of him, of Gideon alive. She preferred to tend to his bones. They stayed still, in one place."

I looked up at the marble bust of the woman. Crow, clutching her hair, spread a wing out to preen, a fan of feathers that shadowed her eyes.

"Remember when I asked you about the red hat? When you told me how you used to eavesdrop on Mama and the stranger up on the walk?"

He nodded.

"That wasn't a stranger. That was Papa."

I told him how I had realized it was Papa who came and went, and how I hadn't wanted to tell him back at Circe's cove, when he was already so disappointed about not finding the sperm.

"But she called him another name, not Benadam. Tayles. Captain Tayles."

I flipped through the diary.

"I know. She uses that name sometimes in here. Only it wasn't spelled Tayles, it was Talos. Don't you remember?"

On the worktable, under Mordecai's strewn papers, were a few of the red-leather books. In the volume stamped with the silver face of Jason, I found what I was looking for: a giant made of bronze, straddling a harbor between two points of land. I turned the book so Mordecai could see.

"He was one of the Titans, remember? He had a single vein, from neck to foot, closed at his heel with a bronze nail. Medea deceived him into believing that he would become immortal if he removed the nail. Or some versions say she hypnotized him so that he tripped and fell, driving the nail from his heel, and the hot oil poured out into the sand." I looked at the sea that Talos straddled, which the artist had etched in stylized waves that rose and fell in a perfect rhythm. "He wanted to prove that he was stronger than the whales, than the sea. But Mama kept pulling him back." I smoothed the page with my hand; the sea, printed with gold ink, shimmered as the paper moved. "And I think it was guilt that always drove him away again. Guilt over losing Gideon."

Mordecai stared down at the engraving.

"You know now, don't you, why Mama and Papa put you here, in the attic?"

Mordecai looked puzzled, then his face cleared, and he nodded slowly.

"They had to keep you up here, out of the light, so it couldn't hurt you and . . . they didn't want you to know the truth about your father."

Mordecai was so quiet. Crow hopped from my shoulder to Mordecai's and settled there. He had never done that before.

I pulled Mama's little book from my pocket and flipped through the pages to the back. I hadn't told Mordecai everything. There were other, later entries in the diary, other things he didn't need to hear, about Gideon and me.

She wrote that we were as alike as two otters, as strong and as quick. We both could swim before we could walk. Papa would take us, one in each hand, and skim us through the surf, then toss us on his back and dive in and out of the waves and Mama would laugh. She wrote of an old seaman bouncing us, one on each knee, on the dock on a fine summer day, spoiling us with rock candy and boiled sweets from a little paper bag. Rowing together in the blue skiff, with small oars to fit our hands — gliding along close to shore at dusk, the sky going dark, the sea quiet under us, Mama calling to us, saying it was time to come inside. A warm and cloudless day when Gideon's baby frock was changed for knee breeches and he ran laughing down the pier, the water sparkling on either side as he ran.

I had strained to remember what Mama remembered, but it had been too long ago.

Each of her memories — only pictures to me — stayed separate, like tide pools too high on the shore, never joined by a sweep of sea into something deeper and broader. Gideon had been away more than he had been home.

I sat up and looked down at Mordecai's face. The purple-black blotch had spread farther, down his cheek and along his neck, dark seaweed on a white beach.

I saw too, now, Gideon's face before me, not salt-white but bright brown and full of life, smiling, his green eyes so like mine.

Gideon was like Papa. Gone or longing to be gone when he was right beside me. I had found Gideon, as much as I would ever have been able, in finding my sympathy with the sea. I had found something I wouldn't lose.

Though Gideon was my twin, though his face rose before me, it was Mordecai I was thinking of. It was Mordecai who was my true brother. I had looked into the distance so long that I hadn't seen what was near at hand. If we don't cherish those who stay near, what do we have? Only longing. Longing which we grow to love because it's all that we have.

Mordecai's pale-green eyes had drained to nearly clear. His breath rattled faintly. He might have had something left to say, but he couldn't speak it.

I pulled down the blanket that covered Mordecai. I looked at his thin mottled body and felt for a moment that I had no choice. I felt the same tidal pull that my forebears had, that Mama had. I forgave her, a little. I wanted to sail with Mordecai one last time.

Instead I drew the blanket back up, and waited with him until he was gone, and kissed him goodbye.

Chapter Twenty-Seven:
Mama Sets Sail

{in which Mama shines bright}

She would have liked her funeral. The boat of bones, her bier; the sail I sewed from her gowns, its deep blue billowing against a like sky; Gideon by her side. I dressed her in her corset, and in the muslin gown in which she was married and whose cloth had cushioned Gideon's bones in the trunk.

The trunk went, too, stowed in the stern. In it I neatly rearranged, on a fresh bed of kelp, the objects that Mama had provided to keep Gideon company: a flute carved of bone; a soft kid glove of her own; a little round tin with a ship on its lid, filled with sweets, a snack for the afterlife. To these I added my dead crow and the woven bracelet.

I considered carving a headstone of whalebone for her, and consigning her to the worn wives for burial in the graveyard behind their house, where all the Rathbone women who lived on Mouse Island are buried. The island being of solid granite, the graves were made in packed earth brought from the mainland long ago, which the sea is slowly reclaiming; at high tide the stones are partially sunken, and the water will take them all in the end. But I knew Mama would rather be in the sea, where Papa always was.

After I set the boat aflame and pushed it off from shore, before the flames took hold, Crow flew down and plucked a few hairs from her head for his nest. She burned clear and bright for as long as I could see her. With her boat sailed a flotilla of crates, unopened crates, all labeled "For Mordecai." I found them in the attic after he died. For all his hunger for the bones and specimens sent to me, Mordecai hadn't wanted to open any gift from Papa to him. He never received the only gift he ever wanted: a place on Papa's ship. A space in his life.

As I watched her go I knew why Mama had invited the suitors on that last night. She wasn't searching for a substitute for Papa, or trying to forget him with a landsman who found no siren call in the sea. She meant to make him jealous, to lure him home with the threat of finally giving him up. And I think, too, that she knew how it would end.

She had been so lonely. If she lay with every sailor who knocked at our door, she was little different from those old Rathbones who bedded the worn wives so generously, but for her sex. Maybe it was less a choice she made than a map written in her blood. Fish, after all, thoughtlessly scatter their spawn in the sea; they must be profligate to make sure something sticks in their watery world to make more of them. There's a kind of comfort in knowing that it's not all up to us, that we must swing to and fro with the tides. We are all still subject to the ocean's coming and going.

Watching her go, I hoped I was made more from the stuff of my great-great-aunts than that of Mama. Like those early Rathbone men, the wives, too, borrowed of the whale, not in any showy gleam but in their mute fortitude. My great-great-aunts passed each day from dawn to dusk at their loom; Mama, too, spent her time in making, but where my aunts brought together, she scraped away, trying with her blade to plumb the mysteries of the sperm. I think it made her feel closer to Papa, in keeping close to what he had loved more than her, or me. Close not to that vast creature that swam the oceans, huge heart pumping, breath spouting, strength unreckonable, but to that which remained when all else had been hacked and burned away, reduced to irreducible bone, quiet and still. Then she moved into it, under the surface, looking for what was lost.

Watching Mama sail away, I didn't notice when he arrived; when I looked out Papa was just there, standing in the bow of a whaleboat, balancing easily, rising and falling with the waves, a ship's length away. He wore the blue jacket, salt-crusted, buttons missing. He wasn't the giant in the attic dangling me from one hand, or the colossal shadow on the sinking island, or Talos, bestriding the harbor of Crete. He was just a man in an old blue coat.

He raised his arm to me.

I could see the longing in his face. Gideon must have looked so much like me.

I knew the longing was for my brother, not for me. But I raised my arm, too.

When Mama's boat had slipped over the horizon, I looked out again to find Papa gone. I reached around and touched the place on my back where the birthmark shaped like a ship had so long floated to find that it had sailed.

Chapter Twenty-Eight: Golden Child

{in which the tide swings back}

It was only after the knocking had gone on for some time that I made my way down the stairs. Even then I hesitated before opening the door. The sound was so loud in the empty house, and I had not spoken a word in a month; I liked the silence. I opened the door a crack and peered around its edge. Roderick Stark startled me, standing at the door, dark against the glare of the sky behind him. In shape and bearing he looked, as he had when I first saw him, much like Mordecai. Crow, too, was startled; his claws sank into my shoulder and with a loud croak he flew off and up the stairs. When Roderick stepped closer I saw that he had shed his Oriental garb for a sober coat of dark wool and a soft felt hat, though his face was no easier to look at.

"Miss Rathbone." He pulled off his hat.

The powdered wig was gone. I was surprised at his hair, a dark gold, thick and wavy, tied simply at the back of his neck. His face had lost its gray cast, his cheeks reddened by the wind. "Forgive me for just showing up like this, I only . . . I wondered if there's anything I can do for you, any service I can offer?"

I opened the door a little more and stood blinking at the glare.

"How did you know?"

"Captain Avery happened to mention —"

"Of course."

It would be polite to invite him in, I thought, standing there. He took a step back and put his hands behind him.

"You're alone here?"

I nodded. Larboard and Starboard had disappeared the day after Mama died.

We both stood in silence.

"Well. If there's anything, anything at all I can do."

I watched him walk away, down to the landing below the rocks. Beached there was a craft that strongly resembled a barge of ancient Egypt, with a gilded hull and long striped oars. Its crew were walking back and forth on the strand hugging themselves, bare-chested men in pleated skirts, shivering in the winter air. The Starks, I saw, continued to plunder the epochs of history for fashion, though Roderick seemed by his plain clothes to now be following some other course. He climbed into the barge, looking back at the house as the oarsmen pulled away.

He didn't knock again in the months that followed, but I would often wake to find packages on the stairs outside. I knew they came from the Stark kitchen by the dishes inside, which were patterned with jackal heads and lotus blossoms. They held not useless bric-a-brac but wholesome food for which I was grateful, being an indifferent cook: fruits and vegetables from the Stark gardens, still-warm bread (those oarsmen must have rivaled my ancestors in speed to come such a distance with bread still warm), nourishing soups unembellished with birds' nests.

It was a year later when I next opened the door to Roderick. I watched him arrive from the window of my room, this time not in a royal barge but in a handsome little cutter crewed by men in warm pea coats and watch caps. It was an icy morning, early in the new year. The sound was a pale frigid green, like the sky; an easterly wind beat the sea into whitecaps.

Roderick was dressed like his crew. He pulled off his watch cap.

"You look cold, Mr. Stark. Would you like some tea? I've just made some."

I led him up the stairs, through the round hall, and into one of the parlors. His step slowed as he took in the golden walls, tarnished but still dully gleaming, and the room's sparse furnishings: Lydia's settee; the spinet on which Claudia had played. I gestured at the settee. On a small table next to it I had already placed the tea tray.

"I'll just get another cup."

When I returned from the dining room, Roderick popped up from his seat. I sat at the end of the settee and poured our tea. He lifted his cup tentatively, sniffing at it.

"My aunts make it. Rose hips, mostly, a little nettle."

Roderick took a few polite sips and set his cup down.

"It must be healthful. You're looking very well."

I looked down doubtfully at my musty gown, the algae-brown one my aunts had made, and put a hand to my hair, which was loosely coiled on my neck.

"Oh. Well. If I do, I have you to thank, Mr. Stark. If it weren't for your kind gifts,

I'm not sure how I would be surviving this winter."

"I'm so glad. I mean, not that you're barely surviving. It's just, is there anything else I can do for you?"

"No, I manage quite well. Thank you."

I looked at him sidelong as he fumbled with his teacup.

"You're looking well, too, Mr. Stark."

I was surprised that it was true. His grim face could now be better described as rugged, browned by sun and smoothed by wind. His lank frame had acquired muscle, his thin hands, sinew. Those dark blue eyes, sad before in his gray face, now sparkled.

"Please, call me Roderick." He looked down at himself. "If I look well, it's my turn to thank you. If you hadn't started me thinking about what I wanted to do, what I really wanted to achieve —"

"Me? What do you mean?"

"When we were looking at the old portraits that day, you spoke of my returning to the family trade, of doing something useful. It struck me that I'd never allowed myself to think of doing something I actually wanted to do. But not being a merchant, buying and selling. I wanted to make something useful, something real."

To his family's chagrin, he had given up

581

his studies in the arts in Boston and now spent his days in the warehouse on the wharf, teaching himself woodcraft with his great-grandfather Calvin's old saws and adzes and plumb bobs.

"The old Rathbone ships were built by Starks. Did you know that? The *Misistuck* was built by my great-grandfather and his brothers in 1772, the *Sassacus* and the *Paquatauoq* . . ."

We talked of the ships, and how they were rigged, and how it felt to be out there on the sea, and the hours slipped by.

"What are you reading, Mama?"

"It's only an old journal."

"Can I see?"

"Maybe later."

Little Mordecai shrugs and runs down the lawn and off and away to the point. He shimmies up a tree, a young pine springing from among the charred trunks above the tide line, where the sheds burned. He clings to the top of the tree, swaying, fearless, waving to me and shouting; his voice is carried away to sea by the wind. He's brown from the sun, nimble and hardy, as keen-eyed as me. In him live the Rathbone gifts and the golden beauty of the Starks. It seems the tide has finally swung back; I hope it has. I fold the chart and close his uncle's journal.

Mordecai lies in Circe's cove, in a grove of slim white birches, where the stilts nest each spring. Circe lives on in her cave and keeps Mordecai's grave free of droppings. Captain Avery helped me bury him there. I considered sending him to sea with Mama but there wasn't room for more than one on her boat of bones. And Mordecai wouldn't have wanted to go with her.

A warm arm comes around my shoulders and squeezes them. Roderick still, sometimes, reminds me of Mordecai. His way of striding stiffly, hands clasped behind his back, when he's thinking; the light that comes into his eyes when he's excited about discovering some new, better way of pursuing his craft. I like to imagine that Mordecai, given a different path, might have been as content.

"Is it that time of year again?" Roderick smiles at me, brushing wood chips from his hair, taking the journal gently from my hands. "Maybe you should put this away for good."

"Someday, maybe."

We watch as the first of the skiffs and dories arrive down at the dock for the day's work. Little Mordecai Stark also watches from his tree. And now my name is Stark, too. I'd never carried my father's name. My mother had christened me Mercy Rathbone, after her forebears, but I've decided to strike out on my own path.

"Two new orders this week!" Roderick shouts down to the men now striding along the dock toward the boat shed.

The men raise their arms and cheer — local fishermen, who have been learning shipbuilding with Roderick in the off-season. With the new orders, Roderick will be able to take on a few of them full time. A saw begins to whine from the boat shed and the sharp scent of pine wafts up to the house. The first new brig is being built on the Rathbone dock — not the dock of the elder Starks, who still cannot bear to hear my family's name. Maybe they will relent when they know that soon there will be a new little Stark (a girl, I know) who will likely look much like her brother, and so may remind the elder Starks of their own lost golden girls and warm even their chill hearts. Euphemia and Thankful will come to help, as they did when Little Mordecai was born. There's a nursery now on the third floor. We moved curtains from the hall of beds — my favourite pair, those woven with twin octopi — to hang from the crib, and my aunts have made bedding of fresh-loomed wool and soft rugs of sheepskin. The nursery is next to Mama's old room, where Roderick and I now sleep. The long black table is back in the library, where the shelves are slowly filling; Captain Avery brings us a box or two of books each time he visits.

The workmen's wives head up the lawn, chattering, greeting me as they pass into the house. They come each morning to help me in the kitchen; the men breakfast with us. My cookery improves, though I would still prefer to stand atop a cold crosstree than before a hot stove, and the house fills with pleasant aromas and lively voices. It pleases me to see all our china and silver shining around the table, and a man at each place. All nine of my great-great-aunts come once a month for dinner, rowing over and back in a single whaleboat, three to each bench. I visit them often.

Crow flies out of the house and lands on Roderick's shoulder. Crow has taken to Roderick, perching on his head or napping in a corner of the boat shed while he works. Roderick enlists him to carry small tools or blocks of wood, though Crow soon tires of the work and carries off bright nails and hinges to his nest. He visits the attic now, too, where I still keep all of the things that Mordecai so long preserved, those that were not lost on our voyage.

When the new brig is finished, it will join a merchant fleet in Boston. There have been no orders for whaling ships. Captain Avery, who often stops by, told us that he sees fewer and fewer whalers at sea. He's heard that men are building towers on the land now, out on the prairies, not to look for whales but to draw up oil from deep in the earth. Black oil that will replace the white spermaceti.

"You and I will take her out in a month or so." Roderick gazes down at the brig, smiling. "You can teach Little Mordecai the names of all the sails." He kisses me and heads down to join the men.

I watch the men working for a while, then turn toward the point, to where the trying sheds stood. They, too, burned on the night that Mama died; it was their red glare that had shone through the knot-holes in Mordecai's attic. Papa must have set them on fire as he left. The last of the old gold went with them, the gold which had, in Bow-Oar's time, brimmed, molten, in one of the great cauldrons in which the whales' oil was rendered.

When the tryworks were abandoned, the cauldron of gold was left there to cool and stiffen, alongside a cauldron half full of old sperm oil. Plenty of other gold was kept in those days in the house, gold minted into coin; the men had no need for the gold in the cauldron and later forgot it. I had once, when a child, rowed my skiff up to the great doors and peered into the gloom inside. The shed was built over the water, the cauldrons suspended on chains high above the sea. The vast iron vessels, each large enough to hold the oil of a seventy-foot sperm, hung too high for me to see into them, but light entered through the gap between the doors and played on the surface of the cauldrons, and on the water below, bright ripples of gold. When the sheds burned the chains gave way and the cauldrons tumbled into the sea. The stiff gold lies shining on the ocean floor. The spilled oil rejoined the sea it came from.

There was some gold left in the house, a few hoards of coins that we found in drawers and cabinets, where the crows had hidden them. Just enough to furnish Roderick in the tools and materials of his craft, with a little left over to get by until the boatyard begins to yield a profit, with which I am more than content.

I touch the three bones at my throat and think of both my brothers. They are the bones of Gideon's finger, the ones that

Mama wore, but I think of them as Gideon's, and Mordecai's, and mine.

I turn back to the open sea. A whale blows there . . . no, it's only clouds. But it could be a school of sperm just under the surface, looking up, casting their own clouds into the sky from the deep with great long breaths.

Crow, who had been away somewhere at sea, flies down to me. In his beak he carries a folded piece of blue paper, the letter Mama always kept tucked in her sleeve, trailing straw from his nest.

Naiwayonk, Connecticut, September 10, 1845
My Talos —

When you are out on the full blue of the ocean, with no land in view (surely sailors have a word for that), distances must be deceptive. When you see a ship against the sky, on the horizon, how can you tell its true distance or size by eye, when no landmarks guide you and nothing else sails near? The horizon line must, in clear weather, be some absolute distance from you on the open sea — is it twenty miles as the crow flies? The distance a gaze can travel undisturbed by the curve of the earth is only a short line, a tiny segment of her circumference. Can you be sure, though it has the shape of a thousand-ton schooner, that such a ship may not be much smaller, much closer? If you had only one eye and could poorly judge space, and suffered a little from fever, besides: Couldn't that eye mistake a child's toy, carved of balsa wood with handkerchiefs for sails, bobbing lightly by, for a grand galleon?

Though the books tell me that the earth is round, I would rather think of her as flat, as she was for so long, until one of the Greeks came along and made her into a sphere. I would rather think of you, with the heavy body of the ship beneath you, moving straight and true, steady against wind and whale alike, sighting with your sextant as far as you wish, no curve blocking your gaze. You might then, standing on the forecastle, look back in a straight line to me, while ahead your goal stays always in sight. Though but a speck at first, you would only need to squint hard enough to see it.

When I think of the earth in her cloak of ocean, turning her back to every kind of weather, always spinning, I wonder what would happen if she suddenly stopped to rest, while your ship sailed on, unknowing; and when the sea reached the topmost point of the stalled globe, it would slide on, unable to stop, spilling off the edge into the ether with all its travelers. How barren the earth would be then. If she were still flat you would see your end coming, whatever its distance, however small its signal. Perhaps she's better round.

But still, when I look out to sea from shore on a clear day and watch a ship approaching, when I first spy the tips of her masts, I prefer to believe that, rather than rounding the curve of the world, she rises straight upward, from the depths of the sea, like Aphrodite.

Ever Yours I Am
— Verity

— The boy grows stronger, more beautiful each day. The girl, too, is fine.

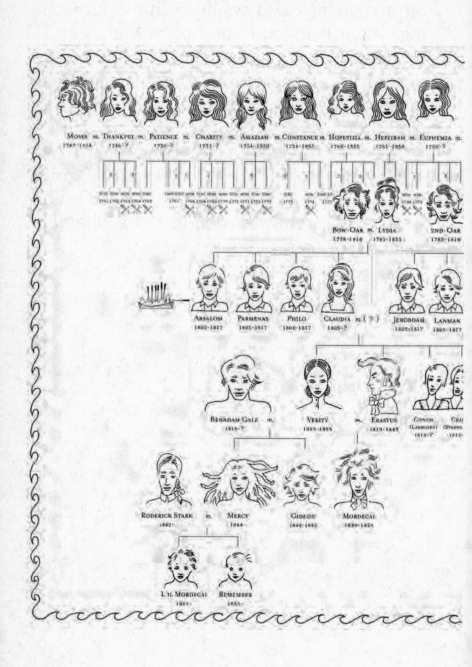

EUNICE *m.* FELICITY *m.* BEULAH *m.* EXPERIENCE *m.* DESIRE *m.* TRIAL *m.* HUMILITY *m.* SILENCE *m.* KATURAH
1763–? 1765–? 1766–? 1771–? 1778–1857 1780–? 1779–? 1781–? 1786–1858

MIRIAM 3RD-OAR *m.* PRISCILLA
1784–1833 1784–1818 1788–1834

CLAYMAN SOPHIA *m.* (?) EZEKIEL SILAS JULIA *m.* (?)
1809–1817 1805–? 1802–1817 1805–1817 1805–?

ABALONE WENTLE LIMPET SCALLOP PERIWINKLE COWRIE CORAL
1820–? 1820–? (CIRCE) 1821–? 1821–? 1821–? 1821–?
1820–?

THE RATHBONES

ACKNOWLEDGMENTS

My agent, Mollie Glick, believed in this novel early and late; I'm so thankful for her insight, energy, and dauntlessness. I'm deeply grateful to my editor, Alison Callahan, for her masterly hand and warm support throughout. Many thanks to Katie Hamblin at Foundry Literary + Media, and to James Melia, Bette Alexander, and all of the wonderful team at the Knopf Doubleday Publishing Group.

The graduate creative writing community at NYU provided invaluable support and inspiration. I'm especially grateful to Breyten Breytenbach, Chuck Wachtel, Irini Spanidou, Garth Risk Hallberg, E. A. Durden, Martin Marks, and all my workshop comrades.

Many thanks to PJ Mark, Drenka Willen, Jill Schoolman, Molly Daniels-Ramanujan, and Lorin Stein for early encouragement.

For their support and love along the way I

thank my father and mother, Kenneth and
Maureen Clark; my sisters, Karen Clark and
Barbara Clark-Greene; my son, Bryson
Clark; Joan Bassin; Gigi Buffington; Steve
Evans; Kristin LeMay; Sue Pak; Ann Snow-
berger; Dino Stoneking; and Michael Tir-
rell.

Many thanks to Emily Mahon for the
jacket design and to Michael Collica for the
book's interior design.

I'm forever indebted to Diane Cole for
helping me learn the profound value and
joy of making art.

My deepest gratitude to Eric LeMay,
without whom I would not have become a
writer.

Sources

Thank you to the New Bedford Whaling
Museum for permission to use part of a
verse from a scrimshaw whalebone busk in
their collection for Claudia's song: "This
bone once in a sperm whale's jaw did rest /
Now 'tis intended for a woman's breast"
(whale panbone busk, NBWM Collection,
gift of the heirs of Nathan C. Hathaway,
1923.6.35). Mystic Seaport's online collection of logbooks and journals provided
models for Benadam Gale's journal entries.
"Blood Red Roses," which Mordecai sings

596

on the deck of the *Able,* is a traditional sea chantey. "A night in the arms of Venus leads to a lifetime on Mercury," the caption to an image in the fictitious booklet *Diseases of the Seaman* from the Rathbone library, is an anonymous saying about the nineteenth-century practice of treating syphilis with mercury. Apologies to the ghost of Matthew Fontaine Maury (American oceanographer and astronomer, nicknamed "Pathfinder of the Seas," 1806–1873) for appropriating his *Wind and Current Chart of the North Atlantic* as Mordecai's invention; certainly Mordecai, given opportunity, might have created such a wonder.

ABOUT THE AUTHOR

Janice Clark is a writer and graphic designer. She grew up in Mystic, Connecticut, a nineteenth-century whaling port, and has lived in Montreal, Kansas City, San Francisco, and New York. She currently lives in Chicago.

6- 14